D1442690

# KING ARTHUR'S BONES

## A Historical Mystery

### By

### The Medieval Murderers

Susanna Gregory
Bernard Knight
Michael Jecks
Philip Gooden
Ian Morson

**POCKET
BOOKS**

LONDON · SYDNEY · NEW YORK · TORONTO

First published in Great Britain by Simon & Schuster UK Ltd, 2009
This edition first published by Pocket Books, 2010
An imprint of Simon & Schuster UK
A CBS COMPANY

1 3 5 7 9 10 8 6 4 2

Simon & Schuster UK Ltd
1st Floor
222 Gray's Inn Road
London WC1X 8HB

www.simonandschuster.co.uk

Simon & Schuster Australia
Sydney

A CIP catalogue record for this book is available from the British Library

ISBN: 978-1-84983-456-8

Printed by CPI Cox & Wyman, Reading, Berkshire RG1 8EX

# THE MEDIEVAL
# MURDERERS

A small group of historical mystery writers, all members of the Crime Writers' Association, who promote their work by giving informal talks and discussions at libraries, bookshops and literary festivals.

**Bernard Knight** is a former Home Office pathologist and professor of forensic medicine who has been writing novels, non-fiction, radio and television drama and documentaries for more than forty years. He currently writes the highly regarded Crowner John series of historical mysteries, based on the first coroner for Devon in the twelfth century; the thirteenth of which, *Crowner Royal*, has recently been published by Simon & Schuster.

**Ian Morson** is the author of an acclaimed series of historical mysteries featuring the thirteenth-century Oxford-based detective, William Falconer, and a brand-new series featuring Venetian crime solver, Nick Zuliani, the first of which, *City of the Dead*, has recently been published.

**Michael Jecks** was a computer salesman before turning to writing full time. His immensely popular Templar series, set during the confusion and terror of the reign of Edward

II, is translated into most continental languages and is published in America. His most recent novels are *The King of Thieves* and, the 27th in the series, *No Law in the Land*. Michael was chairman of the Crime Writers' Association in 2004–5 but balances that by Morris Dancing enthusiastically – and badly.

**Philip Gooden** is the author of the Nick Revill series, a sequence of historical mysteries set in Elizabethan and Jacobean London, during the time of Shakespeare's Globe Theatre. Among the titles are *Sleep of Death* and *Death of Kings*. He also writes 19th century mysteries, most recently *The Salisbury Manuscript*, as well as non-fiction books on language. Philip was chairman of the Crime Writers' Association in 2007–8.

**Susanna Gregory** is the author of the Matthew Bartholomew series of mystery novels, set in fourteenth-century Cambridge, the most recent of which are *A Vein of Deceit* and *To Kill or Cure*. In addition, she writes a series set in Restoration London, featuring Thomas Chaloner; the most recent book is *The Westminster Poisoner*. She also writes historical mysteries under the name of 'Simon Beaufort'.

# The Programme

**Prologue** – In which Philip Gooden describes how at Glastonbury Abbey in 1191 the remains of King Arthur are believed to have been discovered.

**Act One** – In which Susanna Gregory describes how the bones are stolen during a violent skirmish between the Welsh and the invading Normans.

**Act Two** – In which Bernard Knight relates how in 1282 a band of patriots retrieve the relics after the darkest day in Wales's history.

**Act Three** – In which Michael Jecks describes how a chance encounter with a pardoner and quack healer causes problems for Sir Baldwin de Furnshill, Simon Puttock and the church.

**Act Four** – In which Philip Gooden's player Nick Revill becomes involved with Arthur's bones, William Shakespeare's younger brother and a murder at the Tower of London.

**Act Five** – In which Ian Morson recalls how rumours

of Napoleon Bonaparte's escape revives the old myth of King Arthur's return.

**Epilogue** – In which Bernard Knight returns to an archaeological dig near Tower Bridge, where the experts find something unexpected in the foundations of Bermondsey Abbey.

# PROLOGUE

## *Glastonbury, 1191*

The first he knew of it was the noise, like the sound of leaves rustling across dry ground. The abbot looked up from the parchment he was studying. It was a list of estimates, the costs of rebuilding. Listening more carefully, he heard not the sound of leaves but of voices. He wasn't sorry to be distracted from his task. He got up and opened the window of the parlour. It was an overcast afternoon in mid-autumn. The air was still.

Monks and lay brothers as well as ordinary workers were converging on an area of grass a few dozen yards from the abbot's first-floor window. They were crowding around a tent-like structure of drapery curtains, crowding with such force that the whole construction quivered as if about to topple down. What surprised the abbot was not the fact that the workers or even the lay brothers should be running to reach the spot – obviously something had been discovered behind the dirty white curtains, and word had spread fast – but that his fellow Benedictines in their black garb were also moving at such an undignified rate. Whatever the *something* was, it must be significant. Almost despite himself, the abbot felt a tremor of excitement.

Henry de Sully fastened the window. He moved towards his chamber door at a deliberate pace. There was no one to see, but it would not do to betray any sign of agitation, even to himself. Before he could reach it, there was a clatter and the door banged open. In the entrance stood Brother Geoffrey, his chaplain and secretary.

The man was out of breath. He was not so old that a few stairs should have exhausted him. He clung to the door frame, with an expression on his face that was close to confusion. Henry de Sully smiled and made a calming gesture. He waited while Geoffrey regained control of himself, but the other was too impatient. His secretary-chaplain got as far as 'They have found . . . have found . . .' before being overcome by a bout of gulping and swallowing.

'It's all right, Geoffrey. Calm yourself. Whatever they have found I will discover for myself,' said de Sully.

The chaplain shifted to let his superior through the doorway and followed him down the stone steps to the lobby. The abbot moved without hurry although it cost him an effort to do so. Over his shoulder he heard the monk stuttering, 'It's . . . it . . . it is . . .'

'Yes?' said de Sully, halting at the foot of the stairs. 'It is . . . what?'

'Extraordinary,' Geoffrey managed to get out.

'We'll see.'

The abbot and his chaplain emerged into the open. The crowd around the tent was growing all the time, with monks and labourers still arriving from every quarter. They moved at a run or a brisk walk. There could not have been such a stir in the place, thought Henry de Sully, since the great fire of a few years ago, the fire which destroyed the old church and much of the abbey before his own arrival in Glastonbury. At the thought, he glanced towards the Lady Chapel, which stood, fresh and fine, near the site of the original church. He'd never seen the church but had been told frequently of that simple wattle-and-daub edifice, many centuries old and transformed to ash in minutes.

Abbot de Sully and Brother Geoffrey drew nearer to the tent-like construction. Located halfway between a pair of stone pillars, it consisted of discoloured white drapes slung over crosspieces supported on wooden uprights. It enclosed an area of a few square yards. The tent might have been primitive, but it was sufficient to give some protection from the weather and a measure of privacy to whatever was going on inside.

No one noticed the approach of the abbot or his chaplain. Instead, the monks and lay brothers jostled each other to get closer to where the drapes had been pulled back to allow the workers to come and go past piles of earth and rubble. The buzz of questions and exclamations was like the sound of bees.

Henry de Sully halted. Geoffrey clapped his hands several times and silence slowly fell as the crowd realized the abbot had arrived. They moved aside and left a passage to the entrance of the 'tent'. At first sight it was hard to imagine what the exitement was about. Four men were kneeling or crouching by the entrance. On the ground between them lay a couple of stone fragments. Two of the men were labourers, identifiable by their caps and coarse clothing. Their faces were streaked with mud and sweat. The other two men were monks, Brother Frederick, who was the sacrist of the abbey, and Brother Owen, the cellarer.

Brother Frederick looked up at de Sully and clambered creakily to his feet. There was the same mixture of confusion and excitement on his face which the abbot had seen on his chaplain's. The sacristan brushed away the dirt from the knees of his cassock and came towards Henry.

'I knew this must be the place!' he said.

'You have made a discovery?'

'About six or seven feet down, we found ... well, they found ... come and see.'

Forgetting himself, Brother Frederick tugged like a child at the abbot's sleeve. Henry de Sully moved forward and looked down at the pieces of stones. Owen the cellarer stood up. Like Frederick, he raised himself with an effort, though more on account of his size than ageing joints. There was a strange, vacant look in his eyes. The two workmen remained on their knees but shifted so that Henry could have a better view.

What the Glastonbury abbot saw first was a slab of stone. It was like a large piece of paving, apart from an indented section in the shape of an irregular cross. On the edges of the indentation were some rusting bands of iron. The other item was not stone at all but made of lead. It was the cross itself, not large, perhaps a foot in length. Lettering was inscribed in a straggling fashion on the side facing him. He stooped down. The light was poor from the overcast afternoon and the shadow of the tent, but Henry de Sully was able to pick out some of the Latin words despite the mud and grit embedded in the capital letters. One word in particular he could read, a name inscribed in Latinate style. Henry felt his heart thumping hard.

His chaplain had been right. It was extraordinary. He looked around at the circle of monks who were standing at a respectful distance. He smiled at no one in particular. There was something disconcerting about the abbot's smile, which was humourless and even threatening because of his rather pointed teeth. He was startled by a sudden grunt near him. It was Owen the cellarer. Lost in a world of his own, the man had said nothing so far.

'Are you well, Brother Owen?' said the abbot.

Owen seemed to shake himself before saying, 'The cross

was attached to the underside of the stone by those brackets, isn't that right, Michael?'

One of the workmen raised his muddy face and pointed to the rusting iron bands.

'The cross fell away, sir,' he said, addressing the abbot. 'When we lifted up the stone, the cross fell away.'

'Is there anything else down there?'

'Don't know, sir. We stopped digging. We thought it best to report what we found.'

The other labourer nodded in vigorous agreement.

'Very well. Do no more digging today. You have done enough. Get a couple of your fellows to stay here and keep watch. Carry both the stone and the cross to the Hall.'

'They're dirty, sir. Should we clean them up?'

'That doesn't matter. Bring them straight away.'

Henry de Sully turned away from the makeshift tent. He moved at his usual deliberate pace, his face composed. He indicated to the sacristan and the cellarer as well as to Geoffrey that they should accompany him. He needed time to consider the implications of this find.

But if he'd hoped to keep the principal part of the discovery secret, it was too late. For, as the Abbot of Glastonbury moved towards his quarters, the hush that had fallen while he examined the cross was broken by a fresh outbreak of questions and whispers among the monks and the lay workers.

One word stood out from the buzz. It was a name. Not in the Latin form that was etched into the cross but in its English version.

'Whose is it? *Who* is it?'

'Arthur,' said the buzz. 'King Arthur.'

An hour later Henry de Sully, Owen, Geoffrey and Frederick were peering down at the cross. It had been laid on a table in the abbot's parlour, with a cloth to protect the surface of the table. But, of course, the cross was infinitely more valuable than a mere tabletop.

It was shaped like a great key, with a slope-sided head, stubby arms and a squared-off section at the end. The letters were quite crudely formed, almost crammed to fill all the available space. Frederick the sacristan had transcribed them – his veiny hand shaking with excitement – but each monk had the legend already fixed in his mind as if the cross-maker had inscribed it there himself: *HIC IACET SEPULTUS INCLITUS REX ARTURIUS IN INSULA AVALONIA*.

'Here lies buried the renowned King Arthur in the Isle of Avalon.'

This was Owen the cellarer. There was reverence in his lilting voice as he repeated, for the sixth time at least, the English meaning of the words. For all their seniority and air of wisdom, the four men had been reduced to little more than head-shaking and mute examination of the cross for several minutes now. They traced out the letters with disbelieving fingers. They stood back to marvel at the item.

One peculiarity was that the face of the cross had been placed inwards against the stone.

'Why should that be?' mused the abbot.

'Perhaps those who buried Arthur needed to keep his grave secret,' said his chaplain-secretary Geoffrey. 'His enemies would have despoiled his resting place if they found it, so the slab of stone was used to hide the face of the cross. That would also account for the small size of the cross. A great leader should have a fine grave, but Arthur was buried almost in secret.'

'Remind me, Brother Frederick,' said the abbot, 'why you ordered the men to dig in that spot.'

He knew perfectly well but felt it important to recapitulate events, to get a sense of order into the story. The sacristan, who had charge of the abbey library, was the obvious person to ask. He was an elderly, spare man but, apart from some stiffness in his joints, he had the stamina and memory of a man twenty years his junior.

'As you know, Father, it was the late King Henry himself who passed on to your predecessor a story concerning the burial at Glastonbury of Arthur and his queen, Guinevere.'

'And yet Robert of Winchester did not attempt to find the burial place, despite having a king's directions?'

'They were not directions, Father, so much as . . . as a fable told to Henry years ago by a bard from Brittany.'

'A bard from Wales,' said Owen.

'It doesn't matter,' said de Sully, smiling in his humourless way. 'Go on, Frederick.'

'According to Abbot Robert, King Henry could not recall much except that the body was reputed to be buried between two pyramids near the Old Church. The last abbot was not inclined to investigate any further. A "fable" was how Robert referred to it.'

'But this is no fable,' said Owen, brushing his hand over the surface of the cross.

'We did not look for the tomb in earlier days because the hints from the late king were vague. It was not until *you* came to Glastonbury, Father, and told us to begin the search . . .'

'The king has an interest here,' said de Sully. 'Our present king, I mean. He feels that the remains of his famous forebear should be more fittingly disposed of . . . if they can be found. I took my cue from him.'

The others were silent for a moment, no doubt contemplating the fact that de Sully came from a noble family, a very well-connected one. King Richard himself had recently elevated de Sully to Abbot of Glastonbury.

'It was Brother Frederick who thought that the "pyramids" in the old story might be the obelisks, the remains of ancient memorial crosses on the grass outside,' said Geoffrey. 'It was he who directed that the digging should start exactly midway between them.'

'That is so,' said Frederick, unable to hide his pleasure.

'If this is truly Arthur's cross, then why is it buried so deep?' said the abbot.

'In St Dunstan's time, we were running short of burial space,' said Frederick. 'Dunstan ordered that layers of fresh earth be heaped over the old cemetery. It is possible that the stone and the cross were themselves buried then.'

The sacristan talked as if he had witnessed Dunstan give his command a few years ago, yet the sainted abbot of Glastonbury had been dead for more than two centuries.

'So Arthur or his remains, and perhaps those of his queen, should be further still below the same patch of ground?'

'I do not believe so,' said Brother Owen. 'I do not think he will be found.'

The other three looked in surprise at the cellarer. Owen, an easy-going, gregarious individual – as cellarers tended to be – rarely expressed himself so directly. The abbot waited for him to explain. Owen seemed uneasy. He glanced out of the window at the gathering darkness.

'There is a story that Arthur is not dead but merely sleeping . . .' he said at last.

'All of the dead are merely sleeping . . . until they rise on the day of judgement,' said Henry de Sully.

'. . . and that he will return in the hour of his country's need,' said Owen, ignoring the interruption. He added quickly: 'I am only saying what I heard at my mother's knee.'

The abbot and the others had often heard such tales of

King Arthur, the past and future king. They dismissed them as credulous talk, popular on the western fringes of England and over the border in Wales, the parts of the country which had held out longest against the waves of invaders since the days when Arthur was supposed to have flourished. The surprise was that an educated man like Owen should even give voice to the belief. But then he was from Wales and would have swallowed the legend of Arthur's return with his mother's milk.

'So, in your opinion we will not find the remains of the king or his queen, Brother Owen?' said the sacristan.

'Even if we did unearth some bones,' said Owen, 'how would we know that they are Arthur's or Guinevere's? As you reminded us, Brother Frederick, the place we are excavating is the site of an old cemetery. It must be littered with human bones. We should explore no further; it is a sacrilege to all who lie at rest out there. We must be content with this cross.'

Once again he grazed his fingers over the leaden object.

'Our community in Glastonbury might be content with the cross,' said the abbot after a pause. 'It is a fine relic and will doubtless draw pilgrims and visitors to our abbey. But I have a living king to account to, a fact which may be more important than our scruples about a dead one. King Richard has personally urged me to dispose of King Arthur's remains more fittingly if they can be found. And we are nearer to finding them now than we were this morning. Surely, Brother Owen, you would wish to see the mortal remains of this great monarch and warrior bestowed with all due ceremony, not lost for ever in a common graveyard?'

'The fame of Glastonbury would sound across the land,' said Geoffrey.

Henry de Sully said nothing. Geoffrey was right, but it was not for the abbot to make such an expedient remark.

For his part Owen said nothing either. It was obvious that he did not wish the bones to be uncovered but he would not contradict his superior outright or disagree with Geoffrey.

Further discussion was not possible since they were interrupted by the early-evening call to vespers. Wrapping the leaden cross in the blanket, Henry ushered the others from his parlour. He made a show of locking the door. They left the Hall and walked out into the darkness, now suddenly sharp and cold. As Henry passed the tent, he was reassured to see a couple of the abbey labourers keeping watch over the entrance, their faces illuminated by flaring torches. He must order an all-night vigil to be maintained at the place.

In the Lady Chapel, the abbot was aware of a subdued excitement that seemed to make the air shimmer with more than the heat and smoke from the candles. This was no ordinary evening; these were no ordinary prayers and chants. He had to struggle to keep his own mind and heart on his devotions.

To an extent, and no doubt like the other senior Benedictines, Henry de Sully felt there was some justice in the Welsh cellarer's remark about the sacrilege of disturbing long-buried bones. But he was aware of other considerations. It was noble of King Richard to want Arthur's bones uncovered and then buried more reverentially; it was a desire befitting a monarch. But Henry de Sully, who was well versed in the ways of power, knew that another of Richard's motives wasn't so high-minded. By proving Arthur dead and gone, once and for all, King Richard would be able to stamp on those troublesome legends which asserted that the legendary leader was going to return. It might help to calm an occasionally rebellious spirit in the far-western fringes and corners of the country.

The abbot had his own reasons for uncovering the remains of Arthur and Guinevere. De Sully had been elevated from the grand but dour Thames-side abbey at Bermondsey to this great foundation in the west country. The origins of Glastonbury were lost in time, but one story held that Jesus himself had walked through this watery landscape. Another tradition was that the Old Church, the very one destroyed in the fire that also laid waste to other monastic buildings, had been the handiwork of the apostles of Jesus.

The abbot did not know whether this was true. He hoped it was true. In any case it had proved a useful tradition, drawing pilgrims and worshippers as well as the merely curious to Glastonbury. De Sully glanced around the interior of the Lady Chapel, with its bright patterning of reds and blues and yellows, the dyes and paints so recent that they seemed to glisten in the candlelight. For sure, this church was far removed from the simple wattle-and-daub construction of the disciples. It had cost money to build. To restore the abbey to its former glories would cost a great deal more. At the very moment when he had been disturbed by the buzz of voices beyond his window, he had been studying estimates for repairs and rebuilding. The unearthing of King Arthur's remains would be . . . convenient . . . in ensuring the continued flow of money into the abbey's coffers. To say nothing of keeping King Richard's benevolent attention fixed on Glastonbury.

So there was no question of halting the excavation just as they seemed to be on the verge of a discovery. He would order the workmen to continue their labours the next day.

These were the worldly and practical thoughts of Henry de Sully as he listened to evensong.

As he slipped quickly out of the abbey precincts after vespers, Owen the cellarer was gripped by rather less worldly considerations. He was not joining the other monks in the fraterhouse for supper. Instead he wondered how many of them would allow their thoughts to drift away from the scriptural passage that was read aloud during the meal. He wondered how many of his fellows would instead be as preoccupied as he was with this day's discovery.

Owen paused by the main gate to catch his breath. He wasn't used to moving at such a pace. Or perhaps it was the strain and excitement of the day's discovery which were leaving him breathless. Owen nodded towards the lay brother who acted as porter. He didn't have to explain his movements. With the exception of de Sully, the cellarer had more licence to come and go than anyone else in the abbey. Among other affairs, he was responsible for buying in provisions and so he had the most contact with the world beyond the monastic walls.

Owen gazed out and down from the slight slope beyond the gatehouse. Directly overhead, the night was clear with a waxing moon even though cloud was gathering in the west. The moon glinted off the lakes and rhines which dotted the land as it fell away from Glastonbury towards the great channel dividing England and Wales. As often, the Welsh cellarer had the impression that he was gazing out at a sea, broken by tiny islands scarcely more than reedy marshes and peat bogs. Glastonbury tor, on the lowest slopes of which perched the abbey and its small town, was the biggest of these islands.

Like his fellow monks, he was familiar with the story that Jesus had walked this watery region and that his disciples had constructed the first church with their bare hands. But Owen was thinking now of a quite different tradition, one which said that King Arthur had not only visited Glastonbury but had been brought here to die. That he had been buried in the Isle of Avalon.

The leaden cross excavated this afternoon was surely proof of the story. Gazing on it for the first time, seeing something which he had never dreamed of seeing in his lifetime, kneeling by the cross in the shadow of the makeshift tent, reading the Latin inscription, putting out tentative fingers to touch what had been so carelessly handled by the workmen, all this had affected Owen almost as much as if he were handling a piece of the True Cross on which the Saviour hung in his agony.

The letters *HIC IACET SEPULTUS INCLITUS REX ARTURIUS IN INSULA AVALONIA* swam before Owen's eyes. The cellarer had been unable to utter a word while Frederick the sacristan was exclaiming in wonder and Geoffrey was rushing off to give the news to Henry de Sully. It was only when Abbot Henry arrived and asked Owen whether he was well that he came back to himself.

Had anyone noticed? He didn't think so. Everyone was distracted by the discovery of the cross. He feared, however, that he might have drawn attention to himself in the abbot's parlour by announcing they should not dig down any further in the graveyard, that it would be sacrilegious to disturb the last resting place of Arthur – or of anybody else. He did not say so aloud but, as far as Owen was concerned, the king's bones must not be found. If they were, it would demonstrate that Arthur, the once and future king, could never return to reclaim his kingdom.

Better to find an empty grave. Better still not to dig any deeper and to be content with the cross, to treat it with the reverence which it deserved and to install it in a privileged place on display in the abbey. Where it would doubtless draw those pilgrims and visitors so desired by the abbot. Owen didn't despise the idea of visitors. He was almost as conscious as de Sully that such guests frequently made offerings and, as cellarer, he had a clearer idea than most of the abbey's finances and the costs of restoring the place after the ruinous fire of six years before.

It was surely right too, as Brother Geoffrey claimed, that the uncovering of Arthur's bones and perhaps of Guinevere's would not only guarantee the wealth of the abbey but cause its name to go down in history.

Yet none of these things weighed very heavily with Brother Owen as, guided more by instinct than the moonlight, he drew nearer the cluster of low dwellings, shops and taverns composing the town of Glastonbury. Like the now-vanished Old Church, they were mostly constructed of wattle and daub. There was the smell of woodsmoke in the crisp air. Doors were shut tight against the night. In the distance sounded the howl of a melancholy dog.

Owen reached the entrance to a building slightly larger and more solid than the others. Above the door hung a withered bush, the sign of a tavern. From within came male voices and bursts of laughter from a woman. He recognized the laughter.

Brother Owen put his hand to the latch and then hesitated. He could go back now and retreat to the abbey precincts. He could return and attend to his proper business before compline, the final summons of the day to prayer. Yet, he told himself, he was going about his proper business now. King Arthur must not be found. And he would be found if the men continued digging, for after evensong Owen had asked the abbot what his intentions were, whether he intended to order the hole filled in and the ground made level once more out of respect for the dead. Henry de Sully, slightly impatient with the cellarer's scruples, put his hand on Owen's arm, employed his pointed teeth in a kind of smile and said: 'Of course not. We cannot afford to leave things as they are. We must dig down and find whatever God permits us to find. If there is nothing there, so be it.'

Owen made no reply and inclined his head slightly in deference to the abbot, but at the same time the resolution hardened inside him. This was a moment he had long awaited. A moment of discovery that had been predicted in some quarters. But the bones of the king should never be claimed by the English.

So Owen grasped the latch and opened the door of the tavern.

When he entered, a few faces turned towards him through the gloom. The light provided by the handful of tallow candles was almost cancelled out by the smoky stench which they emitted. A couple of the drinkers nodded in recognition of Owen. As cellarer, he was a familiar enough figure in the little town whose suppliers and artisans depended on the abbey's patronage. Nevertheless, his appearance in the tavern was hardly usual. The monks could drink better wines and ales within the abbey, in the company of their own kind and in greater comfort too. Even the beeswax candles that Owen burned in his workroom gave off a more pleasant odour than the tallow ones in here.

But Owen had not come to drink or to compare the cost of candles. He had come to speak to the tavern-keeper, an individual called Glyn. Like the monk, Glyn was from Wales and he too had been brought up on stories of Arthur and that king's inevitable return. The tavern-keeper was serving a customer, pouring ale from a jug. His wife Margaret was in an opposite corner, getting familiar with a couple more customers, laughing with them. She was English. She caught Owen's eye. He nodded almost imperceptibly at her. Margaret's fair hair gleamed in the smoky candlelight. The Glastonbury cellarer had memories of that hair, of lifting the inn-keeper's wife's heavy tresses and allowing them to trickle through his fingers. He recalled the weight of her breasts against his cassock, he remembered their snatched hours together. Owen had been breathless often enough in the company of Margaret. She too in the monk's company.

Owen indicated to Glyn that he wished to see him, alone, and the taverner showed him into a curtained-off cubicle at the back of the room. There was almost no light, only what leaked through the thin fabric. It was a fusty sleeping area for all the family, Glyn and Margaret and four or five smallish children, Owen couldn't remember how many children, except that he rather thought one of them was his. So Margaret had informed him, and since she'd never asked for anything in return he had never had cause to doubt her word.

A bed big enough to hold the entire family occupied most of the space. There were snuffling, whimpering sounds as if the two men were standing amid a litter of baby animals. It occurred to Owen that it might have been better to have talked to Glyn in the tavern itself rather than draw attention by seeking privacy. Too late now.

'You've heard?' he said to the tavern-keeper.

'Everybody's heard. We had that Michael in here earlier, getting himself plastered on account of how he'd dug up the cross. Is it true, Father Owen?'

'Yes.'

'The cross of Arthur?'

'It seems so,' said Owen with a caution that the abbot would have approved of. 'It seems that the moment has arrived.'

'If the cross is found, what else is down there?' said the tavern-keeper. 'The king?'

The two men had been conversing in whispers, but Glyn's

voice dropped even further when he referred to the king. From beyond the curtain came voices, Margaret's renewed laughter.

'The king's bones *may* be there,' said Owen.

'How can they be? Arthur is not dead,' said Glyn.

'One part of us, my friend, believes that he is dead, as all men must be in the end. The other part of us knows that Arthur can never die, can never be allowed to die.'

'That's a bit deep for me, Father.'

'No, it is not, Glyn. You and I come from the same land; we are not like the English around here.'

'You're right there. Margaret's told me that often enough.'

'*We* understand why Arthur must live; *we* understand why he can have no grave,' said Owen. 'Or if he does have a grave, then it must be empty. Or it must be found empty.'

'How will that happen?'

'We need a little time. We cannot employ anybody around here. How long will it take to get help from—' Owen gestured vaguely over his shoulder. He might have been indicating somewhere a few yards away – or many miles to the west. In any case, the gesture went unseen in the darkness of the curtained room.

'Three days at least, maybe four days at this time of year.'

Owen sighed. It wasn't long enough. Excavation of the supposed burial place of King Arthur would be resumed tomorrow; the abbot had as good as said that. It might take the labourers another day, possibly longer, to dig down to the right depth and discover the remains. But they'd certainly do it within three days.

'Send nonetheless,' said Owen. 'Send for help.'

'They will not reach here in time.'

'Then pray for a miracle.'

'Who should I pray to, Father?'
'The spirit of King Arthur, of course.'

A miracle was what happened on the next day, or that very night to be precise. The westerly clouds which had been gathering in the evening rushed in later, bringing autumnal gales and unceasing rain. The ponds and rhines filled up, the abbey stews rose higher, the monastic gutters and gargoyles gurgled and spouted. And work on King Arthur's burial place had to stop. The flimsy tent was blown down by the wind, and the sides of the excavation fell in, covering up the previous day's work.

Henry de Sully watched impatiently from his parlour in the Hall, although there was nothing to see apart from mounds of glistening black earth and a hole that was turning into a pond. The leaden cross remained up here in his personal care, locked in a chest. It was an extraordinary discovery, but now he was expecting something yet more extraordinary, and even an hour's delay frustrated him. He had already written to King Richard, telling him of Arthur's cross and hinting strongly that this was only the first of several discoveries, all of them destined to reflect glory on the abbey and on the reigning monarch.

Meanwhile, Frederick the sacristan had been researching in the library with a vigour that belied his age. He assembled a quiverful of references showing that Arthur had close ties to Glastonbury. In his enthusiasm, he was inclined to lecture the abbot on these – to babble about Caradoc and *The Life of Gildas*, to tease out riddling verses by obscure Celtic bards, to talk knowingly of William of Malmesbury and his *Deeds of the Kings of the English* – until the abbot had trouble concealing his weariness with history.

While this was happening, Owen the cellarer attended to his duties. But he was always conscious that, by ordering

Glyn to summon 'help', he had set in motion a process whose outcome was uncertain and possibly dangerous. It wasn't that he did not trust the tavern-keeper. Not only was Glyn from Wales but he was well aware – so Owen believed – of the cellarer's relationship with his wife Margaret. He had never said a word, however, never dropped a hint.

Two days passed from the first unearthing of the cross until the skies cleared and the water in the excavation began to drain away. By the time the hollowed-out space was dry enough for work to start again it was decided to erect a more substantial shelter to protect the area, and so a further twenty-four hours had elapsed. And by that stage a small band of men was arriving on the waterlogged fringes of Glastonbury from across the wide channel that separated England from Wales. They did not stay in the town, fearing to draw attention to themselves, but found lodging in villages and settlements outside. They waited for word from Glyn. And he was waiting for word from Owen.

The abbot detailed extra men to dig in the burial ground, although it was hard to increase the work-rate much because of the cramped space. They did turn up more than a few bones, showing that the spot had indeed been a graveyard, itself buried under fresh earth. These bones were carefully removed and stored in a temporary coffin in the Lady Chapel. But the workmen reached a depth of fourteen feet or more without finding anything that might clearly signify the remains of a dead king. No sign of a ceremonial interment, no elaborate sarcophagus, no finely wrought coffin.

Henry started to regret the letter to King Richard. Was it possible that the cross denoting the presence of Arthur was a fake relic or that the fabled king was buried somewhere else altogether or that – as the legends of the Celts had it – the king would never be found because he had never died in the first place. The abbot remembered his cellarer expressing some such belief.

Then, almost as he'd begun to lose hope, the labourers toiling in the old graveyard seemed to reach their goal. This time there was no buzz of excitement, no crowd of monks and lay brothers hastening towards the enclosed space on the grass. Henry de Sully had instructed Michael, the most reliable of the workmen, to tell no one else but to inform him personally of any discovery. This Michael had done, his seamed, mud-streaked countenance alight with excitement and privilege as he stood on the threshold of de Sully's quarters. The abbot, acting with his customary calm, summoned only Frederick, Owen and Geoffrey. So it was the same quartet of Benedictines – the sacristan, the cellarer, the abbot and his secretary-chaplain – who gathered about the excavation, now completely shielded from prying eyes not only by the curtained sides of the tent but by the piles of soil surrounding it.

The hole was both wider and deeper, so much deeper that three men standing on each other's shoulders would scarcely have reached the rim. A long ladder was required to clamber down to the bottom where, amid a slurry of mud and bones and wood fragments, stood a couple of artisans. Their faces pale and sweaty, they looked up expectantly at the monks.

'There is a log down there, sir,' said Michael, 'a tree trunk which has been hollowed out. There are bones in the hollow. They have the form of a body.'

'That is an old method of interment,' said Frederick. 'It is all of a piece with the hidden cross. We are not looking for a grand mausoleum; we are looking for a hidden burial site.'

'Some of the bones in the tree hollow are very large,' said Michael. 'Look.'

With a conjurer's flourish he produced what appeared to be a shin-bone. He placed it beside his own lower leg for comparison. It was true: the bone was visibly longer – and Michael was not slight.

'Careful, man! Do not handle it so carelessly.'

This was Owen. He took the bone as reverently as if he were handling the host.

'There was this too, sir, down among the bones.'

Michael produced a leather pouch, shrunken and dirty, and handed it to the abbot. Henry unwrapped its stiff folds. Inside lay coiled a golden tress of hair, human hair. It was fresh and bright as if it had just been cut off. As when he had first seen the cross, the abbot felt the hammering of his heart. Beside him, Owen stumbled in excitement and would have fallen into the hole had not the wiry sacristan held him back with a restraining hand.

'A woman's, I'd say,' said Michael, who was starting to feel himself on an equal footing with the monks.

'A queen's, you mean,' said Owen breathlessly.

'Do not be so hasty,' said the abbot.

Then Frederick said: 'That is from a royal head. Whose else can it be except . . . ?'

'Except Queen Guinevere's,' said Henry de Sully.

The monks and the workmen conveyed the bones and the precious fragment of hair to the abbot's Hall. The golden tress was tightly secured again within the pouch lest exposure to the air should cause it to perish. Yet even this find had been outmatched by another discovery in the hollowed-out log: a man's skull with a great dint to one side. It indicated a sudden, violent death.

The great bones were not sufficient to make a complete man but rather to suggest the possibility of such a giant. Each of the individuals who stared at these remains in the abbot's parlour was lost for a time in his imagination, seeing a great and final battle in which a warrior-king had been fatally struck down. They put out their hands – even Michael and the other labourers – to touch the skullcap, the jaw-bone, the mighty shin-bone, the fragments of a ribcage, as if some trace of Arthur's spirit might be transmitted to their own blood and sinew.

Then, in a humble mood, the monks went to the Lady Chapel to pay their devotions. All of them, in addition to their public prayers, sent up silent thanks to God for having blessed Glastonbury with such legendary relics.

When they returned to the abbot's parlour, the bones and the pouch containing the golden tress had gone.

There was a council of war late that night in the same chamber from which the relics had disappeared. At first it seemed as though the bones and the pouch containing the Guinevere tress had been spirited away by some supernatural means. The door to the abbot's parlour was locked; he had made sure of that, the last man out of the room as they proceeded to vespers. There was no sign of forced entry and no other access except the windows, which were glazed and fastened from the inside. Besides, the parlour was on the first floor of the Hall.

Fortunately the cross was still secure in the locked chest, but its presence seemed merely to mock the monks with what they had so recently found and lost again.

Theft was rare in the abbey, despite the number of pilgrims and outsiders who frequented the place. It was unheard of in the abbot's own quarters. So Frederick assured Henry de Sully. In fact the shock of the vanishing of the bones and hair was so dreadful that it caused one of their number – Brother Owen the cellarer – to collapse on the floor as if he was about to have a fit. He was now being cared for in the infirmary.

So it was just the three, the abbot, chaplain and sacristan, who sat by the fire, musing over what had occurred and wondering what to do next.

'Did we dream this?' said Geoffrey. 'Did we dream that we had found those bones?'

'Of course not,' said Henry. 'Nor have they been taken by magic.'

'Brother Owen seemed to think so,' said Frederick. 'He has been more affected than any of us.'

'It is the Celt in him,' said Henry. 'But we shall all be affected if we do not act to remedy this situation. I mean, the good name of Glastonbury will suffer if it ever becomes known that we had Arthur's bones in our care . . . and then mislaid them. Or allowed them to be taken from under our noses.'

'No one knows yet that we have found the relics,' said the sacristan.

'No one apart from we four,' said Geoffrey, pedantically counting on his fingers, 'and Michael and the others who were present when they were exhumed. How long do you think *they* will keep it a secret?'

'There is only one thing to do,' said Henry de Sully.

He stood up so that his back was to the fire. He smiled without humour at the other two. He outlined his plan. There were, he said, other pieces of bone which had been disinterred during the excavations. It should not be too hard to find some larger-than-usual items that might be substituted for the missing ones belonging to the king. Even a skull which, by dint of artful bashing, might be given a blow simulating a fatal wound. They would pick among the bones in the coffin in the Lady Chapel and select those that might be fit for a monarch. 'And after all,' added the abbot, 'we still have the cross signifying that Arthur was buried here.'

'With respect, Abbot, it is an imposture,' said Frederick the sacristan.

'Good Brother, how is anyone to say with absolute certainty that the bones we choose are *not* a king's?'

'What about the lock of hair?' said Geoffrey.

Henry de Sully turned and gazed into the depths of the peat fire. When he turned back again, his face was flushed from heat or inspiration.

'There is a woman in the town, Margaret the wife of the tavern-keeper, I mean. She has a fine head of hair, fair hair. Brother Owen . . . talks to her from time to time, doesn't he?'

The other two exchanged glances.

'Our brother hears her confessions, yes,' said Geoffrey.

'He shrives her,' said Frederick.

'Well, then,' said the abbot, 'nothing could be simpler. When he has recovered, get Brother Owen to see what he can do to get a tress from this Margaret. Remember, meanwhile, that we do this not for personal profit or glory but for the sake of the abbey; we do it to protect our future.'

So it was that under the brightly coloured vaulting of the Lady Chapel and in the secrecy of night, the abbot, the sacristan and the chaplain rummaged among the human remains that had already been disturbed in the graveyard. They found what they were looking for: large bones for a man, even a skull that might be taken for the king's, especially after it was given a great tap with a hammer.

Meanwhile, in the infirmary, Owen sighed and sweated with guilt. He turned on his side on his hard, narrow bed and remembered how he had copied the key to the abbot's parlour, how he had slipped it to the tavern-keeper as he walked across the green on the way to evensong. He had already alerted Glyn, knowing from the abbot's earlier summons that something of significance had been found.

Lying on his sickbed, eyes staring into blackness, he had visions of men stealing into the abbey precincts while the monks were occupied at vespers, of dark shapes scurrying on the edge of the cloisters and the back of the kitchen quarters. It would not have taken the group long to get into the abbot's parlour and scoop up Arthur's relics.

Where were the bones now, he wondered?

But if he did not know exactly where they were, he knew in which direction they were going. They were being ferried across the marshes and peat bogs to the great channel separating England from Wales, they were being carried to the west under the protection of the guardians.

Once Arthur's bones were safe from discovery by the English, Owen the cellarer did not much care if his own role in this affair was discovered. He had played his part, he had done his duty. Even so, once he was out of the infirmary the next day, he took the precaution of disposing of the duplicate key by throwing it in a stew in the abbey grounds. A large fish swam towards the surface to inspect Owen. Its mouth gaped. Owen was reminded of the abbot's teeth.

There was no sequel to the disappearance of the bones. No one mentioned it. In fact, to his amazement he was invited to feast his eyes on those very items once again in the abbot's quarters. Nods and hints gave him a good idea of what had occurred. As did Henry de Sully who, drawing him aside, explained that he should use whatever influence he had with the tavern-keeper's wife to get her to surrender a lock of her golden hair.

'Do you think you can manage that?'

'Yes,' said Owen cautiously.

'Suggest she give it up as an act of penitence,' said the abbot, smiling. 'Her hair is a snare in which the hearts of men are caught. I refer to secular men, Brother Owen, who must be protected from the perils of golden hair. Penitence, I say.'

'Yes, Abbot.'

'She has much to be penitential about, I dare say.'

'We all have,' said Owen the cellarer. 'We all have.'

Many miles across the water and among the hills to the west, at the time when Brother Owen was gazing open-mouthed on the substitute bones, a similar scene was taking place in an isolated, long-abandoned church. A second group of men was assembled in a circle around the genuine relics which had been taken from the abbot's Hall in Glastonbury. They spoke little but their words were solemn. The men were dressed in the garb of artisans, which some of them were.

The church was a shell rather than a building, with ragged walls and a roof which was more holes than thatch. Tucked away in a fold among the hills, it had fallen into disuse when the village it served had withered away through sickness and migration. All that remained inside was a stone altar, as rough and fissured as a boulder newly tumbled from a hillside. The bones of Arthur and the leathern pouch containing the tress of hair were spread across the altar, illuminated by nothing more than the light of the moon and the stars which soared above the gaping roof.

Yet to each man in that place the relics of the king seemed to shine with their own light.

They had paid their homage to the bones and now their leader – a slight man whose name was Meurig ap Rhys, a man with a widow's peak as sharp as a flint dagger – gave his instructions on the safeguarding of the remains of the great king. When their duties ended, which they surely must at the conclusion of their own mortal existences, the task would pass to their offspring, he said. They were the Guardians. They held in trust the future lives of their race. He predicted that the day would come – not in their lifetime, nor that of their sons or even their sons' sons, perhaps, but come it would – when the bones of the great warrior-king would be required once more. The crisis when the descendants of the present company would be called on to throw off the invader's yoke. He swore them to silence on pain of those same lives.

Ap Rhys may have been slight of stature but his word was law. Two of his own sons were among the group. He nodded at them with particular emphasis as he bound the group to silence.

None of those standing in a ring about the bones doubted him. When the ceremony was finished, ap Rhys dismissed everyone save for his sons. He waited until the sounds of footsteps and horses' hooves had died away on the still, frosty night. Then the three men retrieved the bones and leather pouch from the top of the altar-stone and reverently folded them in silken wrappings and deposited them in a small chest which had been brought to the dilapidated chapel for this very purpose. The chest was not large, certainly not large enough to draw attention, being no more than the length of a man's arm and about two-thirds as wide. Placing the chest in a cart to which was tethered a small but sturdy pony, the men bowed their heads under a moon which was nearly at the full. After a moment's silence, with the father leading the horse and the sons on either side of the cart, they paced off down the track towards the lowlands.

# ACT ONE

## I

### Carmarthen, February 1196

Meurig was dying. The battle to repel the invaders was lost, and the castle was ablaze. The town rang with victory cries from Lord Rhys's men, screams of terror from hapless civilians, and the roar of flames. The billowing smoke was making it difficult for Meurig to breathe, but an arrow had lodged in his spine and his legs no longer worked – he could not move to a more comfortable place to die. In an agony of despair, he wondered what would become of King Arthur's remains now.

He had thought the bones he had spirited away from Glastonbury would be safe in Carmarthen. The pretty little town in southern Wales was under Norman control, it was true, but this paled into insignificance when its history was taken into account. It was said – and Meurig believed the tale with every fibre of his being – that Merlin the magician had been born there. And Merlin had always been Arthur's protector.

He thought back to the perilous journey from Glastonbury, some five years before. It had taken weeks to trek through the wet countryside, always travelling at night so as not to be seen. All three of his sons had been with him – Hywel the eldest, jealous and brooding; jovial Young Meurig in the middle; and shy Dewi, his favourite. The box he had fashioned for the precious cargo was not very large – as long as a man's arm, two-thirds as wide, and high enough to accommodate Arthur's impressive skull. The wood was hard and black, and Meurig had coated it with a damp-repelling resin.

Once the bones were safely in Wales, he had dismissed the other men he had appointed to be Arthur's Guardians – too large a party would have attracted attention – and continued the journey with only his sons for company. Naturally, the others had objected. Arthur was so important to Wales that they were appalled at the notion of leaving him, but Meurig had insisted. And they, dutiful souls, had deferred to his wishes and had returned to their homes, to carry on with their lives until they were summoned again. As the son of a Welsh prince, Meurig had always been a leader, and the Guardians – trusted friends, close kin and long-time allies in battle – were all men who acknowledged him as such.

Of course, he had paid a terrible price for his decision. A robbers' ambush near Dinefwr had almost seen the bones lost, and afterwards . . . Meurig bit back a sob. When the raid was over, and the villains had been successfully repelled, his beloved Dewi lay dead. He was not sure he would ever forgive himself for that.

He took a deep, shuddering breath, pushing the painful memories from his mind as he focused his thoughts on his current predicament. What was he going to do about Arthur? How was he to protect the bones if he could not even climb to his feet? And why had Merlin failed to watch over his erstwhile protégé? Meurig closed his eyes in despair. Carmarthen had been a *good* choice. The ancient king *should* have been safe there.

But Meurig had reckoned without the Lord Rhys, who had always resented the fact that Normans occupied the strip of land south of his stronghold – and who had finally elected to do something about it. It was ironic, Meurig thought bitterly, that the hope of Wales should be put at risk, albeit unwittingly, by one of Wales's greatest heroes. It was even more ironic that the feisty old warrior-prince was Meurig's own father. Bitterly, Meurig ap Rhys reflected on the events that had seen him racing to defend the treasure he had hidden – and that had resulted in him being mistaken for a Norman and shot by Welsh bowmen.

Lord Rhys had attacked Carmarthen in the darkest part of the night, when most of the garrison was asleep and the sentries were handicapped by a bank of clouds that blotted out the moonlight. His small but efficient force had swept into the town before the Normans realized what was happening. By the time the alarm was raised, Rhys's men had gained control of the castle bailey. The ensuing fighting was ferocious and had lasted all morning. Meurig had not joined in – his sole objective was to protect the ancient oak under which he had buried Arthur.

Hours had passed, and he began to hope that the worst was over. But then the invaders had swarmed into his part of the town, and they had seen not a Welshman standing sentinel by a tree, but a stranger with a sword. Before he could open his mouth to say he was a son of Lord Rhys, he had been cut down by archers.

Afraid they might return to see what he had thought worth protecting, he had dragged himself the short distance to his house, where he had hidden among the ivy that grew around his door. He wished he could go inside, because night was approaching and it was bitterly cold. But his strength was spent: he would now die where he lay.

He closed his eyes and wished with all his heart that his father had chosen another Norman-held settlement to harry. After hiding the bones in Carmarthen, Meurig had settled there, and he was fond of its winding streets, busy riverside dock, stalwart castle and handsome buildings. His pretty little cottage had a Welsh cheese-maker on one side and an English grocer on the other. He liked them both, and hoped they would survive the raid.

Of course, there was another reason why Carmarthen was attractive to him: his favourite sister, Gwenllian, lived there. Ten years before, Lord Rhys had forced her to marry the town's constable – Sir Symon Cole was one of King Henry II's favourite soldiers, and it had suited Rhys to forge an alliance with his Norman neighbours at the time.

Unfortunately the alliance had died along with old King Henry, and Rhys had either forgotten or did not care that the castle he was now attacking was held by his son-in-law. Meurig could hear Cole in the distance, yelling to his scattered troops. Was he preparing a counter-offensive? Meurig hoped not. The battle was lost, and futile heroics were likely to get him killed – and then Gwenllian would be inconsolable, because although she had objected to the match at first, she had grown to love her brave, if not overly intelligent, spouse.

Meurig opened his eyes and looked towards the end of the street, where the old oak stood. Legend said the tree had been planted by Merlin himself, and although most people dismissed it as a fairy tale, Meurig felt it was true. Whenever he touched its ancient bark, he could almost feel the magic coursing through it.

So, shortly after he had arrived in Carmarthen, he had taken Arthur's chest and gone out alone one night, to dig between the tree's gnarled roots. It had been an evening when the town's richest merchant had invited everyone to celebrate a daughter's marriage, so Meurig knew he would be safe from prying eyes. The box had fitted into the hole as snugly as a babe in a cradle, and putting it there had felt so innately right that Meurig had the peculiar sense that the tree had been waiting for it. Even the memory was enough to make him smile, in pain though he was.

But he did not smile for long. Through the swirling smoke, he could see that the tree had been damaged – a branch had fallen. He experienced a great lurching fear in the pit of his stomach. Was this the beginning of its end? Was it no longer able to provide a haven for his secret? Gradually it dawned on him that the bones would have to be moved – taken somewhere they would be safe.

But how? He did not have the strength to stand, let alone excavate a chest. He felt sick with self-recrimination. He had told no one where he had hidden Arthur, not even his sons, because it had seemed an unfair burden to foist on young men – and the prospect of his own premature death had never occurred to him. He had not even sent word to the Guardians, although he had always intended to; somehow, he had never managed to get around to it. He berated himself as he lay there. How could he have been so negligent?

He thought about his two surviving sons. Young Meurig was away in Gwynedd, learning to be a warrior. And Hywel? Where was he? Meurig had not seen him since the fighting had started, and hoped he had not been harmed. Had he taken part in the battle? Meurig was sure he had. Hywel was cold and brutal, and would have relished the opportunity to wage war against Normans. Or rather, against Cole. For reasons Meurig had never fully understood, Hywel hated Gwenllian's constable husband with a cold and deadly passion.

As he lay in his doorway, Meurig wished Dewi had not died and Young Meurig was to hand. Could Hywel be trusted with the secret, even if he did come home? Meurig had to pass it to someone, so word could be sent to the Guardians. But what if Hywel did not come? Who else was there? There were people around – the street, just beyond his veil of ivy, was full of them, racing this way and that, howling at the top of their voices, some in triumph and some in fear.

Now most of the skirmishing was over, the prince's men had turned to looting. Priory Street, where Meurig lived, was home to several wealthy men, and the invaders were beginning to congregate there, like flies around meat. He could see his neighbours, Spilmon the grocer and Kyng the cheese-maker, barricading their homes. Kyng's was like a small fortress already, with a great, thick door and sturdy window-shutters, but Spilmon was offering increasingly wild sums of money to any local man willing to help him repel thieves. Could they be trusted with the secret? Gwilym Kyng was Welsh, so he should welcome the chance to serve his country. Regrettably, though, Meurig knew Kyng would be more interested in defending his own possessions than in rescuing ancient relics.

Next he saw the constable's clerk, a timid, diffident Englishman named John. But John was far too feeble to be of use – he was trembling so violently he could barely walk, and Daniel, the castle chaplain, was almost carrying him towards the sanctuary of the priory. What about Daniel, then? He was said to be a decent man. But he would not do either – his first loyalty would be to the Church, and Meurig was afraid he would hand the bones to his Norman prior, in a monkish act of obedience.

Behind them was another Carmarthen resident, generally known as Gilbert the Thief. Obviously *he* was not a suitable candidate, but what about the fellow with him, Sir Renald de Boleton? The Norman knight was acid-tongued and lazy, but he was a competent warrior and unquestionably intelligent. Would he accede to a dying man's last wish and carry a message to the Guardians? Meurig supposed he would and opened his mouth to call out. But suddenly someone was pushing his way through the ivy. It was Hywel.

'Father!' Hywel gasped, dropping to his knees and seizing Meurig's hand. 'I have been looking for you all day – I did not see you among these leaves when I was here earlier. I thought . . .'

'Not dead yet,' Meurig said with a wan smile, indicating his wound. 'But it will not be long now. No! Do not carry me inside – it will only hasten my end, and there are matters to discuss.'

Hywel glanced around quickly, to ensure that no one else was close enough to hear. 'You refer to Arthur's bones? You appointed me a Guardian, but never told me where they are hidden. You had better tell me now, because they may not be safe here much longer. They must be moved.'

'But moved where?' Meurig's voice was full of anguish. 'Wales is full of tiny kingdoms, all unstable and constantly at war. How can we know which ones will prevail?'

'Then give them to Lord Rhys.' It was not the first time Hywel had suggested this solution, and hearing it again made Meurig uneasy. 'My grandfather is a good man and a great leader.'

'He is old and has too many enemies – putting Arthur's bones in his care runs the risk of them falling into the wrong hands. And that must never happen.'

Hywel was about to argue, but there was a movement behind him. 'Your sister is here,' he said with a resentful scowl – he had always been jealous of his father's affection for Gwenllian. 'We joined forces when we realized you were missing and have been searching together.'

Meurig felt a great surge of relief. His shrewd, beautiful kinswoman would know what to do, and there was no one in the world he trusted more. He smiled when she knelt next to him. There were cinders in her black hair, and her face was smudged with soot, but she was still the loveliest woman in Carmarthen. She turned to Hywel.

'Fetch Brother Daniel from the priory,' she said urgently. 'Hurry!'

'Fetch him yourself,' retorted Hywel indignantly. 'I am not leaving. I need to hear—'

'This is no time to be thinking of yourself,' she interrupted sharply. She fixed him with an imperious glare, looking every inch a princess of Wales. 'Go!'

Lesser men than Hywel had been cowed by that expression, and he began to back away. Gwenllian watched him go, then turned her attention to Meurig, smoothing the flint-sharp widow's peak from his forehead with gentle hands.

'There is something I must tell you,' he whispered. 'It is a terrible secret, and I am sorry to burden you with it, but there is no one else.'

Gwenllian tried to stop him from talking, to save his breath for his confessor, but he would not be silenced.

'You remember the stories of Arthur?' he asked, his words coming in an urgent rush. 'How he will lead our people out of oppression and into an age of peace and prosperity? How he represents all our future hopes? For the proud nation we shall be when we are free?'

Gwenllian thought he was rambling. 'Of course,' she said soothingly. 'You told me these tales when I was a child on your knee, and I will never forget them. But rest now, because—'

'It means Arthur did not die,' Meurig pressed on, eyes boring into hers, trying to make her understand. 'If he had, he could not be sleeping in a cave, ready to wake and lead us to victory.'

'No,' agreed Gwenllian, bemused. She wondered if he was delirious, and tried to quieten him a second time.

'But what if his bones were found?' whispered Meurig, riding across her concerns. There was nothing he would have liked more than to close his eyes, content in the knowledge that she was with him, but it was a luxury he could not afford. 'What would that mean for Wales?'

Gwenllian shrugged, the puzzled expression on her face telling him she had no idea what he was talking about. 'I do not know – that we have no hope, I suppose.'

'Quite. So they—' Meurig faltered when there was a faint sound behind his front door. Was someone there, listening? But there was no time to ask Gwenllian to investigate. He pressed on. 'So they must *never* be discovered. Or, if they are, then they must be delivered into the hands of people who will know what to do with them – for the good of Wales.'

'Then if ever I hear of them excavated, I shall—' Gwenllian began reassuringly.

'But they *have* been excavated,' Meurig whispered. 'Arthur's body was exhumed at the abbey in Glastonbury five years ago.'

Gwenllian gaped at him. 'How do you know? And how can you be sure it is Arthur's—'

'One of the monks is Welsh,' interrupted Meurig, speaking even more urgently, because he could feel the darkness of death approaching. 'He told me what had happened, and together we managed to spirit the bones away. I brought them here, to Carmarthen. Because of Merlin.'

'Arthur's protector,' said Gwenllian, understanding immediately. Meurig gave a brief smile – she always was quick-witted. Then her face clouded. 'Is that when poor Dewi . . .'

Meurig winced, then nodded. 'Yes, Dewi was killed bringing him here.'

There was another sound behind the door, and this time Gwenllian heard it too. She started to move towards it, but Meurig grabbed her hand and held it tightly. There was simply no time.

'Listen to me, carefully, Gwenllian. The future of Wales depends on it.'

He described the bones from the abbey, the hank of hair discovered with them, and listed the men he had chosen to act as Guardians. She nodded her approval at his choices, although he could tell from her expression that she thought they should have been closer to hand.

'I buried Arthur under Merlin's oak,' he concluded, lying back exhausted. 'On the far side of the tree. But it has been damaged, and he is no longer safe. So you must retrieve him and put him somewhere secure. *You* are a Guardian now.'

'And take him where?' Gwenllian was appalled by the responsibility being imposed on her.

But Meurig did not reply. Her voice seemed a long way away, and when his head lolled to one side he was unable to stop it. With his vision fading, the last thing he saw was a pair of feet – someone *was* hiding behind the door by which he was lying, and that person had heard every word he had said. He tried to speak again, but his strength was spent. He closed his eyes and died without another word.

Gwenllian was numb with grief. Although Meurig was many years her senior, she loved him more than her other siblings, and their relationship had grown deeper still when he had made his home in Carmarthen. What would she do without him? Who would talk to her about the old Welsh ways, and teach her little-known snippets of her nation's history? And what was she going to do about the bones he had entrusted to her care? The other Guardians were miles away – and messages to summon them were unlikely to get past Lord Rhys's sentries anyway.

Hywel arrived with Daniel, the Norman monk from the nearby Augustine priory who served as castle chaplain, but she barely heard his muttered prayers. Daniel did not stay long – there were many others who needed his services. Hywel, pale with shock, carried Meurig inside his house, then went in search of a coffin.

'A coffin?' asked Gwenllian dully. 'Why?'

'They will be in high demand today,' Hywel explained in a choked, broken voice. 'And I am not letting *my* father go to the grave without one – he was the son of a prince, and I am going to ensure that he is buried as such. Stay with him until I return.'

'Please do not be long,' begged Gwenllian, too distressed to argue. She did not tell him why she could not linger long with her brother's body. Hywel was family, but she had never really liked him, and felt Meurig had been right to entrust her, not his son, with his secret.

But it was fully dark by the time Hywel returned, two men at his heels toting the most handsome casket money could buy. By then, Gwenllian had been kneeling by Meurig for so long that she could barely move, and Hywel was obliged to help her stand.

Yet her mind had cleared, and she knew what she had to do: go to Merlin's oak and inspect the damage. Then she would send for her husband, and they would excavate Arthur that very night – Symon would be full of self-recrimination for losing the castle, and digging up bones would take his mind off the debacle for a while. There was a risk of being seen, of course, but the tree cast its own shadows, and its far side was not overlooked by houses – unlike the near one, which she could see from Meurig's window.

She left the house and started to walk along Priory Street towards it; even from a distance, she could see that the tree had indeed lost a branch.

She turned when she heard her name being called. Three men were hurrying towards her. One was John, her husband's mousy little clerk, and the others were Meurig's neighbours – Spilmon and Kyng. She liked Spilmon, but Cole had fined Kyng for selling underweight cheeses, and the man had been unpleasantly hostile to them both ever since.

'There you are,' Kyng said irritably. 'We have been looking everywhere for you.'

'Why?' she asked. The other two men were refusing to meet her eyes, which was making her uneasy. 'What is the matter?'

Kyng's expression was vengeful. 'Your husband would insist on fighting on when it should have been obvious that all was lost. He has been wounded, and Daniel says he is going to die.'

Gwenllian regarded the cheese-maker in mute horror, and Spilmon shot him an uncomfortable glance. 'That was roughly done, friend. Could you not have found a gentler way to—'

'It is not true!' cried Gwenllian, cutting across him. 'Symon surrendered hours ago, and I went with him to discuss terms with my father. He is rounding up his troops to *prevent* more violence, not to continue it. And he gave Lord Rhys his word that there would be no more skirmishing anyway.'

'Well, he must have broken it, then,' said Kyng spitefully.

'Who can blame him?' asked Spilmon, gesturing at the

chaos around them. 'It is dreadful, being forced to stand by and watch these louts rampage through our town, stealing and burning.'

'Go to him, My Lady. Now,' urged John. He was trembling violently, still terrified even though the fighting was over. 'Or he will slip away before you can say your farewells.'

Gwenllian gazed at them. Surely they were mistaken? Symon would never break an oath solemnly sworn. 'Where is he?' she demanded.

'St Peter's Church – not far,' replied John. His finger shook when he pointed towards it. 'He was asking for his friend Boleton too, and it is bad luck to neglect a dying man's last request, so I had better do as I am bidden.'

He scuttled away, aiming for Merlin's oak and the priory beyond, where many Carmarthen folk – civilians and soldiers – had taken refuge. Gwenllian began to run in the opposite direction, stomach churning. She was vaguely aware of Spilmon escorting her. Kyng was not – he had waddled off towards his own home, confident that his iron-studded door and well-made window-shutters would protect him from harm, and eager to hide himself behind them. The moment she reached the church, Spilmon muttered an apology and was gone too. Gwenllian pushed open the door with unsteady hands and entered the darkness within.

Cole was in the Lady Chapel, guarded by a grizzled sergeant named Iefan and several soldiers. Daniel was there too. The monk shot to his feet when Gwenllian hurried towards them. A distant part of her mind noted that his habit was now torn and bloody, leading her to wonder whether he had ignored his order's injunction against violence and had exacted his own vengeance for the havoc that had been wreaked on his town.

'I am sorry,' he said in a choked voice. His face was white, and she knew his distress was genuine – he and Cole were friends. 'I have done all I can.'

Gwenllian dropped to her knees next to her husband. 'What happened?' she asked, struggling to keep her voice steady. Symon was barely breathing, and the light from Daniel's candle illuminated an unnatural pallor.

It was Iefan who answered. 'He and I were rounding up the men, ordering them into the forest lest they felt like fighting again, but we became separated. Then I heard Daniel yelling for help.'

'I had found Symon lying on the ground,' explained Daniel in a whisper. 'I think I saw someone running away, but I cannot be sure.'

'Kyng accused us of picking off Lord Rhys's best archers under cover of darkness. But we were not – it never occurred to us.' Iefan reflected for a moment. 'It might have occurred to Boleton though – he was livid when we surrendered, because he thought we could still win.'

'Then he was wrong,' said Daniel harshly. 'Symon did his best, but we never had a chance. Lord Rhys's men were simply too strong and too well organized.'

But Iefan was still thinking about Boleton. 'Maybe *he* was picking off the enemy, and the prince's men mistook the two of them in the dark – both are knights, of roughly the same size. Or maybe Boleton convinced Sir Symon to join him, although if he did they were not doing it for long – Sir Symon was gone from me for only a few moments.'

A decade of marriage to a soldier told Gwenllian that a dagger was responsible for her husband's injury, but she was shocked to note its position: he had been stabbed in the back. What had he been doing to sustain such a wound? *Had* he and Boleton been waging a small war of their own? It did not seem likely, given Symon's low opinion of truce-breakers. But Boleton had a sly tongue, and it would not be the first time he had used mangled logic to bring his slower-witted friend around to his way of thinking.

But it was no time to ponder. The cut was deep and had bled profusely, but it was also clean, and she thought she could repair the damage – with care and warmth, Symon might yet survive. She stood, feeling the horror and helplessness recede as grim resolve took over. She had lost a brother that day, but she was damned if she was going to lose a husband too.

'We are taking him to Kyng's house,' she announced. 'It is the nearest safe place.'

'It is safe here,' objected Daniel. 'No one will attack a house of God.'

Gwenllian was not so sure about that, especially once the invaders got at Carmarthen's copious supplies of ale and wine. And the church was a large building – too large for Iefan and his men to defend effectively. But no good would come of alarming them with grim predictions. 'It is too cold,' she said instead. 'And Symon needs a fire. Lift him gently, and follow me.'

Kyng's door was barricaded when they arrived, but she hammered and yelled until the cheese-maker had no choice but to answer – the rumpus was attracting attention. He was furious.

'You cannot bring him in here!' he hissed. 'He broke the prince's ceasefire, and *that* is why he was stabbed. I do not want *my* property incinerated as punishment for sheltering the enemy.'

'I do not care what you want,' snapped Gwenllian. 'Stand aside.'

Kyng opened his mouth to argue, but there was something in her regal glare that warned him against it. Muttering venomously, he did as he was told. Iefan and his men carried Cole inside, and Gwenllian followed, heartened to note that there was a good fire burning in the hearth.

'It is not as if Kyng has a family to consider – he is unmarried,' muttered Iefan resentfully. Then he glanced around uneasily. 'Where has he gone? It had better not be to bleat to the enemy that the constable lies here – the constable who was injured after the fighting was supposed to have stopped. Perhaps we had better move—'

'We are not going anywhere,' said Gwenllian firmly, acutely aware that Symon would not survive any more jostling. 'We shall set a guard on the door – you can take it in turns.'

'*I* cannot,' said Daniel apologetically. 'Others are dying too, and they also need my prayers. But you have Iefan, and Boleton will be about somewhere. When I see him, I shall send him to you – he will help.'

'Assuming he is not fighting,' muttered Iefan under his breath.

For everyone's sake, including Boleton's own, Gwenllian sincerely hoped he was not.

The night was one of the longest Gwenllian could remember. There was an orange glow in the sky where the castle still burned, and the street outside was full of noise – the raiders were drunk and growing increasingly wild. Skirmishes broke out as they squabbled over spoils, and the sound of clashing arms and screams made her want to put her hands over her ears. But no one attacked Kyng's home. Iefan thought the thick door and shuttered windows were responsible, but Gwenllian knew the truth – that Lord Rhys had somehow learned his daughter was within and had ordered the place to be left alone.

Cole failed to improve as the hours dragged by, and she

began to think Daniel might be right – he was going to die, and her determination to save him was not enough.

'He keeps asking for Boleton,' she whispered to Iefan, distressed by the patient's agitated entreaties. 'He would rest easier if Boleton were here, so where *is* he? Why does he not come?'

'He must be with the men in the forest,' replied Iefan. 'He cannot know what has happened, or wild horses would not stop him from being here. He and Sir Symon are closer than brothers.'

During a quiet spell, Gwenllian went to the door for some fresh air. The priory had been set alight, illuminating Merlin's oak in a stark silhouette. It was oddly lopsided, and she recalled Meurig's fear that it was no longer capable of protecting the bones.

It occurred to her that she should send some of Cole's men to guard them – it was not a good idea to leave them unattended when the town was full of men who were of a mind to steal. Obviously she could not tell them *what* they were minding, but she was perfectly capable of fabricating a tale they would believe. Unfortunately she knew they would refuse to leave their master. And she could not go herself – not only would she not abandon Symon either, but she could hardly excavate a heavy chest and spirit it away by herself.

Then her eye lit on a familiar, lanky figure. Gilbert the Thief was not the first man she would have turned to for help, but she was hardly overwhelmed with choices.

'Gilbert,' she called softly. 'Come over here.'

The thief looked around uneasily, as if he imagined there might be another Gilbert in the area. By rights, he should have been hanged years before, but Cole disliked executions and preferred to incarcerate him in the castle prison instead. And Gilbert was not very good at his trade anyway – what he stole was invariably recovered – and people tended to regard him more as a lovable rogue than a criminal.

'Will you do something for me?' she asked when he was close enough to hear. 'Will you stand by Merlin's oak until I send someone to relieve you? I will pay you for your trouble.'

Gilbert's eyes widened in surprise. 'Why?'

'Because of the legend,' she lied. 'The one that says Carmarthen will cease to exist if the tree should fall. I thought you might like the honour of making sure that does not happen.'

Pride filled Gilbert's face but then faded away. 'I am sorry, lady, but I cannot. I have things to do, and it is more than my life is worth to ignore them.'

'What things?' she demanded indignantly. 'What is more important than saving your town?'

Gilbert became flustered. 'Just things, lady. It is best you do not ask – what you do not know cannot harm you. Just go back inside and pretend you never saw me.'

He left abruptly when shouts indicated the revellers were coming back. Gwenllian put her face in her hands and wished the night was over.


It was almost a week before Lord Rhys adjudged his warriors to be sufficiently sober to march to the next Norman castle he wanted destroyed. During that time the townsfolk – Norman, English and Welsh alike – were ordered to remain either in their homes or the priory. Cole hovered at the brink of death for four days, but then his fever broke and he slipped into a more natural sleep. When he woke, he asked for Boleton again.

'He is in the forest, keeping our men in order until the prince leaves,' replied Iefan with more confidence than Gwenllian felt was warranted.

Cole accepted the explanation though, and it was one time when she was grateful for his ingenuous habit of believing everything he was told. Then, before she could stop him – it was hardly a suitable subject for a sickroom – Iefan began to recite the names of everyone who had died in the raid, and she felt tears scald her eyes when Meurig's was among them.

'Meurig?' echoed Cole, shocked. He groped for her hand. 'Oh, Gwen! I am so sorry.'

She took a deep breath to compose herself. Symon hated to see her cry, and she did not want him upset. 'Never mind that – we should talk about you. Do you recall what happened?'

'Kyng said you were picking off the enemy's best archers,' promted Iefan. 'Were you?'

'No!' exclaimed Cole, appalled. 'I had surrendered, and the prince had accepted my pledge of good behaviour. Of course I was not fighting!'

'Then tell us who attacked you,' urged Iefan grimly. 'I will see he answers for his crime.'

'It was dark – I could not see.' But Cole was a poor liar, especially to anyone who knew him.

'Who was it?' demanded Gwenllian, thinking she would strangle the culprit with her bare hands; the murderous attack had come far too close to succeeding.

'All men look alike in winter cloaks,' Cole murmured, closing his eyes so he would not have to meet hers. 'It might have been anyone.'

His face was ashen, so she did not press him. He fell into a doze and was still asleep when the prince rode away the next day, taking with him a hefty chunk of Carmarthen's portable wealth.

The moment the dust settled, the townsfolk began to emerge from their hiding places. Gwilym Kyng was among the first to arrive, anxious to see whether his house was still standing, although he refused to acknowledge that it was Gwenllian's presence that had saved it from the torch. Spilmon and his insipid wife, whose name Gwenllian could never remember, had accompanied him.

'Where have *you* been?' demanded Iefan coolly. 'You slipped away like a snake in a—'

'Of course I fled!' snapped Kyng. 'What did you expect? For me to die with you, when Lord Rhys set fire to the place where his enemy lay? But Rhys has gone thank God, and now I want you gone too. Your clerk has arranged you accommodation near the castle, so please leave.'

'We cannot move Symon yet,' said Gwenllian, aghast. 'He is too weak.'

'I do not care. It is his fault the town lies in ruins – he should have protected us.'

'Easy, friend,' whispered Spilmon, embarrassed. 'He did his best – and almost died for it.'

'Well, his best was not good enough,' said Kyng angrily. 'It will take years for the town to recover from this disaster – if ever. Moreover, the raiders have not only stolen all my cheeses, but they burned my dairy into the bargain. I am ruined! And I want him out of my home. Now!'

'We are not moving him until he is strong enough,' said Gwenllian firmly. 'So I suggest you lodge elsewhere, if you find his presence so objectionable.'

'You can stay with me, Gwilym,' offered Spilmon generously. 'I am missing a roof, but my downstairs rooms are relatively unscathed.'

'We cannot accept guests,' whispered Spilmon's wife. 'We have only one bed left.'

Spilmon shot her a pained smile. 'Then you can lodge with your sister while Gwilym and I stay here in Priory

Street. These are trying times, and we must all make sacrifices.'

Mistress Spilmon grimaced, as if she thought her sacrifice was rather greater than her husband's, but she bowed her head and accepted his decision. Gwenllian raised her eyebrows, thinking she would have strong words to say to Symon if he ever treated *her* with such rank disregard. She watched the two merchants march away arm in arm, while Mistress Spilmon trailed along behind them.

Daniel was the next to seek them out. He looked exhausted and said he had spent much of the week either burying the dead or absolving the dying. Atrocities had been committed by both sides, and he estimated that more had died during the pillaging than in the initial attack.

'But at least Symon is not among them,' he said with a tired smile. 'I thought he was lost when I saw his wound, but God saw fit to spare him.'

Eventually Boleton arrived, breathless and dishevelled, claiming he had spent the entire time of the occupation rallying Carmarthen's garrison in the woods, ready to drive the invaders out.

'I was about to spring into action when I saw them riding away,' he declared. 'So I decided to let them go. Why risk the lives of our men when the enemy was leaving anyway?'

'I am glad you stayed your hand,' said Cole. The relentless stream of visitors was taking its toll, and his voice was weak. 'We had surrendered – promised we would not fight again.'

Boleton waved a dismissive hand. 'That was before Lord Rhys started looting. It would have been he who broke the terms of the truce, not us, and I am sorry I did not get the chance to tackle him.'

'Boleton's tale *is* true,' said Iefan in a low voice to

Gwenllian, seeing the doubt in her face. 'He *did* move troops about in the forest – the men told me.'

'I am sure he did. But moving and intending to attack are two different things.'

She studied Boleton carefully. He was a handsome man in his thirties, who might have done well for himself had he not been so unashamedly lazy. Cole liked having his friend to hand and had created a post for him at the castle, thoughtfully ensuring it was one that did not entail too much work – Boleton's duties revolved around investigating crime, but as Carmarthen was relatively law-abiding, the effort required to fulfil them was negligible.

*Was* Boleton telling the truth about what he had been doing for the past week? He did not look as if he had been sleeping rough, and Gwenllian was sceptical of his next tale too – that he had fought off a large band of vicious forest-dwelling robbers single-handed.

John the clerk arrived halfway through it, bursting with administrative matters that required urgent attention. Unfortunately for him, Gwenllian decided Symon had had enough at that point, and ushered everyone out.

'I cannot leave until I know what to do about the supplies that were stolen,' objected John in dismay. 'And there is a missive from the Sheriff of Hereford that requires an immediate answer.'

'It will have to wait,' said Gwenllian firmly. 'My husband needs to rest now.'

'It is not him I want – it is you. You make all the important decisions anyway.' John raised his hands defensively when she started to object. 'I mean no disrespect, My Lady. It is an arrangement that works very well – your brains and his authority.'

Gwenllian knew it was true, but it sounded disloyal coming from John. Knowing nothing would be gained by sending the man away with a flea in his ear, she dealt with his questions, then walked to Merlin's oak, grateful for the opportunity to stretch her legs at last.

Like the town, the tree bore the ravages of battle. There was a gash of pale wood where a branch had been hacked off, and some of its leaves had been singed. But even so, it stood tall and strong. She ran gentle fingers over the crusty bark and thought her brother had been right to entrust his secret to its care. It exuded an air of comforting permanence, and she had the strange sense that Merlin's power still coursed through it. She started to walk in a slow circle around its trunk, then stopped in horror when she reached the other side.

There was a gaping pit in the ground. The roots had grown to form a protective cocoon around whatever had been placed there, and someone had used an axe to hack through them.

She stared into the empty hole as she thought about Meurig's last words. She had tried to stop him from speaking, partly because she had not wanted him to die before Daniel could absolve him, but also because she was sure someone else had been listening – someone who had slipped into Meurig's house and lurked behind his door. But who?

She racked her brains, trying to think who might have spotted her kneeling next to her brother and come to see whether he was confiding details of hidden money. Everyone with sense had buried what they could when the attack had started, so it was not inconceivable that someone had surmised that he was telling her the whereabouts of hastily concealed wealth.

She closed her eyes, recalling the people she had seen – Kyng and Spilmon; John the clerk; Boleton, before he had escaped to the forest; Gilbert the Thief. Meanwhile,

Hywel had gone to fetch Daniel but had taken longer than he should have done – perhaps he had returned to listen to what his father had to say. Or was the villain one of Lord Rhys's men, and the precious relics were even now being toted east?

But would anyone have the audacity to lay thieving hands on King Arthur's bones? Of course they would, she thought grimly, because such items were worth a king's ransom – no religious foundation would pass up the opportunity to buy such a prize. And there was Glastonbury to consider – its abbot would no doubt be delighted to receive back what had been taken from him.

Trying to track them down after so many days would be impossible, and she dropped to her knees and wept when she saw she had let Meurig down – she had lost what he had given his life to protect.

# II

## *Summer 1198*

It was more than two years since Lord Rhys had attacked Carmarthen. Buoyed up by the ease of his victory, he had gone on to sack Colwyn and Radnor, and the Normans had been hard-pressed to contain the grizzled old warrior. Then he had died suddenly, and his heirs were more interested in sparring with each other than harrying Marcher lords. Peace reigned, albeit an uneasy one, giving Carmarthen a chance to recover.

The first task was to repair the castle. The Marcher lords had learned their lesson with fortresses made of wood, so Carmarthen was rebuilt in stone. It was not long before the keep had been given a sturdy curtain wall studded with towers. The bailey was extended too, and deeper ditches dug for defence. Meanwhile, the townsfolk plundered the surrounding forest for wood and pilfered nails from the castle-builders, so houses and shops were soon restored as well. Apart from a grassy knoll in St Peter's churchyard, where those killed in the raid had been buried, there was little to remind the inhabitants of the horrors of Lord Rhys's visit.

It was a busy time for Gwenllian. As constable, it was Cole's responsibility to oversee the building work, and once he had recovered he flung himself into the physical side of the operation with great enthusiasm, leaving his wife to manage what he considered the mundane tasks – organizing labour rotas, commissioning supplies and hiring suitable craftsmen. With his brute strength and her talent for administration, the work proceeded apace, and she had scant opportunity to dwell on Meurig's death or the loss of Arthur's bones.

One day, when the project was nearing completion, they stood together on the new battlements, enjoying the warmth of a summer evening as the sun set in a blaze of red-gold over the Tywi Valley. By standing on tiptoe, Gwenllian could see the topmost branches of Merlin's oak, just visible between St Peter's Church and the towers of the priory beyond. Some judicial pruning had corrected its lopsided appearance, and the great gash in its bark had healed.

Although she rarely thought of the chest Meurig had buried, she did consider it then, wondering again who had stolen it. She had expected to hear of the relics being offered for sale – Lord Rhys had sired a number of children, legitimate and otherwise, which meant Gwenllian had a large complement of half-brothers and sisters to supply her with news and gossip, and little happened that was not reported to her. But there had not been so much as a whisper about the bones. It both puzzled and irritated her – she did not like mysteries.

She had been pondering the matter for some time before it occurred to her that Cole was unusually quiet. He was normally full of chatter at the end of the day, eager to tell her whom he had met and what he had done, and it was rare for him to be silent. She regarded him in concern.

'What is wrong, Symon?'

He pulled himself from his reverie and shot her an unconvincing smile. 'Nothing.'

She narrowed her eyes. 'Do not lie – we both know you are hopeless at it. So tell me what is the matter. I am sure we will be able to find a solution – we usually do.'

'*You* usually do,' he corrected glumly. 'Very well, then. Daniel was murdered last night.'

'Our chaplain?' she cried in horror. 'Why would anyone kill him? Who have you arrested?'

Cole grimaced. 'No one – I do not know who was responsible.'

'Then what are you doing to find the culprit? I cannot imagine Daniel had enemies – he had his faults, of course, but he was a tolerant, patient confessor and that alone made him popular.'

'What faults?' asked Cole, a little sharply. Daniel was his friend – two Normans a long way from home, who shared a fondness for horses and fine wine.

Gwenllian touched his arm sympathetically, seeing it was not a good time to remind him that the monk had been rather worldly for a man sworn to poverty – he preferred the rich foods available at the castle to the simple fare of his priory, and never declined gifts from his flock. But his gentle compassion in the confessional meant people tended to view his weaknesses with indulgent affection. She doubted anyone would have killed him over them.

'He was wealthy for a monk,' she mused, trying to think of another motive. 'Perhaps he was the victim of a robbery.'

'No, because he still had his purse – it was the first thing I checked. It contained six pennies and a little phial of something I assumed to be holy water.'

'Tell me what you know of his death,' she ordered, not bothering to point out that felons tended to run away if they were disturbed, so the presence of the purse proved nothing one way or the other.

'He celebrated a special Mass for the castle carpenters last night. Afterwards he and I shared a jug of wine in the hall, and it was dark by the time he left. He was killed on his way home.'

'How did he die?'

'He was hit over the head with something heavy.'

'Where did it happen?'

'By Merlin's oak, which is within spitting distance of his priory.' Cole's voice broke as he added: 'He was almost home.'

'When was he found?' asked Gwenllian, touching his arm a second time.

'This morning. His brethren did not worry when he failed to return last night, because his duties as castle chaplain often keep him out late. His body was discovered at dawn, by my clerk.'

'What was John doing there at such an hour?' Gwenllian was immediately suspicious. 'He lives here in the castle and has no reason to be on the other side of town at dawn.'

'I did not ask. I suppose I shall have to interview him again.' Cole did not sound enthusiastic.

'Are there any witnesses to this horrible crime?'

'If there were, they would have told me the name of the culprit, and he would be in my prison,' replied Cole, uncharacteristically curt. 'So, no, Gwen. No one saw what happened.'

But she knew what was really troubling him. 'You offered to escort him home after the wine was finished. I heard you. But he refused. Do not even think of blaming yourself.'

He stared morosely into the bailey below. 'I should have insisted. The people of Carmarthen have a poor bargain in me – I fail to protect them from raiders, and I fail to protect their monks.'

'They could do a lot worse,' she said briskly before he could grow too dejected. 'And we shall avenge Daniel's death by bringing his killer to justice.'

Cole regarded her doubtfully. 'And how will we do that, when the villain left no witnesses and no clues as to his identity?'

'By using our wits.' She shot him a mischievous glance. 'Well, *my* wits and your authority as constable, to be precise. No wicked murderer shall best *us*.'

Gwenllian spent a restless night reviewing all Cole had learned about the murder, although it was frustratingly little. Daniel had left the castle at roughly nine o'clock, and John had found him dead just after first light. Priory Street was a major thoroughfare, and although there was a curfew during the hours of darkness it was not very rigorously enforced, and she was sure *someone* must have seen something that would help them solve the crime.

She decided her first task would be to question John, to ascertain what he had been doing out discovering bodies at such an hour, and her second would be to inspect the scene of the murder. Cole claimed the culprit had left no clues, but he would have been thinking along the lines of dropped weapons or easily identifiable items of clothing, and it would not have occurred to him to look for more subtle evidence. And if grilling John and examining the place where a man had been bludgeoned to death did not provide answers, then she would interview the residents of Priory Street. Cole said that Boleton – whose remit it was to investigate crime – had already done that, but Boleton's legendary laziness meant Gwenllian could not be sure he had been sufficiently diligent, and she felt it needed to be done again.

She was awake and dressed long before dawn, and she and Cole ate a hurried breakfast of bread, cheese and summer berries in the hall, both eager to begin their search for answers as soon as possible.

'Is Daniel's body in the priory?' she asked, wondering whether anything might be gained from examining it. She doubted Cole – or Boleton, for that matter – would have thought to check it for clues.

'I brought him here.' Cole hesitated, but then pressed on. 'Mistress Spilmon said it was wrong to foist a bloodstained corpse on his brethren, and asked if she might be allowed to ... She will come to tend him this morning.'

'Mistress Spilmon?' asked Gwenllian, mystified. The wives of wealthy merchants did not usually volunteer to prepare bodies for the grave – that was a task performed by impoverished widows who needed the money. 'Why would she do that?'

Cole shrugged sheepishly, in a way that made her sure he was holding something back. 'He was her confessor – perhaps she wanted to perform this one last service in return. Did you want to see him?'

Gwenllian followed him across the bailey to the chapel, an unassuming building with wooden walls and a thatched roof. Daniel lay on a trestle table, and someone had covered him with a clean blanket. Cole removed it, then rolled the monk on to his side, so she could see the back of his head. The wound was not as fearsome as she had anticipated, and it seemed Daniel had been unlucky – the blow had caught him at an odd angle and he might have lived had it struck a little higher or a little lower.

'Mistress Spilmon must have tended him already,' she remarked. 'There would have been *some* blood, but someone has washed it away. And his hair is damp.'

'I did that last night,' said Cole. 'There *was* blood, and I did not want her to see it.'

Gwenllian regarded him askance. 'She offered to lay him out, Symon, so I doubt she is squeamish about gore. But it was kindly done, and it certainly helps me, because I can see the wound has a very clear imprint. Can you?'

Cole bent over the body, squinting in the unsteady light of the lamp. Then he looked at her in confusion. 'It looks like a cross. There is a long mark that leads from his crown towards his neck, and a shorter one that transects it.'

'Precisely.'

He continued to regard her uncertainly. 'Are you saying the culprit is another monk – that a cross from the priory was the murder weapon?'

His face was pale, and she understood this was not a very desirable solution – the Church was powerful and would object to a secular official accusing one of its members of heinous crimes.

'Not necessarily, although we should bear it in mind. But crosses are not the only cruciform objects in existence. Look at your sword, for example. Were you to strike someone with its hilt, it would produce a wound shaped exactly like this one.'

He glanced at it. 'I am not the killer – I was tucked up in bed with you when Daniel died.'

She said nothing, but his claim was not entirely true.

She had heard Daniel leave, but it had been some time before Cole had joined her upstairs. She had asked him where he had been, and he had mumbled something about a raid on the kitchens for food. It was something he did not infrequently, and she had thought no more about it.

'If Daniel *was* killed with a sword, then none of your soldiers is responsible,' she went on. 'Their hilts are too thick to have made this mark. In other words, the murder weapon would be a knight's blade, not one owned by a common man.'

'Then Daniel was killed with something else,' said Cole firmly, 'because the only knights in Carmarthen at the moment are Boleton and me. What else might it have been?'

Gwenllian was not surprised to hear him dismiss the possibility that Boleton might be responsible, given their close friendship. Personally she disliked the man, and had still not forgiven him for what she saw as his abandonment of Cole during Lord Rhys's raid – not to mention his unattractive habit of running up debts and persuading Cole to settle them. Fortunately, though, a recent inheritance had made him comfortably wealthy, so he was currently paying for his own wine, whores and fine clothes.

'Some pots have bases that are cruciform,' she suggested. 'Spilmon showed me one only last week, which he had bought in Bristol. It was very heavy, and might well kill a man.'

'Spilmon,' mused Cole. He did not add anything else, but his expression was troubled. 'Can the body tell you anything more?'

She wished he had not washed it, feeling all manner of clues might have been lost in his misguided attempt to be sensitive. She inspected the rest of Daniel, noting that his habit bore two muddy patches where he would have fallen to his knees, and dust on the chest and stomach – from pitching forward into the dirt.

Then she picked up his purse, and emptied the contents into her hand. As Cole had said, it contained six pennies and a small phial. And there was something else too, caught in some loose stitching at the bottom. It was a finger-bone – one that suggested its owner would have been enormous.

Gwenllian's mind reeled as she stared at what lay in her hand. Then she flung it away, frightened by it. Cole regarded her in astonishment, but it was a moment before she could speak.

'Do you remember me telling you how my brother hid King Arthur's bones under Merlin's oak?' she asked unsteadily. 'And how someone overheard, and got them before I could do as he asked, and move them somewhere safe?'

Cole grimaced. 'Yes – you were delayed, because you were nursing me. You had several suspects, although I cannot recall them all now.'

She began to list them for him. 'I virtually told Gilbert the Thief that the oak held something worth stealing, while your clerk John has a nasty habit of eavesdropping. Did you know he was listening to you and Daniel two nights ago, by the way? I saw him in the shadows when I went to fetch a cup of water from the kitchen.'

Cole blinked. 'Why would he do that? All we talked about was horses and the recent spate of thefts that have been plaguing the town.'

'Have you asked Gilbert about those?' asked Gwenllian dryly.

'Of course. But Boleton and I searched the caches he usually uses for his stolen property, and they are empty.

Besides, Boleton has been watching him, so he cannot be the culprit this time. Personally I suspect outsiders – outlaws from the forest, who sneak into the town after dark.'

They were getting away from the subject. 'Boleton was on my list of suspects too,' she said.

Cole scowled. 'He was rounding up our men, to prevent trouble. He did not take your bones.'

Gwenllian did not argue, but she had her doubts. She had given the events of that fateful night a lot of thought, and could not escape one obvious conclusion – that Symon had been knifed to create a diversion, to prevent her from retrieving Meurig's chest. She had done everything in her power to make him talk about what he had seen, but he had resisted, doggedly maintaining that it had been too dark to be sure of anything. Why would he keep his silence, unless he suspected the culprit was someone dear to him – a friend he was determined to protect?

'Spilmon and Kyng own the houses on either side of Meurig's,' she continued, prudently steering the discussion away from murky waters. 'That in itself is no reason to suspect them, but they recouped their losses very quickly after the raid. Is it because they sold valuable relics?'

'The invasion started at the opposite end of the town from Priory Street,' Cole pointed out. 'Perhaps that gave them enough time to bury their own treasure – in other words, they did not lose as much as they claimed.'

'Perhaps,' acknowledged Gwenllian. She hesitated, but then pressed on. 'I hate to include a family member on such a list, but Hywel has always been an enigma to me. He does not work, but never lacks for bread, and will not explain how.'

'He has changed since his father's death.'

It was an understatement of enormous proportion. Hywel had never been particularly amiable, but since the raid he had grown surly and withdrawn. It was entirely possible that he had delayed fetching Daniel in order to eavesdrop, and had then hurried off to attack Cole and steal the bones once his father was dead. Gwenllian recalled his curious insistence on acquiring a coffin – surely not a priority for most recently bereaved sons. And then what had he done? Sold the relics to the first religious house willing to buy them? Was that what kept him in ale when he did nothing to earn an honest day's pay?

She closed her mind to the awful possibility and turned to the last of her suspects – the one who suddenly loomed larger than the others because of what she had just found in his purse.

'Daniel was in the vicinity too,' she said quietly. 'He came to pray over Meurig's body.'

Cole's jaw dropped. 'You suspected Daniel? But he was a monk!'

'And monks cannot steal?' Gwenllian pointed to where the bone had fallen. 'I wager anything you please that this huge finger belonged to Arthur – Meurig said the bones in the chest were massive, and there cannot be *that* many enormous relics in existence. So how does it come to be in Daniel's purse?'

Cole bent to retrieve it. He was a large man, but the bone dwarfed his hand. He stared at it for a while, and she could almost hear his mind working.

'Do you really believe King Arthur was so vast?' he asked eventually. 'I have listened to dozens of ballads about the man, but none says he was a giant. Surely, if he were, *one* account would have drawn attention to the fact?'

It was a valid point. Could he be right, and the fact that Meurig said his chest contained a behemoth meant it was *not* Arthur? Gwenllian tried to recall what her brother had told her about the discovery at the abbey in the English marshes.

'When Arthur's leg was measured against that of a Glastonbury workman, it was almost twice as long. And the skull was so large that the distance between the eye sockets was more than the width of a hand. This was seen as proof that the skeleton belonged to a special man.'

'Very special!' remarked Cole caustically. 'If you are right, then Arthur would have towered over his fellow warriors, and that would have made him very vulnerable in battle – any common bowman could have picked him off. Personally I do not believe he was a monster.'

'Those were ancient times,' she suggested tentatively. 'Perhaps everyone was bigger then.'

'In that case, you cannot use their unusual size to contend that they belonged to a special man,' he argued with uncharacteristically impeccable logic. 'They might belong to anyone. Was there anything in this Glastonbury tomb that might make identification certain? A sword, for example – perhaps one with an engraving on it?'

'Well, there was hair,' recalled Gwenllian. 'Meurig said it belonged to Arthur's queen. Apparently some of it fell to dust when it was grabbed.'

Cole looked dubious. 'I saw ancient hair in France, but that did not disintegrate when *I* touched it. And it does not prove anything one way or the other anyway.'

She did not ask how he came to be handling old corpses – not all his soldiering stories were very salubrious. 'Well, Meurig said the bones were Arthur's, and that is enough for me,' she said firmly. She nodded to the bone in his hand. 'Can we be sure that it is human?'

'Who knows? But may I make an observation about the phial in Daniel's purse? I assumed it was filled with holy water – he was a monk and usually had some to hand –

but I have just remembered that the priory uses round pots for that purpose. His is oval.'

Gwenllian was bemused. 'What are you saying?'

'That if his bottle does contain something holy, then it is not water blessed at the priory.'

Gwenllian narrowed her eyes. 'So his purse held two relics, not one? This phial might contain something else from Meurig's chest? Is that what you are suggesting?'

'I am not suggesting anything; I am stating a fact. Interpreting it is for you to do.'

It was still dark when they left the chapel. Cole was regaling Gwenllian with descriptions of grisly relics he had seen on his various travels, but she was not listening. Her mind was full of what they had learned. *Had* Daniel overheard Meurig, then stabbed Cole in order to prevent her from claiming the bones? And was he really callous enough to have pursued a friendship with Symon afterwards, spending hours in his company and enjoying his generous, open-hearted hospitality?

She frowned, trying to recall precisely what had happened when. She had ascertained at the time that Symon had been knifed not long after Meurig had died. And who had found him? Daniel! The monk had summoned Iefan, and together they had carried Cole to St Peter's Church, where he had ordered Spilmon, Kyng and John to find her. She recalled how his habit had been torn and bloody, and how she had wondered whether he had ignored his vocation and joined in the fighting. But now it occurred to her that he might have been stabbing his friend instead. Or was she maligning the man? He had, after all, been ministering to those hurt in the fighting, so some stains were going to be inevitable.

She spotted Sergeant Iefan in the bailey, and beckoned

him over. 'You were with Symon very quickly after he was attacked two years ago. Will you tell me what you remember?'

'Not this again, Gwen!' groaned Cole. 'Do you not think it is time to forget about it?'

'Willingly,' said Iefan, ignoring him and addressing Gwenllian. She was not the only one for whom the incident still rankled, even if the victim had put it from his mind. 'It occurred not far from the castle, and there were a number of people milling about – Lord Rhys's men as well as townsfolk. But no one saw it happen – and, believe me, I asked around afterwards. Daniel found Sir Symon – it was he who told us to take him to the church, because it was the safest place.'

'Do you recall seeing blood on Daniel's habit?' she asked.

Iefan nodded. 'And it was not his own either. But I turned a blind eye – if he was seized by the urge to knock a few raiders' heads together, then good luck to him, I say.'

'He joined in the fighting?' Cole was startled. 'But he told me he spent the whole time on his knees, praying. I remember thinking that it had been a waste of a strong pair of arms.'

'Then he lied,' said Iefan bluntly. 'Not that I am accusing him of anything untoward, you understand. He was probably just embarrassed to admit there was a warrior beneath his habit.'

'He did not linger long once we had arrived at Kyng's home,' mused Gwenllian. 'He left with almost indecent haste.'

'To minister to the dying,' said Cole. 'Not to excavate bones while you were otherwise engaged. He was a good man, and he was my friend. I refuse to believe anything bad about him.'

Gwenllian inclined her head. He was entitled to his

opinion, as she was to hers. However, Cole was too trusting for his own good, because any number of people had seen the monk wandering around when he claimed to have been at his devotions. And if Daniel had lied about that, then what other untruths had he told? And why?

It was time to speak to John, the clerk who had discovered Daniel's body. Cole sent a boy to wake him, unwilling to waste a single moment now the investigation was under way. John arrived yawning and rubbing the sleep from his eyes. He looked tired, as though he had spent a disturbed night, and Gwenllian wondered why – his duties at the castle were hardly onerous, so his fatigue was unlikely to be due to overwork.

'I will finish the stores inventory today,' he bleated in alarm when he saw Gwenllian. He was far more intimidated by the constable's wife than the constable. 'I have been busy of late.'

'Doing what?' asked Gwenllian evenly.

John became flustered. 'Going through old documents – there is no point in keeping records of ancient transactions, as I am sure you will agree, sir.' He gazed at Cole, hoping to elicit his support – the constable was well known for having scant patience with administration.

'Really,' said Gwenllian sweetly, before Cole could respond. 'Perhaps later, you will show me what you have done, and we can admire the fruits of your labours together.'

John's consternation intensified. 'It is tedious stuff, My Lady,' he babbled. 'Normally I would delegate it to one of my underlings, but it seemed unfair to foist such a dull task on them.'

'I see,' said Gwenllian, not sure what to make of the tale. She decided to investigate, but not that morning. Daniel's murder was a far more pressing matter. 'But my husband did not summon you here to talk about your work. He has questions about what happened yesterday.'

'You mean when I found Daniel?' John gulped uneasily. 'But I already told him about that.'

'He would like you to tell him again. To iron out one or two inconsistencies.'

'Inconsistencies?' John was now seriously discomfited, and Gwenllian could see Cole frowning; clearly this had not happened when the clerk had been interviewed the previous day.

'Well?' she asked, when John did no more than stare in alarm.

'I discovered Daniel just before dawn,' John replied shakily. 'He was lying face down under Merlin's oak. When I saw the blood on his head, I guessed he had been unlawfully slain, so I ran to the priory to raise the alarm. Then you and Boleton arrived, sir, and I told you my tale.'

Gwenllian mulled the information over. 'The wound was on the back of Daniel's head, and he was lying on his front. That suggests he did not see his assailant coming – or he trusted the fellow enough to turn his back on him. He stumbled forward and died where he lay.'

'Yes.' John was nodding. 'There was nothing to say he moved after he was hit.'

Of course, Gwenllian had already surmised how Daniel had fallen from the marks on his habit – the two muddy smears at knee height, where he had been knocked from his feet, and the dust on his chest where he had pitched to the ground. Then she frowned. Something was amiss. The answer clicked into her mind: the weather. She filed it away, to discuss with Cole when John was not there.

'What do you think happened to Daniel?' she asked of the clerk.

John swallowed. 'That is not for me to say, My Lady.

Sir Symon pointed out that his purse was not stolen, so it cannot have been robbery. Perhaps he was assaulted by someone who does not like foreigners – Daniel was Norman. Or it was a case of mistaken identity.'

Gwenllian raised her eyebrows. 'You do not think his bulky figure in its monastic habit made him distinctive?'

'Not if it was dark,' John flashed back. 'And there are several taverns near Merlin's oak. Perhaps his killer was drunk – his judgement impaired.'

'Why were you out at such an hour?' demanded Gwenllian. 'To walk there before anyone else means you must have risen very early – far earlier than you woke today. And it is common knowledge that you start work late.'

'Yes, but I finish late too,' John objected defensively. 'I am still at my books long after everyone else has gone home.'

'Even more reason to answer my question, then.'

John spread his hands in a shrug. 'I could not sleep, so I went for a stroll to clear my mind. It is something I do not infrequently.'

Gwenllian nodded to the writing equipment the clerk had brought with him, having assumed, not unreasonably, that he had been summoned because his clerical skills were needed. He carried a sheaf of parchment, an inkwell, some pens and a portable desk.

'You tote this wherever you go, do you not?' she asked, taking the desk from him and turning it over in her hands. It was a heavy, well-made piece, built to last a lifetime.

The clerk stiffened, as if he had been accused of something. 'Of course. I am a scribe. I cannot work without the tools of my trade. It is—'

'Why were you listening to the discussion between my husband and Daniel two nights ago?' interrupted Gwenllian, aiming to disconcert him. There was something about the diffident Englishman she had always found unappealing, and she had never really trusted him.

John regarded her in horror. 'I was not—'

'You were. I saw you,' she said harshly. 'Now answer my question.'

John's cheeks burned. 'They were talking about horses,' he mumbled. 'I am interested in horses, and could not help myself.'

Gwenllian asked one or two more questions, but it was clear the clerk had no more to add – or no more he was prepared to share, which, as she remarked to Symon when John had gone, was not necessarily the same thing.

'Do you think he killed Daniel?' asked Cole worriedly. 'You certainly treated him as though he were a suspect.'

'Only because he behaved like one.' Gwenllian tapped her chin thoughtfully. 'And I am unconvinced by his tale of early-morning walks. But despite his reluctance to cooperate, I still garnered a few interesting snippets from his answers.'

'You did? The only thing I learned was that he likes horses – which surprises me, because he has never expressed an interest in them before. And he rides with all the grace of a sack of corn.'

She regarded him askance, amazed he should have believed the tale. 'I think you will find that was a lie, *cariad* – he was listening for some other reason. Did you notice his portable writing desk, by the way? Its base is formed by two strips of wood that meet in the middle.'

Cole raised his eyebrows. 'A heavy implement with a cross. Do you think it is the murder weapon?'

'If so, then he cleaned it well, because there was no blood. And something else occurred to me as he spoke, although it is not something that points to his guilt – or lack thereof, come to that. It was fine yesterday – we have not had rain in days.'

'For more than a week. What of it?'

'The marks at knee level on Daniel's habit were muddy. *Muddy*, Symon, not dusty. The surface of the ground is dry, although it will be damp deeper down. The stains on his chest were powdery, consistent with him falling face forward on to the hard ground. But what of his knees?'

He regarded her blankly. 'I have no idea what you are talking about.'

'Then think! He was not on his knees because he stumbled on to them when he was hit, as I first thought – he was already on them.'

'Praying?' suggested Cole tentatively.

'Digging!' Gwenllian failed to understand why he could not see what was so obvious. 'His knees came into contact with soil from deep within the ground – *muddy* soil – but his chest was only dusty. Moreover, he died at Merlin's oak. And what was buried at Merlin's oak?'

'Arthur's bones. But they are no longer there. Or are you saying you were careless and did not look as closely for the wretched things as you might have done? You overlooked them?'

'I was careful – they had certainly gone. But that was two years ago, and now we find Daniel in possession of a relic that almost certainly came from Arthur's chest.' Gwenllian began to stride towards the gate. 'So I suggest our first port of call this morning should be the place where Daniel was murdered.'

Bewildered and hopelessly out of his depth, Cole turned to follow her.

The questioning of a clerk at an hour when he was usually abed did not go unnoticed. The castle was a small community, and very little happened in it that was not soon common knowledge, so they had not reached the gate before Renald de Boleton intercepted them. Cole beamed a welcome at the knight he regarded as a brother, although Gwenllian's greeting was rather more restrained.

'What has poor John done that you felt compelled to haul him from his slumbers at such an ungodly hour?' Boleton asked. He was wearing a fine new tunic that Gwenllian had not seen before. 'The poor man is still shaking.'

'Gwen asked him some questions,' replied Cole, giving his friend the kind of look that said that should be explanation enough. It was not unknown for the princess to home in on some aspect of castle management that did not meet her approval and interrogate someone about it.

'Questions about what?' pressed Boleton. 'The fact that he spends more time on personal matters than on his duties?'

'Does he? I had not noticed.' Cole's shrug suggested he did not care either.

Gwenllian did. 'What personal matters?' she demanded.

'He talks of taking the cowl,' explained Boleton. 'But decent clerks are hard to come by these days, so we should all try to dissuade him – for the good of the castle.'

'John a monk?' asked Cole, startled. 'Will anyone accept him? He is such a quiet mouse.'

Boleton laughed. 'He wants to join a monastery, not an army, brother! Quiet mice are no doubt highly prized in abbeys, especially ones who can write so prettily.'

Cole pondered the notion of anyone yearning for a monastic existence for a moment, then dismissed it as incomprehensible. 'We were asking him about finding Daniel's body.'

Boleton's eyebrows shot up. 'Investigating crime is my job. Are you telling me I am relieved of my responsibilities?'

'Just Daniel's death,' replied Cole. 'Gwen is going to solve that. But it is good news for you – it will leave you more time to deal with the burglaries that have the town in such an uproar.'

'True,' agreed Boleton. He frowned. 'But surely you do not suspect John of killing Daniel? The monk was a large man, and an unfit scribbler like John could never have bested him.'

'It takes no great strength to hit someone from behind. Especially if he is kneeling.'

Gwenllian winced, and wished Cole had not shared this particular piece of information, although she could not have said why.

'Kneeling?' pounced Boleton. 'You mean he was killed while he was at prayer? But he was struck down under the tree in Priory Street. What are you suggesting? That he was dabbling in some pagan rite that had him on his knees under Merlin's oak in high summer?'

'Of course not,' said Cole, before Gwenllian could stop him. 'He may have been digging for something. In fact we are going to see what can be learned from the scene of the crime now.'

'Intriguing,' mused Boleton, rubbing his chin. 'May I come with you? I am bored with looking into these dull thefts, and this sounds like an amusing diversion.'

'Hardly a diversion,' said Cole reproachfully. 'Or amusing either. My friend is dead.'

Boleton, unrepentant, snorted his disdain. 'A man who liked you for fine wine and chatter about horses, brother. I would hardly call him a *friend*.'

Gwenllian knew Boleton had resented the easy companionship between Cole and Daniel, but the knight's words made her consider the fact anew. Was he jealous enough to take steps to put an end to it? He had gone out on the night in question – to hire a prostitute, he had said – and she had not heard him return. So he would have had the opportunity, while his fine hilt would almost certainly match Daniel's injury. She wondered how she could question him without Symon realizing what she was doing – Cole would never entertain the possibility of one friend harming another and would try to stop her.

'I should have walked home with him,' Cole was saying quietly. 'He would not be dead if I had done my duty.'

'I am not so sure,' said Boleton. 'Have you considered the possibility that you have had a narrow escape? That *you* might have suffered a blow to the head, too, had you accompanied him?'

Cole regarded him in horror. Clearly the possibility had not occurred to him.

'Are you saying Daniel had enemies?' asked Gwenllian, not sure what to make of the remark.

'Well, he was unlikely to have been killed by someone who wished him well,' drawled Boleton, regarding her steadily. She found his expression impossible to interpret.

'But who would mean him harm?' asked Cole. His face was pale, and Gwenllian could tell the notion of the monk having enemies disturbed him deeply – in his code of honour, friends were supposed to protect each other from those.

Boleton shook his head slowly. 'I do not know. No one relieved him of his purse, so he was not the victim of a robbery. And do not tell me the thief was disturbed before he could complete his grim business, because the body lay under a tree all night. When no alarm was raised, any self-respecting villain would have returned to finish what he had started.'

It was a good point, although Gwenllian declined to acknowledge it. 'Then what would you say *was* the motive?'

Boleton held her gaze. 'I really do not have the faintest idea. But I am sure that if anyone can find out, it will be you.'

Wondering why she felt as though she had been insulted, rather than complimented, Gwenllian followed the two knights towards the gate. She found herself staring at the hilt of Boleton's elegant sword. Was it wishful thinking, or was it a better match for the imprint on Daniel's skull than Cole's more robust one? She edged closer, but a thread of cloth suggested it had enjoyed a recent cleaning. Was that significant? Boleton was usually lax about weapon maintenance, and Cole was always berating him about it. She was not sure what to think, but Boleton was firmly at the top of her list of suspects.

To reach Merlin's oak from the castle entailed heading towards St Peter's Church, then continuing on past it into Priory Street. The tree stood at the far end of the road. When they arrived at the tree, Cole and Boleton began to poke about in the long grass with sticks, although not very systematically, while Gwenllian stared up at the shady green canopy.

'What have you seen?' she asked it softly. 'Who killed Daniel? Who stole the bones Meurig hid – and almost murdered my husband into the bargain?'

A summer breeze whispered through the branches. Then a leaf fell and spiralled slowly to the ground. Gwenllian followed it with her eyes, watching it come to rest on a patch of grass. She bent to inspect it. It was healthy, shiny and green, and she wondered why it should have dropped. She started to pick it up, but her fingers closed around some blades of grass as well as its stem, and when she lifted the leaf the grass rose with it.

'Symon!' she shouted, excited. 'Come and look!'

'Weeds,' drawled Boleton, when the two knights had darted around the tree to find the constable's wife brandishing a fistful of vegetation. 'How very fascinating!'

'Turf,' explained Gwenllian curtly, not liking his tone. 'Grass excavated carefully, so it could be replaced and no one would know a hole had been dug.'

Cole was on his knees, hauling up clumps of sod. He tossed them to one side, until he had cleared a neat square that was roughly the length of his arm. The soil below was damp and hard and had clearly been stamped into place. Before Gwenllian could stop him, Boleton had stepped into the hole.

'The digger had average-sized feet,' he announced authoritatively. 'Smaller than mine. Do you see the print he left?'

'Not really,' replied Gwenllian acidly. 'Your trampling has just obliterated it – along with any clue it might have yielded.'

Boleton sighed. 'How foolish of me! It was a very clear impression too.'

Gwenllian studied him hard but could not decide whether he was mocking her or was genuinely contrite. She opened her mouth to say something sharp, but Cole spoke first.

'It does not matter, brother. I saw the mark before you trod on it, and it was unremarkable. I doubt it could have told us anything useful.'

Gwenllian scowled at them both and heartily wished they had stayed in the castle. Cole she could control, but Boleton was obviously going to be a nuisance. She fought down her irritation and knelt, hoping to find some other clue. Unfortunately there was nothing to see but recently excavated earth.

Cole borrowed a spade from Spilmon the grocer, whose

house was nearby, and began to dig, relishing the opportunity to indulge in the kind of physical exercise that was generally frowned on for royally appointed officials. Boleton offered to take a turn, but not with much conviction, and was more than happy to lie in the shade while his friend did the work. He tossed a boy a penny to fetch him a jug of ale and settled back with an indolent sigh.

The sight of the constable wielding a shovel was enough to attract attention, and it was not long before a crowd had gathered. Hywel was among them, so Gwenllian went to greet her nephew, pleased by the chance to abandon Norman French and speak her native tongue. But Hywel was not of a mind to exchange pleasantries. He scowled towards Cole.

'What is he doing?'

'Investigating Daniel's murder.'

'By digging holes?' Hywel asked incredulously. 'I know he is stupid, but I did not think he had lost his wits completely.'

Gwenllian fixed him with a glare that had him stepping back in alarm. 'He is not stupid.'

'He was stupid two years ago,' muttered Hywel. He was drunk, as usual, and did not know when it was more prudent to stay quiet. 'If he had done his duty, my father would still be alive.'

'I am tired of hearing this,' said Gwenllian. Hywel started to raise a wineskin to his lips, but she slapped it down. 'I miss him too, but it is time you pulled yourself together. Do you think he would be proud, seeing what you have become? A drunkard, wallowing in events of the past?'

Hywel regarded her through bloodshot eyes, then turned abruptly and shouldered his way through the crowd. She closed her eyes, temper subsiding as quickly as it had risen. She had not meant to be cruel, but she was weary of his recriminations, and someone needed to tell him the truth about himself. She dragged her thoughts away from Hywel when Cole cleared away the last of the loose soil, and his spade chopped towards the harder earth around the tree's roots.

'Stop!' she cried. Was it was her imagination, or were the leaves shivering in agitation above her head? 'The hole is empty. You have proved someone came a-digging, but whoever it was has left nothing behind.'

Cole leaned on his shovel and wiped sweat from his eyes with his sleeve. Then he frowned, leaned down to pluck something from the grass and handed it to Gwenllian.

'A phial,' she mused. 'Oval – and identical to the one we found in Daniel's purse.'

'Not identical – this one is empty,' he said. 'What do you think it means?'

Gwenllian considered. 'I think you were right to assume the contents of Daniel's little bottle were special. Perhaps someone believes the tree under which Arthur lay is sacred, and has been filling phials with rainwater that has dripped from its leaves.'

Cole's expression was dubious. 'But why should such a thing be in Daniel's purse? I cannot see *him* falling for such foolery. He was a monk, not some superstitious bumpkin.'

Gwenllian did not know what to think. 'If you are sure there is nothing else to find, we should refill the hole. I do not think the tree will appreciate being left with its roots exposed.'

It took Cole considerably less time to fill the hole than it had to dig it. When he had finished, Gwenllian replaced the turf and stamped it down. Despite their care, the grass still stood proud of the surrounding vegetation, and it told her that whoever had excavated the original pit had gone to considerable trouble to ensure his handiwork remained hidden. She wondered why.

Cole wiped his hands on his shirt, then accepted a drink from Boleton's jug. 'I am not sure that was worth the effort. We still do not know how the hole is connected to Daniel.'

'It is *not* connected,' said Boleton scornfully. 'Obviously. *He* did not dig it – unless someone waited until he had patted it all back in its rightful place before killing him, which seems unlikely. Perhaps he just had the bad luck to spot the digger at work and was murdered for his silence.'

Gwenllian drew Cole away from him. 'This hole is dug on the town side of the tree,' she whispered, 'but Meurig buried Arthur on the far side. Two different pits, two different places.'

He regarded her uncertainly. 'What are you saying? That whoever tried to steal the bones two years ago dug in the wrong location? That Arthur has been here all along?'

'No, I could tell by looking at Meurig's pit that it had held a chest – the tree had wrapped its roots around it like a cradle. I have no idea why anyone should have been digging on the opposite side now. Perhaps it is nothing to do with Arthur, although . . .'

'Although it is an odd coincidence. Poor Daniel. I wonder what he stumbled across.'

Gwenllian frowned. 'I cannot believe the culprit did not make some kind of noise. So it is time to ask the people of Priory Street what they heard or saw.'

Gwenllian did not want Cole or Boleton with her when she spoke to potential witnesses, because no one was going to be free with information when a pair of Norman knights were looming behind her. Unfortunately she could not think of a way to be rid of them, and when she suggested they separate to ask questions, Boleton made a casual remark about an official investigation sending the murderer into a panic. It was cleverly done, because once the seed was planted in Cole's mind there was no way he was going to let his wife conduct an enquiry on her own. And where Cole went, so went Boleton.

Trying to look on the bright side, telling herself that people would be less inclined to lie when two warriors with sharp swords were at her back, she knocked on the door of the first house.

It was owned by a cobbler, who was visibly alarmed by a visit from the constable and his henchman, and would certainly have been forthcoming had he had information to share. Unfortunately he had none, other than that Daniel had died on the eve of the Feast of St Peter. It was an important festival – a patronal one – and there had been a vigil in St Peter's Church. The cobbler had remained all night, devoutly on his knees, and so had many other Priory Street folk.

'But not Kyng and the Spilmons,' mused Gwenllian as they left. 'We will talk to them next.'

'Hywel was not there either,' said Boleton challengingly. 'Or are we overlooking kin?'

'We are not,' replied Gwenllian frostily. 'We shall speak to *anyone* who was home on the night of the crime.'

'Then let us start with Hywel,' suggested Boleton. 'He has a military past, and he was all but unhinged by the death of his father. It would not surprise me to learn he killed a monk.'

'He has a point, Gwen,' said Cole in a low voice, when Boleton stopped to exchange greetings with one of the town's prostitutes – the most expensive one, Gwenllian noticed; his recent inheritance was allowing him to enjoy all manner of costly treats. 'Hywel *is* a ruffian.'

'He is,' agreed Gwenllian with a sigh. 'But I had better

speak to him alone. He is unlikely to be very forthcoming if you are there – you know he does not like you. So stay here and—'

'No,' said Cole immediately.

Gwenllian touched his arm. 'He is family, Symon. He would never harm me.'

It was rare that Gwenllian lost a battle of wills with her husband, but Cole's distrust of Hywel ran deep, so it was three people who knocked on her nephew's door. Gwenllian noticed how the house, like its occupant, had turned shabby since Meurig had died.

'What do you want?' demanded Hywel. He seemed less drunk than he had been shortly before, as if his aunt's hard words had sobered him. They had done nothing to improve his temper, though. 'If it is ale you're after digging that hole, you can go to hell. Norman curs do not deserve my piss.'

He spoke Welsh, sufficiently rapidly that Cole could not follow, although it was obvious from his hate-filled expression that he had not said anything polite. Boleton inspected his fingernails, feigning boredom, although his eyes were alert, and his right hand rested on the hilt of his sword.

'We only want to talk,' replied Gwenllian quietly in Norman French. 'I need to know if you heard or saw anything that might help us catch Daniel's killer.'

Hywel continued to scowl. 'I was in the tavern that night.' He spoke Norman French in a way that said he did so unwillingly. 'I came home when it was dark, and heard and saw nothing.'

'But Daniel left the castle after dark,' said Cole hopefully. 'Are you sure you—'

'Yes, I am sure,' snarled Hywel. 'Of course, Daniel would not be dead if you had escorted him home. You know there has been trouble with thieves in the town, and you should not have let him wander around alone. His death is *your* fault – like so many others.'

Cole flinched, and Gwenllian did not like the flash of spiteful triumph in her nephew's eyes when he saw the barb had gone home. She put out a restraining hand when Boleton took an angry step forward.

'What trouble with thieves?' she asked.

'The spate of petty larceny,' explained Boleton. His voice was tight, suggesting his temper was only just under control. 'Cole believes outlaws from the forest are responsible.'

'It is not *petty* larceny,' argued Cole. 'Spilmon lost a box of coins, while the priory was relieved of valuable altar dressings. The culprits know exactly which places to target, and when. It is uncanny.'

Gwenllian looked from one to the other. 'Then surely it is possible that Daniel was attacked by these felons? Perhaps he saw them hiding their ill-gotten gains under the tree, and they killed him to ensure he could never identify them.'

'I doubt it,' said Boleton. 'Personally I believe the culprit to be a local man – I am *sure* you are wrong about the thefts being the work of outsiders, brother. You and I have spent days scouring the forest, but we have found no trace of outlaw camps.'

Cole frowned. 'But I have spoken to witnesses who have seen strangers—'

'Drunkards and beggars who will say anything for a penny,' interrupted Boleton. 'We have no *credible* witnesses – and you will waste your time if you follow their testimony. But we are wasting time now – we want to know what happened to Daniel, and this discussion can wait.'

Cole turned back to Hywel. 'Please think carefully. Are you sure you did not see anything—'

'If I did, I would not tell you,' said Hywel tauntingly. 'Daniel got what he deserved anyway.'

'Hywel!' exclaimed Gwenllian, shocked. 'What a terrible thing to say! Daniel was a gentle man who took his vows seriously.'

'Only the ones that suited him,' said Hywel, oozing malice. 'Just ask your husband.'

And with that he turned on his heel and marched back inside his house, slamming the door behind him. It made a crack like a thunderclap, and echoed along the otherwise peaceful street. Gwenllian looked at Cole and raised her eyebrows to indicate that an explanation was in order.

'I did not want to tell you,' he said sheepishly.

'Tell me what?' demanded Gwenllian, hands on hips. She was aware of Boleton looking equally bemused – Symon had not confided in him either.

'Daniel had a lady,' Cole mumbled uncomfortably. 'I learned about it the night you and I were married, but it was their secret, not mine.' The last part was spoken defensively, as if he imagined his wife might think less of him for keeping silent for so many years.

Gwenllian regarded him in exasperation. 'But the identity of this lover might have a bearing on his death. You should have told me about her last night.'

'You should,' agreed Boleton. 'So you had better tell us now. Do not look troubled, brother! Hywel knows about her, so it will not be long before Daniel's secret is out.'

'Meurig knew,' hedged Cole. 'He was an observant man, and noticed comings and goings. We discussed it once, then agreed to forget about it. It was not our business.'

'Who is she, Symon?' asked Gwenllian, although facts were coming together in her mind and she thought she had the answer. 'Is it Mistress Spilmon?'

Cole gaped at her. 'How did you know?'

'Because she offered to tend Daniel's body, and because you were considerate enough to wash it for her, to spare her the sight of his blood.'

'Well, then,' said Boleton, looking towards the grocer's house. 'Perhaps there is your culprit for Daniel's murder. No man likes to be a cuckold.'

Gwenllian did not need to knock on Spilmon's door, because the grocer was already hurrying towards them, Kyng at his heels. Cole saw the scowl Gwenllian directed towards the cheese-maker and the malevolent expression she received in return, and he shook his head in incomprehension.

'Lord Rhys attacked Carmarthen more than two years ago,' he whispered to her. 'Do you not think it is time to forget what happened?'

Gwenllian raised her eyebrows. 'I do not – especially not today. My brother confided his secret to me on that fateful night, and someone stabbed you in order to steal Arthur's chest from Merlin's oak. And now Daniel is brained under that very same tree with a large bone in his purse. It is a time for *remembering*, not forgetting.'

'Not if Boleton is right, and Spilmon has just learned his wife has had a lover for the last ten years. That would make Arthur's bones irrelevant, while the relics in Daniel's purse might be a coincidence.'

'Of course they might,' said Gwenllian flatly, wondering how he could even suggest such a thing. 'But Boleton might be wrong, and Spilmon may still be in blissful ignorance. In which case I suggest that nothing can be gained from incautious words. You had better leave this to me.'

'All right,' said Cole, not bothering to hide his relief. He was not very good at the kind of subtle probing necessary to elicit answers without revealing what he knew. 'I will just listen.'

'I hope you are not planning to chop down Merlin's oak,' said Spilmon when he was close enough to speak. 'You know the legend, do you not – that the town will fall if it is destroyed?'

'A branch was lopped off two years ago, and look what happened then,' added Kyng. 'Lord Rhys stormed in and almost killed us all. We are lucky we survived – no thanks to some.'

'The cheese-maker thinks to blame us,' said Boleton to Cole, hand resting threateningly on the hilt of his sword. 'But the raid was carried out by *his* countrymen, not ours.'

'Actually the branch came off *during* the raid,' said Cole to Kyng, although Gwenllian was sure the man knew it – he had just twisted the facts to make accusatory remarks. 'It did not come down in advance, to warn of pending disaster. It was an accident.'

'The tree does not allow accidents to befall it,' said Spilmon. He sounded indignant on its behalf. 'Everything that happens around it happens for a reason. Take Daniel, for example. His death was not a random act of violence, but will have a greater meaning.'

'Really?' asked Gwenllian, putting on her most winning smile. 'What sort of meaning?'

Spilmon leaned towards her conspiratorially. 'I heard odd sounds the night he died, and I am sure he was scrabbling about by its roots. Merlin's oak does not appreciate tampering.'

Gwenllian glanced at Boleton. Cole had given the impression that the knight had already interviewed the residents of Priory Street about Daniel's death, so why had Boleton not mentioned Spilmon's testimony? It represented an important clue, after all.

'I did not manage to speak to Spilmon yesterday,' Boleton said, seeing her look and understanding what it meant. He was unconcerned by her immediate exasperation. 'He was out when I did my rounds, and I forgot to return later.'

Gwenllian did not know whether to believe him. She turned to the grocer. 'Did you see Daniel with a spade?'

'No, but he walked past my house not long before these strange noises started, so it must have been him. The man was a fool, wandering about in a town that is the domain of violent robbers.'

'Violent robbers?' echoed Boleton, regarding him contemptuously. 'Do you refer to the minor thefts that have occurred of late? Really, man! You exaggerate!'

'And you understate!' countered Kyng, stepping forward belligerently. 'But I know why you make light of the matter – because you have failed to catch the culprits.'

'Those scoundrels stole a fortune from me,' added Spilmon before Boleton could respond to the charge. 'And they are growing increasingly brazen. Did you hear that they had the audacity to attack the priory and make off with its finest cross – a great heavy gold one?'

'A cross?' asked Cole sharply. 'I thought they had lost some altar dressings.'

Kyng sneered at him. 'A cross *is* an altar dressing, *constable.*' He managed to inject considerable scorn into the last word, and might just as well have said 'stupid'.

But Cole was looking at Boleton. 'You visited the priory and recorded their complaint. Why did you not tell me an item of such great value was taken?'

Boleton shrugged. 'Because the *modus operandi* was different from the other thefts – it took place in a crowded priory and the culprit stole only the one piece. There was no need to bother you with it, not when you are so busy at the castle. And I am quite capable of investigating the business myself.'

Cole nodded acceptance of the explanation, although Gwenllian frowned. Why had Boleton used the term 'altar dressings' to describe the stolen property, when 'cross' would have sufficed? And was his intention really to save a busy man from worry? But there were more important issues to ponder than Boleton's curious behaviour.

'Where were you the night Daniel died?' she asked of Kyng. 'We understand you and Spilmon were notable by your absence at the vigil in St Peter's Church.'

'We had other business,' Kyng replied smoothly, although the flash of alarm in Spilmon's eyes did not escape Gwenllian's attention. 'Spilmon and I stayed in his house all night, going over ledgers. We can account for each other, but there is no one else to verify our tale.'

'What about your wife?' asked Gwenllian of the grocer. 'Was she not with you?'

'She was at the vigil,' replied Spilmon.

But the cobbler had told them she was not, and he had had no reason to lie. Gwenllian could only assume that Mistress Spilmon had taken the opportunity to spend time with Daniel. But then how had Daniel come to die? Surely, if she had seen the attacker, she would have spoken out? Or had she tired of her monastic lover, and murder seemed a good way to end the situation?

'No,' said Cole, when Gwenllian pulled him to one side and suggested Mistress Spilmon as a culprit. 'She was distraught when I told her what had happened. And I do not see her offering to clean his corpse if she were the killer either. She would have been keen to stay away from it.'

He had a point, and Gwenllian was beginning to feel

frustrated. There were simply too many questions and too few reliable answers. She nodded a curt farewell to the merchants, and saw their relief. It aroused her suspicions, but she did not want to raise the question of Mistress Spilmon's infidelity without good cause – not to spare the grocer's feelings, but for the sake of the shy, colourless woman who was his wife.

Gwenllian happened to glance back at the two merchants when she was halfway down the street and saw them jump away from each other. Spilmon looked positively furtive, but Kyng had the audacity to wave. She was not sure what it meant, but there was something about their odd behaviour that set the glimmer of a solution burning at the back of her mind.

Her thoughts were interrupted by the sudden appearance of Gilbert the Thief, who immediately shoved a cloth-wrapped bundle behind his back. Cole regarded him wearily.

'What have you stolen now?' He held out his hand. 'Come on. Give it to me.'

'I found it,' said Gilbert defensively.

'Oh, let him be,' said Boleton impatiently. 'It should be beneath your dignity to treat with such creatures, and he is not worth your time. Leave him, and I will deal with him tomorrow.'

'Good idea,' said Gilbert, beginning to edge away. 'Thank you, sir. Feel free to come any time. I shall be waiting for you. We might even have a mug of ale together.'

'Do not push your luck,' growled Boleton, although Gwenllian could see he was amused by the man's cheek.

But Cole did not find the situation funny. He moved suddenly, faster than the thief anticipated, and grabbed him by the scruff of his neck. Gilbert squealed in alarm and tried to keep his prize out of the constable's reach, but to no avail. Cole snatched it from him, shoved Gilbert into Boleton's arms and began to pull off the wrappings. Then Boleton yelped suddenly, wringing his hand, and Gilbert darted away, disappearing down a nearby lane. Immediately Cole started after him, but Boleton yanked him back, hard enough to make him stagger.

'Remember your dignity,' he hissed. 'Knights of your standing do not hare after felons like common foot soldiers, and we know where the man lives. I shall visit him later and invite him to spend a few days in the dungeons. He is due for a spell under lock and key anyway – for biting me, if nothing else.'

But Cole's face was white with anger. He leaned down and retrieved the bundle he had dropped. 'It was different this time,' he snapped. 'Look at what he stole!'

He hauled the last of the sacking away to reveal a heavy jewelled cross.

'We wasted a day,' said Cole gloomily as he sat with Gwenllian in their bedchamber that evening. The daylight was fading, sending an orange glow around the little room. She was straining her eyes to sew, and he was honing his sword. 'We learned nothing useful, and Daniel will go to his grave unavenged.'

'Nonsense,' she exclaimed, surprised he should think so. 'We discovered a great many interesting facts. For example, I have narrowed my list of suspects down to six men – all of whom had the opportunity and a reason to want Daniel dead.'

'Six men?' he asked doubtfully. 'Do you mean the robbers from the forest? Witnesses tell me they come to do their sly work in a pack.'

'Not them – Boleton is right about that, at least. I asked a few questions around the castle this evening and learned that they have been disturbed at least twice – their response is not to stand and fight but to run away as fast as their legs will carry them. They are not killers.'

'Then who are these six? One must be Spilmon. His motive would be that he learned about the affair between Daniel and his wife, while you told me that he owns a pot with a cruciform base. Another will be Kyng – he wore a heavy dagger in his belt today, which might well match the wound in Daniel's head.'

She smiled. 'That was observant of you – I did not notice it. And Kyng, like Spilmon, has no proper alibi for Daniel's death. Of course, there is the question of Kyng's motive.' She tapped her chin thoughtfully. 'Perhaps he did it to avenge Spilmon's injured pride. Or perhaps he resented the fact that Daniel was your friend – you know how he hates you.'

'Perhaps.' Cole did not sound convinced, but Gwenllian would not put anything past the vitriolic cheese-maker.

'My third suspect is Gilbert, for obvious reasons,' she went on. 'He is an inveterate thief, and Daniel may well have caught him stealing. And he had that cross from the priory. Were they pleased to have it back, by the way?'

'Very – they said it is the most valuable thing they own. But I wish Boleton had kept a firmer hold on Gilbert, because the wretched man has disappeared. I know he will not stay away long – he never does – but I want to talk to him now, not in several days' time.'

'My fourth suspect is John,' Gwenllian continued. 'His writing desk has a cruciform bottom, and he was furtive when he spoke to us earlier. He eavesdropped on you and Daniel on the night of the murder, and I am unconvinced by his tale of being interested in horses. He listened for some other reason.'

'What about Hywel? Does he feature on this list?'

Gwenllian nodded unhappily. 'Yes, although it grieves me

to say it. He is sullen, bitter and unpredictable, and he owns a sword with a cross-shaped hilt. My last suspect is Boleton.'

A pained look crossed Cole's face. 'No. I will not entertain—'

'He exhibited a curious desire to dog our footsteps today, and his sword looks a better match for the murder weapon that any of the other items we have seen. Moreover, he was jealous of your friendship with Daniel – he likes to think *he* is the constable's indispensable confidant.'

'No,' repeated Cole angrily. 'You are wrong. Boleton is not a cold-blooded killer.'

Knowing there was no point in arguing with him, she let the matter drop. 'These men are the same ones I suspect for stealing Arthur's bones,' she said, aiming to dilute his irritation by piquing his interest in another matter. It worked, as she knew it would.

'Really?' he asked, mystified. 'How in God's name did you reach that conclusion?'

'Because of the reasons we have already discussed. Kyng and Spilmon recouped their losses suspiciously quickly after my father's raid – perhaps they sold the relics. Meanwhile, Hywel has access to money that allows him to drink all day and never lift a finger.'

'And you essentially told Gilbert there was something valuable under the tree,' mused Cole. 'While John likes to listen to other men's private discussions. You said at the time that all five were in the vicinity when Meurig told you about the bones.'

She nodded. 'Any one of them could have overheard him. As could Daniel.' And so could Boleton, she thought, although it did not seem a good idea to mention it.

Cole yawned. 'Well, I can make no sense of it, and it has been a long day. Perhaps answers will come tomorrow.'

\*

It was in the deepest part of the night when the alarm was raised. Iefan burst into the bedchamber to announce that something was happening in Priory Street. Snapping into instant wakefulness, like the warrior he was, Cole dragged on tunic and hose, and was buckling a sword around his waist as he ran from the room moments later.

Because it was Priory Street, and she thought it might have a bearing on Daniel's murder, Gwenllian threw a cloak over her nightshift and followed him down the stairs.

'No,' he said, seeing she intended to accompany him. 'The thieves have been spotted creeping about, so this is our opportunity to catch them red-handed. You cannot come with me this time.'

'Then be careful.'

But Cole did not hear, because he was already halfway across the bailey, sprinting to catch up with the party of men who were heading out under Iefan's direction. They were all armed to the teeth, grim-faced and determined. She waited until they were out of sight, then followed, fixing the guard on gate duty with one of her regal glowers when he tried to stop her.

She kept to the shadows, although the soldiers did not once look behind them. They moved quickly, and she found herself obliged to run to keep up. The town was silent, other than their soft footfalls. They passed the dark mass of St Peter's Church, with its spacious churchyard and grassy knoll, and slowed down when they reached the town end of Priory Street.

Cole issued a series of low-voiced instructions, and the soldiers split into two groups – he led one down a nearby alley, while the other stayed with Iefan. It did not take Gwenllian long to understand his plan – furtive shadows could be seen massing near Kyng's home, in the middle of the street, and Cole aimed to ambush them in a pincer-like movement. A quick count told her that there were probably a dozen thieves, all cloaked and hooded against identification. By contrast, Cole and Iefan had eight soldiers, four in each little band.

Blissfully unaware of the trap that was springing, the burglars approached Kyng's house. Gwenllian was mystified. With its iron-studded door and sturdy window-shutters, it was by far the most secure house in the town, although she knew it was stuffed to the gills with treasure – she remembered seeing it when she had commandeered the place after Lord Rhys's raid.

The felons seemed to be looking at the large window on the upper floor, but it was a long way off the ground and would be unreachable by all but the very longest ladder. She wondered what they intended to do.

Then one villain, taller than the others, beckoned his cronies towards him and began to mutter. When he had finished, a handful went to crouch directly beneath the window. As soon as they were in position, others moved forward and began to climb on top of them. Fascinated, Gwenllian saw a human pyramid begin to form. Despite his disguise, Gwenllian knew it was Gilbert the Thief who was assisted to the top, because she recognized his lanky frame. He opened the latch with consummate ease and disappeared inside the house.

Moments later, a bundle was handed out, followed quickly by another. With silent efficiency, they were passed down to the leader, who deftly packed them into sacks. More items followed, and Gwenllian was amazed by the skill and speed of the operation. It was not long before several bags had been filled. Then there was a low whistle, and Gilbert began to climb out.

With a blood-curdling yell, Iefan leaped into action, tearing forward with his dagger raised. The pyramid immediately disintegrated, leaving Gilbert dangling from the window-ledge by his fingertips. He began to screech, but his accomplices were more interested in saving themselves than rescuing him. As one, they turned from Iefan and began to run towards Merlin's oak. But it was to find themselves facing Cole and his men, who stood in a line across the street, weapons at the ready. A few tried to jig around them, but most seemed to accept that the situation was hopeless and offered no resistance as they were rounded up.

But their leader fought like a tiger. Unlike his accomplices, he had brought a sword, and he slashed viciously at the soldiers who tried to bar his way. Unnerved by the ferocity of the attack, they fell back. Cole dived towards him, and they exchanged a series of brutal blows that made both men stagger. Iefan hurried to help, but his timing was poor and Cole was obliged to twist awkwardly to avoid striking him instead. The leader took advantage of the constable's momentary loss of balance to escape down a nearby alley.

Cole set off after him. Seeing their leader make a bid for freedom encouraged several burglars to do likewise, and Iefan was hard-pressed to keep them in order. Meanwhile, the sudden racket had woken Priory Street's residents. Lights gleamed under window-shutters, and doors opened as people came to see what was going on. Their curiosity turned to outrage when it became known that here were the thieves who had been relieving decent folk of their belongings, and then Iefan was obliged to turn protector, as well as captor.

Gwenllian stared at the alley, heart thumping as she willed Symon to return unscathed. It was not long before he did, empty-handed and furious. He growled to Iefan that his quarry had backtracked unexpectedly and ambushed him. He had managed to deflect the killing blow, but it had sent him sprawling, granting the felon vital moments to disappear into the night.

'These vermin say they do not know his name,' said Iefan, jerking his head towards the subdued prisoners. 'They claim he just appears in the forest and guides them to the houses he wants them to burgle. A likely story!'

Cole did not reply. He strode towards Kyng's house, flung open the door and marched inside, appearing moments later at the window from which Gilbert still dangled. Gwenllian abandoned her hiding place and moved forward to help – she could tell by the stiff way Cole walked that he had jolted his old stab wound, and he would not be able to rescue Gilbert one-handed.

'Your leader,' Cole said, making no attempt to reach down to the thief. 'What is his name?'

'No, I will never betray him,' cried Gilbert. He sounded terrified. 'His secret is safe with me.'

'Really?' said Cole. His voice held an odd timbre that Gwenllian had never heard before. She froze, uncertain and uneasy.

'Please!' wailed Gilbert. 'My fingers are numb – I will fall at any moment!'

'Then you had better give me a reason to help you,' said Cole coldly.

He leaned forward when Gilbert whispered something. For a moment he did nothing, but then he reached out of the window and gripped Gilbert's wrist, hauling him upwards until the thief was able to gain a better purchase on the window-sill. He could not manage more with one arm, but it was enough for Gilbert to gasp his gratitude.

Gwenllian heaved a sigh of relief, afraid Symon might really have let the man fall for refusing to cooperate, but sure it would have plagued his conscience later.

She was not sure what happened next. Suddenly Cole bellowed John's name in a voice loud enough to have been heard at the castle, and she turned just in time to see the clerk slinking along the opposite side of the road. He was cloaked and hooded, like the burglars. Cole's yell had stopped him dead in his tracks, but then he started to run, aiming for the alleys that led to the river. Next, there was a cry and a thump, and when Gwenllian whipped around to look back at Kyng's window, it was to see Gilbert crumpled beneath it. Cole shot through the door moments later, and tore after his clerk.

John had a head start on the constable, but Cole was faster and fitter and caught him with ease. In the faint lamplight from one of the houses, Gwenllian saw the glint of steel as a dagger was wielded. Without stopping to consider the consequences, she raced towards them.

By the time she arrived, John was lying on the ground and Symon was standing over him. A spreading stain of red seeped from under the clerk, and he was gasping for breath. He saw Gwenllian, and murmured just one sentence before he went limp.

'Beware the one you love.'

'Damn!' muttered Cole angrily. 'He killed himself rather than face justice. But what are you doing here, Gwen? I thought I told you to stay in the castle.'

Gwenllian gazed numbly at him. 'Face justice? You mean he was one of the thieves?'

Cole gestured to the clerk's clothing. 'Apparently so. Why else would he run when I called?'

'What happened to Gilbert? Did he also kill himself, rather than face justice?'

Cole swivelled around, looking towards the unmoving figure under the window. 'He fell? I thought I had pulled him far enough inside to save himself. I suppose his hands must have been too fatigued to hold him. What a nuisance! Now there are no witnesses to identify the leader.'

'Not the other burglars?' asked Gwenllian. But then she recalled what Iefan had said.

'He disguised himself – they would not know him if he stood in front of them.'

'I see,' said Gwenllian, aware of a cold hand of fear gripping her heart. The only two witnesses were permanently silenced, and Cole had been near both when they had died. And John had warned her to beware the one she loved. What was going on?

When Gwenllian said nothing else, Cole took her hand and tugged her towards Kyng's house. She tried to pull away, but he was too strong. He did stop, however, and turn to look at her.

'If you have been watching,' he said impatiently, 'you will be aware that Kyng is the only Priory Street resident who is not out demanding to know what is happening. Something is wrong, and we need to investigate. As you are here, you may as well come with me.'

As he spoke, Gwenllian saw that the cheese-maker's house *was* the only one not ablaze with lanterns, and although the stairs to the upper chambers could be negotiated using light from outside, the parlour was pitch black. Cole fiddled with a tinder and lit a lamp. It illuminated a scene neither could have anticipated.

Hywel was lying on the floor, grey-faced and immobile. With a cry of horror, Gwenllian ran towards him. There was a cup near his hand, and when she picked it up she saw a frothy residue at the bottom. Poison.

'Kyng offered me wine,' Hywel said in a low, strained voice. 'And, like a fool, I accepted.'

'Why should you not have accepted?' asked Cole, puzzled. 'Drinking with neighbours is—'

'Not with neighbours you have wronged,' interrupted Gwenllian quietly.

She knelt next to her nephew and rested his head in her lap. She could tell by his pallor and laboured breathing that he was dying, and she was grateful the cheese-maker had used a substance that did not seem to be causing his victim pain.

'I only learned about Mistress Spilmon and Daniel yesterday,' she went on softly, 'but Meurig knew, and so did you. You acquire money, but not by working. It is obvious now that you earn it from blackmail – you have been extorting money from Spilmon. And from Kyng too.'

'Kyng?' echoed Cole, hopelessly bewildered. 'What does Kyng have to do with it?'

Gwenllian recalled the strange behaviour of the two men earlier, when they had jumped apart as she had turned to look at them. She had known then that their reaction was significant, and she had been right.

'A woman cannot possibly deceive her husband for so many years,' she began. 'At least, not in a functional marriage. But Kyng and Spilmon are always together, which is probably why Spilmon's wife turned elsewhere for affection. They are respected merchants, and no doubt paid handsomely to keep their relationship quiet.'

Hywel inclined his head, but there was no sign of remorse. 'Their sordid secret has kept me in ale and meat for more than two years. But then I decided to leave Carmarthen, and needed a more substantial sum. I should have been suspicious when they agreed and poured wine to seal our bargain . . .'

Gwenllian was full of sorrow for what Hywel had become.

'Your father did not teach you to capitalize on the vulnerability of others. You soil his precious memory.'

Hywel looked away. 'Why should I care about his memory? He did not love me. He should have told *me* where he hid the bones, but instead he chose you – his favourite.'

Gwenllian smoothed the hair from his forehead. 'Actually, I believe he *did* tell you. I think he knew it was you who was listening behind the door when he gave me his secret.'

'The eavesdropper was Hywel?' asked Cole, startled. '*He* stole the bones?'

'I did not *steal* them,' objected Hywel weakly. 'I—'

Cole ignored him and addressed Gwenllian. 'How did you guess it was him?'

'Because he has just admitted to knowing that Meurig told *me* about the bones – you are the only person I have ever told about that, which means Hywel must have been the eavesdropper. There is no other way he can have known.'

'I was listening behind the door,' acknowledged Hywel. 'But how did my father know?'

'After I discovered the bones were missing, I went to the place where he had died and lay down there. He would have been able to see shoes from where he lay.'

'And he recognized mine,' breathed Hywel. 'He trusted me after all.'

'I should have guessed this years ago,' Gwenllian went on. 'Because it is obvious now that the bones have been in the custody of someone who cares about them. They have not been sold for a quick profit, but have disappeared – kept safe. My other suspects would not have been so restrained.'

'Where are they, Hywel?' asked Cole, adding bluntly: 'You are dying, so you had better tell someone, or they will be lost for ever.'

'I will confide in Gwenllian,' said Hywel softly. 'But not you.'

Cole shrugged. 'As you please. I will hunt down Kyng and Spilmon instead – they have committed murder here and must answer for their crime.'

When Cole's footsteps had died away, Hywel shot Gwenllian an anguished look. 'I have been so bitter and angry. I might not have tormented Kyng and Spilmon had I known . . . Things could have been so different!'

'Perhaps you would not have stabbed my husband either. No, do not deny it – I know he was attacked to distract me while the bones were removed. You pretended to hunt for a coffin, but instead you hunted Symon – and you almost killed him!'

'He started to turn when I came up behind him, and panic made me strike harder than I intended. I was about to fetch you, but Daniel arrived and took over. So I went to dig up the chest instead.'

'What did you do with it?'

'Buried it in the priory. But the whole business preyed on my conscience, and one night, in an agony of guilt, I went to my confessor.'

'Daniel,' said Gwenllian, beginning to understand at last.

'He was not a good man, although he hid his dark nature well. He wanted me to tell him where I had put the bones, and when I refused he began to follow me.'

'I know he was deceitful,' said Gwenllian softly. 'He said he tended the wounded on the night of the raid, but no one saw him praying. And he escaped from Symon's sickroom with unseemly haste. I suspect he spent his time stealing – for a monk, he had expensive tastes.'

'You are right.' Hywel coughed wetly, struggling for

breath. 'Your fool of a husband considered him a friend, but Daniel was interested only in the fine food and wine available at the castle. And he stole in his capacity as chaplain too. John suspected, and he was going through old accounts to learn how.'

'Is that why he eavesdropped on Symon and Daniel?' asked Gwenllian, more of herself than Hywel. 'But John was a thief himself – in league with forest felons, no less. Why would he work so hard to catch a fellow criminal?'

'John was a reluctant villain – he stole because he was bullied into it. But he did not like the notion of Daniel cheating the castle.'

'Why did John not tell us what he was doing? We could have helped.'

'You? Do not be a fool! He was terrified of you, while Cole was Daniel's friend. You were the last people on Earth he would have confided in. He was probably frightened of Daniel too. Incidentally, it was Daniel who stole that big gold cross from his priory.'

Gwenllian stared at him. 'How do you know?'

'Because the chapel is locked up as tight as a prison at night – no common thief could ever get inside. The thief *had* to be a monk. Besides, I saw it next to his body.' Hywel's voice was growing weaker.

Gwenllian frowned. 'But you told me earlier that you saw nothing suspicious that night.'

Hywel looked away. 'I lied – I did not want to help Cole. The cross was just lying there, so I took it, and Gilbert offered to sell it for me.'

He was fading fast, but Gwenllian still needed answers. She spoke more quickly. 'I found a bone in Daniel's purse. Was it one of Arthur's? Did Daniel find where you buried him?'

Hywel managed a wan smile. 'I gave him an animal

bone – told him it was Arthur's finger in the hope that it would make him leave me alone. He dipped it in water, which he decanted into bottles to sell as relics. But I do not have long left, so I had better tell you where I hid the chest.'

'You have told me – in the priory grounds.'

'I was afraid of Daniel, so I moved it. I was going to take it to Abbey Dore tomorrow – their sexton is sympathetic to Welsh interests, and where better to hide Arthur's bones than right under Norman noses? But I came here first, to get my blood money from Kyng and Spilmon.'

Then he whispered his secret, much as his father had done two years before. After that, it was not long before he began to slip away. Just before he died, he opened his eyes.

'Have you asked Cole for *his* whereabouts on the night Daniel was murdered?'

'What do you mean?' she demanded, recalling uncomfortably that Cole had not come directly to bed after Daniel had left – he said he had been raiding the kitchens for food.

But Hywel was dead.


Gwenllian wept when her nephew had gone, although few of the tears were for him. The night had exposed so many dark secrets that she wished she had done as Cole had ordered and remained in the castle. She came to her feet when she heard footsteps outside, and her heart began to hammer in her chest. Was it Symon, coming to ask the whereabouts of Arthur's bones? Kyng and Spilmon, to see whether their victim was dead? But it was Boleton.

'My husband is not here,' she began. 'He—'

But Boleton put his finger to his lips, and she saw that his face was pale and filmed with sweat. 'Do not give me away,' he whispered. 'Please! He is hunting for me.'

She regarded him in confusion. 'Who is?'

'Cole. He has accused me of being the forest thieves' leader.'

Gwenllian felt her jaw drop. 'Why would he do that?'

'Because the real leader is *him*. But he knows the game is up, and intends to evade justice by having me blamed in his place. And I thought we were friends!'

Gwenllian's thoughts whirled. 'But he—'

'Just *think* about it,' urged Boleton desperately. 'Who, as constable, is well placed to round up outlaws and make a bargain with them – they burgle Carmarthen homes and he looks the other way for a share of the proceeds? Who else could force malleable locals, like John and Gilbert, to join his vile game – to say which houses to rob and when? But they have been arrested, so he is covering his tracks by saying *I* am the one who organized the whole affair.'

'But John and Gilbert are dead. One from being stabbed and the other from a fall. And Iefan said the forest folk do not know the name of the man who recruited them. Symon has no need—'

'Dead?' echoed Boleton. His face was ashen. 'Was Cole nearby when they met their ends?'

'Yes.' She was unable to control the tremble in her voice.

'Then he has eliminated the only witnesses to my innocence,' breathed Boleton.

'I do not understand,' she said, backing away. She was beginning to be frightened.

'Surely you must have worked it out by now? Why do you think I have not shared details of my investigation with him? Why do you think I have tried to keep him away from Gilbert – an important witness? Why do you think John was so terrified when he was summoned at the crack of dawn yesterday? And why do you think I insisted on coming with you while you asked questions about Daniel's murder?'

Gwenllian felt sick. 'Are you saying *Symon* killed Daniel with the priory's cross?'

Boleton nodded. 'He is a dangerous man and must be stopped. Will you help? He is a better swordsman than me, and I cannot best him alone. You must distract him while I—'

He broke off when there was a clatter of footsteps. He drew his sword and stepped behind the door just as Cole burst in, breathless and gasping.

'We caught them! They were on a ship, ready to sail for Ireland. They confessed everything – how they were lovers and Hywel blackmailed them. How they poisoned him and were discussing how to dispose of the body when my soldiers arrived – they did not realize the rumpus was for someone else's crime, so they tried to escape. I doubt they will hang, because they can claim benefit of—'

'Symon! Watch out!' Gwenllian screamed.

Only Cole's instinctive duck saved him from decapitation. Boleton's blade smashed into a table, which flew into pieces. Cole's sword was in his hand even before he had recovered his balance, ready to do battle.

'Why did you warn him?' cried Boleton, ripping his weapon from the shattered wood. 'Did you not hear a word I said?'

'He is not this criminal mastermind,' shouted Gwenllian, tears spurting. '*You* are.'

For a moment no one moved. Then Boleton backed away from Cole, sword held defensively.

'You are making a terrible mistake, My Lady.' He was pale and his voice shook. 'He has just killed the two men who can testify to his identity – you told me that yourself.'

'Gilbert is not dead,' said Cole, looking from one to the other in confusion. 'He is knocked out of his wits. Perhaps I should have pulled him further through the window, but I saw John—'

'And you knifed him,' finished Boleton. He appealed to Gwenllian. 'Help me make an end of this evil—'

'John knifed himself,' said Cole, his face a mask of bewilderment. 'His weapon is still embedded in his stomach, if you care to look. But my dagger is here, at my side.'

'Mistress, please,' begged Boleton. 'You were beginning to be convinced by my reasoning—'

'Actually I was encouraging you to talk, to give Symon time to rescue me,' said Gwenllian coldly. 'He is *not* the leader of these thieves, and you will never make me believe otherwise. So put up your sword, and let us be done with this nonsense before someone is hurt.'

Cole regarded his friend in shock. 'You told her *I* committed these burglaries?'

'Yes, he did,' said Gwenllian, going to stand next to him. 'But there are many reasons why that cannot be true.'

'Then name them,' challenged Boleton, gripping his sword in both hands.

She might have said Symon did not possess the wits for such sly subterfuge, but she refused to denigrate him to his treacherous friend. She began to outline what she had deduced instead.

'First, you accuse him of being in a position to forge an alliance with outlaws, but the same applies to you – more so, because *you* are the knight in charge of solving crime and you often meet villains. Second, he can barely persuade John to raise his pen, let alone join a criminal fraternity. Third, you did not dog our footsteps yesterday to prevent him from destroying evidence, but to protect yourself.

Fourth, look at your fine new clothes. I do not believe your tale about a recent inheritance.'

'That *did* seem odd, brother,' said Cole quietly. 'We have been friends for years, and you never mentioned this dowager aunt before.'

'Then there is your relationship with Gilbert,' Gwenllian went on. 'You stopped Symon from arresting him yesterday, and you were in his company during Lord Rhys's raid – like Daniel, you stole at a time when it would be blamed on the invaders. Gilbert said he had things to do that night and seemed frightened – *you* were using him to make the most of the chaos.'

'You draw ridiculous conclusions,' shouted Boleton angrily. 'It is not—'

'Afterwards, when theft became too dangerous, you fled to the forest,' Gwenllian cut across him. 'You spun a wild tale about single-handedly fending off forest-dwelling robbers, which I did not believe. But I should have done, because *that* part was true – and later you decided to put your new acquaintances to good use.'

'This is arrant rubbish,' objected Boleton hotly. 'I am not a—'

'Gilbert betrayed you before he fell,' Gwenllian forged on. 'I saw the distress on Symon's face when the name of the leader was whispered, although I could also tell he had already guessed it – it was confirmation of what he feared. Meanwhile, Gilbert misunderstood his reason for asking – he thought he was being tested, to see whether he would inform on the constable's closest friend.'

Cole regarded him unhappily. 'I *had* already guessed, brother. You see, you doubled back to ambush me when I chased you towards the river, and I recognized the manoeuvre – we used it together many times in France.'

'And then there was poor John,' Gwenllian went on. 'You

recruited him to your nasty cabal, knowing he did not have the strength of character to resist. Was he really so useful?'

'He was about to expose Daniel as a villain.' Boleton rounded on Cole. 'Your so-called friend, who was stealing from the castle. Another few days with the accounts, and John would have had all the evidence he needed.'

'You always were jealous of Daniel's relationship with Symon,' said Gwenllian in distaste. 'You must have been delighted to learn he was dishonest. No wonder you did not want John to take holy orders – who else would trawl through old records on your behalf? But you drove him to suicide.'

Boleton was outraged. 'It was not me at his side when he died. It was Cole.'

'John's last words were meant for you,' said Gwenllian, turning to her husband. '"Beware the one you love." I thought he was speaking to me, but he was warning *you* of Boleton.'

Cole looked sadly at the knight. 'I wish I knew what led you to this.'

Boleton opened his mouth to protest his innocence again, but then closed it. He regarded Cole sullenly. 'Is it not obvious? I am more suited to high office than you in every way – I am a better administrator, I am infinitely more intelligent and I have ambition. *I* should have been constable, but the king gave the post to you, just because you are good with a sword.'

'You did not have to come with me,' said Cole reasonably. 'You could have—'

'I thought I could be content here, with a life of indolent leisure,' spat Boleton. 'But I was wrong. I am bored, and the more I think about it, the more it is apparent that the king made a mistake. You are a brainless fool who lets his wife make all the decisions.'

'Symon, no!' cried Gwenllian, when Cole took a firmer

grip on his weapon and stepped forward. He did not care about the affront to himself, but no one insulted his wife. 'Do not kill him in anger. Disarm him. Let the law be his judge.'

For a moment she thought he was going to refuse, and although he was the better swordsman of the two, his old wound was clearly paining him that night. He might lose.

'Gwen is right,' Cole said eventually. 'We should not fight each other. Yield to me.'

Boleton also hesitated, but then did as he was told, dropping sword and dagger on the floor. Cole sheathed his own blade and indicated that Boleton was to precede him out of the house. It was too easy, and every one of Gwenllian's senses clamoured that treachery was in the air. It was not long in coming.

With a sudden roar, Boleton spun around, stabbing wildly with a knife he had concealed in his sleeve. Cole managed to duck away, but the manoeuvre unbalanced him and he fell. Boleton's face was an impassive mask as he moved in for the kill.

But he had reckoned without Gwenllian. She darted towards the table, grabbed a pot and brought it down on Boleton's head. He crashed to his knees. Cole was quick to take advantage, and by the time Boleton's wits had cleared there was a knife at his throat. Cole regarded his friend in silence for a moment, then stood back and nodded towards the open door.

'Go, brother,' he said softly. 'Ride to the coast, take a ship and do not return.'

'No!' cried Gwenllian. 'He will—'

'I hate this house,' interrupted Cole, looking around unhappily. 'I almost died here after Hywel stabbed me, and now my dearest friend tries to complete the business. It has an evil aura.'

Gwenllian gazed at him. 'How long have you known Hywel was your attacker?'

'I have always known – I saw him. But it seemed unkind to tell you when you had just lost your brother.'

'Dear Symon.' Gwenllian felt tears scald her eyes. 'You kept your silence to protect me?'

Cole shuddered as he surveyed Kyng's parlour a second time. 'There has been enough death and deceit in this house, and I do not want more of it.' He gestured to the door, but he did not look at Boleton. 'Go, and never come back.'

Without a word Boleton slunk away into the night.

# III

In the weeks that followed, Gwenllian was acutely uneasy, sure it was only a matter of time before Boleton came to wreak vengeance on his erstwhile friend. But then a cousin brought her some news. He spoke rapidly in Welsh, too fast for Cole's meagre grasp of the language.

'The sly knight tried to make the surviving forest folk attack the town, to create a diversion while he killed your husband, but they turned against him. Shall I tell you where they buried his body?'

Gwenllian glanced at Symon. 'No. I think it is better to believe he escaped. My husband has endured enough treachery, and he does not need to hear more of it.'

Cole had placed a guard on the place where Hywel had hidden Arthur's bones while Gwenllian made some enquiries about Abbey Dore. Within a month word began to trickle back that the Welsh sexton was indeed a man who could be trusted, so she resolved to follow her nephew's plan and take them there. A Norman abbey in

Herefordshire would not have been her first choice of hiding places, but Lord Rhys's warring sons meant that southern Wales was currently an unstable, uncertain place. It was certainly time for Arthur to be moved – and to enlist the help of the men Meurig had appointed as Guardians.

The moment she made her decision, she and Cole went to Merlin's oak. It was a beautiful autumn evening, with the scent of the harvest in the air and the sun bathing the land in a warm, golden light.

'It was clever of Hywel to put the bones back in Meurig's original hiding place – the cradle of roots – after Daniel began to suspect they were in the priory,' Cole remarked. 'But why was there a pit on the *other* side of the tree too – the one Daniel was kneeling by when he was murdered?'

'It was a decoy hole. Hywel dug it because he was afraid Daniel might guess where he had moved them. And he was right to be cautious, because Daniel *was* poking around it when he died – the mud on his knees attested to that.'

'Meurig should not have told you his secret when he knew Hywel was listening,' said Cole resentfully. 'He should have known better.'

It was a curious thing to say. 'What do you mean?'

'Dewi – Hywel's brother – was shot by would-be robbers on the way from Glastonbury. Or so Meurig told everyone. But I saw Dewi's body, and it was no arrow that killed him. He was stabbed.'

Gwenllian's mind reeled. 'Stabbed?'

Cole nodded. 'I knew Hywel was the culprit from some incautious remark he made. But Meurig said it would upset you if I arrested one nephew for murdering another. It was a clever ploy – he knew exactly how to stay my hand.'

Gwenllian stared at him. 'You knew this terrible secret but did not think to share it with me?'

'Meurig asked me not to. It was a nasty business – Hywel killed Dewi because Dewi was Meurig's favourite. Meurig was deeply ashamed. He did not want you, or anyone else, to know.'

Gwenllian shook her head slowly. She had wondered why Hywel had stabbed Cole in order to prevent her from claiming the bones – why not attack her, who was smaller and posed less of a threat? The answer was obvious now – he wanted revenge on the man who knew his dark secret. It explained why he had spent his dying breath trying to implicate Symon in a murder too.

'But Meurig should not have told you about the bones when he knew Hywel was listening,' Cole was saying. 'It might have put you in terrible danger.'

'Oh, Symon!' said Gwenllian, exasperated. 'I might have worked out what had happened to the bones years ago, if I had known all this! Do you really think I warrant such cosseting?'

Cole considered the question carefully, then nodded, smiling as he did so. 'There is nothing I would not do to protect you. And Meurig felt the same way.'

There was nothing to say to such a remark, and they walked in silence for a while. Gwenllian found herself thinking about the people who had been touched by the events of the summer. No one missed Hywel's drink-fuelled bitterness or Boleton's acid tongue, but the castle clerks grieved for John, and the town's merchants had been sorry when Kyng and Spilmon were banished from the realm.

Meanwhile, Gilbert had recovered from his fall and, in exchange for his freedom, told Cole where Boleton kept the proceeds of his crimes. It had all been returned to its grateful owners.

And people mourned Daniel as a good man. Gwenllian had completed what John had started, and had been appalled by the extent of Daniel's dishonesty. But Cole, ever loyal, even to friends who did not deserve it, had persuaded her that nothing could be gained by exposing the monk's penchant for the castle's money. So Daniel's reputation as a fine, generous, upright man remained unsullied.

'We searched for one villain in all this, but it transpired there were many,' she said ruefully. 'Daniel stole from us and his priory, Hywel was a blackmailer, Kyng and Spilmon plotted murder, John and Gilbert joined forces with criminals, and Boleton—'

'Boleton was the worst of them all,' finished Cole flatly. 'You were right about him all along. I should have listened to you more.'

'If you had listened to me less, he might not have turned against you – it was the fact that I help you with your work that annoyed him.'

'But then my men would have mutinied instead,' he said with a rueful grin. 'They know who organizes their regular pay, decent meals and clean bedding. No, Gwen. Listening to you is a very good idea.'

When they arrived at Merlin's oak, Cole unbuckled his sword and dagger, placing them on a wide, shelf-like branch to keep them out of the way. Then he touched the spade to the soil and began to dig. The soil yielded easily, as if the tree knew it was time to give up its treasure.

'We never did learn who killed Daniel,' said Gwenllian, settling down to watch him. The leaves whispered in the breeze, creating dappled patterns of sun and shade on the grass below. Then there was a rather harder gust, and Cole gave a yelp. The branch had swayed, causing the dagger to drop and strike his shoulder.

'It was a good thing it was not the sword that fell,' he grumbled, rubbing it. 'Or you might be finishing this on your own.'

'Daniel!' exclaimed Gwenllian, as all became clear. 'He stole the priory's cross and Hywel found it next to his corpse. I understand now! No one killed him – it was an accident!'

She hurried to the other side of the tree and saw a similar shelf-like branch over Hywel's decoy pit, although it was much higher. Cole climbed up to see scuffs on the bark, where something had rested.

'He must have set his stolen property here,' he said, 'while he dug for the bones—'

'Lest someone walked by and caught him with it . . .'

'But it fell on him as he was patting the last of the turf back into place. It was a heavy thing, and you told me it caught a vulnerable point on his skull.' Cole shivered suddenly and lowered his voice. 'But it was not an accident, Gwen – the tree killed him.'

'Perhaps,' said Gwenllian, walking around the mighty trunk to their own hole. She could already see the top of the plain, dark-wooded chest that contained the bones, and it would not be long before they had it out. 'But I do not think it means *us* harm – it is willing to let Arthur go this time.'

'I hope you are right,' said Cole, glancing uneasily at the branches above. 'The sooner he is in Herefordshire, the better. I hope he will be safe there.'

'He will be,' said Gwenllian softly, thinking of the sexton in Abbey Dore and of the group of silent, sober men who were even now waiting in the forest – the Guardians were ready to do their duty. One was Meurig's middle son, Young Meurig, who had always been her favourite nephew. From now on, Arthur's bones would be watched over by them and by their descendants.

She rested her hand on her belly, smiling as she felt the kick of life within. And by her own sons, of course. After ten years she had all but given up hope of a child, but suddenly she was pregnant. She could not help but wonder whether she owed the miracle to Arthur, or perhaps Merlin, who wanted *her* heirs to guard Wales's most precious treasure. She knew it was a son that grew inside her, and she also knew what he was going to be named – Meurig, after the brave, noble man who had set Arthur's bones on the road to their rightful destiny.

## Historical note

Norman-held Carmarthen was attacked by Rhys, Prince of Deheubarth, in 1196, when he sacked the town and burned the castle. The constable at the time was Symon Cole. Lord Rhys died the following year, and his sons turned on each other, giving the Sheriff of Hereford (William de Briouze) ample time to rebuild the fortress in stone. Rhys is thought to have sired at least eighteen children, although tracing them is difficult due to his penchant for giving them the same names (he had at least three Maredudds and two Gwenllians). As was the custom of the day, his daughters were married off to politically important allies.

An entry in the Cartulary of St John, Carmarthen, dated between 1194 and 1198, refers to a deed in which de Briouze donated the church of Ebernant to Carmarthen's priory. Ebernant had belonged to Lord Rhys, and the gift was to compensate the priory for his attack. The writ's witnesses include Renald de Boleton, knight, John the clerk, Gilbert, Robert Spilmon, William Kyng and Daniel Adam the chaplain. King Street and Spilman Street are still extant in the town.

There was a famous tree in Carmarthen called Merlin's oak, but it was probably planted in the seventeenth century, perhaps to mark the Restoration. But local legend maintains it was put there by Merlin, who is said to have been born in the town. The last remnants of the oak were removed from the end of Priory Street in 1978.

# ACT TWO

## The Welsh Marches, December 1282

The tavern-keeper filled a pottery mug with a pint of ale and reached up to place it almost fearfully on the centre of the blackened tree trunk that arched across the *simnai fawr*, the great fireplace that was built into the thickness of the wall.

'On a night like this, the devil needs his brew!' he muttered, crossing himself as paradoxically he pandered to an ancient superstition meant to placate Satan in such foul weather as this.

'No need, Eifion!' growled one of the dozen men hunched around the fire on benches. 'The devil is safe up in Anglesey tonight – the bastard who calls himself King of England!'

The snarl of agreement from the throats of the company was tinged with despair, as it competed with the howl of an icy wind that rattled the shutters and flickered the flames of the few candles and rushlights.

'Almost two hundred bloody years we've fought those swine – and now it's all over,' groaned one old fellow, his voice ending in a sob.

A much younger man, in his late thirties, with black hair and deep-set dark eyes, slammed his ale-jar down on a rough table.

'No, it doesn't have to be over, damn you! Prince Dafydd

is still fighting on up in the north. It's up to folk like us to give him all the help we can.'

Another man, with a face scarred by old cow-pox, shook his head. This was Dewi, who worked in a fulling mill just up the road. 'You mean he's *cut off* in the north, Owain! And most of our army was massacred at Builth, after Llewelyn was ambushed. What's the point of carrying on?'

There was a rumble of dissent from some, but others sided with the speaker.

'What can we few do down here in Erging?' said one. 'It's a hundred miles or more to where Dafydd's forces lie in the mountains – and Edward's armies have them squeezed in tighter than an abbot's arse!'

The drinkers subsided into a doleful silence, hunched around the great hearth like a group of mourners around a coffin – which in reality was fairly near the truth. The main difference was that they had no corpse to mourn, as no one knew for sure where Llewelyn's body lay, though his severed head was already stuck on a spike at the Tower of London.

Eifion, the landlord, kept an anxious eye on the wooden screen behind the great oak door. He had stationed his unfortunate pot-boy outside, a lad of ten who, though wrapped from head to toe in a smelly sheepskin, would have to be called in soon before he perished from cold. The lad's task was to scan the moonlit track outside and warn of any strangers on the road from Abergavenny to Hereford, though this seemed unlikely this late on such a freezing, blustery night, three days before the eve of Christ's Mass. A warning was vital, as the group of men in the bleak taproom were all former Welsh soldiers, and their assembly could well be considered treasonous if the Sergeant of the Hundred or one of the lordship's servants from Grosmont took it into his head to visit the Skirrid

Inn that night. Even though this was geographically Wales, the Norman-English Marcher lords and their client landholders considered it their territory. Even the Welsh name 'Erging', for the area of what was rapidly becoming south-west Herefordshire, had been eradicated by the English, who now called it 'Archenfield'. It was true that many folk, even some English, accepted that the little river Monnow marked the border in this area, but the endless to and fro of frequent Welsh raids and relentless English acquisition made the idea of a frontier meaningless.

The black-haired man broke the silence. 'So what are we going to do about it?' he growled. 'If we could gather enough support, I'm willing to lead a party through the mountains to reach Dafydd in Eryri.'*

Out of the muttering that this provoked, another voice dissented. 'You may well say that, Owain ap Hywel! You have no wife or children left to starve while you go off to be killed.'

Then Dewi, the scar-faced man, added his own caution. 'Before you do anything rash, Owain, you had best take your father's advice. He fought alongside our prince many times, though it was twenty years past.'

'And got a spear through his chest for his trouble,' added the inn-keeper. 'You said Hywel was dying, Owain? This awful news must be breaking his heart?'

The black-haired man nodded sadly. 'My father has been sickening all autumn; his cough gets worse each day. I knew he could not last the winter, but this tragedy will kill him before Christ's Mass.'

He got to his feet and swallowed what was left in his pot. 'I promised to call in on him tonight. There may not be many more chances before God takes him.' He pulled

* Snowdonia

117

a shoulder-cape of dark leather over the belted tunic of coarse brown wool that reached to his thighs, covering serge breeches pushed into thick boots. The cape had a hood, which he pulled up over his head as he made for the door.

'I'll see what my father has to say and we'll meet here again on the eve of Christ's Mass,' he promised, passing behind the draught screens and tugging open the massive iron-banded front door.

A blast of icy wind swirled a few flakes of snow past him, as he pushed the freezing pot-boy inside and heaved the creaking door shut behind him. For a moment he stood in the bright moonlight, checking that the road of frozen mud that went past the hamlet of Llanfihangel Crucorney was empty in both directions. The Black Mountains, the edge of Wales, loomed close behind him and a mile or two to the south he could see the strange silhouette of the Holy Mountain, Ysgyrid Fawr, the English corruption of which gave its name to the 'Skirrid Inn'. The great cleft in its side was said to have been caused by an earthquake that occurred at the hour of Christ's Crucifixion. Owain wondered bitterly what earthly disaster might have occurred somewhere in Wales at the dreadful hour of Prince Llewelyn's ambush and assassination.

His father lived a mile up the road at Pandy, a cluster of cottages around the fulling mill, whose wheel was driven by the Honddu stream. He was looked after by his daughter Rhiannon, whose husband also worked at the mill, which treated all woollen cloth woven in the surrounding area.

Owain was a self-employed carter who carried much of the mill's produce around the neighbourhood and often further afield. His two patient oxen were tethered out of the wind in the lee of the tavern and, huddling against the cold on the driving board, he drove the plodding beasts and his empty cart up to Pandy, where he left them in the shelter of the mill yard.

His sister's *bwthyn* was a hundred paces further, on the banks of the millstream. It was a two-roomed cottage built of cob, a mixture of clay, straw and dung plastered on wattle panels between oak frames, the walls capped by a steep thatched roof.

Rhiannon was expecting him, late as it was, but her husband was asleep in the inner room, snoring in the box-bed with their two small children cuddled under blankets on the wide shelf above him. There were glowing logs in the fire-pit in the centre of the main room, the wispy smoke being lost beneath the high ceiling of plaited hazel twigs that supported the thatch.

'How is he tonight?' murmured Owain, as his sister opened the door for him.

'Weaker than ever, poor man. He can hardly catch his breath.'

Propped against the far wall, slumped on a hessian mattress stuffed with raw wool and goose feathers, was their father, Hywel ap Gruffydd. At seventy, he looked a score of years older, a gaunt skeleton of a man, unable to lie down because of shortness of breath. His old chest wound had collapsed one lung and now the other was giving up as well. His sparse white hair overhung a cadaveric face, the same deep eye sockets that his son possessed being like dark pits above sunken cheeks and blue-tinged lips.

Owain went across and knelt on the floor rushes alongside the pallet. He took his father's hand in his, feeling the coldness of the claw-like fingers, in spite of the profusion of blankets that lay on the bed and around his shoulders.

'I've no more than a day or two left, my son,' he whispered

between heaving breaths that drew air into what little remained of his lungs. 'But there's nothing to live for now that our last prince has gone.'

His son gently stroked the bony fingers. 'Don't strain your voice, *Tâd*,' he said. 'We'll all come to see you in turn, the whole family.'

Briefly the old man's eyes flashed. 'Idwal's sons are most welcome,' he hissed between gasps. 'But is it likely that Ralph and his brood care much if I live or die?'

Rhiannon, standing on the other side of the bed, clucked in disapproval. 'Now, *Tâd*, that's not true. They'll be here tomorrow, no doubt.'

Hywel had had three sons, as well as a daughter. The eldest, Idwal, had been killed many years before, during Llewelyn's attack on Caerphilly in '68. Idwal left two sons and when, later, their mother had died, Owain had looked after them until they were old enough to fend for themselves.

Hywel's remaining elder son was Ralph, though he had been baptised Rhodri. Now a prosperous man in his forties, he had 'gone over to the English', as his father put it bitterly. He had abandoned his patronymic of 'ap Hywel' and become 'Ralph Merrick', a common anglicization of one of his forebears, 'Meurig! As a youth, he had entered the service of the Scudamores, a notable Norman family, and had risen to be their bailiff at nearby Kentchurch Court, one of the Scudamores' main estates. Ralph had married an Englishwoman from Hereford town and their three children were John, William and Rosamund, all thoroughly English names.

Relations between the two parts of the family were cool and, though there had never been any outright enmity, Ralph and his family looked down on the others as rude yokels who had failed to make the best of their lives by siding with the invincible invaders who were inexorably pushing the Welsh border further westwards.

Owain and his sister crouched for a while on the floor alongside their father's bed, soothing him and talking quietly about old times. None of them made any attempt to avoid the fact that the old man had not long to live, for death in those rural communities was commonplace and accepted. Hywel had already lived much longer than most men, though it was hard that he must go now, knowing that his revered prince had been killed – and along with him the last hope of maintaining Welsh independence.

Rhiannon fed him some warm bread in milk, and their father seemed to gain a little strength, struggling to sit up further on his deathbed. 'Go to bed now, good girl,' he commanded. 'I will talk to Owain for a while.'

Reluctantly, but accustomed to doing what she was told, the middle-aged woman left them, putting a few more oak logs on the fire as she went. As soon as the heavy leather flap that served as a door to the bedroom fell back into place, Hywel seized his son's hand in a surprisingly strong grasp.

'I cannot die before telling you something, Owain *bach*,' he wheezed. 'Our family carries a secret which must be passed on from generation to generation.'

His son frowned, wondering if the old man's mind was failing along with his body, but he felt he must humour him. 'Why me, *Tâd*, for Ralph is the older one?'

Hywel scowled and gripped his son's hand even harder. 'I cannot trust him with this; he panders too much to our enemies.' He paused to cough, white spittle appearing at the corners of his mouth, then continued, though it was an effort to do so.

'Listen, you know the legend that in times of great crisis Arthur of Caerleon, ancient king of the Britons and

Hammer of the Saxons, will come again to save the country in its hour of need?'

Bemused, Owain nodded in the firelight, wondering what this had to do with some family secret. 'The bards say he never died,' he conceded, recalling the fairy tales his mother had told him as a child. 'He is supposed to be sleeping in a cavern with his men, awaiting the call to arms.'

His father slowly shook his head. 'Wishful thinking, my son. Our bards liked to make a romance out of everything,' he murmured cynically. 'Arthur died on the Isle of Avalon and was buried there, long ago in Glastonbury. But the damned English monks dug him up almost a century ago, to prove that the champion of the Britons was really dead and gone, so could no longer be looked to as a future saviour.'

'Why are you telling me this now, *Tâd*?' muttered Owain, becoming a little impatient when there were far more immediate troubles to be considered.

'Because the bones of Arthur are no longer in Glastonbury, to be mocked by those who want him proven dead. They were stolen by us and are hidden very near here.'

Owain's eyebrows climbed up his forehead in puzzlement. 'What do you mean, *stolen by us*? Who are "us"?'

Hywel struggled to sit up even straighter, the effort causing him to gasp for breath. When he had recovered, he explained. 'A band of brave men took them from Glastonbury – a band led by Meurig ap Rhys, your great-grandfather. He swore that the secret of their hiding place must be handed down through each succeeding generation, and so it came to me from my father, Gruffydd ap Meurig.'

'And you are loath to pass this on to Ralph?' asked Owain.

'He is not to be trusted with such a secret,' wheezed

Hywel contemptuously. 'Being a creature of the Scudamores and even known to Edmund Crouchback of Grosmont, he might tell them in order to curry more favour. No, it is you, Owain, a true patriot and a fighter who must carry this trust onwards.'

'But I have no sons. You well know that my wife died barren years ago.'

'Then pass it to Idwal's sons! That would be fitting, as he was my eldest boy.'

Owain was dubious. He felt that this must be some romantic fantasy, perhaps with a basis of truth, but exaggerated by the dying mind of his father. Yet the old man was speaking clearly and rationally, with no sign of mental confusion. 'But what use is this knowledge to us – or anyone else?' he asked.

Hywel's dark eyes flashed briefly in the light from the flickering logs and briefly he became almost animated. 'This may be the time, Owain!' he hissed. 'God knows that if ever there was a moment when Wales was in mortal danger, this must be it! With Llewelyn slain, we need Arthur's return as the only hope of salvation.'

'But you said that he was dead – he must be, if you have his bones! This old story about him sleeping in a cave is just a fairy tale!'

The old man became agitated, grasping at the blankets with an emaciated hand. 'Of course it is, boy! But think what a rallying point it would be for Prince Dafydd's army up north, if it were known that the relics of King Arthur were carried before their host when they marched to battle! Even these Norman-English bastards are fascinated by Arthur, which is why they revered the remains in Glastonbury. It was even old King Henry, curse his black soul, who told the abbot where they were to be found.'

The effort of this long speech exhausted him, and he slumped back against the pillow behind his head.

Suddenly Owain could see what his father was driving at, and a wave of love and admiration swept over him at the clear-sightedness and cunning of the dying old warrior. 'You think I should take them up north, then, *Tâd?*' he asked, anxious to get a firm direction from the head of the family.

'I know you meet the local patriots in the Skirrid and other places,' gasped Hywel. 'Discuss it with them, but hurry! Every day makes Dafydd more hard pressed in Gwynedd. Take the great king's remains to him at his castle of Dolwyddelan and trumpet their magic to every minor lord, archer and foot soldier in the country, for them to rally to the aid of our dear land!'

His desperate enthusiasm was infective, and Owain bent closer to the frail figure on the pallet.

'So where are the bones hidden, *Tâd?*' he whispered.

In the flickering light of the fire-pit, father and son bent their heads together as the secret was passed on.

'They'll have you dangling from that, if this becomes known!' warned Dewi. He pointed at the wooden staircase that wound its way to the upper floor of the tavern, where a rope with a noose on the end hung ominously in the stairwell from a beam above. The large upper chamber was used for the monthly court of the nearby Hundred of Ewyas Harold. Summary justice was carried out on the premises for a whole variety of offences, including hanging for the theft of anything worth more than twelve pence.

'Supporting Prince Dafydd is now treason, from what we hear,' confirmed Eifion, the inn-keeper. 'That sod King Edward has decreed that any Welshman found in arms will be hanged.'

It was now the eve of Christ's Mass, and a few of those who had assembled two nights earlier were back to meet Owain. Dewi from the Pandy mill was there, with his twenty-year-old son, Caradoc, who was trying to court Owain's niece, Rosamund Merrick, against the violent objections of her father Ralph.

The dejected patriots huddled together in a corner this time, as there were some other villagers from Llanfihangel crouched around the hearth, also rather despondently celebrating the birth of the Saviour with a few jars of ale.

Owain had patiently explained to his fellow conspirators the substance of his father's disclosure, eventually overcoming their incredulity. In a low voice he finally asked their opinion on what should be done. 'I already had half a mind to go up to Gwynedd to join Dafydd's forces. Now this seems a formidable gift to take him, if it puts more mettle into his men,' he argued.

As Eifion collected the empty ale-pots, he gave his opinion before going back to his line of kegs at the back of the taproom.

'I'd say leave well alone, Owain. Keep your head down and it may remain on your shoulders,' he muttered.

Dewi lifted his cow-pox-raddled face to follow Eifion with his eyes as the inn-keeper walked away. 'I'd be careful what we say in front of that man,' he advised. 'I've got my doubts about how true he is to our cause.'

'He is beholden to the Sergeant of the Hundred who rents his room upstairs for their court,' added the old man with the rheumy eyes. His reddened lids leaked tears, as the cold was still intense, though the wind had dropped.

As no one had answered his question, Owain repeated it impatiently. 'So what are we to do? Are we to retrieve these relics and try to get them up to Dolwyddelan?'

The half-dozen looked at each other uneasily.

'So where are they now?' ventured Caradoc.

Owain shook his head. 'That secret has been guarded for over ninety years. I'm not going to divulge it in a public alehouse, especially when we've not yet decided what to do about them.'

After some further muttered discussion, Dewi's son Caradoc and two of the younger men agreed that they would support Owain if he really did intend trying to smuggle the relics up to North Wales to join the prince's depleted army. The others decided that their lives and their families outweighed the slim chance of success for such a hazardous journey – and the even more doubtful outcome of trying to defeat the massive forces of Edward Plantagenet that now formed an iron ring around Snowdonia.

'Come with me a moment, while your wives sit and gossip in the church,' Owain commanded, beckoning his two nephews into Garway's sloping churchyard. It was after morning Mass on this special day of Christ's birth, and their feet crunched through a thin layer of frozen snow that lay on the grass outside the strangely shaped building. The Knights Templar, who had a preceptory in the tiny village, had recently built a circular nave on to the old chancel in imitation of the Holy Sepulchre in Jerusalem, with a separate fortified tower a few yards away.

'Where are you taking us? It's damned cold today,' grumbled Madoc, at twenty-five a couple of years older than his brother, Arwyn. He was a big-boned young man with abundant brown hair and the family's deep-set eyes.

'Let's walk down to the Holy Well, out of earshot of those nosy folk,' growled Owain, looking at the trickle of parishioners coming out of the south door.

As they trudged the hundred paces down to the bottom

of the churchyard, Arwyn pulled his heavy woollen cloak more tightly around him and shivered. 'Don't be too long, Uncle, for Bronwen has a goose to cook for us all.' He felt the cold most, as unlike his brother, he was thin and wiry, with darker hair.

'This is more important than a damned goose, even for dinner on the day of Christ!' retorted Owain, and the two younger men fell silent. He had been virtually their father since they were children, and his word was not to be questioned.

In the corner, against the boundary wall, a small stone-lined well normally provided water that was claimed to cure eye ailments, but today it was frozen solid. A couple of raised slabs formed benches, but today they were too cold to sit on, so the three men stood by the well, the two nephews waiting expectantly for Owain to speak.

Gravely he explained the whole history of Arthur's bones and their removal from Glastonbury by their great-great-grandfather, as well as the solemn vow of the Guardians to pass on the secret of their hiding place through the generations. At first incredulous, the two younger men were by no means lacking in intelligence and quickly grasped the significance of the relics.

'But that swinish king, Edward Longshanks, caused them to be moved to a new shrine near the High Altar in Glastonbury only four years ago,' protested Madoc. 'He went with all pomp and ceremony to the abbey there and made sure that everyone knew that Arthur was really dead and unable to rise again to save the true Britons.'

Madoc was more aware of current news than most people, as he was the reeve to the Templars' farm at Garway and often had conversations with the three monkish knights who lived in the nearby preceptory.

Owain grinned, the first time he had smiled since the

news of Llewelyn's fatal ambush. 'Then they are fakes, substituted by the Benedictines there. *We* have the real bones of Arthur.'

He went on to tell them that as he had no sons himself to whom to pass on the secret, he was going to impart it to them. 'It is fitting, as your father, Idwal, was the eldest son and he would have told you, had he lived.'

'Why are you telling us this now, Uncle?' asked Arwyn. 'You are not all that many years older than us, and you have a long time before you need contemplate death.'

Owain began to explain the present crisis and his intention to take the relics north to Prince Dafydd. 'I may never return, either because I will be killed before I reach Gwynedd – or die in the battles that must come. In that case the bones will be lost and your duty will never be called on.'

'So why are you telling us?' persisted Arwyn.

'The relics are still in the hiding place where they have rested for almost a century. There are many people in this area I do not trust, and it may be that I will be prevented from retrieving them – possibly prevented by death!'

He banged his hands together to get some warmth into them.

'In that case someone must still keep the knowledge of where they are, for some future occasion. You are the only ones I can trust, as Ralph and his brood cannot be relied on not to go running to their English masters.'

Madoc frowned. 'My masters are the Templars and they are Normans. Why do you trust me?'

'Because you are the son of Idwal, and grandson of Hywel, who, thank God, still survives, though he cannot last for long.'

He turned to Arwyn. 'And that goes for you too. You are both true Welshmen, and if I can't trust you both I may as well lie down and die this minute.'

Madoc looked at his uncle in concern. 'Are you going to ask us to leave Garway and go with you to fight in Snowdonia? We both have wives and children.'

Owain placed a fatherly arm around their shoulders. 'No, never fear, I'll not prise you from your Bronwen and Olwen. It may be that I will need you to help me hide these bones, which are within a few miles of here. But that is all, apart from learning of their hiding place, in case I am killed tomorrow!'

He pulled them closer and their heads bent together so that they almost touched, as he whispered the old secret into their ears.

On the morning after the day of Christ, the hooves of a pony clattered to a halt on the frozen track outside Owain's cottage in the tiny hamlet of Hoadalbert. This was a handful of dwellings midway between Pandy and Grosmont Castle.

The carter, who lived alone in the single-roomed *bwthyn* that used to belong to his father, rose from putting fresh logs on his fire to peer through a crack in the boards of the door. Seeing a lad slide off a shaggy mountain pony, his first thought was that this was a message to say that his father had died, until he realized that the boy had come from the direction of Grosmont, not from his sister's home. In fact the messenger was a stable-boy from Kentchurch Court, just beyond Grosmont on the English side of the Monnow.

Owain opened the door and waited for the lad to come in. His nose was bright red from the cold, and he was beating his arms to get warm. Around his thin shoulders he wore two oat sacks as a cloak, and his hands were wrapped with rags in lieu of gloves.

'I come with a message from Bailiff Merrick, sir,' he announced, using the English language. 'He says that he wishes you to come to a family meeting at his house at noon and bring your sister with you.'

'Is that all he said?' Owain was surprised, as his elder brother rarely communicated with him and never invited him to his home, which was in the grounds of the large fortified manor house where the Scudamore family lived.

Taking pity on the lad's frozen appearance, Owain ladled some *cawl* from an iron pot at the side of the fire and handed him a wooden bowl of the leek and mutton stew. Gratified, the groom fished a spoon fashioned from a cow's horn from his pouch and, between appreciative slurps, confirmed that Ralph Merrick had said nothing else at all but had appeared to be in a bad temper – though this seemed to be his usual state of mind.

The boy knew nothing else and after warming himself at the fire for a few moments, he rode off towards Grosmont, this being the *caput* of the barony, held by Prince Edmund Crouchback, brother of the hated King Edward.

Owain pondered for a while, wondering what crisis could have caused his brother to deign to summon him. Possibly their father's imminent demise had prompted Ralph to talk about the division of Hywel's property, though there was precious little of that, as he had not been able to work on his smallholding in Hoadalbert for years, due to his chest troubles. He had given it to Owain for his home and had moved in with Rhiannon.

Owain shrugged and thought he would let events take their course. He decided not to use the cart to take his sister to Kentchurch, but instead saddled up his old mare. Rhiannon could sit behind him on the blanket that underlaid the simple saddle. When he reached Pandy, she was as surprised as he was to learn of their brother's invitation – or rather command – but she refused to leave her father, who was getting weaker and was now only half-conscious.

Her husband was working in the mill, and she would not leave her two children alone with a dying man.

Owain knew better than to try to persuade her, for she was a strong-willed woman – and indeed, by the looks of his father, he was not likely to last the day.

'I'll come back as soon as I can, *cariad*,' he promised, 'to tell you what our dear brother wanted and to sit with *Tâd* for the rest of the day – and night, if needs be.'

As it was approaching mid-morning, he rode back along the track, taking care to avoid the worst patches of ice so that his mare would not lose her footing. The wind had dropped and it was a clear, still day, with patches of pale blue sky appearing between the clouds. As he passed through the village of Grosmont, he saw that work had already restarted on the castle after the holy day break. Prince Edmund was strengthening the fortifications of the compact but menacing fortress and increasing the living accommodation. Edmund Crouchback, so called from the Cross he had emblazoned on his shoulders at the Crusades, was Earl of Lancaster and Leicester and, though he had numerous possessions elsewhere, he seemed intent on making this remote corner of the Welsh Marches his principal home.

Cursing Edmund, Edward and all the damned Plantagenet brood as he rode past, Owain crossed the little bridge over the Monnow and turned down the long track that led through the wide Scudamore lands to Kentchurch Court. However, he did not need to ride that far, as his brother's house was near the barton, the demesne farm that served the domestic needs of the Scudamores. As bailiff, the controller of all outside work at the manor and overseer of all the bound and free workers, he had a substantial dwelling. It was a stone building with three rooms and a stable at one end. A chimney protruded from the other end, as there was a hearth instead of the cruder fire-pit, and it was in this room that Ralph Merrick had assembled his family for the meeting.

His wife, Alice, a thin woman with a sharp face and a tongue to match, sat on a settle near the fire, with her pretty daughter, Rosamund, seated alongside her, looking pale and nervous.

The two sons sat on a bench opposite, looking ill at ease in their father's presence. The elder was John, at twenty-five a huntsman for the Scudamores, in charge of the hounds. He was a stocky fellow, with fair hair inherited from his Saxon mother, and a narrow rim of beard running around his jaw. He wore a dark green tunic over breeches and riding boots, with a hunting horn hanging from a thick leather belt.

His brother, William, two years younger, was heavily built like his father. He had a mop of dark brown hair, shaved up to a line above his ears in the old Norman style. A jerkin and serge breeches were usually covered by a thick leather apron, but he had left this in the stable, as his job as the estate butcher and slaughterman had fouled it with bloodstains. His otherwise comely features were marred by a bad turn in his left eye, which failed to follow the movements of the other.

The focal point of this family gathering was Ralph Merrick, a tall, erect man with a permanently truculent expression. He was forty-five, born seven years before Owain. Heavy features and a ruddy complexion made him unlike his brother, apart from the deep-set eyes that were a family trait.

'I told you to bring our sister,' he snapped as a greeting. 'Where is she?' He spoke in English, though he also had a fair grasp of Norman-French, the language of his masters.

'She cannot leave our dying father, and her husband has

to be in the mill all day,' replied Owain, deliberately speaking in Welsh.

'For God's sake, speak in English,' snapped his brother irritably. 'You know Alice can't understand the peasants' talk.'

'It was good enough for you when you were young!' retorted Owain. 'You never heard a word of English until you were ten years old.'

He suspected that Alice understood far more than she admitted, but this pretence was all part of their craven attachment to the Marcher lords and their tenants, who were ruthlessly annexing what for untold centuries had been Welsh lands.

'Why have you asked me here today?' he demanded, never one to be overawed by his domineering brother. 'Our father cannot live much longer, so I trust you are going to come to visit him while he still breathes?'

'I was there last week,' growled Ralph. 'And if my duties here permit, I will ride over in the morning.'

'You may well be too late,' retorted Owain. 'Since Idwal died, you are the eldest son and must lead the family.'

Ralph dismissed this with a wave of his hand. 'I summoned you here because I have heard very disturbing news about your activities,' he began ominously. 'It has come to my ears that you are encouraging men to go with you to join the rebel Dafydd. Are you mad, brother!' His voice had risen to a shout.

Owain was shocked, for this meant that someone had betrayed him. 'Who has told you this? I am a Welshman, as you are, and I am free to fight this oppression against my homeland!'

'The king has declared all such rebels as traitors and the penalty is death,' thundered Ralph. 'You say I will soon be the head of this family, so I intend to prevent it from falling into disrepute by having a traitor as a brother!'

Owain, now in a rage himself, pointed a quivering finger at Ralph. 'You'll not tell me what I can or can't do, Rhodri ap Hywel!' he shouted, deliberately using his brother's real name. 'If you were not so besotted with crawling around the English who have settled on our land, you would join me on this journey to Gwynedd!'

Alice squealed her protests at the quarrel that had flared up, and the two sons had risen to their feet, looking aggressively at their uncle. Ralph, bright red in the face, advanced on Owain, shaking a fist at him.

'This part of the March is now at peace. Would you see all our efforts wasted by your mad schemes? We are prosperous, both Welsh and English. Why would you wish to stir up conflict once again?'

'And what's this nonsense about taking King Arthur's bones to the north?' cut in the son John. 'Everyone knows that they lie in Glastonbury, so are we going to suffer you as a charlatan as well as a rebel?'

His uncle was too aghast at this further disclosure to censure his nephew for his insolence in speaking in such a way to a family elder. How in God's name did they learn about the relics?

'Who told you this?' he demanded. 'Was it Eifion at the Skirrid?'

To his further surprise, Rosamund suddenly burst into tears, bending over where she sat and sobbing into her folded arms.

Ralph threw out a hand dramatically towards her as he continued to rant at his brother. 'See how you and your treacherous friends cause such anguish to my family?' he rasped. 'Some common fellow of your acquaintance has had the impudence to try to pay court to my daughter. It was from him she has heard these tales of rebellion, before I forbade her today ever to lay eyes again on the ruffian.'

This provoked a fresh outburst of sobbing from Rosamund, which caused her mother to give her a good shaking rather than to comfort her. Owain, though incensed at the way in which his secrets had been bandied about, felt obliged to come to the defence of the culprit.

'The lad is no ruffian! Caradoc is the son of the fuller at Pandy, a respectable and prosperous freeman,' he protested.

Privately, if Owain had had Caradoc here now, he would have boxed his ears soundly for his loose mouth, even if it was to his girlfriend.

'I care not if he has a chest of gold, he will not approach my daughter ever again!' snarled Ralph. 'I have given orders that if he sets foot on this estate again, he will be flogged!'

Rosamund wailed again and got another shaking from her mother.

'I suppose he is another of your rebellious knaves – so let him go off to Gwynedd and be killed, and good riddance to him! All who are foolish enough to rally to Dafydd ap Gruffydd will be slain,' ranted the bailiff. 'But I forbid any member of this family to sully our name by turning to treachery!'

Owain glared at his elder brother, containing his anger with difficulty. 'Is that why you called me here today?' he demanded. 'Dragging me from the side of our dying father to lecture me on your craven obedience to the people who have stolen our land and our heritage?'

'Don't speak to our father like that!' bawled William. 'The Scudamores have been good masters. We live better now than we ever did before.'

John, emboldened by his brother's defiance, weighed in

with his denunciation: 'A damned sight better than you who live across the Monnow and up into the hills – squalid shacks to live in, scratching an existence from stony ground and few sheep!'

Owain ignored them and continued to glare furiously at his brother. 'So what are you going to do about it? Denounce me to your English overlords and have me hanged? Edmund Crouchback's castle is just down the road, and he has the highest gallows in these parts!'

'Of course not, you foolish man!' glowered Ralph. 'You are my brother and for all your wrongdoing you are still my kin.'

He swept his hand around the room to indicate his wife and offspring. 'But look what danger you have brought on me and my family, damn you! By concealing my knowledge of your folly, I risk being branded as a traitor myself.'

Owain shrugged. 'None will hear it from me – so if you tell your daughter to keep her chattering mouth closed, no one will be any the wiser. I'll deal with Caradoc. He'll say no more to anyone.'

He turned to go, convinced that staying would only worsen the antipathy between them. As he reached the door, he turned to face them again. 'Whatever has passed between us, remember that your father is dying, Ralph. If he could walk or even crawl, he would be with me on this venture, but, as it is, he at least deserves to hear his son say farewell!'

With that, he stalked back to his horse and rode away.

Ralph and his two sons did come to Pandy the next day, but they were too late. Hywel had died peacefully in his sleep in the small hours and now lay in the Church of St Michael, near the Skirrid alehouse, until he was buried in the churchyard the next day. Owain walked out of the cottage near the mill when Ralph appeared, too incensed at his brother's dilatoriness, leaving Rhiannon to exchange a few stilted words with him.

He took his empty cart, which he had used to carry his father's body to the church, down to Llanfihangel and sought out the priest to make arrangements for the burial.

'The ground is rock hard with frost, Owain,' said the parson sadly. 'How will we dig the grave? Our sexton is sick with a fever, though in any case he's too old to hack his way through such ice-bound earth.'

Owain promised that he would come himself with friends and with picks and iron bars, to lever away the topsoil to get at the softer earth beneath. The priest, Father Samson, was Welsh-speaking, unusual in this area. When Owain had gone with his nephews to Christ's Mass in Garway, the priest there conducted the whole service in Latin, of which no one apart from a couple of Templars understood a word. Owain knew that this was the usual practice everywhere, except that often the short sermon was delivered in English. Here in Llanfihangel, still within the diocese of Llandâf, the incumbent was a native, and Owain suspected that his sympathies were similar to his own. It would have been difficult for Father Samson not to have been aware of the politics of some of the men in the parish, such as those who met covertly in the Skirrid.

Later that day he returned with Dewi, Caradoc and Islwyn, another of their coven, and began the arduous task of digging a grave pit near an old yew in the corner of the graveyard. They had to avoid the roots, but the shelter of the tree had slightly lessened the depth of the frost, and within two hours they had gone down a sufficient depth to accommodate the rough coffin that one of the mill workers had fashioned. As they finished digging the hole,

Owain took Dewi and Caradoc aside and gave the younger man a stern warning about his loose mouth.

'But it was only to Rosamund!' he protested. 'How was I to know she would carry tales to her father?'

'Well, she'll carry no more, by the looks of it,' snapped Owain. 'Ralph Merrick says he'll have you whipped if you set foot in Kentchurch again – and probably he'll have you hanged if you try a second time!'

Dewi responded by giving his son a smart clout across the ear, which made the young man stagger. 'You silly fool, you put all of us in danger with your idle chatter! Let's pray that none of this comes to the ears of those in Grosmont!'

Their altercation was cut short by the return of the parish priest, who came to see if they had finished the grave. After he had inspected it, and declared it better than their sexton could have done, Owain took him aside and spoke in a low voice. 'Father, talking of sextons, do you happen to know who is the sexton at Abbey Dore now? Is it still a Welshman called Meredydd?'

The parson looked at him covertly, suspecting this was no casual enquiry. 'I think he is still there, but why do you ask?'

Owain became evasive, still not sure of where the priest's sympathies lay. 'Digging this hole made me think of sextons – and I had heard that that post at the abbey was almost a family benefice, handed down from father to son.'

'I would not know about that, Owain, but certainly the fellow there now is called Meredydd. It is not often I go there, as local priests are not always welcome at Cistercian houses.'

Abbey Dore was a large and very rich abbey at the bottom of the Golden Valley, which ran down the eastern edge of the Black Mountains.

Owain was on the point of letting Father Samson into the secret, but after having castigated Caradoc for the same indiscretion he decided to keep quiet.

The diggers adjourned to the Skirrid for well-earned refreshment, during which Owain was beset with people offering their sympathy for the loss of his father. Eventually he was able to retire to a corner of the taproom with Dewi, his son and two others, Alun and Cynan, who had offered to go with him to Gwynedd.

'We have to see my father safely into the ground tomorrow,' he began soberly. 'Then we need to carry out his last wishes, by recovering these relics and taking them to our prince up north.'

Dewi nodded in agreement. 'The will of a dying man, especially one with the courage of Hywel ap Gruffydd, must be respected. So what are we going to do?'

'It's time to tell you where the bones of Arthur rest,' said Owain. 'And this time, no one – and I mean no one,' he added, glaring at the abashed Caradoc. 'No one breathes a single word until our task is accomplished . . . is that understood?'

There were nods and grunts from the four heads that were inclined close to his. Then he stood up and swallowed the rest of his ale. 'Come outside. I'll not reveal the hiding place in an alehouse, as I said before.'

They trooped out into the cold afternoon, but there was no wind and even a weak winter sun made it just bearable to sit on the tailboard of his heavy two-wheeled cart while he related the story he had heard from his father.

'Hywel told me what he had learned from his father years ago,' he began. 'After the relics were retrieved from Glastonbury by a group of patriots, they were taken to Carmarthen, where they were hidden for a few years. The leader of the group was Meurig, one of the sons of the

Lord Rhys, but ironically, when Rhys attacked the Normans in that town, they were in such danger that they were moved on to a safer place.'

'What happened to this Meurig?' asked Alun.

'He died of wounds in the fighting at Carmarthen but managed to pass the secret to his sister, who called the remaining Guardians – I don't know how. His half-brother, also called Meurig, led these men, and he was my great-grandfather!'

Dewi nodded wisely; for a miller he was well versed in Welsh history. 'It was common for brothers to have the same name, as so many died in infancy. That same Lord Rhys, who is your ancestor, had no fewer than three sons called Meredydd.'

'But where did they take these relics?' demanded Caradoc impatiently.

Owain looked around cautiously at the empty countryside. 'Abbey Dore!' he murmured.

'The abbey! What the hell did they take them there for?' exclaimed Cynan, sounding indignant. 'Those Cistercians were all Frenchmen then! They would have no truck with anything to do with Arthur, unless perhaps they were from Brittany.'

Dewi shook his head. 'They came from Burgundy, that lot.'

'And they must have known that the real bones were still in Glastonbury,' objected Cynan. 'The abbot there made great play with the news of their discovery, so that he could attract even more pilgrims and their pennies.'

Owain held up his hand to placate them. 'Don't fret over that! This ancestor of mine, this Meurig, was a drover and he knew many people between Carmarthen and Hereford. One was a Welshman, who became sexton at Abbey Dore.'

'What good was that?' muttered Alun.

'It seems that this man was sympathetic to all things Welsh. Meurig took the box of bones on a packhorse when he was driving the next herd of cattle to Hereford and prevailed on this sexton to hide them at Abbey Dore.'

'But why there, of all places?' persisted Cynan.

'Meurig felt that it was right for a Christian king to be buried in consecrated ground, as he was in Glastonbury,' said Owain. 'It would not have been seemly for him to be stuffed into some unhallowed field or bog.'

Dewi nodded sagely. 'Arthur was certainly a devout man – he bore the image of the Virgin on his shield at the battle of Mount Badon, where he defeated the Saxons.'

Caradog became impatient with his father's tale-telling. 'So how are we going to get him back?' he demanded.

Owain shook his head at the impetuousness of youth. 'Straight after the funeral tomorrow, I'll go over to the abbey and see how the land lies.'

With that, the others had to be content.


The whole village turned out to the funeral and, as legally he was the chief mourner, Hywel's eldest son Ralph grudgingly attended, with John and William but not his wife or daughter.

The priest droned the Mass in poor Latin and then unusually gave a more sincere eulogy in Welsh at the graveside, to Ralph's annoyance. There were no formalities after the coffin had been lowered into the frosty ground, but all the villagers filed past Ralph and Owain at the church door, briefly offering their sympathy and respect. With hardly a word to his brother, Ralph left as soon as propriety allowed, leaving the small group of conspirators to fill in the grave with the lumpy, frozen earth.

Owain stood for while with his two nephews, sadly

contemplating the tumbled soil in the bare patch among the winter-shrivelled grass of the churchyard. Then he pulled himself upright and sent Arwyn and Madoc back to their homes and wives in Garway. When they had gone, he went over to the yard behind the Skirrid tavern, where his fellow conspirators were waiting.

'Are you sure you don't want us to come with you?' asked Dewi anxiously.

Owain shook his head. 'This is only a scouting visit, to make contact with the sexton,' he said. 'I can do it quicker on my old nag than with the cart – though we may have to take that to fetch the box.'

They watched him ride off, trotting up the Hereford track in the clear cold of the December day.

'I've got a bad feeling about all this,' muttered Dewi. 'God grant that my resolve holds, to leave home and hearth to risk my life for a desperate cause up in Gwynedd.'

It took Owain the better part of two hours to cover the eight miles to Abbey Dore. A mile or so short of the monastery, he passed the small castle of Ewyas Harold, sitting on its mound. He half-expected some challenge to be called out by the sentinel on the gate, but the man thankfully ignored him.

'The bastard probably thinks the Welsh are finished for good now that Llewelyn's dead,' he muttered, but it gave him pause to think about returning with the casket of bones. There was no way he could get past here with the cart, as its creaking wheels could be heard a quarter of a mile away in the stillness of the night, when there was supposed to be a curfew. Either they would have to come back in the day, with a load of legitimate goods in the cart, or else carry the box across country, though he had no idea of its weight or size.

Soon the huge abbey came in sight, nestling in the lush

Golden Valley, with the slopes of the Black Mountains on one side and the fertile land stretching away into England on the other. The great church, with its square tower and huge nave was surrounded by numerous stone buildings that housed the chapter house, dormitories, refectories, guest rooms, hospital and all the other accoutrements of a prosperous monastery. The surrounding land was dotted with sheep and held strip fields which, in season, would be filled with corn, barley, oats and vegetables.

Owain was cautious in his approach, not wanting to attract too much attention to himself, but played the part of a traveller seeking rest and refreshment. He walked his horse into the guest-house yard and offered two pennies to a lay brother who was the ostler in the stables. For this subscription to the abbey treasury, the man readily agreed to water and feed the mare, telling Owain to go into the hall kept for travellers to get some potage and ale. When he came out, he asked the ostler if Meredydd was still the sexton.

'I knew him some years ago,' he lied. 'I wondered if he was still here.'

The man grinned. 'He can hardly go anywhere else, being as his father before him did the same job,' he chuckled. 'And his eldest son will succeed him one day, no doubt.'

'I'd like a word, for old times' sake. Where could I find him?'

'This time of day, he'll most likely be in the parish graveyard. A babe was buried this morning, so he's probably tidying up there.'

There were two cemeteries at the abbey, one for the monks and priests, the other for the lay brothers and their families, as well as for the villagers who lived in the surrounding area. Owain was directed to this one, which lay against the eastern boundary wall. Here a tall, thin man of about fifty was hacking at frosted clods of turf with a mattock and placing them against a pile of earth which was obviously the pitifully small grave of an infant. He wore a coarse brown robe, quite different from the white habit and black scapular apron of a Cistercian monk, and he had no shaven patch on top of his greying hair.

'Meredydd? God be with you!'

He spoke in Welsh, and the man jerked around suspiciously.

'Who are you? I don't recognise you from the village.'

He replied in the same language, but stiffly, as if he rarely used that tongue.

Owain explained who he was and cautiously opened up the reason for his visit. 'I think we both have family obligations concerning the same matter,' he began. 'My great-grandfather was Meurig ap Rhys, and he brought something precious here from Carmarthen.'

Meredydd's long face creased into a beatific smile. He dropped his hoe and advanced on Owain, gripping him on the forearms with both hands.

'Many years ago, my father told me that he knew of a man in these parts who was descended from the Guardians, but he never approached him. That must have been your father?'

Owain nodded sadly. 'Hywel ap Gruffydd, whom we put in the ground only this morning. That's why I'm here, as he charged me with taking the relics to Gwynedd.'

The sexton's eyes widened as his eyebrows rose. 'The time has come, then? It should not be a surprise, given the evil news from Builth. If ever there was an hour of need, this must be it.'

Owain explained the hope that his father had, that the possession of Arthur's bones might spur the remnants of the Welsh army to greater feats of courage in the coming battles with the English forces. Meredydd nodded enthusiastically and, picking up his mattock, steered Owain back towards the guest house, where he insisted on plying him with more ale, though Owain resisted his offer of food.

'I apologize for my rusty Welsh,' said the sexton as they sat on a bench near a large fire. 'Since my wife died and my sons all married, I have lived in the lay brothers' quarters near the farm, where everyone speaks English, so I am out of practice.'

'Where are the relics now?' asked Owain in a low voice, though there was no one within earshot in the near-deserted hall. The midday meal was long over and, with no guests travelling the winter roads so soon after Christ's Mass, only two serving lads were in sight.

'They are buried in the monks' graveyard on the other side of the church,' answered Meredydd. 'I have never seen them, nor did my father or his father! But I know where they are.'

Owain frowned. 'But I saw no stones or grave-markers in that place you were digging just now.'

The sexton shook his head. 'Only eminent people like abbots and priors get an inscribed slab inside the church, though a wooden cross is often placed on the grave straight after the burial, but it is not meant to last long. A grassy mound is good enough for eternity, for God certainly knows where they are.'

'So how can you be certain where Arthur's remains lie? You say no one has seen them for three generations!'

Meredydd smiled and tapped the side of his long nose. 'My father dinned it into me, as his father had done to him. There are sight lines with various parts of the abbey that mark that particular grave mound. I have often checked on it, just for curiosity. Now I am fated to be the one who actually uses those directions.'

Owain was still not completely convinced. 'It may be that we will have to do this in the dark. Can you still find the box?'

The sexton shook his head. 'There is no need for that. I can remove it in daylight and hide it nearby until you collect it.'

'What if you are seen?' said Owain, aghast at the man's nonchalance in the face of such vital issues.

'Unless there is a burial, no one ever goes in there, except me. And if they were to see me digging and pulling things around they would think nothing of it – that is part of my task in life.'

Before Owain left to get home before the early-winter dusk fell, he arranged with Meredydd that the sexton would dig out the casket and conceal it near the abbey farm, under a pile of hedge trashings that were waiting to be burned.

'I can take it across on my wheelbarrow hidden under a heap of old leaves from the cemetery,' he said confidently. 'Then you can bring your cart and pick it up tomorrow.'

As Owain left, he fervently hoped that no one at the farm decided to have a bonfire that night.

Dewi was the one who accompanied him on the cart next day, as the miller was a freeman who operated the fulling mill for the Lord of Abergavenny, who owned it. No one breathed down his neck every hour of the day to see that he was there, and as long as the wool was washed and beaten by his three workers he could get away for most of the day. This was just as well, as Owain's ox-cart was a slow, ponderous vehicle which took three hours to make the journey to Abbey Dore. Both Dewi's son Caradoc and Alun wanted to go with them, but Owain felt that too many on the cart might arouse the interest of the sentries at Ewyas Harold, for, since the momentous events at Builth, the Marcher lords were nervous about possible reprisals from the Welsh and were checking on the movements of strangers.

They set out an hour after dawn, the weather having changed from its icy calm to a blustery west wind and a sky filled with heavy grey clouds. Their load was a pile of woven hazel hurdles, made in Llanfihangel and destined for Monnington, ten miles beyond Abbey Dore. Owain had to deliver them in the next few days but felt they were useful camouflage for his journey. He could leave them at the abbey farm and pick them up later, before he set off on his crusade to North Wales. As it transpired, his subterfuge was unnecessary, as the guards at the wayside castle took but a cursory glance at the wagon as it passed.

'We'll come back with a load of straw that I'll buy from the abbey,' said Owain. 'That can conceal the box well enough, without drawing any attention.'

This plan worked well, for the straw had to be purchased from the demesne farm, where the box had been concealed overnight under its pile of hedge cuttings. When they met Meredydd, who seemed to be enjoying the intrigue immensely, he arranged for the three pennyworth of straw to be collected from an open barn and helped Owain and Dewi to load it into the cart.

'You found the box?' muttered Owain, as they dumped armfuls of yellow straw into the wagon.

'It's in my barrow. I took it from the waste heap an hour ago,' replied the sexton. He trundled his conveyance nearer and with a quick heave slid a wooden box on to the tailboard of the cart and deftly pulled straw over it. Owain just had time to see a rectangular casket of dark oak, about the length of his arm and two-thirds as wide and deep, streaked with smears of earth.

'Pile more straw on top of it!' Meredydd commanded, and Dewi and Owain dropped further armfuls of last year's wheat stalks into the cart so that there was no sign of their illicit cargo.

They gave their sincere thanks to the sexton, who Owain suspected would have joined them on their trip to Gywnedd, given the chance. 'If anything goes wrong, you can always bring it back here,' said Meredydd as they prepared to leave. 'I can still pass on the sacred trust to my sons.' He stood gazing after them as they trundled away, his Welsh fervour reawakened after all these years.

'A good man. A pity we don't have twenty thousand more like him,' growled Dewi, as Abbey Dore slowly faded from view behind them.

They reached Garway without incident, the guards at Ewyas Harold taking no more notice of them than they had on the outward journey. Owain decided that he could not leave for Gwynedd for several days yet, as there were arrangements to be made with his sister and nephews. He needed to make sure they would not suffer for being linked with a felonious rebel and intended to slip quietly away with the three others. With luck, no one at Grosmont or Kentchurch would notice their absence for some time.

Madoc, who was the reeve at the farm run by the Templars at Garway Preceptory, lived in a cottage just outside the tiny cluster of houses that formed the village. The land sloped down from there towards the Monnow, the preceptory being between the village and the church. The home of the three Templars was a collection of stone buildings, with quarters for the knights, a sergeant and several lay brothers, including a few clerks, as the preceptory acted as the administrative headquarters for all the Templar properties and farms in South and West Wales.

Owain's ox-cart creaked its way to the farm, which was separated from the preceptory by a few acres of pasture, where Madoc anxiously awaited them. They unloaded their straw into a barn, which already held a large amount, and unobtrusively slid the precious box beneath the large mound.

'It'll be safe enough there for a few days,' said Madoc. 'No one will need any of that straw. We have a different store for the horses' bedding.'

They went over to Madoc's dwelling where his handsome wife Olwen warmed them before the fire and fed them *cawl* and fresh bread.

'Have you looked inside the box?' asked Madoc, who was fascinated by the thought that he had actually carried the remains of the greatest figure in the ancient history of the Britons.

Owain shook his head. 'I have kept it out of sight ever since we collected it,' he answered. 'But I'm not sure I want to look. These are powerful relics!'

'Best make sure, Owain,' said Olwen 'You don't want to struggle all the way to Dolwyddelan and then find you've given the prince a load of stones or beef bones.'

They talked it over for a while and eventually, with Dewi's added persuasion, Owain saw the sense of Olwen's caution and agreed to open the box briefly before taking it away.

With the evening approaching, they took their leave and the cart rumbled away, leaving the great king to slumber under a pile of straw in a Templars' barn, perhaps an appropriate place for such a devout warrior.

When they reached Hoadalbert, Dewi left to walk the couple of miles to Pandy. After settling his oxen, Owain threw a few logs on to the smouldering ashes in his fire-pit to warm the room for the night, then he wrapped himself in a couple of blankets and, after offering up a prayer for his father's soul, settled down on the hay-stuffed mattress in the corner.

It would be the last time he ever slept in his house.

Next day Owain was back at Madoc's cottage and went with him down to the barton, the home farm of the Templars, to check on the bones. Owain's presence there would cause no comment from the few lay brothers and outside labourers, as being a carter he often came to the farm. In fact the preceptory was one of his main customers, as he brought in much of their supplies and carried a lot of their produce to market in Abergavenny, Monmouth and Hereford.

They went into the barn and pulled out the large box, handling it with some reverence. Though almost a century old, the hard oak looked in good condition despite being buried for so long.

'Just a quick look, to make sure there really are bones in there,' said Owain, rather hesitantly.

'It's not locked – just a tight-fitting lid,' observed his nephew, tentatively poking at the top edge. It took more than that to open it, as the wood had swollen and distorted over the years, and Owain had to use the edge of a large, rusty hay-knife to prise it apart. Eventually the lid creaked open on its corroded brass hinges, revealing a layer of mould-stained linen covering the contents. Gingerly pulling that aside, they gazed down on a jumbled heap of mottled brown bones, some of which even their inexpert eyes recognised as human, especially as they glimpsed the rounded calvarium of a skull. They stared for a moment in awe, then spontaneously crossed themselves and mumbled a prayer in Welsh.

'That's enough!' said Owain abruptly and pulled the linen back across the remains. 'Let greater men than us do what they must with them.'

As he was about to lower the lid, Madoc pointed to something lying between the cloth coverlet and the side of box.

'There's a pouch there. It might be important.'

Owain lifted it out, a damp leather bag with a drawstring, patches of green mould growing thickly on its surface. Loosening the string, he looked inside, but there was nothing there but a small quantity of yellowish slime at the bottom. With a shrug, he put the pouch back again and closed the lid, pounding the warped wood until it sat firmly in place.

They pushed the heavy box back under the straw and returned to Madoc's house, but just as they reached the door they heard the sound of hooves coming at a canter, and a brown gelding dashed into the yard, bearing Arwyn on its back. He almost fell off in his haste and rushed across to them.

'Owain, you must hide. They are searching for you!' he gasped, grabbing at his uncle's sleeve. 'A man I often employ to help me with the thatching is working at Grosmont, and he came just now to tell me that Crouchback's sergeant-at-arms has gone out of the castle with a couple of men to arrest you!'

Owain stared at him in surprise. 'What the hell for?'

'It seems someone has denounced you as a traitor, intending to join the rebels fighting the king!' gabbled Arwyn. 'You must flee at once – hide yourself, for when they know you are not at home in Hoadalbert, my house and this place will be their next targets!'

'Bloody Ralph Merrick, that's who it will be!' snarled Madoc. 'He'd sell his own brother to curry favour with those bastards at Grosmont.'

The two nephews hustled Owain away, urging him to vanish into the countryside for the time being and hide somewhere until he could slip away to North Wales.

'We'll meet you after dark at the dead elm on the banks of the Monnow,' promised Arwyn. 'I'll bring some food and a blanket for you. Now go, for God's sake. We'll put them off with some tale about you having already gone away!'

Dazed, but responding to their genuine fears, Owain trotted out of the barton and then downhill past the church, keeping going until he reached the thickly wooded strip of land that ran along the river. He vanished into the trees and loped for a mile deeper into the woods until he found a badger sett and sank into it gratefully, pulling his cloak around him as tightly as he could. Thankfully, the really icy weather had moderated and the wind was coming from the west, which meant rain by tomorrow. He sat there pondering who might have given him away, to send him scurrying into the forest like a hunted animal. Though Madoc had immediately put the blame on Ralph, Owain could hardly believe that his own brother would denounce him to the English.

Others knew about the plan to go up to Gwynedd to join Dafydd's army. There were the two sons, William and John, who had never got on with Owain and looked down on him as a peasant. Ralph's wife and daughter knew of the plan, thanks to Caradoc's big mouth, but of course there could be many others. At the Skirrid, Dewi had warned him against the landlord, though again he found it hard to accept that Eifion would knowingly betray him. What about the priest? He was a Welshman but, as far as Owain knew, he was not aware that they were planning to join Dafydd.

The culprit was probably someone working at Kentchurch, who had picked up the gossip from Ralph or one of his family. Maybe they had not denounced him directly, but gossiped with folk at Grosmont, which was very near and had close connections with the Scudamore estate.

There was nothing he could do about it now, except try to keep out of sight until he could slip out of the district and make his way north. Accepting this philosophically and giving thanks for the fact that he had no wife or children to abandon, he settled down into his badger hole and waited for dusk.

'The swine's not here, so let's see if he's holed up with his kin in Garway,' growled the sergeant, aiming a kick at a stool, sending it flying in pieces across the room. He and one of his men had already trashed the place, ripping up the mattress and overturning the table in frustration. Outside, the others had pulled out the oxen's hay from the byre and chased the pig from its sty, in a futile search for Owain ap Hywel.

They mounted their horses and cantered off back to Grosmont, then on past Kentchurch towards Garway, where Sergeant Shattock burst first into Arwyn's cottage half a mile outside the hamlet and then into Madoc's at the barton. Neither of the men were at home, and after terrifying the wives and children, who genuinely knew nothing of what was going on, they scoured the neighbourhood until they found the two brothers, who professed similar ignorance of anything amiss.

'What our uncle intends doing is none of our business,' protested Arwyn. 'He never tells us anything about his own affairs.'

'His father has just died. You shouldn't be hounding him like this!' declared Madoc. 'What mischief-maker told you these lies?'

Shattock, a heavily built, florid man with a surly nature, gave the reeve a shove in the chest. 'Watch your tongue, damn you! None of your business who told the steward. If we find you've been hiding him, you'll both be wearing rope necklaces down at the castle gallows!'

They soon lost interest and rode away, the sergeant complaining that he had missed his dinner because of this futile mission. It was obvious that they were not going to take this allegation about Owain all that seriously, unless the steward, Jacques d'Isigny, sent them out once again to hunt him down.

Back at Grosmont, the sergeant went for his food before seeking out Jacques to report their failure. The castle was in state of chaos, and it was just as well that the recent defeat of the main Welsh forces had reduced any risk of a local attack, for a length of the curtain wall and one of the main towers had been pulled down in order to rebuild them according to the ambitious designs of Prince Edmund.

The steward, the principal officer of the barony and ruler of the castle when Edmund Crouchback was absent, took Shattock's news calmly.

'If the bastard turns up, just arrest him and then we'll hang him,' he said casually. 'With the prince arriving in a few days, I've got better things to do than chase some local peasant.'

Jacques d'Isigny was a tall, smooth-faced man of forty, with an olive skin that suggested a family origin in southern France. He dressed in clothes that were modest in style, but of the very best quality. His calm manner hid a ruthless nature, which made him a most efficient administrator. The fact that he was the senior civil servant of the king's brother gave him a status well above the usual steward.

As his lord was coming soon to check on the progress of the remodelling of his favourite castle, Jacques was understandably more concerned with this than catching some local renegade. If it had not been for a message from Sir Vincent Scudamore's manor at Kentchurch, to the effect that he had been given news of this man's seditious intentions, he probably would not have stirred himself to bother with the matter.

But by the following morning Jacques d'Isigny would be very keen to lay hands on Owain ap Hywel.

That night, Arwyn and Madoc met their uncle at the prearranged spot on the banks of the Monnow, about two miles from Garway. They took him food and a *carthen*, a thick woollen blanket, and sat with him in the dark while he ate his fill.

'We'll take your pig down to your sister and bring the oxen up to the farm,' said Madoc reassuringly, though in fact he was worried sick, not only about Owain's plight but also about the risk to him and his family if they were found to be giving aid to a rebel.

'What about the relics now?' asked Arwyn. 'We can't leave them in the barn for long. They're bound to be discovered sooner or later.'

Owain shook his head sadly. 'There's no way I can take them up to Gwynedd now, even if I can get there myself. I doubt Dewi and the others will risk coming. It will be obvious after this treachery where they've gone, and their families would suffer.'

'So what shall we do with the box?' persisted Madoc. 'Take it back to Abbey Dore?'

Owain considered for a moment. 'No, not yet anyway. Find somewhere safe to hide the bones, preferably in consecrated ground. It may be that I can come back and collect them later, if Prince Dafydd thinks it's worth while.'

They agreed and left their uncle to a solitary night, apart from the indignant badgers whose sett he was blocking.

But a couple of hours later and a couple of miles distant, greater trouble was brewing.

A shadowy figure lurked within sight of the bailiff's house at Kentchurch Court, patiently waiting in the gloom. Though there was a half-moon, the gathering rain clouds often blocked its light, but eventually the watcher's persistence was rewarded. Before going to bed each night, Ralph Merrick did his rounds of the farm buildings to make sure everything was secure. At the stables, the bailiff checked that the hurdles were in place across the doorways and that the two ostler-boys were sleeping in their proper places on piles of hay. He had to make sure that the chicken pens were locked against foxes and the fire damped down in the kitchen shed.

Ralph carried a lantern to light the interior of the buildings, a candle within a case that had thin sheets of pared horn as windows. As he began to walk back to the house, he thought he heard a noise in the bushes that ringed the yard. Holding up the lantern, he tried to see if there were the shining eyes of a fox or even a wolf, but the dim light of the single candle was too feeble.

Shrugging, he turned away, but after only a couple of steps there was a commotion behind him and a heavy cudgel smashed down on the back of his head. He fell like a poleaxed bull, and by further ill chance his forehead landed on a large stone embedded in the pathway.

Though the noise brought the stable-boys running to his aid, they found him deeply unconscious – and within the hour he was dead.

'It's that evil brother of his,' sobbed Alice Merrick, sagging against her daughter in a melodramatic fashion. 'He did this awful thing!'

Jacques d'Isigny motioned to his wife to help the woman to a chair, and the silent, black-haired woman moved forward to assist Rosamund in settling her mother in a leather-backed chair. They were in the first-floor chamber of the north tower of Grosmont, the sound of hammering and sawing coming through the window-slits.

'Tell me again what happened,' commanded the steward.

Alice related her brief tale through her sobs. 'My husband went out to close down for the night, sir, as he always did,' she blubbered. 'Then one of the stable-hands rushed in to say that he was lying in the yard. There was a wound on the back of his head and a great bruise on his temple. We brought him in, but he died without recovering his wits.'

A grey-haired man, dressed in a sombre but good-quality cote-hardie, nodded his agreement. 'I can confirm that, steward, as they came rushing up to my court to tell me my bailiff had been assaulted and I was there when the poor man died.'

This was Sir Vincent Scudamore, and Jacques was careful to be deferential to a man who was second only to Prince Edmund in the hierarchy of the district.

'It seems this carter is the obvious suspect, sir. We were already seeking him as a renegade Welshman intent on continuing their hopeless fight.'

Sergeant Shattock, lurking near the doorway with one of his men, was bold enough to speak up. 'We'll get him today, sirs, never fear. I already have all my men-at-arms out seeking this Owain.'

Scudamore nodded his approval. 'I suggest that you use my hounds in your search – their master is the son of the dead man, so he will have an added reason to succeed.'

This brought forth a fresh bout of howling from Alice Merrick, and her daughter Rosamund tried to soothe her, though the girl herself did not seem unduly distressed at the loss of her father.

Vincent Scudamore walked to the door and jerked his head at the steward to accompany him. Outside, with the sergeant in attendance, he spoke to d'Isigny in a low voice.

'This man Owain had a dispute with my bailiff a few days ago, so one of his sons tells me. On the eve of Christ's Mass he came to their house and uttered threats if they disclosed that he intended to go off to join the rebels in the north.'

The steward nodded. 'So I heard from the other son, the butcher, who came with the news of the murder earlier today. Obviously the miscreant must have decided that his elder brother had revealed his treachery to us – as, of course, was his duty.'

'And had he?' asked Vincent bluntly.

'No. As it happens, it came from someone else. But nevertheless, the carter exacted his revenge on your bailiff with the sin of Cain on Abel.'

The Lord of Kentchurch shook out the heavy riding cloak that he had been carrying over his arm and swirled it about his shoulders, ready to leave. 'This is damned inconvenient, losing such a good servant,' he snapped. 'Now I shall have to find another to take his place.'

As he started down the steps to the cluttered bailey, which looked more like a builder's yard, he gave an exhortation to the steward. 'Do everything you can to find this bloody man! I'll send John down with his hounds as soon as I get home.'

As Scudamore went to his horse, Jacques made a mental note to have the gallows put back up in the bailey, in spite of the builder's objections.

While more than a score of soldiers and a pack of hounds were beating the countryside, Madoc and Arwyn were worrying about the box of bones as well as the safety of their uncle. The news of the bailiff's death had already reached Garway by noon, and they had realized that Owain would immediately be the prime suspect.

'With all this searching, that chest is not safe under the straw,' declared Madoc. 'We need to hide it somewhere well away from here, best of all back in Abbey Dore. There's no chance now that Owain will be able to take it to Gwynedd as he'd planned.'

'He'll be lucky to get there himself,' growled Arwyn. 'But how are we going to move it? It's too big to go in the pannier of a packhorse.'

'I'll have to bring the oxen back here, or they'll starve. We can use them for the time being. The preceptory has to have some transport when our uncle's gone.'

They were standing outside Madoc's cottage, well above the church and the preceptory, and he stared out westwards across the undulating countryside to the dark mountains that formed the edge of Wales. They agreed that Madoc would go to Hoadalbert to fetch the oxen, take the pig to Rhiannon's house and give her the disturbing news about Owain now being a fugitive.

'You'd better have a quiet word with Dewi in the mill,' advised Arwyn. 'Tell him to keep his head down for a while.'

The two brothers moved to sit on a log outside the door, each with a quart of ale brewed by Madoc's wife Olwen. They were silent for a while, staring out over the countryside, which today at least lay under a watery sun.

'You don't think he could have done it, do you?' said Arwyn eventually. 'His mood has been desperate since Llewelyn was killed.'

Madoc looked indignantly at his younger brother. 'For God's sake, man! Of course not! He wouldn't harm Ralph, other than perhaps with his tongue. He was his brother, objectionable though he might have been!'

'Well, who did it, then?' persisted Arwyn. 'Someone lay in wait for Ralph and it must be a local, otherwise they wouldn't know he had that regular round of the farm each night.'

Madoc was implacable in his defence of the uncle who had virtually brought them up.

'Anyone with bad intentions could spy on the place for a couple of nights and discover that . . . and almost every bailiff does the same. And how could Owain get up there last night, when he's holed up in a badger sett two miles away?'

Arwyn muttered something about two miles being nothing for a tough man like Owain, but he wanted to be reassured that his fears were unfounded. When their ale was finished, he went off to repair the thatch on one of the preceptory outbuildings. Madoc returned to his duties at the farm, checking on two labourers who were whitewashing the back of the calf shed, before he went for the ox-cart. In the yard he met one of the three Templar Knights who lived in the preceptory. This was Brother Robert de Longton, a thin, cadaveric man who had returned from the Holy Land some years before, following a severe illness.

'What are all those men doing down in the lower fields, Madoc?' he demanded.

The reeve had no option but to tell him that they were searching for his uncle, in the mistaken notion that he had murdered the Kentchurch bailiff. The Templar clucked his tongue in concern.

'A sad thing to disturb the peace of this village. We cherish the serenity of this innocent place.'

Gathering his heavy black cloak around him, he stalked

away, the eight-pointed red cross on his shoulder glowing in the pale sunlight. Madoc wondered how many Saracens he had killed in his time, which was seemingly at odds with his present pacifism.

As the warrior-monk reached the gate leading into the grounds of the preceptory, he saw that the two other Templars had appeared, John de Coningham and the preceptor himself, Ivo de Etton. They began talking earnestly and de Longton's gesturing hand told Madoc that he was relaying the latest news to his brothers-in-God.

Later, as he set out on his pony to Hoadalbert, he saw more evidence of the soldiers from Grosmont. At the end of the strip fields sloping down to the river, iron helmets were bobbing among the bushes at the edge of the woods. As he neared the castle he saw another dozen men-at-arms marching out with menacing clubs dangling from their wrists, and when he had gone a little way along the road beyond Grosmont towards his uncle's house the baying of hounds came clearly across the still winter air.

Saddened at the turn of events, Madoc carried on with his task, all too conscious that there was no way he could warn Owain of the new hunt for him. They had arranged to meet again at the elm, for them to give him more food. To try to find him deep in the woods along the Monnow, with all these soldiers around, would be futile and probably suicidal.

With a sigh he carried on to collect the pig in the cart and take it down to Rhiannon, who would be devastated to hear this new turn in their lives.

Owain never had any realistic hope of eluding capture, especially as he was not even aware that he was being hunted for murder rather than for being an alleged renegade.

Late that afternoon he was woken from a sleepy reverie in his badger hole by the distant sound of baying hounds. At first he thought that it was probably a hunt for deer or foxes out of Kentchurch and decided to lie low and let them pass him by.

But soon it became apparent that they were closing in, and he began to hear men shouting and the crack of snapped branches.

Owain got up and listened more intently, then decided to make for the river, to wade across and lose any scent of him that the hounds may have picked up.

He was too late. Before he had got fifty paces, a dozen hounds broke cover, including several lymers and running-dogs, which hunted by scent rather than sight. Though they did not attack him, they surrounded him and began barking and howling, so that soldiers soon crashed through the undergrowth and seized him roughly, throwing him to the ground. As he managed to look up as they lashed his wrists behind his back, he saw his nephew John Merrick calling his hounds back, managing to avoid looking at his captive uncle.

'John, for Christ's sake!' he called in a strangled voice, for a burly soldier had his boot planted on his back. 'What's this all about? Was it you who denounced me?'

The fair-haired man dropped his gaze to Owain, with a look of hate on his face. 'Denounce you? You mean accuse you! You killed my father, you cowardly swine!'

As he was pulled to his feet by a couple of men-at-arms, Owain stared at John in bewilderment. 'Killed Ralph? He is dead?'

'Don't play the innocent! You struck him a cowardly blow from behind! Could you not fight him like a man, face to face?'

Before he could respond, Owain was dragged roughly

by the rope around his wrists towards the nearest path, where Sergeant Shattock appeared, out of breath.

'Good work, lads. You've got the bastard!' He accompanied his words with a vicious punch to Owain's face, before turning and leading them away from the river, up towards the church and the village.

'What are we going to do with him?' asked one of the soldiers, a rough-looking man with a face like a pig.

'Until he's hanged, lock him up,' snapped the sergeant.

'The castle's no good, then,' grumbled the ugly man. 'The tower that had the lock-up has been pulled down and half the outer wall of the bailey is missing.'

'Do you think I don't know that!' rasped Shattock, who until that moment had not given it a thought. He rubbed his bristly chin as he strode forward, then made up his mind. 'We'll use the church tower for now, until the steward decides what to do with him. That's used as a lock-up for drunks and poachers.'

It was true that a room at the base of the massive, squat tower of Garway was sometimes used for securing petty offenders and was known by the villagers as 'the prison'. The tower had been erected some years earlier by the Templars when they rebuilt the ancient church and added their circular nave. It was a few yards distant from the church itself and intended more as a defence against marauding Welsh than for any religious function.

Owain was dragged out of the woods and across the now-bare strip fields towards Garway. The sergeant marched ahead, then dismissed most of his men, telling them to return to Grosmont, leaving himself and three soldiers to handle Owain. After a few pointless struggles against his captors, he gave up and stumbled along behind them, staggering now and then as they gave a malicious tug to the rope that bound him.

Below the tiny hamlet, they struck up the hillside, past the grey buildings of the preceptory, to reach the church. The familiar surroundings crowded into Owain's consciousness: the farm, which he visited so often with his cart, and the church itself where he had taken the sacrament only a few days ago.

The sergeant and his men hustled him into the churchyard and across to the tower, which stood alone like a massive stone thumb, with its four-sided conical roof and a pair of arrow-slits high up on each side.

'Hold him there, while I get that door open,' snapped Shattock and left them pressing their captive against the cold stone alongside a heavy door. He marched into the church through the south door and returned with a large key, almost as long as his forearm. An elderly man followed him out, with grey hair and full beard, wearing the brown habit of a Templar lay brother. Recognizing Owain, he demanded to know what trouble he was in.

'He's a rebel and a murderer!' snapped the sergeant. 'We must keep him confined until he's hanged.'

'Are you sure you have consent for this?' called the sexton, as the sergeant thrust the key into a hole in the tower door.

'It's at the command of the steward of Grosmont – and will be confirmed by Prince Edmund when he arrives,' lied Shattock brusquely. 'We have no means of keeping a prisoner at the castle while the building work is going on.'

The sexton was not impressed by this, as the Templars acknowledged no one except the Holy Father in Rome as their ruler and were unlikely to take orders from a castle steward. He went muttering under his breath towards the preceptory, to see what the knights thought of the situation.

Inside the tower, which was even chillier than outside, Owain's wrists were freed, then he was thrust into a small side-room. Its door was slammed shut and a bar dropped into stout brackets. It was entirely empty, with some mouldy straw on the floor and a low window-opening the size of Owain's face running through the massive wall like a tunnel. He heard the big key being rattled in the outer lock and Shattock's harsh voice telling a guard to stand outside until he was relieved.

Then there was silence.

As dusk fell, Madoc and Arwyn came into the churchyard and bribed the freezing soldier on guard with two pence to let them talk to the prisoner. Though he had the key, the man would not let them into the tower and they had to hold a conversation through the hole in the wall. They also used it to pass in the food and drink that they were going to take to him in the woods.

'Has anyone been to see you?' whispered Arwyn to the shadowy figure at the other end of the tunnel.

'Brother Robert came and brought me some milk and bread a few hours ago. He asked if I wanted to confess, and I told him I had done nothing wrong, apart from wanting to fight for my country.'

Arwyn sighed. 'For the blessed Mary's sake, Uncle, he's from Normandy! He's on the side of the bloody king. You shouldn't admit anything to him.'

'I swore on the Cross that I had not harmed my brother, and I think he believed me.'

'Do you know what is going to happen tomorrow?' asked Arwyn tremulously, for he already knew the answer.

'They'll take me down to Grosmont, no doubt. The steward will hold a mock trial in the name of Prince Edmund, then they'll hang me.'

His voice sounded dull and resigned, as if he'd already given up any hope. His nephews could think of nothing to say that would deny his morbid anticipation, so they turned to Arthur's relics instead, telling him of their intention to get them back to Abbey Dore when the present emergency was over – presumably when Owain was dead and buried.

He agreed, but impressed on them the need to pass on the secret of the chest's whereabouts to their family when the time came. Arwyn had a baby daughter, though Madoc so far had no children, but they both swore that the family obligation would be honoured.

'Tell Rhiannon to come to Grosmont when I am arraigned,' pleaded Owain. 'I must see her one last time before I join my father.'

But once again fate took a hand.

Next morning Madoc and Arwyn mournfully intended to follow their captive uncle down to Grosmont Castle to meet his accusers. A couple of hours after dawn, they went to the church expecting to see Owain being taken out of his cell by his gaolers, but apart from a different soldier stamping his cold feet outside there was no sign of activity. Ignoring the guard's eavesdropping, Madoc called through the tiny opening in the wall. 'Owain, has anything happened yet?'

His uncle's face appeared dimly at the other end, slightly more visible now in the eastern morning light. His voice was almost eager, different from the resigned apathy of the previous day. 'That Father Samson from Llanfihangel Crucorney came here at first light, God bless him!'

'What did he want? To shrive you before you hang?' said Arwyn bitterly.

'Not at all! He was trying to save my life.'

Owain explained that the Welsh priest had exhorted him to claim sanctuary, as he was in a church! At first he had not taken him seriously, but Father Samson was emphatic in claiming that being on consecrated ground made it legal for him to be a sanctuary-seeker and to demand his forty days' grace, free from arrest.

Madoc gave a great shout, which startled the guard, but they ignored him. 'I recall one of the old men in the village telling of such a case here years ago,' he said excitedly. 'He'd stolen a sheep from up on Garway common, but he ran to the church here and sat in the chancel, holding on to the altar for weeks. I can't recall what happened to him.'

'The priest says they have to call the county coroner, then after performing the right rituals, the accused can be sent out of the country,' called Owain through his diminutive window. 'He's gone over to see the preceptor about it now.'

Arwyn was doubtful about this ray of hope. 'I can't see those swine in Grosmont accepting this! They'll just drag him out of there – after all, it is a prison.'

'Well, let's go into the church, brother, and pray that it does come about,' suggested Madoc.

Half an hour later a heated argument was going on in the preceptory yard, across the lane from the church. Sergeant Shattock had arrived on horseback with two men-at-arms and a spare horse to carry the prisoner back to Grosmont, about three miles away. Father Samson, in a rather threadbare cloak over his cassock, stood in the gateway where he had patiently awaited the expected escort and then informed them that they could not take Owain ap Hywel, as he had claimed sanctuary.

'Don't be damned silly, begging your pardon, Father,' growled Shattock. 'The fellow's in gaol and we mean to take him out.'

'He's also in a church and, having declared himself a sanctuary-seeker, you can't have him!' said the priest stubbornly. 'There are severe penalties laid down for violating that sacred right.'

'He's in bloody gaol!' yelled the sergeant furiously. 'Now get out of my way!'

He pushed the slightly built cleric aside and waved to his men to follow him to the church, but a stern voice rang out behind him.

'Stop, fellow! Come back here.'

Shattock was not accustomed to being spoken to in this fashion, even by the steward or Edmund Crouchback. He swung around, ready to shower blasphemies on the speaker, but they died in his throat when he saw who was addressing him. A tall Templar Knight, flanked by two of his fellows, stood in their forbidding black winter cloaks with the red crosses. They formed an impressive sight as they regarded him impassively.

He walked back towards them, his eyes on the preceptor, Ivo de Etton, whom he knew by sight and reputation.

'Sir, I am but carrying out my duty. I have been commanded by the prince's steward to bring this man to the castle for trial.'

'Well, you can't!' the preceptor responded flatly. 'He is in a church and has claimed sanctuary.'

'But he's in the tower, sir – not even joined to the church!'

One of the other knights shook his head at the sergeant. 'That's of no consequence,' said Robert de Longton. 'Anywhere within the consecrated ground is sufficient. If he only crawled through the churchyard gate, he would still be entitled to sanctuary.'

Shattock was not going to give up easily. 'But he's a murderer, not just some serf who's illegally trapped a rabbit!'

'That's also immaterial,' snapped the third Templar, John de Coningham. 'Unless it involves sacrilege, the nature of the crime does not matter.'

'I have to take him back to Grosmont!' yelled the stubborn sergeant. 'They are waiting to hang him. I'll be in big trouble if I go back without him.'

'That's your problem, soldier,' snapped de Coningham. 'And it says little for natural justice that you intend executing this man even before he goes to trial.'

Red in the face with anger, Shattock looked around and stared at the church down the lane. He was contemplating dragging Owain out of the tower and be damned to these monks, even though their reputation for battle was legendary.

The preceptor seemed to read his mind. 'Don't even dare think about violating our church, sergeant!' he barked. 'You will answer to our Grand Master himself if you do. You could suffer greatly – fines, imprisonment, even excommunication!'

In spite of his military calling, Shattock was in awe of the Church and knew that for the moment he was beaten. He was unsure if these Templars carried their swords under their cloaks, but in any event his ingrained discipline ensured that there was no way in which he was going to challenge three knights. Let the bloody steward or the Crouchback sort it out, he decided.

'So what happens next, sirs?' he muttered.

'We will send to Hereford for the coroner,' replied Ivo. 'He has to take a confession from the prisoner and then arrange for him to abjure the realm.'

Shattock's face reddened again in outrage. 'You mean the sod will get away with it?' he roared.

'As he's not been tried yet, we don't know that there's anything for him to get away with,' said the preceptor calmly. 'You should go back to the castle and report what has happened, and we will get the coroner here as soon as possible. I'll send a man to Hereford straight away.'

The sergeant stomped towards the gate. 'Prince Edmund is due shortly. He will have something to say about this!' he warned.

'He can say what he likes,' responded Ivo placidly. 'The refuge of sanctuary is older than Christianity itself, and no king or prince has any power over it. You can petition the Holy Father in Rome if you like – you might get an answer within six months!'

'But your man will be gone long before forty days have passed,' added Brother Robert maliciously. He had taken a marked dislike to the soldier's arrogance.

Shattock bristled. 'I'm not taking my guard from the door,' he snarled as he walked into the lane. 'If I do, that Welshman will be off quicker than a scalded cat!'

When he had gone, still fuming with injured pride, the preceptor sent John de Coningham over to the church tower to explain to Owain what was going to happen. John knew the carter well enough after Owain's years of service to the farm and was solicitous about his well-being, checking that his nephews had brought him sufficient food and drink for the day.

'Do I have to stay in this damned cell, sir?' asked the captive. 'There's not even a bucket in here for me to use.'

The Templar considered this for a moment. 'I see no reason why you should not move into the church. I have read in our records that there have been several sanctuary-seekers here over the years, and they have all sojourned there.'

In spite of the guard's feeble protests, Owain was released and taken to the round nave a few yards away, where he could sit or lie on the shelf around the walls, built for the feeble and aged parishioners, as there were no chairs or pews on the floor of beaten earth.

'I'll send a bucket over for your use,' promised the knight

as he left. 'Understand that if you leave the confines of the church grounds, you are liable to be slain on the spot – that is the law.' He forced the reluctant man-at-arms to stand outside the churchyard gate, telling him that he could only act against the accused if he put a foot outside it.

Satisfied, he left the reprieved Welshman to his thoughts.

In the tower room of Grosmont, Jacques d'Isigny listened impassively to the sergeant's ranting. Though he was annoyed at the interference of the preceptory monks in his administration of justice in the area, he had more pressing matters to deal with than some peasant who may have assaulted his own brother. Furthermore, he had no intention of standing up to the Templars, who were virtually immune from interference from Church or state, being accountable only to the Pope. If Edmund Crouchback wanted to make an issue of it when he arrived, that was up to him, but with the spectre of Thomas Becket and the consequences to Edmund's great-grandfather still hovering, violation of sanctuary was hardly to be contemplated for such a trivial matter.

'Make sure he does not escape from the church, but do nothing else,' he commanded Shattock. 'We will see what Prince Edmund advises when he comes. Until then, let the coroner deal with this lout. Maybe he will refuse to take a confession, in which case we have to wait forty days, then the coroner will close up the church and let him starve.'

The sergeant scowled, still smarting from his loss of face at Garway.

'And if the coroner does allow him to abjure, are we to let the bastard walk away?' he demanded.

The steward stroked his smooth chin. 'Then we let his

family and their friends know which route he is given. Maybe they can engineer some unfortunate accident on the way.'

This was Jacques' only concern, that allowing the Welshman to escape would anger the Scudamores, who were an influential family in these parts. To see the alleged killer of their bailiff escape to a port and sail away might not be something that Sir Vincent would appreciate. His ruminations were broken by a clerk demanding his attention, as the master mason was clamouring for the steward's attention about some problem with the grand new chimney, and Jacques put away the irritation of a Welsh felon for more immediate concerns.

Back at Garway, Madoc took time from his duties in the farm to go over again to the church, where he found Owain sitting against the wall in the peculiar round nave, staring at the great Norman arch that led into the chancel, which was the original old church.

'I didn't kill Ralph, you must know that,' he said, turning his face to his nephew.

'I never thought for a moment that you did,' replied Madoc loyally. 'Though I'm damned if I know who did.'

'Much as my brother and I had our differences, I'm sure he didn't denounce me to the castle as a rebel,' he said bitterly. 'It must have been his scrawny wife or one of those sons of his.'

Madoc shrugged and spoke of more immediate matters. 'The Templars, bless them, seem to be on your side. At least they don't make judgments without any evidence.'

'What's going to happen to me, lad?'

'The preceptor has sent Edwin on a horse to Hereford, to notify the coroner. He should be back with news by tonight.'

Owain was hazy about how the English legal system worked. 'What happens then?'

Madoc had questioned Robert de Longton about this, as he was the most approachable of the three Templar Knights. 'It seems the coroner has to take your confession, then send you to a harbour to take ship out of England, never to return.'

'Suits me, though where the hell am I to go?'

'France or Ireland are the usual places, now that Wales has been declared part of England by that evil king of theirs,' replied Madoc. 'But you could get back to Gwynedd from Ireland.'

'How can I make a confession when I didn't do anything?'

His nephew shrugged. 'If it saves your neck, does it matter? God will know you are innocent.'

Owain looked up to make sure that no one was within earshot, especially the guard. 'What about the relics? Are they still safe?'

Madoc nodded. 'But we can't leave them there much longer. Someone will soon need straw and then the box would almost certainly be found.'

'Can you not take them straight back to Abbey Dore and get Meredydd to bury them again?'

His nephew nodded. 'That's what we intend doing, but it's a day's work and we can't leave you while all this coroner business is going on.' Deciding that he had better get back to work, he emptied Owain's bucket at the edge of the churchyard and left his uncle to his lonely vigil in the nave.

It was dusk when he arrived back with Arwyn to take Owain more food and tell him that they had sent a message by one of the farm boys to Rhiannon, who would come to see him the next day, walking the miles from Pandy and back.

One of the Templar lay brothers had given him a rushlight,

and he sat in the gloom with the yellow glow illuminating his face as they came in. He had news for them too, as the messenger who had gone to Hereford had returned with the news that the coroner would come the day after tomorrow. He had sent instructions that a sackcloth robe be prepared for the confession and that the sanctuary-seeker should himself fashion a cross from wood found in the churchyard, the standard accoutrements for anyone abjuring the realm.

'Have you heard any news from Kentchurch Court?' asked Owain. 'I'll not be able to go to my brother's burial now. Much as we disagreed about almost everything, he was still of my family.'

'I doubt that we would be very welcome there either,' said Arwyn ruefully. 'They look on us as your sons, rather than nephews, so we'd not be popular at the funeral.'

'So who *did* slay Ralph?' pondered Madoc. 'Though from what I've heard, it was him falling on to a rock with his forehead that killed him, rather than the blow on the back of his head, so maybe the assailant just wanted to hurt him.'

Owain shrugged in the gloom, 'Whatever happened, I certainly had no part in it. I was skulking down in the woods by the river that night.'

'Bailiffs are not popular people,' observed Arwyn. 'He used to hold the manor court quite often and must have sent scores of poachers and other miscreants to the stocks – or laid heavy fines on them. Maybe one of those decided to get his revenge.'

'Let's not concern ourselves with that now,' said Madoc. 'We have enough to worry about with getting Owain out of here alive.'

The coroner, Humphrey de Bosco, was a heavy, short-necked man with a red face and bulbous nose that suggested his fondness for the wine flask. A knight with a small manor near Hereford, he had fought briefly in the Irish wars and then, mainly for lack of any other candidate for this unpaid task, had been appointed coroner, which he pursued with no great enthusiasm.

Arriving at the preceptory on a grey mare, he first accepted some liquid refreshment, then went over to the churchyard with one of the Templar clerks, as he had brought no one to record the proceedings. A small crowd had assembled outside the lychgate that led into the churchyard, including Madoc, Arwyn and their aunt Rhiannon. Several of the preceptory lay brothers were there, as well as their sergeant, in his brown habit and cloak. Standing well apart was another sergeant, Shattock from the castle, holding a watching brief with one of his men-at-arms.

The chaplain from the preceptory, who aided the parish priest in conducting the holy offices, led out Owain, who was dressed in a rough smock of hessian, with a length of thin rope for a girdle. He had made a crude cross from two branches from the churchyard trees, lashed together with twine.

'Let's get on with this. I want to get back to Hereford before nightfall,' grunted the coroner, indicating that the supplicant was to kneel before him at the gate. He was illiterate, but had learned the ritual phrases by heart and began to gabble rapidly in Norman French, before offering a shortened version in English. 'You have to confess your crimes, fellow,' he grunted.

'What am I to confess? I murdered no one!' answered Owain stubbornly. His nephews groaned when they heard him throwing away his last chance of survival.

De Bosco glowered at him. 'Are you going to waste my time after riding all this way?' he bellowed. 'I'm told you killed a man – your brother, no less!'

Owain shook his head vehemently. 'I killed no one. But if it pleases you, I'll confess to being a true Welshman, one willing to fight for his country.'

The coroner was in no mood for arguing. 'Sedition and rebellion!' he grunted. 'That'll do me – you've confessed to that.'

Owain then had to repeat a formal declaration of confession and take an oath of abjuration, before de Bosco again gabbled a long instruction in French, from which Owain was able to pick out enough words to get the gist of what the coroner was saying. He would have to take the shortest route to the port of Chepstow, wearing a white robe and not straying from the high road even to walk on the verge. He must not spend more than two nights at any one place – which was a pointless rule, as Chepstow was less than twenty miles away.

'When you get to the harbour, you must take passage on the first ship,' rumbled the coroner, suddenly switching to English. 'If there is no ship, you must wade out into the tide each day up to your knees, to show your eagerness to depart!'

After muttering some more half-understood phrases, he gave the kneeling Owain a shove with his foot that sent him sprawling on the ground, then he turned and addressed the dozen people watching the proceedings with mystified curiosity.

'Let no man interfere with this man as he abjures the realm. As long as he keeps to the road, he is inviolate. But should he depart from it, he becomes an outlaw and any of you is entitled to behead him without peril to yourselves!'

With this morbid injunction, Humphrey de Bosco left without so much as a glance at Owain, and headed back to the preceptory, where Ivo de Etton had promised him food and especially more drink before he set off back to Hereford.

The onlookers drifted away and Sergeant Shattock took his bad temper back to Grosmont to report. Though the new abjurer legally had thirty-seven days left to stay unmolested in the church, he was keen to be off before anything worse happened, such as the arrival of Edmund Crouchback, who might decide to ignore sanctuary and seize him for his gallows.

'You can't start today. It's well after noon,' advised the chaplain. 'Stay in the church again for tonight, and we'll find you a white robe in which to make an early start for Chepstow in the morning.'

Afterwards, Owain sat in the church porch with his sister, his nephews and their wives, eating and drinking the victuals that the women had brought. It was almost a festive occasion, as although they knew that Owain was leaving, probably for good, at least he was alive. Later, when the women had gone, the men had a serious discussion.

'I don't trust any of those from Kentchurch or Grosmont,' said Madoc. 'They'll not take this as calmly as it seems. I'm sure the bastards will have some plan up their sleeves.'

They discussed contingency plans for a while, then Owain asked about the relics.

'We'll take them back to Abbey Dore the day after tomorrow,' promised Madoc. 'We want to be on hand when you step outside that churchyard gate.'

After a good breakfast, again brought by his nephews' wives, Owain pulled on a plain white tunic supplied by the Templars, though it was bare of their striking red insignia. Grasping his makeshift cross, he went with Madoc and Arwyn to the churchyard gate and, with a slight hesitation at leaving his safe sanctuary, stepped out into the lane. Embracing his sister, as well as Olwen and Bronwen, they said fervent farewells, with wishful hopes that one day he would come back to them from Gwynedd.

Then he set out past the preceptory, where several of the lay brothers stood to wish him Godspeed, and plodded up to the road that ran through the village. The route from Garway to Chepstow first went eastwards to Skenfrith, then south through Monmouth and down the Wye Valley. His two nephews were firm in their decision to escort him for the first few miles. Somewhat to their surprise, Dewi and his son Caradoc arrived from Pandy to join them.

'Like you, I don't trust those sods from Kentchurch,' Dewi growled to Madoc. 'Nor the bastards from Grosmont!'

As they walked steadily down the long incline towards the Monnow, leaving the strip fields for dense woodland on either side, Owain and his escort looked suspiciously around them for any signs of men lurking in the trees. Every few hundred paces, Arwyn looked behind him to make sure that they were not being followed. Owain was careful to keep in the centre of the narrow road, well away from the verge, even though there was no one in sight.

'Once well away from the village, I'll be safe enough,' he protested. 'You can't come all the way to Chepstow!'

'We'll keep with you as far as Skenfrith,' declared Madoc. 'I doubt even those bloody cousins of mine will stray further afield than that.'

He was not sure what they would do even if they were attacked, for since the king's edict they dare not carry swords or maces and had to rely on the usual countryman's knife on their belt and a stout staff or a cudgel in the hand. The five men strode warily onwards, keeping in a tight group, but as nothing untoward happened after the better part of an hour they began to relax.

'A pity about the relics,' said Dewi. 'It would have been a great boost to have got them up to Prince Dafydd. If that swine of a brother of yours – begging your pardon, Owain – had not betrayed you, all this would not have come about and you could have taken the bones up north.'

'We're not certain it *was* Ralph who told Grosmont about him,' said Madoc.

'It was either him or one of his poxy family,' growled the fuller. 'I admit it was the fault of this stupid boy of mine, but no one else there knew of your intention to join the prince's army.'

'At least the bones will be as safe as they were before,' said Arwyn, anxious to damp down any controversy. 'We'll get them back to the abbey tomorrow.'

Further talk was suddenly brought to a stop by a warning cry from young Caradoc, who was walking slightly ahead of them.

Around a bend in the track, between tall trees that came right to the verge, they saw the figures of four men sliding out of the wood and menacingly blocking the road. Owain recognized his two nephews, John and William Merrick, as well as a blacksmith from the Kentchurch barton and a soldier from the castle, now without his uniform jerkin and helmet. This last man brandished a sword, and the others had clubs and knives.

They advanced towards Owain and his friends, yelling insults and threats, though Madoc sensed that they were disconcerted to find Owain escorted by four other men.

'Out of our way, damn you!' yelled Madoc. 'The coroner laid a charge on all men to give safe passage to an abjurer, on pain of the most severe penalties.'

'Yes, he said the highway is a place of safety!' hollered

Arwyn. 'You can be hanged and excommunicated for violating the law.' He felt that stretching the truth a little was justified.

Though the two sons of Ralph hesitated, the soldier and the farm worker seemed indifferent to cautions and rushed at them, waving their weapons, leaving William and John to scream allegations of murder at their uncle, before lumbering after the first two men.

It was five to four, but one of the attackers had a sword. A melee began immediately, and Owain, the only experienced campaigner, reversed his stout cross and began laying about him as his companions also started flaying around them with their clubs and knives. The first casualty was the blacksmith, who made the mistake of attacking Owain with his staff and received a stunning blow from the end of the abjurer's cross, which laid him senseless in the road.

Madoc and Arwyn were not inhibited by family constraints in squaring up to their cousins, and a spirited battle with staves and cudgels began, while Dewi and his son Caradoc took on the man-at-arms with the sword. Caradoc danced behind him and swiped at him repeatedly with the heavy stick he carried, trying to stop the soldier from jabbing his broadsword at his father. He failed, and Dewi received a severe wound across his left shoulder which sent him staggering, blood pouring from between the fingers of his other hand. His son, screaming with rage, belaboured the attacker, managing to land several blows with his cudgel that sent the soldier staggering, giving Owain the chance to land another few on him with his penitent's cross that sent the fellow groaning to the ground.

It was all over within a couple of minutes, as the two Merrick sons, seeing both their accomplices stretched out on the road and their stronger cousins gradually beating them back, suddenly threw down their weapons and raised their hands in the air.

'Enough, we give in!' yelled John, dropping to his knees in supplication. He and his brother were grabbed by Madoc and Arwyn, but there was no fight left in them. Then they were ignored, as Owain and Caradoc shouted for their attention. These two had gone to Dewi, who had slumped to the grass at the edge of the track, his head on his chest.

'My father, he's badly wounded!' wailed Caradoc, dropping to his knees alongside the stricken man.

Owain saw the bright red blood still pumping from between Dewi's fingers, running down his chest on to the ground, and knew that this was a mortal injury. Ignoring the Merricks, he called Madoc and Arwyn to his side. 'We can try to get him back to the hospitaller at the preceptory, but I fear it will be of little use,' he murmured to them as Caradoc cradled his father in his arms, tears streaming down his face.

'He's trying to say something,' he sobbed. 'He wants you, Owain.'

Kneeling in the dirt of the road, Owain put his head near that of his old friend, to catch the words coming from his weakening lips.

'I brought this on you, Owain. I am sorry,' he whispered. 'I had so much hate for that Ralph, who not only shamed my son by forbidding him his daughter, but betrayed you to the English.'

'Are you saying you killed him, Dewi?' said Owain incredulously.

'I didn't mean to . . . just injure him. But he fell on to a rock . . .'

His voice tailed off and his head slumped down again. He was not yet dead, but certainly dying.

Owain rose, leaving Caradoc to try to comfort his father,

and walked over to his other nephews. William and John were aghast at having been involved in a death, even though it was not their hand that had directly caused it.

'Did you hear what he said?' he asked in a voice like steel.

William nodded. 'He killed our father, not you,' he said shamefacedly.

'Dewi attacked your father because he believed Ralph had denounced me,' grated Owain. 'Was he right about that?'

John lifted his bowed head and shook it. 'It was our mother. She never liked you and told that sergeant at the castle, when she saw him at Grosmont market. When father was killed, we all assumed it was you getting revenge.'

Madoc and Arwyn, who had been listening, interrupted them.

'Now that it's clear you are no murderer, you can come back to the village,' pleaded Arwyn.

Owain shook his head. 'Maybe no killer, but still a hunted rebel. I've been granted sanctuary and the chance to leave the country and I'm taking it.'

He turned to the Merrick brothers. 'You'll have some explaining to do about all this!' He swept his arm across the two fallen men in the road and the dying man on the verge.

'Madoc and Arwyn, you had better get these stupid relations of ours to help you carry poor Dewi back to the preceptory – though I fear you will be carrying a corpse for most of the way.'

He embraced them both, then picked up his battered cross and strode away down the road.

After another mile, he checked that the track was deserted, then tossed his cross into the bushes and vanished into the trees.

From the start, he had had no intention of going anywhere near Chepstow and now he went deeper into the forest to wait until dusk, when he would make his way across country back to Pandy. He had already arranged with Rhiannon for her to collect clothes and a hidden cache of money from his cottage. With a backpack of food, he would then slip away into the nearby Black Mountains and work his way northwards to Gwynedd.

It was a pity he was unable to take Arthur's bones, but at least they would soon be safe again and ready to await some future crisis that might afflict the true Britons.

The old ox-cart once again creaked its way back to Abbey Dore without incident, the heap of straw concealing the stout oaken box in the back. Madoc and Arwyn were the Guardians this time and sought out the sexton without difficulty.

Meredydd heard out their tale philosophically and readily agreed to resume care of the relic box and make sure that its position was safeguarded by being passed on to the next generation.

'But I can't put it back in that same grave again,' he announced. 'The soil was disturbed so much getting it out that it might be too obvious if I go digging the same spot up again so soon.'

'Where can you put it, then?' asked Arwyn. 'We want the king's relics to be in consecrated ground.'

The sexton nodded. 'They will be, never fear. There's a convenient hole appeared at the base of the cemetery wall, there on the north side. Looks as if a vixen or a badger was trying to make herself a den.'

They went to the abbey farm and discreetly shifted the chest from the ox-cart to a wheelbarrow, but this time helped to cover it with earth.

'I'd have to fill in this pit anyway,' said Meredydd. 'So the bulk of the box will save me carrying at least one load of soil.'

They watched him contentedly pushing his barrow towards the cemetery and as he vanished through an arch in the wall.

Madoc crossed himself and murmured: 'Pray God will keep Arthur safe until next he's needed!'

## *Historical note*

The extraordinary church at Garway is one of the few in Britain to reveal evidence of the round Templar naves, thought to represent the Temple in Jerusalem. It had a separate fortified tower, the ground floor of which is still known locally as 'the prison'. Garway's preceptory administered all the Templar properties in Wales and had three resident knights at the time of the suppression of the order in 1307.

The Skirrid Inn is the oldest in Wales and a contender for the oldest and most haunted in Britain. It still has a hangman's rope dangling in the stairwell, some hundred and eighty executions having been carried out there, the last in Cromwell's time.

The Scudamore family still lives in Kentchurch Court, after almost a thousand years' residence.

# ACT THREE

*Thursday before the Feast of St Martin in Winter, Fifteenth Year of the Reign of King Edward II,* Abbey Dore, Herefordshire*

Iestyn had learned his job well. No brother knew the tasks so well as he. He had made certain of it.

He still felt that slight crawling of the flesh on his head as he passed by the little mounds in the lay brothers' cemetery. Now, in the middle watches of the night, the ancient superstitions were hard to discard. When a man had grown here in the wild country, he may understand that the wisps of paleness were the normal mists, he may even know that the screeching from the tree at the farm over the wall was an owl, but that seemed to have little effect here, in the lee of the wall of the graveyard. Here all he could think of were the stories of ghouls and ghosts.

Soon he was at the projection in the wall. Here his grandfather had set the stone, carefully tamping it into place, so that the precious box could be found. Back then he had thought his only task would be to pass on the location to someone else. Now Iestyn realized that it could not remain. It must be saved.

* Thursday 5 November 1321

It was the rocks that made movement essential.

The abbey had taken delivery of a pile of rocks to build a suitable altar for the pilgrims who were certain to arrive to view the piece of the Holy Cross which had been given to the abbey by Sir William de Grandisson. The masons were swarming all over this area by day, and one had already found the little hole in the ground. A pile of rubble lay all over here, from the present reworkings, and one large rock had fallen on top of the relics in their box – Iestyn only prayed that the bones themselves weren't damaged.

He must shift some of the smaller rocks that still lay about before he could get to it. An inquisitive man might see the box otherwise – masons weren't above digging where an interesting hole materialized, and most knew that old bones could easily be taken and sold. There were strange fools who would always want to buy such things. Necromancers, alchemists and even simple pardoners were keen to get their hands on bones.

Scraping the soil away, he soon found the corner of the box, and he knelt, staring at it for a long moment before clearing the rest of the dirt about it and bringing it up into the dim light. He could feel a tingle running through his hands, up his wrists, along his arms, down his back, as he clasped it to his chest.

Huw ap Madoc stood waiting in the shadow of the gateway.

'Here, take it, friend, and protect it and the contents with your life,' a voice hissed, and Huw found himself holding the final remains of the king.

'I will protect you,' he said, and felt a mixture of foolishness and pride. Foolishness for talking to a box of bones, pride for knowing that he held here in his arms the future hopes of his nation.

When he was younger, he had sneered at the thought of

the Guardians. The idea that he should be the last in the line of men who sought to protect the bones was laughable. Long dead now, his father: a good man, if somewhat fixated on the relics. He could still remember the way in which his father had drummed into him the story of their ancestors, the vital role they must play in the defence of their homeland. Old Madoc had been consumed by the thought of Arthur returning to their land, bringing fire and sword to evict the invaders. It was a delicious idea to Madoc. At the time it had seemed daft to Huw.

Not now. Now that the land of his fathers had been so devastated by the English, it was much more attractive.

'I won't let you be harmed,' he said.

And for three years and one half, he was right.

## *Wednesday before the Feast of St John the Baptist,* Crediton, Devon*

On the day that Sir Baldwin de Furnshill first met the pair of them, he had already been involved in one altercation, and the sight of the pardoner and his friend was enough to make him want to turn about and hurry in the opposite direction.

Earlier it had been a simple dispute about money due. The Church of the Holy Cross and the Mother of Him Who Died Thereon was a vital part of the town of Crediton, and the twelve canons were known to all the townspeople. But every so often there were little flares of resentment. Such as today.

Such a small matter, but one that could have so easily come to blows. A canon riding along the street with his

* Wednesday 19 June 1325

little cavalcade of servants managed to splash the green skirts and red cloak of a townswoman with muddy water. Yes, it was a small matter, and she would have been happy enough, probably, with a simple apology from any other man: any woman would have been. Except she was Agatha, the wife of Henry of Copplestone, and he already had a claim in the court against the dean of the church for damages. A small flock of the dean's sheep had been left to roam by a lazy church shepherd, and they had consumed the better part of Henry's pea crop. Which was why she shrieked at the canon like one demented.

It was also why Canon Arthur wouldn't apologize, and when Agatha's servant began to berate the man, his ecclesiastical servants came to hold him back and ended up knocking him to the ground. Which was why some townspeople, who naturally supported their neighbour against Church arrogance, surged forward to protect him.

When Baldwin arrived, the shouting had already become incoherent. As always, each resorted to his own tongue, and now Canon Arthur was sneering in Latin, while Agatha and her friends replied in more earthy Saxon. The guards with Baldwin were demanding silence in Norman French, while the servant and his friends were cursing and swearing in fluent Celtic that reminded Baldwin of the Welsh foot soldiers he had met on his travels. It took all his powers of diplomacy to calm the affair, to force the canon to apologize gruffly, against the promise that Baldwin would tell the canon's dean if he did not submit, and then threatened the gathering with a day in the stocks if they didn't disperse and leave the clerical group to continue on their way.

Eventually common sense had prevailed. The cold, aloof canon had doffed his hat to Baldwin, while the wife of Henry of Copplestone had sniffily turned her back on the crowds about. Not without attracting some admiring glances, though, because she was a lovely woman. High cheekbones, slightly slanted eyes, full lips, all added to an allure that was uncommon in Crediton generally.

Yes, he had had enough of soothing troublesome citizens, and the sight of two men, who were to his mind little better than felons, was enough to make him want to fly up the road to the stable where his horse waited, leap on it and ride home at speed. But he was Keeper of the King's Peace, and his sense of duty wouldn't allow him – even though, as he strode forward, he was sure that he saw others bolting at the sight of the two walking towards him. One couple looked shifty and guilty, he thought, as though they themselves were running from the law, they fled off so swiftly, bolting up an alleyway. But no, he recognized the glimpse of a green skirt and a long scarlet cloak and took a quick breath of relief – it was Agatha again, he realized, and then he realized that the man with her was a churchman – he had the robes of a canon – but with that thought his own options for flight were gone. The two were upon him.

'Godspeed,' he said, baring his teeth in almost a smile.

'Good Sir Knight.' The first man hailed him with a bow and made a swift movement of his hand, roughly sketching a cross over his breast, although to Baldwin in his present sour mood it appeared to outline the Arabic numeral that denoted eight, a series of swoops that ended at his right shoulder. 'I hope I see you well?'

His slapdash gesture was irritating, almost an insult to God, Baldwin felt. Not that his ability to make the sign more effectively would have endeared him to Baldwin – nor helped Baldwin to trust him. 'You have the permission of the bishop to sell your wares?' he asked sharply.

'I have the permission of the Pope himself,' the fellow replied and bowed again.

'The bishop takes a dim view of men like you,' Baldwin said.

'A humble pardoner? But all I do is ease the souls of those who need my aid.'

'And by what right do you judge the extent of a man's sin? Are you trained as a cleric?'

'I am licensed, Sir Knight. The Pope has given me the power to offer remission of sins. Perhaps you would appreciate a little something? Remission of sins for thirty days after payment is not to be sniffed at. So long as you are truly penitent, of course. And I can give you a discount for . . .'

'Yes, you would take my money. I know you and your sort, man. I will have nothing to do with you. Take your papers and find someone who's more likely to be taken in. I am not.'

'Oh.' The man looked mournful for a moment, looking Baldwin up and down with the gaze of a man contemplating a poor victim of fate, a man whose soul must inevitably be damned.

It was not the sort of expression that suited him. The pardoner was a stolidly built man, with more about his belly than a humble ecclesiastic should carry. Maybe of Baldwin's height, he had a ruddy complexion, which Baldwin felt owed more to the amount of ale he consumed daily than to exposure to the elements, with a round face and heavy jowls. His hands were moderately clean, with long nails to show he had never been forced to work over-hard, no matter that he wore a threadbare old habit as though he was some kind of poverty-stricken cleric. At his side was a leather purse that had a long strap over his shoulder, and which appeared to weigh no small amount. His feet were booted with good red cordovan leather – better, Baldwin guessed, than his own.

'Are you selling this rubbish too?' Baldwin demanded of the second man.

This second man did not appear so fat. His own business was less profitable, no doubt. He was thinner, with a face that was lined and marked with the weather of several winters. It was the temper of the man, though, which had scored his features. There were lines at the side of his mouth and deep wrinkles in his brow, which came from an ill nature, if Baldwin were to guess. He had seen many men like this in his time. The man was one who wore his suspicion of the world on his face. There was no mask of deceit there. It made Baldwin wonder how the man could make a living, with so grim an appearance.

'You think I sell promises of eternal life? Nay, lord, I am a triacleur, a mere humble trader in potions for the ill and needy.'

Baldwin looked him up and down. A Welshman, then, from his accent. One of those who was so effective in the king's armies, with their long knives and bloodthirsty determination to be first at the rape and pillage, he thought. Except this one was different. A triacleur, he was one of those itinerant wanderers who sold treacle or some similar ineffective medicine to the gullible. At least they didn't make promises about protecting a man's soul. Giving sweet-flavoured draughts to those who sought comfort from their ailments was almost a kindly act, in his opinion.

'Well, if I find either of you near my estates or villeins, I'll have you flogged out of the vill,' he grunted. 'Be off with you!'

'Hardly the welcome we hoped for, eh, Huw?' the pardoner said.

'It is common enough that great men will look askance at us, John,' the triacleur said.

'Well and good. I have enough to deal with without two

such as you,' Baldwin said, and stood aside, watching the two amble on towards the main street.

He was glad to be rid of them. All he hoped now was that he may not see them again. Sadly, he felt sure his hopes would be dashed, but he had no idea how soon that would be.

Further up the lanes, Agatha clutched Arthur's hand and stared back down towards the town's high street. 'Do you think he saw us?'

Canon Arthur looked down at her. Her eyes were glittering with anxiety and dread, her breast rising and falling deliciously. 'No, Mistress. I am sure our secret's safe.'

## *Thursday before the Feast of St John the Baptist,* Sandford*

John the Pardoner sat back against the wall in the little alehouse and rubbed his back contentedly against the stone and cob. It had started disastrously, but ended not a bad day, all in all. At least his purse was full.

He wished he'd not had the row with Huw. Huw had remained in Crediton to sell what he could in the way of potions to a credulous audience, and John had left him there. They had not parted happily.

It was a foolish altercation, but no less poisonous for that. Huw had been asking a little too much about things. He should have known that a man's sources were sacrosanct. Otherwise they weren't uniquely his own any more. Why on earth he should wish to know so much about where

* Thursday 20 June 1325

the bones had come from, John had no idea. They were just old bones, in God's name. It left John wondering whether Huw was himself thinking about moving into the pardoning business.

Ach! In his heart John had hoped Huw would have followed on after him, hopefully meeting him again at Sandford, but Huw hadn't turned up. John would have to get used to walking about the country on his own in future. Well, he'd done it often enough before. Huw had suggested that they stay together because two men on the road were safer than one alone, but down here in the wild country west of Exeter, it was Huw who would be most in danger. At least the folk here were John's countrymen, even if they did sound a little outlandish to his ear. It was a pity, though. Huw had been a good travelling companion.

John had had a good afternoon. The parish priest, an older man with grey hair fringing his tonsure, had appeared to be glad to meet him when he had arrived at the tiny little hamlet of Sandford. He had known he was on to a good thing long before he met Father William, though, as soon as he saw the great church up ahead of him on the rise. A church like that was a guarantee of cash in a pardoner's pocket.

It was a good day for a walk. Made a nice change after some of the weather he'd endured in his time. Sweet Jesu, the march from Wales had been God-cursed. Lousy weather, rain in his face the whole way, his hat, the one he'd bought in Chartres, blowing away and snagging in a tree near a cliff so precipitous he'd not dared attempt a rescue, because all the while he was overwhelmed by the fear that his pursuers might catch him. That was petrifying.

But they hadn't. He had survived again, and reached this delightful little vill with the red-sandstone church. Such a prosperous-looking church it was, too. The sort of place where a man might find people in abundance with money to throw about.

And from his reception, clearly there were more than the average number of sinners there.

He had taken his position with some care, standing before the alehouse with his cross, once he had spoken to the priest. The man was utterly content to have him there, naturally. His eyes had lit up like candles when he heard the proposal. And from that moment, John knew his fortune was made, even if the priest wouldn't let him preach from his own pulpit. The bishop was not eager to have pardoners make use of his churches, but this was only a chapel of ease. This was a fine distinction, John knew, but any distinction was better than none.

Leaving the chapel, he saw an urchin standing with some friends. He was a scruffy, grubby little boy with the face of a demon and the manners of a stoat, but at the sight of a clipped penny the brat took John's drum and began to beat a steady rhythm, following John down the little hill to his post outside the alehouse. Soon he had a small audience with him, and John could begin his sermon.

He had soared to new heights. Usually the feeling of being a foreigner would make him anxious. So often the ignorant churls wouldn't understand what he was talking about, even when he was being as slow as possible, trying to explain every point clearly and concisely. And the mere act of careful enunciation highlighted his sense of strangeness, his alienness compared with the folk here. It made him feel this was a dangerous part of the country.

Country folk were the hardest, of course. They tended to stand by, surly and grim-faced, while he spoke, mistrusting the sight and sound of a different accent. Ach! They'd distrust a man who came from a vill two miles away, most of them. Give him a good city crowd for preference. They would admire his rhetoric, laugh at his sallies, and some would even pay him extra if his delivery had been good enough.

It wasn't generally true of bumpkins. Where a city dweller appreciated that he would sometimes be fleeced, but still enjoyed the spectacle, the countryman would jealously guard his purse. The idea uppermost in his mind was generally that he was being rooked, and no villein liked to feel himself to be a gull.

Not so here, though. The people appeared uniformly cheery. There was nothing thrown at him. The boys, and even some of the women, heckled him good-naturedly, while the men openly laughed at his more risqué jokes. It was reassuring. Such attitudes spoke of money. And only the comfortably off could afford to commit sins, in his opinion. He always preferred wealthier crowds. The poor were too desperate for their next meal to bother with pardons.

When he lifted the parchment, all laden down with seals from bishops, damn his soul if a maid at the front didn't swoon! It was the most perfect day he'd known in a long while. It was all downhill from there.

First the more easily swayed came to the front, some with their money all ready, others with rings or other tokens, and he'd passed out the vellum with enthusiasm. Each promised a period of thirty days, remission of sins after payment. Soon he'd have to buy some more vellum, if things kept going like this.

The second group arrived when the first were flagging. He had seen it all too often. While the first enthusiastic crush pressed forward, others would curl their lips, roll their eyes and otherwise demonstrate their contempt for the poor hopeful fools who were so keen to throw their money at a stranger.

That was when he would bring out his pride and joy. While the women and children snatched at their vellum, he slowly reached into his purse while watching the doubters at the back, and then bring out the feather. 'Behold this! Granted to me by the Bishop of Bath and Wells!' he roared, holding it aloft. Bath and Wells was far enough away, he reckoned, for it to be safe to tell a fib about the bishop down here.

'What of it? A goose feather!'

'"What of it," you say? You dare suggest that this marvellous white plume is that of a common goose? Nay, friend. This is a feather from the wings of the angel Gabriel himself! Aye, but if you doubt my words, like Thomas, then you may leave well alone. Stay there at the back where you are safe, and see what miracles you miss!'

'Get on! It's a quill from the goose you stole – the one you ate last night, from the look of your gut, Pardoner!'

But the comment was jocular, not sour, and the sight was enough to bring a few more forward. Only a few. Others still waited at the back, several of them eyeing him with some admiration, like men who listened to the patter of a street seller, enjoying the atmosphere created.

That was when he brought out the bones, one by one, and let all see them, holding them in his cupped hands. And when he announced that they were King Arthur's, the crowds were hushed in awe.

For a moment anyway, John reminded himself, contentedly rattling the coins in his purse. In his experience the longer the silent hesitation, the more money he would garner later. There was plenty here, and soon he would have more. He was a very happy man that night.

Which was good, because it was his last.

Hob of Oxford pulled the apron from his belly as the last guests left his little tavern. It had been a good day, all in all, what with the pardoner appearing and drawing in all the folk from the vill. They'd listened, and once he'd talked them out of their money they'd all come into Hob's house to spend some more.

There were no two ways about it. The pardoner had made him a goodly sum of money. And while the fellow had taken some of Hob's own in exchange for the little strip of vellum, that was not expensive. Especially for the peace of mind it gave him. He needed it.

Closing the door, he shoved the wooden peg into the wood above the latch to lock it before clearing the last of the cups and jugs from the floor where they had been discarded. He banked up the fire, kicking the embers into a small pile, and sank his backside down to rest on a stool nearby. It had been a long day, and his legs were killing him. A jug of ale at his side, he sipped contentedly, yawning and scratching at his beard while he considered the work he must do in the morning.

He was wryly contemplating an early morning's start when he heard the faint noise. It was a scritching, scratching noise, and seemed to come from behind him.

This was not a large tavern. Two rooms only sufficed for the vill's needs, and while Hob had a bed up in the rafters here, over the fire where it was warm, the room at the back was where he occasionally allowed travellers to sleep. It was where the pardoner was resting. Surely it was only that fellow, he told himself. Probably striking a light with flint and tinder. Needed a light to find his way to the pot. Not surprising, the amount the man had put away. Not many could drink so much. Of course, Hob was to blame. He shouldn't have offered all the ale the man could drink in exchange for his strip of vellum.

Grunting, he rose, emptied the last of his jug over the glowing coals and stepped away as the steam fumed. Only when he was sure the fire was dead did he begin to make his way to the ladder that gave access to his upper chamber.

But there was a curious odour in the air. A scent of burning that was odd. It was not natural. All about him was the fug of his damp hearth, but for some reason he could also smell fresh woodsmoke. It was an abnormal smell. Peculiar, odd, out of place. It was enough to make him pause at the bottom of his ladder, frowning and peering about him. And then he heard another noise, some sort of clattering or something.

He didn't want to check. The man was just soused, that was all. He'd probably fallen over. But if he'd collapsed and puked, he might die. And he could have knocked over his pot of piss. The smell of that would reek in a day or so if he had. Ach! Better to see what the dull-witted prickle had done.

Taking a rushlight from its holder on the wall, he used it to light a candle. There was no need for silence, not if the sot was so mazed he had fallen over. Hob threw open the door, and it was only then, as the light from his candle illuminated the chamber, that he realized what had happened, and Hob began to scream even as he fled, running from the appalled horror in John's dead eyes.

## *Friday before the Feast of St John the Baptist,* Crediton*

Sir Baldwin was accustomed to being woken early.

In his youth he had joined the great Crusade which set off from England to aid the city of Acre in its hour of need. A massive army of Mamelukes had overrun the

* Friday 21 June 1325

kingdom of Jerusalem and all the city states which bounded the sea, and now only Acre itself survived. But in a short time the city fell, and Baldwin was one of a tiny number of wounded men who were rescued by the Templars and brought back to health in their care. It left him with an abiding sense of commitment to the order, and he joined the knights as soon as he could to repay his debt.

Sleeping in the Temple had always been an austere experience, but sleeping here was if anything a little more . . . *rugged*, for want of a better word.

It was the spare bedchamber in his friend Dean Peter Clifford's house in Crediton. Peter, a tall, stooped, white-haired cleric, was always pleased to provide hospitality for Baldwin when the Keeper had a need to stay in Crediton. And he was often about the town – occasionally in his capacity as Keeper, sometimes as a Justice of Gaol Delivery, occasionally for some social reason.

The banging on his door made him frown quickly though. This was not the patient, subtle knock of a servant seeking to gently arouse a sleeping guest. It was the panicked thudding of a servant who thought there was overriding need.

'Sir Baldwin! There has been a murder. A dreadful murder!'

The canon hastened his way along the road from the church, his black robes flapping in the wind. It was cool this early in the morning, but the canon scarcely noticed, his cloak was drawn so tightly about him. In any case, when he saw his breath steaming on the morning air, it did not make him pause. A man in holy orders tended to see too much of stone slabs and tiles, usually in the middle watches of the night, and cool air held no fears for him.

He knew the way as well as he would if it were a part of the church's lands. Up the high street, along the alleyway to the left, and then back on himself along the little track that led up the hill, before turning right again down the little lane. It ended in the large house.

It was a rough place, this. On the outskirts of the town itself, this area was the haunt of some of the poorest, and few would dare to approach without a group of men about them. Canon Arthur knew better than most how dangerous it truly was. He had been visiting this site for some months. Ever since his profitable little arrangement had begun.

The last time he had come he had felt sure that he had been followed. Afterwards the dean had grown frosty towards him, and he felt sure that his little secret was known – but there was no proof. He was sure of that.

He knocked on the door, glancing about him. Soon it opened, and he saw the narrow features of Edward of Newton, the servant of Henry of Copplestone.

It was all over in less time than a man would need to flay a rabbit. The canon hurried away from that evil place with his heart in his mouth, hoping against hope that no one saw him.

'Well, Peter?'

The dean had been up for some while already, and he beckoned Baldwin into his little hall, asking, 'Please, Baldwin, old friend, I am glad to see you well. You slept comfortably?'

'Peter, there has been a crime, this lad tells me.'

Peter Clifford motioned to the boy to leave. 'There has been a message to say that a man has been found dead in the Black Lamb at Sandford.'

'Hob's place? Who was it? A local?'

'No, a foreigner, I heard. He was staying overnight with Hob, and someone killed him.'

Baldwin nodded. 'Very well. I must go there, I suppose.'

Peter nodded and called to his servant to bring breakfast for them both. As Keeper of the King's Peace, it was Baldwin's duty to try to seek out felons. When a crime was committed, his writ commanded him to seek the man 'from vill to vill, hundred to hundred, shire to shire', with all the posse of the county. 'You will eat first?'

'I'd rather not fall from my saddle from hunger,' Baldwin said, smiling.

'I should warn you that the coroner has also been called.'

'That is good.'

Peter lifted his eyebrows and gazed pensively at the jug as his bottler poured two mazers of wine. 'Ah. Perhaps. It is Sir Richard de Welles.'

There were few names that would strike such a reaction in a man's breast, Baldwin reflected later as he jogged along the muddy trail from the church, up the steep hill behind and down past the Creedy manor house to Sandford itself.

Sir Richard de Welles was one of those rare creatures, a king's coroner who was uninterested in corruption. In the years since Baldwin had begun investigating felonies, he had known many of them, and most were little better than felons themselves: mendacious, devious and out to line their own purses. Men with honour and integrity were rare, but Sir Richard was one such. He didn't reject corruption so much as live in a state of blindness to the possibility of it. So long as there was ale, wine and food, he was happy. But woe betide the man who did not see to the coroner's needs.

It was his appetites for wine and ale which had served

to make Baldwin's close friend, Simon Puttock, regret ever meeting the coroner. For some reason, the coroner had taken a liking to Simon which had led to hangovers of a virulence that was quite unlike anything Simon had known before.

Baldwin had seen little of Simon recently. They had both been together much of the year so far, but now the two had been separated for some weeks. Simon had once lived near here, over at the farm north of West Sandford, before he had been given the post of bailiff on Dartmoor, but that had necessitated a move to Lydford. Baldwin missed his company.

Still, no matter what Simon thought of him, Baldwin respected the coroner's judgement and enjoyed his good nature. And did not drink with him.

Not that he would be here yet, Baldwin knew. The journey from Exeter would take him all the morning.

Canon Arthur was anxious when he received the message as he returned to the church. Still, he must obey his master, and he bent his steps towards the dean's house.

'Dean? You asked for me?'

Peter Clifford was seated at his table while a dark-haired, bearded man clad in a threadbare red tunic chewed at a little bread and cold ham. The canon recognized him as the knight who had arrived to calm the crowds when Henry's wife Agatha had been soiled in the roadway. It made him panic for a moment to see the man there.

'Canon Arthur, I am glad you could come here so swiftly,' Peter Clifford said. 'Sir Baldwin here was wondering who might know of the people over at Sandford. Could you help him?'

With that, the dean offered Godspeed to them both and left them alone.

'I feared you might have been here to complain about the dispute the other day,' Arthur said with a slight grin.

'No. These little matters will happen,' Baldwin said. 'Please, will you not be seated?'

His questions were concerned entirely with the running of the little vill of Sandford, the quality of the men there, and especially the reeve, Arthur was pleased to learn. He furnished Baldwin with a full list of the senior men of the vill. 'Ulric the reeve is a strong fellow. Hob is a strange fellow: I cannot ever get away from the impression that he is embarrassed about something when I meet him.'

'You go there often?'

'I am responsible for the manors about there which provide us with much of our foods.' He nodded. 'I often travel up there and beyond to the granges and barns to ensure that all is well. Hob runs the tavern in the vill, and I stop there for lunch on occasions.'

'I see. I trust you avoid West Sandford though.'

'Hmm? Why?'

'Surely you would keep away from Henry of Copplestone's house?'

'Oh, him. Yes. Well, I do for now. But he is a reasonable man, generally. As a merchant, he and I will do business occasionally. I am sure that this affair will blow over.'

'The matter of Henry's wife's dress?'

'No! That was a mere accident. No, I was thinking of this problem about the sheep. A small flock of mine was allowed to wander, and it ate all his pea crop in an afternoon before anyone saw.'

'That was why the dispute, then,' Baldwin said.

'Yes.'

It was a short ride.

Baldwin's road followed the River Creedy, curling around

eastwards for some way, before leaving the manor's park and rising up again. The church was prominent before him, with a scattering of little cottages about it, some with smoke rising from holes in the thatch to give a welcoming appearance in this thin rain. It pattered on his cloak as he rode, and he pulled his hood over his head, musing on the dean's words as he left the church.

'Thank you for your hospitality,' Baldwin had said, tugging on gloves while waiting for his horse.

'You are always welcome here.'

'One thing, though. You have heard of the matter of Henry of Copplestone's troubles. Why do you not compensate him for his losses?'

Peter had been still a moment, and he would not meet Baldwin's eye. 'What did you think of young Arthur?'

Baldwin was baffled, but if his friend chose to change the subject he would not embarrass him by harping on. 'He seemed a pleasant enough fellow. Quite efficient and organized.'

'One must always be aware of younger canons,' Dean Peter said. 'They can be more prone to temptations than older men. And he is very aware of his name.'

It had been a curious comment to make, but Baldwin's horse was being brought to him even as Peter spoke, and in a few minutes Baldwin had mounted and was trotting from the church's precinct.

The journey was mercifully short. Sandford was fortunate in its location. The lands to the south and west were fertile, with the good, red soil of the area, not that much could be seen now. Everywhere was smothered with plants. Beyond there were orchards, with apples, pears, some cherry trees and others. Here at the side of the road was the vill's coppice, and men were in there in the rain, hacking away, and only stopping when they saw him. Some stood still and eyed him suspiciously, dark eyes peering from beneath brims.

The road rose up the next hill, but before the crest was a track that passed off to the left. This was a narrower way that suddenly widened into a broad triangular market space. Uncobbled, it was muddy where the grass had been trampled. A road led up to his right from here, up the hill to the church, while another wound off to the left. That, he knew, led to West Sandford and beyond. Simon's old farm was itself off in that direction. But directly ahead of him was the tavern.

It was not a large building. Little more than a cottage built of cob and thatch on top of a raised mound that sloped steeply down to the muddy roadway. Once it might have been a longhouse, a Devon farmhouse with one area for family living and a second for animals. No longer, though. From the piles of broken timbers and the heap of small stones, it looked as though there had been a structural failure, and the end wall replaced with fresh stones and cob to seal it.

Even had he not known where the murder had been committed the day before, Baldwin would have been able to guess. All about the door to the tavern were the vill's men and women. Baldwin rode to the edge of the road where a small oak stood, and tethered his mount to a low branch before making his way to the men.

The reeve here was a quiet, usually cheery fellow of middle height, with an open, red face like a ripe apple. Unusually for this area, he had blue eyes and straw-coloured hair, which he kept wedged under a woollen cap, but now he removed it as Baldwin approached, holding it in his two hands. 'Sir Baldwin, I hope I find you well?'

'I hope I see you well also, good Ulric.'

'I am well enough, Sir Knight.'

'And your wife?'

'She thrives, Sir Baldwin. And yours?'

Baldwin continued with the lengthy introductions, although he was keen to see the body. There was much for him to be working on when he returned home, and the unpleasant dampness dribbling down his back was a reminder that it would be good to get indoors and out of this downpour, thin though it may be. And yet he would need this man's help. Ulric was the reeve for a wide area about here, responsible for the vill here at Sandford, and the hamlets at West Sandford, and some five miles all about. Ulric knew all the men personally within that area, and he would be essential as a helper. But Baldwin knew that Ulric had one failing: the man was a menace for the correct behaviour. He would panic if there was the faintest hint of impropriety. For him, to hurry through the greetings would be an insult to him and to the visitor.

At last, when Baldwin felt the man should be content with the health of his wife, his children, his hounds, hawks and stables, he felt ready to ask where the body lay.

'He's not been moved, Sir Baldwin. Just in here, if you please.'

He led the way into the tavern. It was a small room, only shoulder height at the walls, but rising up into the thatch overhead. At the middle was a series of planks laid over the beams that held the roof trusses together, which Baldwin knew would be the tavern-keeper's bed. It was a scant foot over his head, and Baldwin only hoped it was safe. It didn't look it.

Ulric continued through the building to where a second low door stood ajar.

Inside was a small storeroom and brewhouse. The further wall held a waist-high furnace, with a copper fitting tightly into the stonework over it. A series of barrels lay off to the left, while sacks of grain hung from rafters nearby, off the ground to prevent them growing damp or getting attacked by rodents. The room held the warm, sweet odour of malt, mingled with the more obvious scents of death. And the smell Baldwin recalled so well – burned human flesh.

Baldwin had seen deaths of all kinds in his life. He had witnessed the easy deaths of older men and women, he had witnessed executions, he had seen the slow, agonizing death throes of those dying of starvation, and brutal slaughter during ferocious battles before he began to investigate murders. But when he saw who had died here, he felt a pang of regret. It was rare that he would meet a murder victim only a short while before his death, and when Baldwin met this man, all he had done was insult him.

'Where's his friend?' he said as he squatted near the body.

'He had none here,' Ulric said. 'He came here alone, and died alone.'

'No? I saw him in Crediton, and there he was travelling with a Welshman.' Baldwin looked down again. 'It was a hard death.'

Ulric shook his head sadly. 'There are few easy ways to die, but whoever did this . . .'

The body was lying near a wall. Gagged with a cloth, his cheeks were distended, his eyes staring madly in a face that was grey and bloodless in the cold light. His left hand had scrabbled madly in the dirt of the floor, while his legs had been held still by a sack of grain dropped on to them. A trickle of malt had run out and now mingled with the blood that had puddled on the ground.

But the right arm was what took Baldwin's attention.

'Have you seen his hand?' Ulric asked in a fearful undertone.

Baldwin glanced at him. Where the hand had been there was only a bloody stump. Nothing more. 'Where is it?'

'Sir Baldwin! Hah! In God's name, I am glad to see you. How is your wife, eh? The daughter still growing strong and fit? I'll be bound your little boy's nothing less than a chip off the old block, eh? Let's hope the little devil doesn't have to rest his head on one himself before he's twenty, though, eh? Ha! No need for the headsman's axe there, eh?'

This was all delivered at a volume that would have drowned the hucksters at Exeter's market. Baldwin could almost feel the words assaulting his ears as Coroner Sir Richard de Welles threw his reins to a boy, lifted his leg over his horse's neck, kicked his other foot free of the stirrup and sprang to the ground as lightly as a man fifteen years younger.

Sir Richard was not so young. Tall, broad-shouldered, with a face that was made to smile, he was a powerful man who wore a thick beard and moustache. He was a kindly soul, though, who had seen much of life. He was often surprisingly sympathetic to victims, because he had seen sadness in his time, losing his young wife when he was still very young, yet he always attempted to see the best in life. There were few situations in which he would not find a grain of humour, and for that if nothing else Baldwin was fond of him. His other traits, bellowing at people as though all peasants were deaf, telling appalling jokes and playing practical jokes when he could, were less endearing.

'Where's the stiff, then, eh?'

'Through here,' Ulric said starchily. He had not yet been introduced, and he felt that this was an insult to his reeve's dignity. A reeve was the most senior representative of his area, and for Ulric to be ignored was bound to have been noticed by some of the local villeins. They would make fun of him for this.

'You are?'

'I am Ulric, reeve of Sandford.'

'Master Ulric, you have my apology. I have travelled far today, and was so glad to see my friend Sir Baldwin that I entirely forgot myself. Master, would you do me the honour of showing me the corpse? And if you could let me know his name and anything else you know of him, I would be most grateful. And while we are viewing the unfortunate, if you would be so good as to suggest to the good alewife here that a man who's ridden close on twenty miles for a sight of a body is likely to have a parched throat, I'd be even more glad. A man could die of thirst here and lose his voice before a body stirred to help him, I dare say.'

Ulric hesitated, overwhelmed by the effusive friendliness as much by the bellowing voice, before waving to Hob and hurriedly leading the way into the back room.

'Not pleasant,' Sir Richard said, peering down at the body. 'Who did it?'

Ulric shook his head. 'We have no idea.'

'Who was he?'

'A pardoner, sir. He arrived here yesterday, no earlier, and came alone. Nobody in the vill knew him, so far as I know. His accent was not local. And I've travelled.'

Sir Richard tilted his head to one side and cocked an eye at Baldwin.

'I think he is right,' Baldwin intervened quickly before Sir Richard could make a joke about a reeve's potential journeys. Few would see more than a radius of some twenty miles about their vill in their lifetime, but he knew that Ulric had fought in the king's wars. 'I have myself met this fellow, only the day before yesterday. He was in Crediton then. I noticed that he had an accent from the north. I would think he might have hailed from Bristol, or somewhere about that way.'

'You get his name?'

'I think it was John.'

'No need to worry about proving he was local, then. Just a murdrum fine and the usual amercements,' Sir Richard grunted.

'He was with another man too.'

'Aha. You interest me, Sir Baldwin. Who was this other man?'

Huw sat at the side of the road and pulled his boot off, staring at his foot with wry discontent. The hole in the side of his boot had grown, and mud had stained his toes red, as though he was bleeding from a cut. It also let in stones, and he tipped the boot up, watching pebbles and muddy water dribble out.

The weather was atrocious this year. Nearly as bad as the famine years, when all the crops withered where they were planted, the rain flattening them to the ground, drowning the grain and leaving many people to die of starvation.

At least the downpour had eased a little over the morning. Now he was more than a part of the way to the place he thought John had mentioned. Somewhere called Sandford. From the look of it, it was well named, he thought sourly. There was indeed a shallow little ford here, with a wooden bridge for those on foot. Hardly any point in his worrying, though, with this hole in his boot.

A loud thudding of hooves made him look up. Even this close to a large town like Crediton, no traveller could afford to be complacent, not with the numbers of cut-throats and club gangs who roamed the lanes, always seeking out the unwary. And status meant nothing. There were all too many noblemen who behaved in the same manner, stealing anything they might from those who passed near their castles.

All the same, these didn't look like outlaws. They were not clad in bright armour, but they were on horseback, which together meant well-to-do and less likely to attack. He hoped so, anyway, because it was clear that they had seen him from the way that they slowed and pointed.

No one was safe in this God-forgotten land, Huw told himself as he pulled his boot on again and slowly made to stand up as they approached.

'You are Huw? The triacleur?'

'I have been called that. Not that I have much in the way of medicine with me just now, friends,' he said, observing how two of the men had their hands near their long-bladed knives.

A third held a billhook in his fist, and he pointed it at Huw. 'He's a bit past your medicine now, you Welsh git.'

'Who is? Friends, I don't know what you mean,' Huw said, his hands held up in a placatory manner. 'I stayed overnight in Crediton, and have only just been in a position to set off to meet John.'

'Who, you say? Your mate, the pardoner. You killed him.'

'John is dead? It was nothing to do with me!'

'Tell it to the Keeper!'

To Baldwin's secret astonishment, the coroner sank three quarts of Hob's best ale before sitting at the table, belching gently and patting his belly. 'Ach, there's nothing so good as a fresh ale on an empty belly. Nothing except a haunch of meat on top of it anyway,' he added, eyeing the capon roasting over the fire.

'Do you never suffer from an indigestion? Liverishness? A sore head?' Baldwin enquired rhetorically. He had never seen the vaguest indication of Sir Richard feeling out of sorts.

'Me? What do you take me for? Some milksop youth? Eh?'

Baldwin smiled to himself. 'What do you think of this killing, then?'

'The entry is clear enough. A man slid himself inside from under the eaves.'

When they had looked about the chamber, the hole at the rear of the room was immediately plain. The cob had fallen away a little, and the thatch pulled apart to leave space for a man to enter.

'He was so drunk he probably never heard his killer enter,' Baldwin said. 'Hob and Ulric both said he was well in his cups and had to leave the room before they went home.'

'So someone entered afterwards and killed him, before cutting his hand free,' the coroner said, and belched.

'Yes,' Baldwin said.

'Come along, then – why burn his hand?'

'I have no idea.'

They had found the hand, scorched and blackened, like some wizened relic, lying in the furnace under the copper.

Coroner Richard grunted. 'If he thought a little fire like that would do more than singe the hair from the fingers, he was a thoroughgoing idiot,' he concluded.

'No man would think a little fire like that would have destroyed the hand. It wasn't thrown there to be destroyed, not on a little fire of twigs and shavings. No man would think it would work for that,' Baldwin said.

'So why put it there?'

'I can hear horses,' Baldwin said, climbing to his feet.

They had sent the reeve and some men in the direction of Crediton on horseback to see if any news could be discovered about the triacleur, but that was only a short while ago. There had been no time to ride all the way to the town, let alone enquire. And yet here they all were, riding at a trot, with a bedraggled man hurrying behind, his hands bound with a stout rope that was gripped in the reeve's own hand.

Baldwin and the coroner walked out to stand near the tree where their horses had been hitched. A trio of young boys were rubbing their horses down and seeing to their water and feed. Baldwin had paid them earlier. His training as a Templar had taught him always to see to the comfort and health of his mount before his own. He walked over and patted his old beast, muttering to him as he gazed along the road at the approaching riders.

They drew up in the market area, and Reeve Ulric clambered down, yanking his prisoner forward. 'Here's your man, Sir Baldwin, Sir Richard. A *Welshman*,' he added, spitting the word.

Before Baldwin or Sir Richard could comment, a priest appeared, striding down the lane from the church. 'Is this the man? Is this the killer?'

'We don't know it,' Baldwin said coolly before turning to the man again. 'What do you say?'

'I am innocent, Sir Knight. These men found me on the road coming here. They saw me and brought me, but I don't know why.'

'You say you don't know what's happened to the pardoner, eh?' Ulric snapped.

There was a flash of fear in the man's eyes, Baldwin saw. 'I don't know what happened to my friend.'

'You call him your friend?' Hob said. He was behind Baldwin, and now he stepped forward. 'Sir Keeper, this man was no friend to the pardoner. The pardoner told me last night that this fellow, who had walked with him all the way from Wales, had said he would see the pardoner in hell before the week was out. They argued, and the pardoner had hoped that they might make amends to each other, but now it's obvious what happened. This Welshman broke into my tavern to murder my guest in his sleep.'

Baldwin looked at the man they were all accusing. He was a tatterdemalion, it was true. His hosen were beslubbered with mud, his coat stained and marked, his cloak ragged where thorns had tugged at it – but a man's appearance after a long journey could be deceptive.

He cast a glance up. The sun was hidden behind clouds, which hurried across the sky with a smooth urgency, but there was no sign of serious bad weather. If anything, it seemed warmer. He looked across at the coroner.

'Do you wish to open your inquest?' he asked.

'May as well, I suppose,' Coroner Richard said, amiably enough. 'You, man. Yes, tavern-keeper, you. What's your name? Hob? Fetch more wine. Priest? You'll have to clerk for me today. I've lost my normal ink-dribbler. Ulric? Gather the freemen of the vill here. *Come on, man*! I don't have all day even if you do!'

Sir Richard cast an eye around and shot a look up at the sky 'Bring me a bench,' he said. 'We shall begin our inquest here.'

Baldwin ordered that the man's hands should be unbound as soon as the coroner and he were sitting. There was no need to worry about Huw escaping from here, for he clearly would have little chance of outrunning the men of the vill. Instead, Baldwin allowed him to rub his wrists where the hemp rope had chafed, and let him take his stand near them both. Ulric stood near at hand, watching the triacleur suspiciously and hefting his billhook, while two men went and fetched out the body. They stripped it naked, before rolling it over and over in front of all the freemen of the vill so the wounds could be noted.

The coroner called out a list of the injuries, examining them closely, pulling the head back to show the depth of the wound in the throat, lifting the arm to show where the hand had been cut away. Letting it fall, he turned to the prisoner.

'Well, Master Welshman, what do you have to say?'

'I can give no story at all, good Knight, for the simple reason that I've no idea what had been done to my old friend. All I can tell is, I was in Crediton last afternoon, and there were many saw me there. One fool had a loud shouting match with me, demanding to know what I was selling, and saying I was selling poisons. That's why I've no bag with me now. I was forced to run and lost all my wares. It was not a good day.'

'Where did you go after that?'

'I found a hayloft over near the church. I don't know whose.'

'Did anyone see you there?'

'How would I know?'

'What of this morning? Did any man see you rise and leave?'

'I was careful no one did! What would they do to a poor pilgrim of the roadway like me?' Huw demanded hotly, staring about him at all the grim faces. 'A stranger and foreigner in a strange land is always suspected, no matter whether he be innocent or guilty. Foreigners are easy to blame, Sir Knight.'

'That may be true. The guilty are also easy to blame, Triacleur,' Baldwin noted. He chose not to comment on the fact that a man with so sour a face might expect to be viewed with suspicion.

'He is the murderer,' Reeve Ulric said. 'Listen to him! You can hear the guilt in his voice.'

'I hear nothing of the sort,' Baldwin said. 'Only a man in fear of his life. A justifiable fear, I have to say.'

'Slipping into a room in the middle of the night – that's a Welshie trick,' the reeve persisted.

'You have experience?' Sir Richard said at last. He had been sitting with his chin on his fist, elbow on his knee, eyeing Huw with a wary lack of enthusiasm, as he might study a rabid hound.

'What?'

'You sound like a man who speaks from experience. Were you in Wales?'

'I fought there for the last king, God save his memory! Edward the First took me and seventeen others from about here with our lord.'

'You fought, eh?'

'We fought much, yes. Pacifying that country was hard work. But we did our duty, although only seven of us came home again.'

'A shame. I have been involved in battles too.'

'Sire.'

'Do you tell me that none of you would slip into a tavern at night to take a swig?' the coroner asked with a grin lifting one side of his beard. There was a twinkle in his eye as he spoke. 'You'd be the only men-at-arms ever to be sober, if so.'

'Perhaps some did take some ale or wine when they may.'

'Sometimes I've known men take more than just a little ale too,' the coroner reminisced. He looked over at Baldwin. 'Once one of me own boys took a set of plates from a wealthy merchant's town house. That was a goodly haul! Too good for that damned churl. Took it meself. Gave him a little coin for it, of course. Damned fool spent it inside an hour at a tavern, I expect.'

'Aye,' the reeve agreed, stony-faced. 'There were some made themselves rich out there. Happy days, for them.'

'So you admit Englishmen were capable of the same thievery, then, and that you have experience of it. So, then, Reeve, am I to think you did this thing? You wandered in there last night, killed the man and slipped out again, putting into practice all the expertise you built up during your war career? No? Then don't be so damned keen to blame another man, eh? Now, then.' He sat upright, glaring about the gathered men with an expression that could have turned ale to vinegar. 'Did anyone see this man about the vill yesterday or yestere'en? Come, now! All you are happy to accuse the man, but has any man a shadow of evidence? Will any man say they saw him?'

There was no response to that challenge, and Baldwin felt an unaccountable sense of relief. He had no cause to think that the man was innocent, after all, and by his own admission he had argued with his companion. But Baldwin was a renegade Knight Templar. He had seen the punishment meted out to so many of his comrades on the basis of evidence they never saw. It was the foundation of his own loathing of injustice.

The Templars had been arrested and accused of crimes, but not allowed to know what the offences were, when they were committed, how they were committed, nor even who accused them – nothing – and yet were tortured until they 'confessed'. They were burned, broken and cut without understanding why. Some had their feet roasted until the flesh fell away, and they still did not know why. The experience had taught Baldwin that in the absence of a lawyer there was no justice.

'Right, then,' the coroner continued. 'Who was last to see the man alive?'

This elicited the response that Ulric, Hob, Father William and two or three others had remained in the pardoner's company. He had grown sleepy some hours after dark, and had gone to his palliasse in the brewhouse before the others had left. Hob had taken the pardoner at his word and continued selling beer on his account, assuming that he would be reimbursed the following morning. Soon his snores could be heard, and then gradually the men had parted. First to go was the priest, then Ulric, and Hob was forced to stay up with the others until he grew bored of their company – and singing – and threw them out in the middle of the night. He had tidied the room, doused his fire and then went to make sure his guest was all right. A scratching noise had made him wonder whether there was a rat in the chamber. As soon as he found the corpse, he raised the hue and cry.

There was more evidence to hear from the men who had been drinking, but little more could be learned. All pronounced themselves moderately drunk and had gone home to their beds.

Baldwin nodded and glanced at the coroner. But there was something in the tavern-keeper's tone which made him a little suspicious. He felt the man was concealing something. But who in these days of violence and hardship had nothing to hide?

'In that case,' Coroner Richard declared, 'this matter is unsolved. I find that this pardoner has been murdered by a man or men unknown, and that he is not of this parish.

The murdrum fine will be imposed, and the weapon used to kill him must have been a knife or dagger. I will say the weapon was worth at least a shilling, and that much is deodand. And now my inquest is closed.'

Father William left the coroner's court with a feeling of sour disbelief.

There were not many men in this vill whom he would trust, but Reeve Ulric was one. He was an astute man, with the clear sight that most others lacked. He was standing up near the entrance to Hob's tavern now, and the priest crossed to him with a determined expression on his face. 'I am sorry that they didn't listen to you. You were right, I believe, in God's name.'

'Well, the coroner didn't seem so sure,' Ulric said, still smarting. 'But I know these Welshies. You can't trust them. Not that he'd listen.'

'I've known enough knights who couldn't find their ballocks with both hands,' Father William said shortly. 'These two are no different. You going to the fields?'

The reeve nodded, and Father William fetched his own hoe from the shed at the bottom of his chapel before the two men walked to the fields together. 'You saw how the man broke into the back room?'

'The hole under the eaves. Must have been easy.' Ulric shook his head. 'If that wasn't a clear proof of the Welshman's guilt, nothing was. The fellow must have woken and seen his mate climbing in, and thought he was there to make up.'

'You think so? I'd have thought the pardoner didn't wake at all. No, if he'd come to and seen the Welshman slipping in, he'd have raised Cain. They separated angrily, didn't they?'

Ulric nodded. They had both heard the pardoner tell

of his fight with his companion, and how he believed that
the man could have meant his threat. 'But I don't think
that mother-swyving—'

William shook his head. 'Enough. I won't listen to such
language.'

'Apologies, Father. I forgot I was talking to you. It just
makes me angry to think of one of those Welshmen making
fools of good Englishmen.'

'You were out in Wales for a while, weren't you?'

'Yes. I saw my own son killed. Some Welsh ambushed
us on the way to join the king. He was slain before he had
even time to draw a knife.'

'I am sorry – may he rest in peace . . . Of course. I had
heard – but that was before I came here myself,' the priest
murmured.

The two stood at the edge of the strips, gazing down
the lines of vegetables. Mud lay thick and bright, and the
rainwater was puddled like blood on the paths between.

Ulric shook his head. 'Look at all this. It's wonderful
land, this. Perfect. Any man could make a living with it.
Rich, fertile land. And what good is it?'

'You mustn't upset yourself, Ulric.'

'Why not? This kind of land is perfect for a man to pass
on to his son. Here am I, a freeman, and yet I have no
son to inherit my land. No one. What is the point of life
when there's no one to take over, no one to carry on?'

'You have suffered much, Ulric.'

'Aye. And for what? It is the saddest thing, to lose your
child, to see him die before you.'

'At least you know his suffering's over.'

'Perhaps. I knew there was no good to come of a
pardoner's visit.'

The priest gave him a long, measuring look. 'I didn't
hear you complain while he was here.'

The reeve wouldn't meet his eye, but kept his gaze fixed on the weeds. 'Aye, well, there are some folks you shouldn't argue against. He might have been an honest pardoner, after all. One of them may be.' He shrugged and began to trudge to his own strip. 'I just haven't met that one yet.'

Baldwin and the coroner demanded some food, and a girl soon brought them a little meat pottage with a loaf of rough maslin, a cheap peasant bread made from wheat and rye.

Coroner Richard eyed the fare sourly. 'This the best you can do? I *am* a king's coroner,' he grumbled, but set to with gusto nonetheless. 'What of him?'

'Him?' she said, and glanced at Huw. 'He's no money to pay for food.'

'Then put it on my slate,' Coroner Richard said with a low malevolence. His spoon stopped, hovering near his mouth as he stared at the girl with a fixed determination. '*Now!*'

Reluctantly she went to fetch food for the prisoner. She had been about to get only dry bread, but catching sight of the coroner's glower she amended it to the same as the two knights themselves were eating.

'I am thankful, Sir Coroner,' Huw said hesitantly as the girl disappeared inside again.

Coroner Richard snorted. 'I'll still hang you, man, if they find you guilty.'

A little later Baldwin walked back inside the tavern to ask for more ale, and saw Hob in the corner, near the great window that overlooked the village green.

'Was he successful here, this pardoner?' Baldwin asked. 'Did he make much money?'

'He took many pennies from the people around here. Some women even threw him their rings and bracelets. I saw a gorgeous enamelled—'

'His purse is still full. What of you? Was it a good evening for you too?'

'He paid me a little, which I have here—'

'Show me,' Baldwin said.

Hob opened his purse and withdrew six silver pennies and a ring. 'I liked it, and he threw it to me for his food last night and this morning. The coin was payment for ales last night. He bought drinks for others.'

There was a strip of vellum in his purse too. Baldwin nodded at it. 'A pardon?'

'I gave him his own ales last night in exchange for this,' Hob said defensively.

'You did well,' Baldwin said with a low whistle.

'He was a generous man,' Hob said. He shot a look through the window at Huw. 'Which is why I want his killer to pay.'

'It wasn't me!' Huw exclaimed indignantly, his mouth full of maslin.

'Someone shaved his throat for him,' the coroner said unperturbably.

Baldwin had returned and shared Hob's words with them. Now he jerked his head back towards the tavern. 'The pardoner's purse is still full, so it does not look as though anything was missing. It's unlikely he was murdered for money. Perhaps someone gave him a trinket for an indulgence, which he later regretted, and he came here to take it back?'

'Possibly. What of you, fellow? Did you see anything else he could have had that may have been stolen?' Sir Richard said to Huw.

Huw stared at him, then his eyes went to Baldwin, before they dropped to stare into his bowl. He said nothing for a moment. Then: 'What of the bones?'

*

Agatha, wife of Henry of Copplestone, was in an indignant mood that day.

She had told her husband to go and demand an apology for the atrocious insult offered to her, but the feeble old devil wouldn't think of it. Not even when she had lifted her hem to show how her skirts had been ruined. He just sneered and told her to get the maid to clean it, so instead she had gone to Crediton to purchase more cloth for a new tunic. Let her useless husband see if he preferred that.

If only she had listened to her mother; then she would have wed Cedric instead of Henry. Cedric was already far wealthier than her husband. He had made something of himself, first being apprenticed to a spicer, and now living in Exeter as a professional man himself. With his money, she could have enjoyed a vastly better lifestyle. But no, she'd taken the fool instead. Henry had been there, and she had, to be fair, been quite overturned by his clear adoration. If only she'd been more sensible . . .

Life was there to be lived though. She wouldn't spend her life dreaming of what might have been. No. She must seek all the pleasure she might, for life was fleeting.

Riding back homewards, to her hall at West Sandford, she saw a stranger riding on the same road. 'Do you know him?' she said to her servant.

Edward, a thin-faced man of some two-and-twenty years, peered over his shoulder, his squint making his face as sharp as a ferret's. 'Him? Nah! Never seen him.'

She was not seriously alarmed, for the man appeared to be riding gently enough. Tall, square-shouldered, but with a paunch that implied his wealth, she had been aware of him ever since they had left Crediton.

'Godspeed, Lady,' the stranger said as he drew near, doffing his hood. 'Simon Puttock at your service.'

'God you keep,' she responded, bending her head carefully so her wimple wouldn't fall. It was always a struggle to keep the cursed thing on.

He was a good-looking fellow, this. Grey eyes, set in a sun-browned face which looked as though he was ever ready to smile. Yet there was a certain sharpness to him too, as though he was a man who might be slightly dangerous. Yes, he was a man to watch, she thought.

'You live near here?' she asked.

'I have been some years away. Ten years ago God saw fit to make me bailiff on Dartmoor, and I've been living there ever since. But I am returning to live here now. Do you live near?'

'My husband is Henry of Copplestone. We live at West Sandford.'

'A good barton,' Simon commented.

'Usually. The church has ruined our crop this year. A lazy shepherd allowed the dean's flock to roam and they got into our peas and ate them all.'

'I am sure the dean would be pleased to compensate you.'

'Dean Peter? You don't know him, then?'

'He has been a friend for many years.'

She snorted. 'He has been a torment to me, sire. He has caused me much misery. Our crops gone, and he all but laughed in my face. Then a canon splashed my skirts. Look! Here! And he made no offer to "compensate" me. Nothing!'

Simon gave a sympathetic grunt. 'But I am surprised. I always found Peter Clifford to be a generous-hearted, good and kindly man. This is a sorry tale, Lady.'

'Aye. And little benefit will I gain from the telling. There seems nothing a woman might do to win recompense for the harm done to her.'

'Did you meet your husband here?' Simon asked, keen to change the subject. He did not like to hear people talking about his friend in such a bitter manner.

'No, I was born at Morchard Bishop. My husband came from Copplestone, and we rented West Sandford when we were wed.'

'It was Saul who used to live there,' Simon recalled. 'He was a good old fellow.'

'He lived to a good age. He was almost two-and-forty when he died.'

Simon said nothing. Being almost forty himself, he was always aware of old age looming. 'Oh.'

They had reached the narrow way that led to the marketplace at Sandford as he spoke, and Simon saw before him the familiar shape of his friend Baldwin. Then he saw the other figure and winced.

Glancing at Agatha, he was about to speak when he saw her frown. 'Lady?'

'That man again!' she spat as she looked at the trio.

Baldwin was soon back with them. 'No, there are no bones in there.'

'Come, fellow. Tell us,' the coroner rumbled. 'What do you know of these bones?'

Huw licked dry lips. 'This is a long tale. I am the last of my line. We serve to protect some objects which we venerate most highly. Relics of a man we revere.'

'Saintly relics all over the place,' Coroner Richard said.

'Yes, Sir Richard, but these are different. They are the genuine bones of . . . a man respected throughout Wales. But a man took some of them. It was him, John the Pardoner.'

'The dead man?' the coroner said.

'Yes. It was some few years ago that Sir William de

Grandisson gave our abbey a piece of the True Cross, in the fourteenth year of our lord King Edward's reign.* As soon as it was given, the abbot, Richard Stradell, decided to make a suitable environment for it, and ordered that a special space should be created for this wonderful relic. Stone was delivered, and it unhappily was stored over the top of the corpse of him whom we serve. The masons began their work, and we must remove the box to another safe place. It was taken to a little chapel where it would be safe. Or so we thought.'

'They didn't realize it was the bones of this man you revere, eh? Wasn't the box obvious?'

'No. To maintain the secret, the box was only a small one. Just large enough to hold the bones within. And a tress of hair. Apart from that there was nothing to declare the sanctity of what it held. Only scratches and gouges from a shovel, they were the only decoration. And it was taken away before it was seen.'

'Except the pardoner saw it?' Sir Richard said. 'And like any other pardoner, he saw a chance for some bones to work with, eh, and grabbed 'em?'

'I fear so. He visited the chapel and the chaplain saw him praying, but later, when the pardoner had gone, the box had been moved. Some of the bones had been taken. The bones of a hand.'

'So you took off in pursuit,' Baldwin said. 'And followed him all the way down here?'

'I had no proof it was him who had taken them. I could not simply accuse him of theft without proof. And then, when I was sure at last, and asked him how he came by the bones, he refused to tell me. That was why we separated in such a manner.'

* 1321

'You mean you didn't learn about these bones until you came here to Crediton?' Baldwin said sceptically.

'He had the bones, I knew, but he kept them about his person. I didn't reach him until I arrived in Exeter, and since then I only saw them at Crediton. I had to stay with him until I could be sure that they were the bones I sought. And then, at last he took them from his wallet and showed them, and I was sure that they were indeed the ones that had been stolen. He had the bones of a hand.'

'So you followed him here and killed him in order to recover them?' Coroner Richard grated.

'No, sire. If I wanted to kill him, I could have done at any time between Exeter and here. Why wait until we came here? I admit, he and I parted on no good terms. He denied that he had stolen them, but declared that they were legally recovered by him. At least, he did at first. It was only later that he sneered at me, saying that I should be glad that he was at least showing the bones to some of the world. It made me angry to hear him joke about the bones, but I didn't kill him. I held my tongue and walked away. You see, I meant to return to his side at Sandford and then to persuade him to give them up.'

'Or to wait until you and he were on the road in a quiet place, and take 'em, eh? Well,—' the coroner shrugged— 'can't blame you. Would've done the same meself. Blasted pardoners are a menace.'

'Perhaps,' Baldwin said. 'But the deed has not been committed. He is innocent. However, I am intrigued. Why did you not take them before? As you say, you travelled all the way here with him. There must have been dozens of places where you could have knocked him on the head and recovered them.'

'I didn't wish to kill him,' Huw said simply. 'I was in his company, but ... well, John was a most engaging companion. I did not want to hurt him too close to Exeter at first, and then I decided not to hurt him until I had seen the bones in his possession, and he didn't get them out until he reached Crediton. And by that time it was too late.'

'You mean you didn't want to kill him?' Baldwin said.

'How could I? He was such a friendly, open, amiable man. I couldn't willingly stick a knife in him. He was a real, flesh-and-blood man, while . . . they were only bones, when all was said and done.'

Baldwin looked at the coroner. 'I believe him.'

'You sure? He could easily have broken into the room at Hob's. Anyone could, even a Welshman. And there's the thing about the hand. Surely returning the favour, when he'd stolen the bones from the abbey.'

'But if Huw did that, he would today be at Exeter or beyond. Why return here? And where are the bones he venerates?' Baldwin asked flatly. 'No. He is innocent. Which begs the question: who *was* responsible?'

'Baldwin! Sir Richard!'

And Baldwin felt some of the burden of anxiety fall from his shoulders as he recognized the voice of his old friend Simon.

Agatha was keen to leave the vill and return to her home, but her curiosity wouldn't let her go straight away. She passed her reins to her servant and dropped elegantly from her mount, making her way into the tavern. The serving maid was there, but Agatha went to Hob to ask for a pot of wine.

'What's happening here?'

'Murder, mistress. A pardoner was killed here last night. The coroner and the Keeper are asking about him. It'll cost us all a pile of silver.'

There was no need to elaborate. All knew how expensive a body could be. There was the fine for the death of a man who wasn't known locally, the murdrum. An ancient fine, it was imposed at the height of King William's reign, when the resistance to Norman rule meant that murder was commonplace. If a body was discovered and no one could assert its 'Englishry', it was assumed to be a Norman, and a crushing fine was enforced on the locality.

She winced. 'What of that fellow they're questioning?'

'Him? He was friend to the pardoner, he says.'

'He's an unpleasant little man,' she said. 'He accosted me in the market yesterday. If it wasn't for a few locals coming to my rescue, I don't know what might have happened.'

As she spoke she peered through the window. The man with whom she had ridden here was greeting the two knights with enthusiasm.

'Tavern-keeper, bring more ale!' the taller, heavy-set knight, whom she knew only as the coroner, bellowed, and Hob hissed to the girl to hurry.

'Has he seen you?' Agatha said quietly when they were alone.

'Don't think so,' Hob replied. He chewed his inner cheek fretfully.

'Let's hope, then,' she murmured.

'Hope what?' Baldwin asked.

Agatha shot a look at Hob. 'Nothing, Sir Knight.'

'That is odd. You see, your maid just told us that she thought you had seen this man outside in Crediton, that he was being a nuisance to you.'

'Yes, he was pestering a number of people, trying to sell his potions.'

'Would you come out here, then? You could identify him, and that would be useful.'

'Why?'

Baldwin lifted an eyebrow. 'If you saw him in Crediton, that would begin to validate his story. If he was in the town when you saw him, perhaps we can find others who also saw him and who can vouch for his being there later. That would mean it wasn't him who later came here to kill the pardoner, wouldn't it?'

She reluctantly nodded and followed Baldwin outside.

'Is that the man you saw?' Baldwin asked.

'Yes.'

Huw gaped. 'I did nothing to the lady! I was only selling some medicines, and she and her companion refused even to listen. I only urged them to listen to my words, nothing more.'

She reddened. 'I had no companion, churl. How dare you say such a thing?'

'But—'

'There was no one with me, other than my servant,' she said with emphasis.

Huw followed her gaze to where the servant squatted on his haunches near the horses. It wasn't the man he'd seen, he thought.

Baldwin saw his look and smiled. 'Mistress, it is all too easy for a man to mistake one man for another when he meets different people all day, just as it is hard for a woman not to feel pressurized when a hawker is only trying to bring a new sweetmeat or pie to her attention. No doubt this man was only being polite in his own way.'

She nodded, and with a curt nod to Simon she left them, striding to her horse. Soon she was mounted, and she and her servant made their way from the vill.

'Well, you didn't make a friend there, Master Triacleur,' the coroner said, eyeing the two as they rode away. 'So who could have stolen these bones, then? Someone who wanted to take on the pardoner's trade?'

'If it were only that, surely the thief would have taken the vellum as well? A pardoner is no pardoner who does not possess pardons,' Baldwin said.

'I must try to find them,' Huw said. He sat, disconsolate, his face drawn into a picture of complete misery. 'I should have knocked him down and taken the bones when I first found him, rather than trying to persuade him to give them up. If I'd just taken them, he could still be alive.'

'Don't waste your feelings on him,' Sir Richard said kindly. 'Worry more about yourself. While no other man appears, you are our most likely fellow for dancing a jig from a rope.'

Baldwin was more interested in Agatha's reaction to Huw. 'She was very certain that she was alone when you saw her.'

'I don't care what she says. There was a man with her in Crediton,' Huw said.

'Do not change the subject by accusing an honest woman of infidelity,' the coroner said sternly.

'You don't understand. I saw him today at the inquest: it was the tavern-keeper.'

The coroner exchanged a look with Baldwin. 'Well, adultery is not the same as murder,' he said with a shrug. 'What of it?'

'It is one more thing to consider,' Baldwin said. 'No more, no less.'

It was a little while later, once Baldwin and Sir Richard had given Huw to a couple of sturdy peasants for safekeeping, that the three repaired to the chapel at the top of the vill to speak to the priest about the pardoner.

'He's not here, sires,' the man in the church told them

after they had all bent the knee and crossed themselves at the cross.

'Who are you?' Baldwin asked.

'Me? I'm Peter the Pauper, lord. That's what they call me, anyways. I keep the church clean for Father William.'

He was a little old man, wizened and with a skin that was tanned deep brown by the elements, with pale grey eyes set in a thin face. His right hand was claw-like from some ancient injury.

'He is a senior priest for a chapel like this, isn't he?' Sir Richard asked, eyeing the altar speculatively. 'Thought he looked quite an elderly man for such a posting. Why does a chapel this size merit his presence?'

'Not all priests wish for ever larger congregations, I suppose.' The man shrugged. 'And some come to a place like this because it is convenient.'

'It is that,' Baldwin said. Close to Crediton and not too far from Exeter, Sandford was a good location for a priest. Far better than some out-of-the-way chapel like Gidleigh, or one of the other churches over to the west of Dartmoor.

'Where is he?' the coroner asked.

'He'll be with the other men, tending the fields, of course.'

'So he is a man of humility,' Simon said.

'Oh, I suppose so. Although he has a need for it.'

'What do you mean?' Baldwin asked.

'He was the rector of a church in Axminster before he came here. Any man who came here from a minster must have been considered due for some humility, wouldn't he?'

They soon left the old man and followed Simon down to the strip fields that supported the vill, and before long the three men were walking down the track towards the working peasants and freemen of the vill. It took little time to find the priest and Ulric, both leaning on their tools and watching as the three men approached.

Father William was of only middle height, but he looked taller with his shock of almost-white hair. It was a while since he had last seen the barber, from the way his stubble had thickened on chin and head. 'You want me again? What, more note-taking? I have work to do, coroner.'

'I know that,' Sir Richard said. 'But first I want to ask you a little more about the pardoner. Did you know he had bones? Apparently he was displaying relics as he went.'

'Not until he got them out, no. Why should I? But I don't care what he was doing. When all is said and done, he was only a pardoner.'

'Who will care about a dead pardoner?' Ulric demanded. 'He shouldn't have been here in the first place.'

'He sold quite a few pardons, I hear,' Baldwin said.

'Aye. What of it?' Ulric asked.

'Did you buy one?'

'No! I have no need of them.'

'But many did,' Baldwin said, looking at the priest.

'Not I.'

'The others who did must have felt that they had something to protect themselves against.'

'Men will always think they have a need of protection,' Ulric said. 'If they have some spare money, and the pardoner gives a good tale, like this one did, then he will have people flock to him.'

'They sell lies and deceit,' the priest said uncompromisingly. 'The Holy Father in Avignon has authorized some few friars and others to give indulgences, but men like this one are mere pedlars in people's hopes – and fears.'

'You sound like a man who has cause to doubt such people, Father,' the coroner said mildly.

'I detest them. Yes, and I hate those who pander to the baser attitudes of the people in the vill. The good Bishop

Walter has shown the way with these people, saying that they are not to be welcomed in any of his lands across his diocese, and I support his ban. What, would you have men think that they might commit any sin with impunity just for the price of a letter of indulgence from another man? The Pope may give such a promise, but a man like this dead pardoner? Why should he have the right? Why should any churl without the education of holy orders think himself able to offer God's own forgiveness?'

'The Pope has made the pardoner legitimate in the matter,' Sir Richard said.

'You find my attitude surprising? What arrogance is it to think that one man alone can appreciate the divine will? I say to you: the pardoners are wrong. They should not be saying that they can help souls. That is the task of priests like me, not secular fellows like that man.'

'And what of you, Ulric?' Baldwin asked. 'Do you think he was as evil as the priest thinks?'

'I think he was a dangerous man. Anyone who dabbles in pardons for sins which he cannot understand is dangerous.'

'Where lies the danger? You mean that he will die like John last night?' Coroner Richard snapped.

'No. I mean that a fellow who seeks to sell an indulgence thinks that he knows God's mind. And that itself is more dangerous than the devil. How can a man know God's will?'

'A good point,' Baldwin said. He had noticed that the priest and Ulric had exchanged a look as the reeve spoke, and they remained staring at each other now. 'The bones, though. They were here on view, I think? Where did they go? They were not there in his bags today, so somebody must have stolen them.'

'You think so?' the priest asked. 'Perhaps they were taken

by God, to save them from that man's perverted, thieving hands.'

There was nothing more that they could, or would, tell him, so it seemed, so the three men thanked the two and returned up the path to the vill.

However, as they reached the market area, Baldwin saw a scruffy little lad, scarcely ten years old, barefoot and filthy, playing with a sling near the horses. As the three appeared, he shot to his feet, a ragged warrior, stuffing his sling into the rope that served him as a belt.

'Masters, are you seeking the pardoner's killer? I can help.'

His name, so he said, was Bar. 'I was here yesterday when the pardoner arrived.'

'Aye? And what did you see, boy?' Sir Richard demanded.

The boy was standing, hands behind his back, facing the three men. Baldwin and Sir Richard sat on a bench, while Simon had an old stool at their side. It was an intimidating environment, but the lad seemed unconscious of the fact.

'He saw me. I was out at the chapel trying to hit a magpie in the tall elm,' he said, pointing, 'when the pardoner walked up. He gave me a drum and told me to beat it to call people here to his "pardon".'

'He had no permission to beat it here, then?' Baldwin said. 'That may explain the priest's animosity . . .'

He saw the lad staring uncomprehendingly.

'Why the priest disliked him,' Baldwin explained.

'No, he saw Father William first. I saw him coming down here from the chapel. Father William approved.'

'That scarce accords with the priest's story,' Sir Richard muttered. 'Aye, so what then, boy?'

'He sold his scraps of parchment while people knelt and kissed his licence, and he showed them his goose feather and his bones, and then people paid more. And then they left him.'

'What did he do?'

'He took me to the tavern here, and gave me two pennies. Silver ones. And he gave me a quart of strong ale, while the tavern-keeper gave him as much ale as he could drink in exchange for a strip of the parchment.'

'So Hob had a pardon too?' Baldwin said.

'Yes, I think he needs it,' the urchin said with a sly smile.

'Why, boy?' the coroner demanded. 'In Christ's name, the people of the vill here speak ever in riddles. Just give us some clear answers!'

'Hob has been swiving the mistress of West Sandford.'

'Does everyone know of it?' Sir Richard demanded.

Baldwin smiled to see the expression on the coroner's face. 'No need to repeat that, lad,' he said. 'And what proof do you have of that rather inflammatory remark?'

'It's known all over the vill. The only man who doesn't is her old man,' the boy said. 'She's always with him – here or in Crediton. Everyone knows about him and her.'

It was all too common, Baldwin knew. So often the last person to hear of adultery was the cuckold himself. Simon was thinking the same thing, he saw. 'The man Hob had a parchment in his purse, just like a pardoner's indulgence,' Baldwin said.

'It would not surprise me,' Simon said in answer to his look. 'She was a comely woman.'

'Hardly what I'd say about the tavern-keeper, though,' Baldwin said.

The coroner glanced at him, then looked up at the inn. 'So this good taverner has bought an indulgence for himself because of an amatory matter with the woman from West

Sandford, then? I thought he said he had no such parchment.'

'We shall need to speak to him,' Baldwin agreed. 'Boy, what else can you tell us?'

'Hob gave the pardoner as much ale as he could drink in exchange for the parchment, but others there wanted his aid as well.'

'The priest is clearly against the sale of pardons here. Why would he allow this fellow John to sell them?'

'I don't know. But he was with the pardoner before he started to sell them. I saw them.'

'It is an odd thing,' the coroner said. 'Why would the priest allow the sale to go on, if he is as vehement against the whole principle as he says he is?'

'There are some who will rail against a thing, but when money is given to them, suddenly their antipathy is turned to quiet reflection,' Baldwin said.

'He maybe took money and regrets it now,' Simon said.

'Perhaps,' the coroner said. 'What of this man at West Sandford though?'

'I don't know who he is,' Simon said. 'Still, it couldn't have been him if he was in Exeter like his wife said, could it? And I fail to understand why he would want to kill a pardoner.'

'The man sold a pardon to his wife's ravisher,' Sir Richard pointed out.

'I think most men would seek the death of the adulterer rather than the pardoner,' Baldwin said gently.

They were outside the tavern now. The boy had been sent on his way, with a half-penny from Baldwin for his information, and now they were staring at the figure of Hob as he toiled up the hill towards them.

'Masters! Can I fetch you more ale? Some food?'

'No, Master Taverner, you can explain yourself to us,' Baldwin said with some harshness. 'You have lied to us, master, and we wish to know why.'

Instantly the man's face fell. 'Lied? My lords, I wouldn't—'

Baldwin shook his head. 'It is no good, man. You will have to speak.'

'I don't know what you want.'

'Try telling us the truth,' Coroner Richard grated, 'if you wouldn't test the comfort of the gaol at Crediton! Do you still say you had nothing to do with the murder of the man in your tavern?' he demanded.

'No! Why would I seek his death!' Hob protested.

'Perhaps he saw you with your woman, just as Huw did,' Baldwin suggested shrewdly.

'No – I swear it on the Gospel.'

'What of others? Last night, did you see anyone who could have had something against the pardoner?'

Hob looked up at all their faces, then down again. 'One man, yes. When I opened the doors and threw out the others, I did see one – or so I thought.'

'Where?'

'Over at the edge of my house. But I never thought it would be him. He had nothing to want to kill this pardoner for . . .'

'Who?'

'Agatha's husband, Henry of Copplestone. I thought I saw him over at the side of my house. That was why I made sure I locked the door carefully before going up to my bed. I thought he could try to enter to kill me. But he would do nothing against the pardoner. Why should he?'

Once outside, Baldwin and Simon exchanged a look. 'Well?' Simon said.

'Clearly pointless. There is much we may say of a married woman who behaves like a whore,' Coroner Richard said uncompromisingly. 'But what of it? It's got damn all to do with the murder of the man in the tavern. At least, so far as we can tell, it hasn't.'

'No,' Simon said, but now he remembered the woman's words on seeing Baldwin and Richard questioning Huw as he rode into the vill. 'Except she clearly had something against the Welshman when we rode into the town. That itself strikes me as odd.'

'He saw her with her lover in Crediton,' Baldwin said. 'Perhaps she realized that he might speak to us – as he did,' but as he spoke a vague memory occurred to him.

'You have a constipated look about you, man,' the coroner said.

'When I saw the pardoner and Huw in Crediton, I could have sworn I saw Agatha running away from me,' Baldwin said, and told of the glimpse he'd had of her and a man flying away up the hill. But even as he spoke he was reminded of the curious comment of Dean Peter – that Arthur was prey to temptations. At the time he had not taken much notice, thinking the dean meant only that a young man's eye could be taken by a comely woman, but now he wondered whether he had taken the dean's meaning correctly. Perhaps the dean knew something about the canon.

'So what do you want to do now?' Simon asked.

Coroner Richard grunted. 'Gentles, there is only one way in which we may ease our concerns in this matter. Let us go to her house and ask the woman's husband whether he was there, as the tavern-keeper thought, or not!'

The journey took little time – it was such a short distance that none of them bothered to mount their horses; instead, the three friends walked along the lane.

'What do you think?' Simon asked as they walked.

Baldwin looked over at him. 'Well, the tavern-keeper was having an affair with Agatha. It's possible her husband learned of it and went to kill him – and yet any man who entered that tavern must notice that the man's bedchamber is up in the rafters. I saw it up there the first time I walked inside. So if he went in and killed the pardoner, that would be because he had a reason to, not because he fell over a new body and killed him in mistake. And why cut off his hand?'

'We can hopefully learn more in a short time,' Coroner Richard said. 'Meantime, Baldwin, do you suspect any other?'

'I would feel sure that Hob himself is likely to be innocent. He does not show any signs of blood about his body.'

'Why would a man cut the pardoner's hand off?' Simon mused.

The coroner shrugged. 'Surely because he had taken another man's hand.'

'But who would have known that apart from Huw?'

'He was hardly in the vill long enough to have told anyone,' Baldwin considered. 'Unless he allowed it to slip when he was in the tavern that night.'

Just then they rounded a corner, and before them lay the long hall of Henry of Copplestone.

It was a large property. A longhouse, with a separate byre behind, two small barns and a stable-block all spoke of Henry's wealth. To emphasize his position, the land all about had been splendidly cultivated, with a series of pastures and good strips of fields dropping down towards the stream at the bottom of the lands.

Silently, the three marched to the door and were welcomed by a maidservant who took them over the threshold and into a large hall, well illuminated by the enormous window in the southern wall.

Soon Henry and his wife were with them.

Henry was a short, swarthy man with the eyes of a seaman, permanently squinting as though peering into a strong wind. His hands were muscular, but Baldwin was not sure whether the man had the strength of will for violence.

His wife was very pretty, although now, seeing her more closely, Baldwin was struck by how her looks melded together to produce a less wholesome picture. His own wife was a perfect combination of imperfections that somehow made her extraordinarily attractive to him. This woman was almost perfect in every way, and he found that his initial reaction to her was of stunned admiration. But the vision of beauty was marred. There was a harshness to her eyes, he thought, and few signs of womanly softness. All was angular, crisp and precise, not comforting. She was shrewish, if nothing else.

'Lordings, you honour my home with your presence. I am only sorry that I don't think I will be able to help you overmuch. How may I serve you?'

'Master Henry, we are most grateful for your gracious welcome,' the coroner began. He wore an unaccustomed look of wariness, as though rather nervous of how to broach a difficult subject.

Baldwin decided to save him any embarrassment. It was a curious word to apply to the coroner, but clearly the man was shamed by the reference he must make to the woman's infidelity. 'This is about the matter of the dead man, you will understand,' he said.

'Of course.'

'We do not have a good understanding of the affair as yet,' Baldwin said. 'We are trying to understand what people here in the vill may have felt about the dead man – and his friend. We have heard that others saw the pair of them in Crediton. Did you?'

'Me?' Henry asked. 'No. I was in Crediton yesterday, but came back early this morning, and didn't see any strangers so far as I know. Mind, I was working in my storehouse in the town, not wandering the streets!'

'That is good,' Baldwin said. 'Tell me, what kind of business do you run?'

'I have a number of little ventures, but I sometimes dabble in purchasing wine in Exeter and send it to different taverns and inns. I have some good Guyennois wines just arrived.'

'I see.' Baldwin considered. 'I have heard that you have experienced troubles with the church. Their sheep?'

'Aye, yes. The black-hearted devils let their flock ruin my crop – and then refused to repay me for the damage!'

'And I think your wife was insulted by the canon two days ago,' Baldwin said.

The scene of that morning blazed with a greater clarity on his mind. He remembered seeing the two men approaching him, the flash of this woman running away from the road, his initial thought that others too would keenly avoid the likes of a pardoner and his companion – and then he realized his error. The surprise made him almost gasp.

Henry appeared not to have noticed. 'She did? Oh, it was him splashed her, was it? He's a pleasant enough fellow. Not the brightest. Lousy negotiator, that I know, for if I weren't so honest I could have gulled him out of a barrel in every ten I sold him.'

'You still have dealings with the church?'

'I'd be a fool not to. But the peas are ruined.'

'Sir, perhaps your wife could show me the crop?' Baldwin suggested. 'I have some little influence with Dean Peter. Perhaps I could . . . ?'

'Yes, by all means. I can show you myself,' Henry said.

'There is no need. You stay here and answer my good friends' questions, and we shall be away from you all the sooner,' Baldwin said smoothly, and was through the door in a moment.

'They're over here,' Agatha said, lifting her skirts as she passed over the muddy paths.

'Have you been carrying on many affairs?' Baldwin asked.

'I don't know what you mean,' she said, but now her face was colourless.

'You saw me that day when the pardoner and his triacleur appeared, didn't you? You saw me and fled rather than let me see you. You and a man in clerical robes. A canon . . . It was Arthur, wasn't it?'

'What of it?' The colour had returned to her now, in bright scarlet at her cheeks. It made her look as daunting as an empress.

'You are having an affair with Hob, I know. However, now I am forced to wonder whether you are also having an affair with the canon too.'

Perhaps that was what Peter Clifford had meant when he said that his young canon was tortured by temptations. This woman had decided to ensnare him too. There were women with voracious sexual appetites, Baldwin knew.

'I . . . I cannot speak without you twisting my words . . .'

'I care not about your affairs,' Baldwin hissed. 'All I wish to know is what happened to the pardoner in that room. Do you know who could have had anything to do with it?'

'No! Why should I?'

'Because Hob thought he saw your husband outside his tavern last night when he was pushing the others through his door.'

'But Henry wouldn't have hurt that man . . .'

'He would have wanted to hurt Hob, wouldn't he? And

how better to do that than to leave all assuming that Hob had killed another in his tavern?'

'Henry wouldn't do that. He's too weak to hurt a man anyway, but if he were to try it, he'd stab a man in the chest while looking into his eyes. But I don't think he ever would. He is the softest-hearted man I've known.'

As she spoke, the servant Baldwin had seen at her side in the vill came out and stared around him.

'He is looking for me,' she said, and there was a tone of fear in her voice.

'What of it? He's a servant.'

'I must go!'

'Why should she be so scared of a servant?' Simon asked as they walked back to the vill.

'Perhaps he suspects her of adultery – or knows of it?' Baldwin wondered. 'He may blackmail her.'

'Did she admit it, then?' the coroner said.

'She did not deny the affair with the tavern-keeper, but she was emphatic about not carrying on with the canon.' Baldwin frowned as he realized that he had not asked what she was doing with the canon in Crediton that day as they ran away. Clearly there was a secret matter being conducted there, whether or not there was a relationship.

'Hardly makes her a saint,' the coroner commented gruffly. His own wife had died some years before, far too young, and he still sorely missed her.

'What of Henry? Did you gain an inkling as to whether he had been at the vill?' Baldwin asked.

'He did not deny it,' Simon said. 'But there was no sign of rage, only a quiet introspection. It was just as though he had some other grievance. He didn't strike me as a raging cuckold – did he you, Sir Richard?'

'No. Just a businessman with a problem to solve. Who doesn't have them now?'

Baldwin nodded.

'All of which gives us little help in this inquest,' Simon said.

'Correct. True, it is hard to understand who may have wished to commit this murder,' Baldwin admitted.

'Surely this matter of the woman and her lover must have something to do with it,' the coroner said.

'I am inclined to the view that the servant is more guilty than she,' Baldwin said. He mused. It was a strange fear on her face when she saw the servant coming to seek her.

'Should we go back to talk to him?' Simon said.

'If we do, and he has some sort of hold over her, it would make trouble for her without reason,' Baldwin said.

'She mayhap deserves it,' the coroner said.

'Perhaps there has been enough passion already in this case,' Baldwin said. 'I would not care to learn that she has been killed by a jealous husband.'

'Hah! That woman reminds me of a joke,' the coroner said. 'A man was talking to a fellow in a tavern and asked if he was married. "Aye, and not once but three times," was the reply. "Oho! How so?" "Because all three hanged themselves from my old apple tree," the man said. The first was quiet a moment, and then asked, "Would you consider selling me a cutting of this tree?" Eh? Ha! And perhaps poor Henry should have a similar tree in his own garden for that harridan.'

'Do not judge her too harshly, Sir Richard,' Baldwin said. 'You were fortunate to be happily married. Who can say but that their marriage is unhappy? I have seen too many women made miserable in constraining relationships.'

'So have I,' the coroner growled. 'But that doesn't excuse a woman whoring.'

'Whom do you suspect, then? The Welshman?'

Sir Richard was about to respond when the three men were stopped by screams from behind them. 'What in God's name ... ?' the coroner blurted, but then he was already running back the way they had all come, Simon and Baldwin close behind him.

They had to run a matter of only two hundred yards, but to Simon it felt like a thousand. Once he had been fit enough to walk thirty miles in a day over Dartmoor, but now he was older, heavier and more prone to sitting on a horse.

It felt as though his lungs must burst as he pelted along, the rough, stone-strewn surface of the track threatening his ankles, their sharpened edges cutting into the soles of his cheap boots, and he was aware of a hissing in his ears, a heat rising to his face, a fading power in his legs. He had to wipe the sweat away from his face as he went, but then to his relief he saw the woman running towards them, and he could bend, take a gulp of air, rest a fist on his thigh and catch his breath.

'Help! Murder! Murder and robbery!' she was crying as she came.

Baldwin and Sir Richard exchanged a look. There was no blood on her, so far as Baldwin could see, and he held up a hand to calm her. 'Mistress Copplestone, what is the matter? We returned as soon as we heard your plea for help, but what is the matter?'

'Henry! He's dead! Edward killed him and ran!'

She collapsed sobbing, and Simon stayed with her while the others bolted back to the house. Gradually her panicky panting calmed, and Simon could persuade her to rise with him and begin to walk back to her house. On the way they found Baldwin returning.

'The good coroner will remain until we have the hue and cry come to seek the murderer. Come, Mistress Agatha, do you have a friend in the vill here?'

'None! None at all!'

'Then at the least we may as well install you in the tavern. You will be able to drink some wine there.'

'What has happened?' Simon asked.

'It was our servant.'

'You were scared of him earlier, I saw,' Baldwin said.

'Yes! He knew of my . . . with Hob. You know.'

'You feared he would tell your master?'

'Yes, of course I did. I thought he would denounce me unless I did all he wanted.'

'Of course. Tell me, though. Huw was convinced that you were not with him in Crediton when he saw you.'

She reddened, but then her chin rose and she met his gaze. 'No. It wasn't him. I was with Arthur, the canon from the church.'

Baldwin shook his head. 'You did seek to—'

'No!' she snapped. 'I was not seeking an affair with him. My husband's servant made me go to see the canon and bring him to my husband's warehouse. There Arthur and Edward were having dealings. Edward bought the church's produce and sold it on to his and Arthur's profit, using my husband's contacts. It impoverished Henry's business, but what might I do? I could only do as Edward told me. I had no choice.'

Baldwin said nothing. It explained much. If this Arthur was conducting business to his own benefit, and submitting to the temptation of money, that could well be what Dean Peter had alluded to. And it explained why the dean was reluctant to compensate Henry and Agatha for losses in their garden if he thought that Henry was already robbing him. And why should he think that Arthur was collaborating with a mere servant? If the dean had suspicions, it was more likely that they would focus on the owner of the house where the goods were being traded.

'I didn't want to help him rob the church,' she said with a little, quiet voice.

'Let us take you to the tavern,' Simon said gently.

Later, they were sitting about a fire in the tavern together while they waited to hear about the posse sent after Edward.

'Could the servant have killed the pardoner?' Simon wondered.

'It would be a cleaner end to the story if he was guilty of all,' Baldwin said.

'Either him or Agatha's husband,' Simon said. 'He was seen here.'

'I cannot forget the man's hand in the fire,' Sir Richard said. 'Why would either of them do that?'

'If a man was disgusted with the actions of the pardoner and thought that the bones were genuine, he may have done that in punishment,' Simon mused.

'What, a hand has touched something sacred so it should be cut off?' Baldwin said with a smile.

'Why not, Baldwin?' Simon said. 'Think of it. The Gospel says "If thine eye offend thee, pluck it out", doesn't it? There are some who'd think the pardoner was an offensive man who was polluting incorruptible relics.'

'Old bones in a pardoner's hands are unlikely to cause so much offence,' Baldwin scoffed.

The coroner was less sure. 'God can give miracles from such things, Baldwin. There are many pieces of Christ's cross throughout Christendom. I once heard a friar say that all are from the True Cross. Even though there is more wood there than would build many such crosses, it matters not. It's like feeding the thousands with a couple of fish and all were full afterwards. He can make things like this happen. These relics may be as potent as any other. If someone thought that, he could have taken off John's hand for the insult he gave to relics. And then taken them for safekeeping.'

'Perhaps so. In which case, who was it?' Baldwin asked sharply. 'There is no evidence to suggest who could have done it.'

'Surely the most religious man?' Coroner Richard said. 'He is plainly the man with the most incentive. And offended by the pardoner.'

'Very well,' Baldwin sighed. 'But he seems so mild-mannered. What sort of a man would . . . ?'

He stopped suddenly, closed his eyes and shook his head.

'What is it, man?' Sir Richard asked.

'I am a fool!'

They found the priest in his chapel, bent almost double before the altar. Under the vill's pall lay the body of the pardoner, wrapped in linen.

He heard them enter but gave them no acknowledge-ment, merely remaining with his hands clasped, until he nodded briskly to himself and stood.

Turning to face them, he looked them over carefully and made his way along the empty hall to the door. Departing by it, he stood waiting for them outside.

'A shame to have no one to stand by the body over the night. I must pay one of the poorer parishioners to sit up with the man.'

'He won't care much now,' Coroner Richard said.

'How do you know?' the priest asked. 'He may be waiting

even now in Purgatory, hoping that someone will sit in vigil and pray for him. God knows, he had enough to pray for.'

'Why do you say that?' Baldwin asked.

'Isn't it obvious? A dealer in trinkets, in false promises of pardon, in fake relics. What would you think of his chances?'

'You hate men like him, don't you?' Coroner Richard said.

'I hate the things they do. Like building up people's hopes by lies. That is a cruel and evil thing to do.'

'You were at the tavern last night,' Simon said. 'Did you return to kill him?'

'Me?' Father William looked at him.

The coroner grunted. 'You know as well as I that, if you did, it would not be to your detriment. You can claim benefit of clergy, entirely safe in the knowledge that you would never face a rope. There is nothing to prevent you confessing.'

'I think any confessions should be made to my confessor,' Father William said.

'He repelled you, didn't he?' Baldwin said. 'That is why you happily shield the man who killed him.'

'Do I?'

'Where are the bones?'

'Perhaps I do not know.'

'Oh, you know, Father,' Baldwin said. 'You may hate men who deal in false pardons, but you'd be keen to look after the relics in case they were genuine.'

'Of course I would – if I knew where they were.'

'You do,' Baldwin said. 'And I think you know who killed the pardoner.'

'Why?'

'Oh, it was a discussion we were having a little while

ago, my friends and I. The good coroner said that you were the clear suspect in the matter, because you made your hatred of the dead man so plain. And that struck me. Because, of course, only you could do that safely. You have the benefit of clergy, so you are secure from serious punishment. No one will hang you.'

'What of it?'

'So you sought to divert us from the man who was guilty.'

'I don't know what you are talking about.'

'Who, though?' Baldwin continued. 'I can only assume that the man was the one with whom you were talking when we spoke to you. You sought to move our attention from him and on to yourself. And we were speaking with you and Ulric, weren't we?'

'He has nothing to do with this. He was an—'

'What? An innocent? Even though he murdered a man? You have a curious attitude to one who would kill an innocent for no reason.'

'He had reasons,' the priest said with chilling certainty.

'And they were good enough to justify letting him go free while we arrested and possibly executed another innocent man?'

'Oh, what do you know of such matters? You have no idea what Ulric went through when he was in Wales. You know he lost his only son there? You prate on about innocence – what about his own boy?'

'What of his boy? The man he killed isn't Welsh. This was no revenge attack on a man who represented the fighters who killed his son. This was a mere pardoner minding his own business, man,' the coroner rasped. He stepped forward, and Baldwin thought for a moment he was about to punch the priest.

'Of course he wasn't – but he had the bones, you fool!'

'What do you mean?' Baldwin asked, restraining the coroner with a hand.

'The bones of King Arthur! The Welsh king who would rise and conquer England!'

They retired to a bench outside the tavern, and Hob brought jugs of cider to refresh them all as the priest reluctantly told them the full story.

'He was in the tavern bragging about the blasted things. A handful of bones, he said, but worth a king's realm, if they were to get into the wrong hands. Apparently he was there at Abbey Dore, when a piece of the abbey floor was taken up. There were many there, because the abbey had been given something to install there, and they wanted to give it a suitable location. No one thought much of it, so John said. But then the workmen brought up this box, apparently. Inside were bones, and it was nothing to him. He thought that they were just a set of human remains, nothing more.'

'What did he do?' Baldwin asked, although he knew the answer.

'When it was dark, he went inside and stole a handful of them. It's what pardoners do, as you know well enough. If there's something they can get for nothing, they'll take it. And so he did. And it caused his death.'

Father William shifted uncomfortably. 'He told us all about the bones that night in the tavern. He hadn't known anything about them, just grabbed what he could and made off, back this way. Somehow he heard that he should beat a retreat, because these bones are those of Arthur, and there were many in Wales who would seek to recover them and kill whoever might have desecrated them.'

'And Ulric did their bidding for them?' Baldwin said.

'Sweet Jesu! Are you so stupid, man?' William spat. 'I am sorry, Sir Knight,' he added quickly, seeing Baldwin's expression change. 'Forgive my words. But no, Ulric killed the man to rescue us from the bones! The pardoner was anxious about them, and even suggested that he should take them back to the grave.'

'Where they would pose an everlasting threat?'

'Exactly. If the bones are kept separate, how could this Welsh Arthur return to life and rescue Wales from the English, rightful king? No, the only sensible route was to rescue the bones.'

'Ulric went in there, took the bones, and all to protect the country?' the coroner rumbled doubtfully.

'He sought to prevent the risk of another war,' Father William said. 'He has lost his own son. He didn't want to see another family lose theirs.'

'That is fine – but why cut off the man's hand?' Simon demanded.

'Ulric is religious. How else would you treat the hand of a thief who had polluted the burial place of an important man?'

'So he cut it off to burn it?' Baldwin said. 'Where is he now?'

'I don't know. He has fled the vill. You won't find him.'

'You underestimate the authority of a Keeper of the King's Peace,' Baldwin said. 'What of Henry? We have heard that he was in the vill that night too. Hob thought he saw him.'

'He was a sad man. He feared that his wife was a harlot. Perhaps he was here to see if Hob was entertaining her? I don't know.'

## Saturday before the Feast of
## St John the Baptist,* Sandford

It was only the middle of the following day when the
murderer of Henry was brought back. His arm was broken,
his face bloodied, but he confessed to his crimes before
Baldwin and Sir Richard.

'The church can afford to lose a little grain, some barley
and wine. I wasn't taking it on my own. Why shouldn't I
do it? I saw how to take it, and was bold enough to try.'

Baldwin said: 'Your accomplice was a canon.'

'Aye, the milksop brat Arthur. Pathetic churl, he is. Scared
of his own shadow much of the time. But he was happy
to take the money. He brought sacks of grain, barrels of
wine and other goods straight to me, and I sold them on
our account through my master's business. We took the
money in our purses.'

'And you forced your mistress to help you?' Sir Richard
said.

'Aye. And did she tell you why? It was because—'

Sir Richard stepped forward quickly, and his gloved fist
swept backhanded across the man's face. 'I won't have you
insulting the poor widow only a day after you killed her
man! Be silent, dog!'

As the semi-conscious man was dragged away, Sir Richard
averted his gaze from Simon and Baldwin. 'Can't have the
poor woman's name dragged through the mud.'

'Indeed not!' Baldwin said, adding: 'And what use would
it serve to have Henry shown to be a cuckold now he is
dead?'

---

* Saturday 22 June 1325

## Morrow of the Feast of
## St John the Baptist,* Sandford

It was three more days before the men returned with the body.

'We didn't want to have to kill him, Sir Baldwin, but he wouldn't surrender. I had three men against him, but he wouldn't submit, no matter how much we demanded that he yield.'

The constable was a short, rather slender youth with the black hair and eyes of a Celt, but now he stood with a broad-brimmed hat twisting in his fingers as he told his tale. 'I didn't want this,' he finished miserably.

'He fought?'

'On foot with only a knife. All of us had staves. We had to do something, so I gave the order, and while two penned him in I thrust at him with mine.'

Baldwin nodded as he stood beside the coroner staring down at the dead reeve. It was astonishing how much damage an oaken staff could do to a man's face. The staff had been thrust hard, and the weight of the oak had driven into Ulric's face at the side, but had slipped into his temple. It had crushed the thin bones. All the side of his head to a point over his ear was bloodied, the skull fractured. 'He would have felt little, friend,' he said.

'But why didn't he just come back with us? Or seek sanctuary in a church? There was no need for him to die.'

'He sought to protect us all,' Baldwin said and sighed. He weighed the little purse in his hand. The contents rattled almost comfortingly, like ivory. 'With your leave, coroner?' he asked.

* Tuesday 25 June 1325

'Nothing to do with me. I'm only the coroner.' Sir Richard smiled.

'Then, Huw, *here*!' Baldwin said, and threw them at their guardian. 'And may you find your journey homewards is easier than the one here. Godspeed.'

## Thursday after the Feast of St John the Baptist,* The Church of the Holy Cross and the Mother of Him Who Died Thereon, Crediton

'So you left him to go on his way?' Dean Peter said.

'Yes. What else might we do?' Baldwin said.

'It is probably for the best. And in the meantime, as you suggested, my good canon, Arthur, is to be left in a cell to contemplate his own part in this sorry tale.'

'He confessed?'

'As soon as he heard that his accomplice had told the full story, yes. It took a little while. He has defrauded the church of moneys ever since he took up his duties. A sad man, indeed.'

'At least you know now that Henry himself was innocent.'

'I suppose so. I admit, however, old friend, that I am surprised you permitted the bones to be sent back to Wales. Did you not fear that they may indeed be those of this Welsh figure?'

'Arthur? Nay, Peter. Why, the real Arthur was found at Glastonbury by the old king, wasn't he? I remember that.'

'No. Not found. The bones were discovered – oh, over

---

* Thursday 27 June 1325

a hundred years ago, certainly. The old king, Edward of blessed memory, took those bones and moved them to the new shrine fifty years ago, so that they could be properly revered.' Peter peered into his goblet and sighed. 'But the men who rally to a saint often don't know the precise antecedents of the relics they possess. Who can say that the bones found originally were still the same as those collected up by King Edward I and reinterred in the choir of the abbey? Who can say the first bones were truly those of King Arthur?'

'True. But I think it is enough to know that a man's bones will be reunited. It may not matter to his soul, but it can do no harm either. Or so I hope and believe anyway,' Baldwin said.

'I only hope Huw makes the journey homewards safely.'

But Huw was not going to return home. Not now. By stages he crossed the countryside to Exeter, where he stayed for two days, walking the streets and thinking about the bones.

The chapel was no longer safe. It would be dangerous to return there with the bones now that he had told others of it. He couldn't in truth remember whether he had ever mentioned the precise location of the chapel to the coroner and his friends, but the fear was there that he had. And if news of the bones of King Arthur came to the ears of those who might seek to destroy any hopes of the Welsh rising against their English oppressors, they could too easily be taken.

He could, of course, take them back to Abbey Dore, but if he did there was no certainty that he would be able to secrete them inside safely. Before, he had Owain, but that had been almost four years ago, and in God's name Owain had looked frail enough then. What if he was dead? There was no one else to whom he could give the bones in the abbey. He knew no one there. The alternative was to find somewhere else to place the bones.

Many cities had their own places to store bones. Here in Exeter there was a great cemetery by the cathedral – but the bones would be sure to be dug up. The cathedral had a monopoly of burials for the city – the graveyard was already crowded, and bones were regularly dug up by the sexton and removed to the big Charnel Chapel near the west door. Huw couldn't bear to think of his bones being separated. They must be kept together.

On the third day he finally came to a decision and walked from the city on the old road to Bristol. Five miles from Exeter he came to a large open field, and here he paused, looking about him. A hill rose on his left, further to his right he recognized a line of trees, and he nodded to himself.

'Not long now,' he muttered to the soft leather package about his neck.

He trudged along the tracks until he had passed a vill which was familiar, and then turned west, down to a stream. Here at the ford, he smiled and grunted to himself. There was a thick mess of brambles, and beneath them a hole such as a vixen raising cubs might make. Carefully he reached into the hole until he felt the sharp edge of the box, almost at the extent of his arm's reach. Before long he was digging with his hands, hauling away the soil which he had piled up on the day when he had first seen the pardoner and taken the decision to hide the bones in order that he might rescue those John had stolen.

Later, sitting at a fire in woods not far from the roadway, he opened the box and reverently laid the leather purse inside.

'My king, I am sorry,' he said. 'I am weak and stupid.

I cannot take you home to Wales, and I can't get you to Dore. I have been too foolish. I have to find somewhere else where you will be safe.'

The choices were too confusing. That night he dined on alexanders with some beans he'd brought from Exeter, and chewed on some rough, dried meat that tasted rank but was better on his empty belly than his watery pottage. He curled about the box, desperate, and passed the night in fitful sleep.

But as morning rose he was filled with a firm resolution. He would take the bones to another land where they would be safe. The danger to the bones lay in the English threat. He would take them to another Celtic land – to Cornwall. There must be somewhere there where he could place them and ensure that they were safe. He knew little of Cornwall, but there was a castle at Tintagel, he knew.

He would take the bones to Tintagel. There must be somewhere safe for them there. He had heard of a place just along the coast – Trevenna? There was a small church there dedicated to St Materiana, so he had heard. He would try there. Surely there would be a safe place to hide the bones in a small parish church like that, he thought.

# ACT FOUR

## London, 1606

*I had never seen the royal animals in the Tower of London before. Perhaps I was not curious enough to want to watch the lions and lionesses or the single tiger and the porcupine or the wolf and the eagle. Or maybe it was that I was reluctant to pay the entrance fee of three pennies, which was three times what it would cost to buy a standing place at our very own Globe theatre. Or else it was simply that, like many inhabitants of our great city, I could not stir myself to go out of my way to see its great sights. Leave that to the visitors.*

*Now that I was here, against my will, I could not see the beasts, but I could hear and smell them. I was in one of the compartments of the Lion Tower meant for animal use. More of a cave or a cell than a chamber, it smelled rank. In the next-door cell was a body, not animal but human and supposedly murdered. The body I had recognized. Likewise the man who was slumped in a corner, his head in his hands. On either side of him stood a keeper whose more usual job would be to guard the lions and the tiger but who now found himself watching over a murderer, cudgel in hand. But it did not appear that the slumped man was going to attempt an escape. Instead he looked up at me and said: 'I did not do this thing, Nick. I am innocent, I swear.'*

# I

It was the first time I'd caught William Shakespeare in the act of writing. Why I say 'caught' I don't know, since it makes WS sound like a felon. But he was always secretive about his work and most reluctant to discuss it. Which was the reason his request that I should call on him in his lodgings in Silver Street came as a surprise. This was his lair, his private place.

Shakespeare was sitting at a desk by an open window. Once he'd glanced around in a distracted way to see who was standing in his doorway and given the slightest of nods, he said: 'Ah, Nick, I'll only be a . . . make yourself . . .'

I never discovered what I was supposed to make myself since, instead of telling me, WS performed a vague flourish with his quill and then reapplied himself to the sheet in front of him. There were no sounds apart from the birdsong in the garden below – the casement was open; it was a sunny morning in May – and the small scraping noises as his pen moved across the paper.

I was interested to see William Shakespeare at work, I'll admit that. Privileged too, maybe, for by this time WS was reckoned to be the finest playwright in London, and not just by us players at the Globe theatre. I'd heard that he wrote with great fluency, rarely pausing to blot his work or cross through a line, and from what I now saw it was true. His pen moved with the regularity of a tailor's needle. Not wanting to pry or hang over his shoulder, I picked up a book from a pile on a table and flicked through the pages. It was a translation from the Latin of Plutarch's *Lives,* and my eye fell on a description of Julius Caesar being murdered in the Senate. Some years before, WS had written his play of Caesar's death at the hands of Brutus and the rest.

I became absorbed enough in what I was reading to be unaware that WS had laid down his pen and turned around to look at me. 'What do you read?' he said. 'Plutarch, is it?'

'The death of Caesar. How Julius falls at the foot of Pompey's statue with his three-and-twenty stab wounds. Do you suppose they counted them?'

'Someone might have done.'

'Or the figure was plucked at random out of the air,' I said.

'Twenty-three knife wounds is a plausible number,' said Shakespeare. 'And it spreads the guilt of the killing, spreads it so thin that no one could say for sure who struck the fatal blow.'

'What are you working on, William?' I said. Since it was he who had asked me to visit him on this fine May morning, I reckoned I was entitled to a query or two, for all his secrecy. 'You are writing more about the Romans?'

'No, my subject now is the matter of Britain.'

I must have looked bemused, for WS said: 'Arthur, King of Britain.'

'Oh, him.'

'Yes, him. As well as Merlin and Queen Guinevere and Mordred, and the Knights of the Round Table. The stories about them are known as the matter of Britain. You can read the account in Thomas Malory. It is a good subject because the king – our King James, I mean – has an interest in Arthur.'

This was true. On his accession, James had wanted himself styled King of Great Britain and to be seen, like Arthur perhaps, as a monarch embracing the whole circle of our island. So it was typically shrewd of WS to choose a subject which would appeal to our new ruler.

Now Shakespeare reached for an object on the far side

of his desk, and I thought he was going to hand me another book. But when he gestured for me to take it, I was surprised, uneasy even, to see that it was a bone. A long bone, a human bone I presumed, part of a limb. I turned it over in my hands as if the owner's identity might have been inscribed somewhere on it.

'Do you know whose it is?' I said, returning the object. A stupid question maybe, but it was for want of anything else to say. I noticed that WS handled the bone with more care than I had done, almost cradling it in his arms before returning it to its position on the desk.

'I know whose it might be. But I am forgetting my manners, Nick. Make yourself easy in that chair and I will get us both some refreshment.'

He gave me a generous glass of sack before pouring one for himself and returning to the desk to sit down. His own chair looked less comfortable than the one I was on, but there was nowhere else to sit in the room. A silence followed. WS's rented chamber was at the back of the house and so shut away from the noises of Silver Street. I wondered whether he'd asked his landlord for a quiet room for the sake of his work. I glanced around. Against the wall opposite the window was a canopied four-poster bed with the curtains drawn shut. A fireplace with ornate figures carved on the chimney-piece occupied the side of the room between bed and window. It was a better place than my own lodgings south of the river, but not so much better.

'My brother discovered that bone,' said Shakespeare suddenly. 'Edmund gave it to me.'

'You've never mentioned Edmund before,' I said. In fact I don't think WS had referred to any siblings in my hearing. I did not know much more than that he was married to a wife called Anne, who remained in Stratford-upon-Avon, and that he had fathered a few grown children, who might be anywhere. Shakespeare was a private man.

'Edmund is my youngest brother. He is younger than you, Nick. He was a late bloom in my parents' lives.'

WS looked away for a moment towards the open casement. I couldn't tell what was running through his head but the ironic way in which he'd mentioned the 'late bloom' suggested he didn't have any very high opinion of this brother. So it proved.

'I do not know Edmund . . . not well. Soon after he was born, I married and then I . . . moved away from my birthplace and so came eventually to London,' said WS. Unusually for him, he was picking a path through his words as if uncertain how much to reveal. 'But I know that Edmund was a trial to my mother and my late father, God rest his soul, even if he was never a trouble to me. In Stratford he had the reputation of a scapegrace. Now he has followed my own course of more than twenty years ago and arrived in this town.'

'To be a player?'

'Yes.'

'A player with us? With the King's Men?'

'I fear so.'

'Is that so bad, William? Wanting to be a player with the King's Men?'

'It is bad for Edmund. He does not have the, ah, discipline to be a player anywhere.'

Considering the way in which most players behaved, at least during their younger days, I thought this was an odd comment. Yes, you needed discipline to learn your lines and, unless you were treated indulgently, you needed discipline not to overact or play the fool on stage (less because the audience wouldn't like it and more because of the reaction from your fellows). But outside the playhouse one could go around drinking and swearing and whoring, within the customary limits.

'I can see what you're thinking, Nick,' said WS. 'What need has a young player of discipline except in the matter of his lines and so on?'

I nodded. He'd read my mind. Not very difficult perhaps.

'You kicked a ball around when you were a boy, Nick? A ball that was made of a pig's bladder, inflated?'

I nodded again.

'They can endure plenty of knocks, those bladders; they are strong, yet they are hollow inside. Any man wishing to become a player should have something of the pig's bladder in him. He should contain plenty of wind in order to mouth his lines but be tough enough on the exterior to withstand the kicks of fortune. I mean those kicks that are particular to our craft, a jeering audience, a playhouse closed on account of the plague, an ankle broken during a sword fight on stage.'

'Players are hollow too,' I said, falling in with the spirit of WS's analogy, 'because they can be filled with others' words and natures.'

'Yes, we are everyman – and no man too.'

And then William Shakespeare laughed, as if to rebuke himself for such a high-flown sentiment. 'My brother Edmund doesn't have that pig's bladder quality. If he's disappointed or frustrated, he will lash out with his fists or go and drown his sorrows in the nearest tavern. If one of the groundlings insulted him, he'd probably jump down and clout him. That's bad for business. To say nothing of being bad for Edmund. He'll end up in the Clink.'

None of this sounded sufficient to prevent Edmund from trying to make his name on the stage. There have been undisciplined, impulsive players before now. Some of them have even served a turn in gaol.

'Can you discourage your brother from becoming a player?'

'Whatever I say will only make him more determined.'

'Then surely one of the other Globe shareholders could turn him down? You need have no part in it.'

'Edmund would see through that. He'd know the decision was mine. It would be cowardly and, besides, there are obligations within a family which have to be acknowledged. No, the only course is to get Edmund to see for himself that the stage is not meant for him. It will take time. We shall have to accommodate him by giving him small parts like any fledgling player.'

'I began as an ambassador in *Hamlet*,' I said. 'I was an ambassador from England, arriving at the end of the action.'

'I remember your ambassador well,' said WS, which was what I'd been hoping he would say. But he was softening me up, for his next words were: 'I'd like you to keep a gentle watch on my brother, Nick. Have an eye on him backstage, accompany him to the tavern and . . . other places if necessary.'

'Why me?'

'Because I trust you and because I cannot think of who else to turn to in our company. You are older than Edmund and have a shrewd head on your shoulders.'

I don't think I'd been called shrewd before, certainly not by William Shakespeare, so this was pleasing. But I must have looked doutbful, for he continued: 'You were once fresh up from the country and you learned the hard way about this city and its snares. Edmund is as ready to be taken in as most newcomers but he might accept advice or a warning from you which he'd reject from me. I don't mean that you should be responsible if things, ah, go badly. If Edmund chooses to ignore you, so be it. But at least you can whisper in his ear that that friendly group of card players in the corner of the Goat and Monkey are coney-catchers . . .'

'. . . or that the new French girl at the Mitre will give you a dose of the pox,' I said.

'You've got the idea,' said WS, suddenly finding something of great interest in the glass of sack he was holding.

'And how is King Arthur involved in all of this? You said your brother found that bone for you.'

'Edmund tells me that he is a reformed man, no longer the scapegrace of Stratford. He wants to stand well with me and, knowing that I am writing about the matter of Britain, he brought me this relic of Arthur. Like a dog acting against nature and wanting to please its master, he gave up a bone, you might say.'

Since Shakespeare disliked dogs, feared them even, this was far from being a flattering remark.

'Where did your brother get it?' I said. 'Is it really Arthur's?'

'From one of the bookshops near St Paul's. Edmund says he was searching for books that might help me in my labours and no doubt telling the seller how he was kin to a well-known playwright whose latest piece is about Arthur of Britain. The shopkeeper had no texts on the subject but offered him this bone instead. He claimed on his mother's grave that it was a true bone. Edmund said he almost emptied his purse to purchase it for me. I think he meant well, but anyone who was not kin to him might call him gullible.'

'But you don't call him gullible,' I said, 'not on this occasion.'

'Why, no,' said WS. He put down his glass and picked up the arm- or leg-bone once more. I noticed that he handled it with the same care as before. 'Tell me, Nick, when you touched this, did you . . . feel anything?'

'Just a bone. It made me feel uneasy, no more. But then I didn't know whose it is, whose it is *supposed* to be, rather.'

'Perhaps that's it. Edmund informed me of the nature of his find before giving me this relic. When I put my fingers on it, I experienced a queer kind of blankness, as though I had walked out of doors and into a mist. It was neither pleasant nor especially unpleasant. But was the sensation produced by Edmund's words or was it some property of the bone itself? For nothing is either good or bad, you know, but thinking makes it so.'

He might have gone on in this vein – an abstracted look had entered his large brown eyes – but he was interrupted by a knock outside. WS barely had time to say 'Come in' when the door opened. I turned around in my seat and saw a figure standing there. Without being told, I knew who it must be. Edmund Shakespeare, WS's scapegrace younger brother.

# II

A couple of days later I was sitting with Edmund Shakespeare in the Mermaid tavern on Bread Street near St Paul's. Although it attracted poets and other scribblers, the Mermaid was a well-run house with a reputation for good fish and wine. It was the place where William Shakespeare's envious rival Ben Jonson, sometimes held court. Jonson haunted the tavern partly because of its food and drink – he reckoned himself a man of refined taste – but mostly because it was half a world away from the common drinking dens like the Goat and Monkey south of the river.

Ben Jonson wasn't in session at the Mermaid today, but Edmund and I were awaiting the arrival of another playwright, Martin Barton, who was eager to meet Shakespeare's brother. Barton was no friend of mine but, encountering him earlier that day, he'd badgered me for an introduction when I let slip that I was meeting Edmund once our playhouse business was done. It was characteristic of the man that he should now keep us waiting. The wait wasn't too onerous, however, since Edmund and I were sitting side by side on a bench and occupying ourselves with a pile of oysters and a flask of wine.

During the past two days I'd been doing as William requested, keeping a 'gentle watch' over his brother. Because of WS's position and authority as a senior member of the Globe shareholders, he had easily procured a role for Edmund at the theatre. Not yet as a minor player but as a general dogsbody, running errands for the book-man or assisting Sam, our little limping doorkeeper. Maybe WS hoped to convince Edmund that the playhouse was really a dreary place in which to work and that he'd be better off back home in Stratford-upon-Avon. If so, it was a forlorn hope, for Edmund was wide-eyed about being in London. He'd have been happy sweeping up the draff from a tavern floor. And he wasn't sweeping up in an alehouse but helping behind the scenes in a playhouse where there is always a touch of magic, even among the wooden swords and the paste jewellery.

The quick picture that WS had painted of his brother – a gullible individual who was too impulsive, too undisciplined for the stage – didn't fit with my first or second impressions of the man. Edmund had some physical similarities to his much older sibling. He was slight but tall and wiry, and his eyes had the same large gaze beneath a tall brow. He did not possess the same easy manners as

WS, the almost courtly style that enabled the playwright to be comfortable anywhere. But then Edmund was fresh up from the provinces, as WS had once been and as I had been too. We've all got to start somewhere. Certainly I had not yet seen any indication of the rapid temper I'd been warned about. Nor had Edmund shown signs of falling prey to any card-playing coney-catchers. But there was a woman in the picture. At least there was one in the Mermaid, a pretty piece who was hanging about his ears when I arrived and whom Edmund daffed away, explaining that he wanted male company. I knew no more about her than that she was called Polly or Dolly and had dark ringlets of hair under a pretty hat and large breasts partly concealed by her dress. Obediently she withdrew, and Edmund and I started gabbing.

I'd go so far as to say that I was enjoying his company more than expected. Or, to be absolutely honest, I was enjoying playing the experienced citizen of London and the senior player.

'You'll come with me to visit this fellow Davy Owen, then, Nick?' said Edmund Shakespeare. He reached forward to help himself to an opened oyster from the pile on a platter in front of us. He tilted his head and I watched his Adam's apple bob as it slid down his gullet.

'Yes, I'll come with you. I'm curious.'

I *was* curious too. Davy Owen was the bookseller from whom Edmund had bought the bone – King Arthur's limb – to present to his brother as some sort of peace offering. Now it appeared as though the St Paul's vendor possessed other items relating to that legendary ruler which he might wish to dispose of. Or so he had told Edmund. Usually I would have dismissed the whole thing as a confidence trick. But William Shakespeare's odd belief in the Arthurian relic that lay on his desk – the queer sensation he had experienced when first touching it – was enough to make me want to see any further items for myself. And if it was a confidence trick, then it would be as well for me to accompany Edmund to St Paul's yard and discourage him from wasting the cash that he'd received as an advance for his menial work at the Globe playhouse.

'You are a curious man altogether, Nick,' said Edmund.

'I am?'

'Curious about my brother William, I mean. All those questions you've been asking about him growing up in Stratford.'

Questions? I suppose so. Had I been asking too many questions? To cover my discomfort, I reached for an oyster myself and gulped it down. I'll admit I was interested in WS's life. But there was such a gap of years between William and Edmund that the latter did not have much direct knowledge of his famous brother. However, he did possess a stock of stories which had been preserved in the family and was happy to pass them on, perhaps because several of them showed WS in a less-than-respectable light. Even so, Edmund had a high regard for his brother. That was shown by his coming to London to emulate WS. And he carried a copy of WS's early poem *Venus and Adonis*, which he showed me with a touch of pride. Indeed, on the title page of *Venus and Adonis* Edmund had inscribed his name as if he were the author as well as the owner of the book (WS's own name did not appear).

Yet now he said: 'Did I tell you about the time he was caught poaching deer? Yes, the great playwright was a schoolboy poacher on Sir Thomas Lucy's estate.'

I was keen to hear more but we were interrupted by the arrival of Martin Barton. It would have been hard to imagine Barton as a poacher or indeed as a person engaged in any kind of outdoor activity. He was a gangly, red-headed individual who wrote rather bitter satirical pieces. One of his plays, *The Melancholy Man*, had gone down well with the Globe audiences but Barton had recently fallen out with the shareholders and he was now a regular writer for our rivals, the Blackfriars Children. Plays that were acted out by boys in all the parts (and not just playing the females) were fashionable in London and had been for some years. Barton was no doubt happier there since a principal reason for his quitting the King's Men was a fondness for our own boy players.

Now he inclined his head towards us in his usual manner – that is, a mildly mocking one – and said: 'Mr Shakespeare, I presume. Mr Edmund Shakespeare.'

I made the introductions and Martin Barton seated himself on the other side of the table, helping himself to one oyster, then another and yet one more for luck. He got the attention of a passing pot-boy and, in an insinuating rather than a mocking manner, requested more drink. Then he said to Edmund: 'You are better looking than your brother, a little better.'

This was typical of Martin, a compliment with a large measure of insult added. A flush rose in Edmund's cheeks, and I wondered whether we were going to see a display of the temper he was supposed to possess. Since Martin Barton also had a mercurial nature, which some attributed to his Italian mother, I could see a dispute in prospect. So while the pot-boy delivered a second flask of white wine to our table and Martin was distracted in gazing at him (he was a strapping lad), I quickly put in: 'How is business at the Blackfriars, Martin?'

It was an innocuous enough question, so I was surprised to see him pull a face. 'Toothache,' he said.

'They say the toothache is caused by unbalanced humours,' said Edmund. 'Or worms.'

Barton ignored him and said: 'Oh, business is very good, Nicholas. We thrive. A more select audience, you know. You should visit us, Edmund Shakespeare. Our boys are more, ah, delicate players than your hulking fellows south of the river.'

'I like it well enough where I am,' said Edmund.

'Protected under your brother's wing?' said Martin. 'It must be a warm and downy place to nestle.'

I sensed Edmund growing tense on the bench beside me. The sooner this session was brought to an end, the better. Barton was being his usual needling self, probably aggravated by his teeth, and it appeared that he wanted to meet Shakespeare's younger brother only out of curiosity. Not benign curiosity like mine, but malevolent.

'William is doing his brother no special favours, Martin,' I said. 'Edmund here is making himself useful at the Globe like any apprentice.'

It was the wrong remark, putting Edmund on his dignity and wanting to show he was more than an apprentice, for he now said: 'I can tell you that I am helping my brother with his work, Mr Barton.'

'Do you write too? Another poet emerges from the wilds of Stratford!'

'I am providing him with material for his next piece. He is writing about King Arthur.'

For the first time Martin Barton looked properly interested. He placed his glass of wine carefully on the table and leaned forward, cupping his face gingerly between his hands. I kept my own face impassive but groaned inwardly. As I've said, WS did not usually talk about the work he was engaged on. Whether out of superstition or because he feared his ideas being stolen, he would not wish

for a member of another acting company to know what
he was doing and certainly not Martin Barton. But the
words had been spoken.

'Is he? I have sometimes thought of dealing with Arthur
myself. A comparison of those golden days with our present
corrupt age of iron. A legendary king set beside our
diminished rulers. Satirical of course.'

Satirical wouldn't do, if Barton wanted to gain favour.
King Arthur was taken very seriously by the present royal
court, as WS well knew. But let Barton find that out for
himself. I was about to say to Edmund that it was time to
go, that we should leave Martin to finish his drink (and
make friends with the strapping pot-boy). But Edmund
was nettled. Before I could stop him he'd launched into a
garbled account of how we were going to call on a seller
in St Paul's yard, a seller who had some relics to dispose
of, relics connected to King Arthur.

In other circumstances Martin Barton might have
laughed or made some slighting reply. But the red-headed
playwright was all seriousness and, learning that we were
intending to make our call on Davy Owen that very
afternoon, quickly added himself to our company,
remarking that it would be a distraction from his face-
ache. It was no good my making any objection. Barton
could be pleasant enough when he chose, and his manner
now switched from mockery to compliment, saying to
Edmund that his brother William must be truly glad to
have a member of his family with him in the city.

We made more small talk, rapidly finished our drinks
and the last of the oysters and set off towards St Paul's
yard. It was a fine late afternoon. The sky was high and
dotted with small clouds that flicked across the sun, while
the streets were full of people finishing their activities for
the day. I half-hoped we might arrive at St Paul's yard to

find the stalls and shops closing up, but this is one of the busiest parts of town, a place where there are always visitors wanting to gawp and buy and therefore sellers willing to serve them. Edmund told us that Owen had a shop on the booksellers' side of the yard and that, although he dealt mostly in books and pamphlets, he also traded in other things.

'Like King Arthur's bones,' said Martin.

'So he *says*,' said Edmund, and I was pleased that he was able to show a touch of scepticism.

'He must be Welsh, this Owen? From his name.'

'He is Welsh. You can hear it in his voice.'

'The old stories link King Arthur with Wales.'

Barton sounded caught up in the subject. Maybe he really was considering a play about Arthur. By now, after threading our way past several stalls and browsers, we'd reached the shop. A group was emerging from the door, talking and pushing their way through the narrow entrance. Once outside they halted as if their business was not concluded. There were three men, one short and sharp-featured, one tall and very thin, the third also tall yet broad. There was a woman, almost the men's height and more attractive than any of them.

'That is Davy Owen,' said Edmund, indicating the little man. The group was so deep in conversation that our presence went unnoticed. I couldn't hear what they were saying since the largest man had his head bent down towards the short bookseller, but their postures suggested that this was not a friendly exchange. Although the woman was silent, her expression showed displeasure as far as I could see it under the shadow of a great hat. The second man, the one as thin as a rail, was gazing not at them but at her.

Davy Owen caught sight of us over the other's shoulder

and, with a nod and the touch of a finger on the large man's sleeve, indicated that they were not alone. The man turned around and looked at us as if we were intruders, although we were all standing in the public space outside the shop. He was an imposing figure, with a wide countenance matching his broad frame and a luxuriant fair beard which spilled out over his ruff.

He turned back to Davy Owen and uttered a few words before he strode off in the opposite direction. The woman nodded at Owen, not in a friendly way, then took after the man with a gait almost as decisive as her companion's. In her wake went the thin man. I noticed Martin Barton looking after the woman in particular. The bookseller gazed questioningly at us before recognizing Edmund Shakespeare. Most shopkeepers would be glad to see a returning customer, but Owen was not. In fact he made to scuttle back through the shopdoor, which was still ajar, muttering something about it being time to close.

'Wait a moment,' said Edmund. 'I have brought some friends to see you, Mr Owen.'

'Business is over. It is late in the day, Mr . . . Mr . . . ?'

I'm pretty certain that Owen knew Edmund's identity, but for some reason it suited him to pretend otherwise. I heard the Welsh lilt in his voice.

'I am Edmund Shakespeare. You surely remember me, Mr Owen? I bought a bone from you the other day and paid handsomely for it.'

'A bone?'

'The relic of . . . of a famous person.'

There was a pause while Edmund glared at Davy Owen. Eventually the bookseller said, reluctantly: 'You may have done.'

'Not only that, but you told me that you had similar items in your possession.'

'Then you must have misunderstood me. I have no more such things under my roof. I'm a bookseller.'

Davy Owen moved once again to retreat through his door. But Edmund wasn't so easily put off. He placed a restraining hand on the bookseller's shoulder.

'I have not come here today, and with my friends too, to be daffed away.'

'I can choose my own hours and my own customers,' said Owen. The lilt had changed to a whine. He shrugged off Edmund's hand. Now it was our companion's turn to intervene.

'I am Martin Barton, the playwright and satirist, you know.'

He sucked in his cheeks, and I saw Owen look curiously at him before saying: 'I believe I may have seen some of your work, Martin Barton. Seen it while I was using it as spills to light a fire. You insulted the Welsh in one of your pieces.'

'Did I now?' said Barton. 'Well, look you, if everyone who'd ever insulted the Welsh was gathered here today they'd need to build a new London.'

Shakespeare's brother, evidently growing tired of these verbal blows, started towards Owen as if to resort to something more direct.

'Come on,' I said quickly. 'Don't let us trouble this gentleman when he has no wish to relieve us of our money. You cannot force a shopman to sell his goods, especially if he does not have them.'

'Good advice, sir. I wish your friends were as sensible.'

'Nicholas Revill, at your service,' I said.

'But he does have what we want,' said Edmund. Seizing the bookseller by the front of his jerkin, he hoiked Owen towards him. The bookseller's hat fell off to reveal a close-cropped head of hair, coming to an arrow-like point on his forehead. 'He's as good as admitted it.'

So this was the quick temper that William had warned me about. I was about to step forward and physically unfasten Edmund's hands from Owen's jerkin when Martin Barton suddenly spoke up again.

'If Leonard Leman and his good lady Alice can be your customers, I do not see why we shouldn't be.'

Martin must be referring to the couple who'd just walked away. How he knew them while they appeared not to recognize him, I've no idea. But his words had an indirect effect on Owen, who said calmly: 'I may be able to help you after all, Mr Shakespeare. But you will have to let me go first.'

Edmund allowed the bookseller to work himself free of his grasp. He ducked down and picked up his hat. I expected the man to invite us inside his shop, but he said: 'I do not have what you are looking for on these premises, but I can direct you towards some more, ah, items which you may inspect later tonight. And your friends too if they please.'

'Where?' said Edmund. 'You had better not be sending us on a fool's errand, Owen.'

'You should go to a house on the corner of Seething Lane and Tower Street, near the Black Swan. A house with narrow windows. Ask there for a gentleman who calls himself Bernardo Scoto. He is Italian, as you may guess. From Mantua, I believe. Do not call on him before ten, however. He works by night.'

'And what the devil has he got to do with this?' said Edmund.

'I have heard of this Scoto,' said Martin Barton, wincing as he spoke. 'He has a mountebank's reputation.'

'Be that as it may, he may be able to help you with the toothache which seems to be afflicting you,' said Owen. 'Signor Scoto also has a collection of relics in his possession which he is willing to part with, for the right fee. Now, if you will forgive me, I must attend to my stock and shut up for the day.'

Before Edmund could detain him again, Davy Owen slipped inside his shop and we heard the sound of bolts sliding and keys turning.

I assumed that was it, that our little expedition had come to an end. No point, surely, in trailing off to some dwelling in Tower Street in search of an Italian mountebank. But I reckoned without Edmund's determination and, more surprisingly, Martin Barton's wish to see the thing through. I asked him why.

'I am curious to vist this Scoto.'

'For your toothache?'

'I collect types, you know, Nicholas. A quacksalver or mountebank might be just the character for one of my satires on human folly.'

'But it is not very likely that he will have any relics of King Arthur.'

'It is not very likely that anyone will have them. So what harm is done by calling on the man from Mantua?'

'Why do we have to call on him late at night?'

'No doubt because it heightens the effect. He is a man of mystery. Come on, Nicholas, we are men of the theatre. We understand all about mysteries.'

I couldn't think of a response, but I still didn't like any of it. I had another question for Barton, which was how he knew the identity of the striking couple who'd been deep in talk with Owen outside his shop. That answer was easy enough. Leonard and Alice Leman were good patrons of the Blackfriars playhouse, and in fact Martin Barton had some hopes that they might become patrons of him. They didn't seem to know you, I said. They weren't looking in our direction, said Barton. And so who was the third man, the one as thin as a rail? Oh, that was their steward, said Barton. A fellow called Jack Corner. Like many stewards, a man of ambition. I wasn't surprised that Martin Barton knew the names of these well-to-do folk, nor that he talked dismissively of the steward but warmly of the Lemans. The satirist was one of those people who affect to despise wealth and influence but who are covertly respectful of them. He made it his business to be familiar with the important faces in the audience.

The three of us agreed to meet in a few hours at the junction of Tower Street and Seething Lane. For the first time I regretted having agreed to watch over Edmund Shakespeare.

# III

Seething Lane is a street of large but unobtrusive houses. Queen Elizabeth's spymaster Francis Walsingham had lived (and died) here, and plenty of merchants occupy these solid dwellings. Tower Street is more of a mixture, but it grows dignified towards the eastern end, on the Seething Lane corner of which Edmund Shakespeare, Martin Barton and I were now standing as a nearby bell rang ten o'clock. The darkness was relieved by gleams of light coming from a few windows, and there was a crescent moon slipping up the sky.

By day you would have seen the slope of Tower Hill further east and, even though the Tower itself was out of sight, you might have been conscious of that great palace or castle over your shoulder. If I chose, I could see it more easily from the other side of the river, since I had lodgings in Tooley Street and had only to turn down a lane leading to the river to catch a glimpse of the mighty walls on the opposite shore. It was comforting, somehow, that the Tower was separated from me by a wide stretch of water. I don't know whether it was the fearsome reputation of the place – at this very moment Sir Walter Raleigh was captive within its walls – or because noble people were executed nearby, but like many Londoners I generally felt uneasy when in the Tower's shadow. And I felt uneasy anyway because of the strange mission on which the three of us were engaged.

We identified the narrow-windowed house on the corner. No light came through the crevices in its shutters, and I hoped we might find it unoccupied or get no answer to the rap that Edmund Shakespeare gave on the door. No such luck. Almost straight away, it was opened by a stocky child.

'You wish to see Master Scoto?'

The voice was no child's but deep, a man's. The little figure was a dwarf. It was impossible to make out his features since the only illumination came from candles in a sconce further down the hall.

'You've guessed it,' said Edmund.

'He is expecting you.'

This was not a question but a statement and did not increase my comfort. Ushering us inside, the dwarfish shape told us to go to a door at the end of the hallway and knock three times.

'Three times. Why not once? What did I tell you, Nicholas?' whispered Martin Barton as we passed the flickering light of the sconce. 'Like the little doorman, it is all to heighten the effect.'

But we did as we were instructed. Edmund knocked thrice on the oaken door. Did I detect a slight hesitation in Shakespeare's brother, as if he too was regretting we'd reached this point? A soft voice said 'Enter' and Edmund lifted the latch.

There used to be a shop off St Paul's Walk owned by an apothecary who styled himself Old Nick, and what I saw now of Scoto's room reminded me of that place. This one was an extensive den, smoky from the few scattered, guttering candles and with a sweet but disagreeable scent. There were shelves crowded with wooden boxes and earthenware pots, and from the beams over our heads dangled withered roots and bladders and large whitish objects. A table in a corner was encumbered with wide books and greasy glass tubes and alembics. Against the left-hand wall hung a tapestry or arras depicting strange, garbed figures and symbols. The figures seemed half-alive as a draught stirred the arras. On the far side of the room was a desk and behind the desk was a hunched figure, presumably Master Bernardo Scoto. A single candle wavered next to a hand that was scrawling something across a sheet of paper. The hand seemed disembodied from its owner, who was in darkness.

'*Benvenuto, signori.*'

The voice out of the shadows was soft, insinuating. It made the hairs on the back of my neck prickle. We stood there, three awkward supplicants.

'Your toothache, Signor Barton, 'ow is it?'

How the Italian was aware of the playwright's bad teeth, I don't know. Martin was not wincing or cupping his hand to his face, and besides it was dim in the chamber, as I've said. But the remark had the effect, no doubt intended, of giving the hunched figure some unusual powers of penetration.

'You should try chewin' 'ore'ound,' said Scoto. 'I can make you up a preparation if you desire.'

'I'll attend to my own teeth, with or without the horehound,' said Barton. 'We have come about other business.'

'You are in search of some bones?'

'We have been told you have them,' said Edmund.

'*Fai attenzione*,' said Scoto. 'There are bones above your 'eads.'

Among the vegetable matter hanging from the ceiling there were indeed some bone-like shapes. Despite the sweet-scented fug of the room, I shivered. It was like being in a charnel house.

'Signor Revill stands beneath the 'orn of a unicorn. Reach up and touch it, sir. It will bring you no 'arm but blessings, *i doni della natura*. It is a protection against the plague. And beside it there are the ribs of a – 'ow do you say it? – *una sirena*. Ah, *si*, a mermaid.'

Wondering how he knew my name, as he had known Martin Barton's, I restrained myself from reaching up to touch either the mermaid's ribs or the horn. This latter bone, long and tapering to a point, might have belonged to a unicorn, although there are those who say that no such creature exists.

'We are not interested in animal remains,' said Edmund. 'It is King Arthur's bones we seek.'

'I 'ave many oddments here. *Una miscellanea.*'

'Oddments? These are relics of England's greatness.'

'*Ha parlato l'oracolo!*'

The words were plainly meant as a snide comment, and Edmund took them in that spirit. Stepping forward, he said in a quavering voice: 'They should not be in foreign hands. If you possess such things, Master Scoto, you ought to surrender them to the authorities. The bones of a great king must not moulder in neglect. You will suffer the consequences otherwise.'

Scoto laughed. The sound was as soft and unsettling as his speech. He moved from his perch behind the desk and came towards us. He was wearing a snug cap and some kind of cloak with geometric figures on it, cabbalistic designs probably. By daylight and in the open, I would have dismissed him as I would any mountebank who sells the elixir of life at a country fair. It wasn't so easy to do in this dim and smoky place. But of course the man from Mantua did not have Arthur's bones. This was a fool's errand. We should quit this darkened house now.

But now was already too late. Instead of seizing Scoto as he had with Davy Owen that afternoon, Edmund Shakespeare produced a little dagger from within the recesses of his jerkin and held it underneath Scoto's bare chin. 'Enough of your double talk, signor,' he said. 'Give us a straight answer or I shall give you a straight jab with this blade.'

'If you are so foolish, young man, you will not leave this 'ouse alive. *Non sono solo.* Not alone, you understand.'

'Oh, that small person who let us in.'

'Nano, 'e is worth three of you.'

I had to admire the man's self-possession as well as his confidence in the little doorkeeper. He didn't retreat in the face of Edmund's threats but held up his arms in a gesture that spread his patterned cloak like a bird's dark wings. I glanced first at the rippling arras, as if Scoto might have attendants hidden behind it, and then at Martin Barton. Without a word we took hold of Edmund Shakespeare, one on each side. I was on his right and so it fell to me to grasp his knife-hand, which I did with both my hands around his wrist as tight as a vice. Meanwhile, Scoto watched us with, I could have sworn, an air of amusement.

Edmund was too surprised to struggle, though he turned a burning look on me. Then he seemed to slacken and allowed Martin and me to half-lead, half-drag him back to the entrance of Scoto's den. All this while he still clutched the knife and, even if I did not think he would have struck at me, I feared a slip. We straggled down the hallway and opened the front door, to let in a gust of cold spring air. There was no sign of the dwarfish porter Nano. We emerged into the street and drew Edmund away from the house on the corner. When we judged that he'd calmed down, we released him. He put away the knife without being told to, but he was still angry.

'Why did you stop me? That charlatan in there would sooner have responded to a threat than a polite query.'

'You might not have been content with a threat,' said Martin Barton, and I was glad not only that the red-headed satirist had kept us company but that he was displaying such good sense. For myself, I'd been shaken by the whole encounter.

'I suppose you are going to go and tell tales to my brother,' said Edmund to me.

'Not a word,' I said, 'if you return to your lodgings now and forget this silly quest for Arthur's bones.'

'You go back to your lodgings if you please,' said Edmund. 'I will go where I like.'

He turned on his heel and stalked off up Seething Lane, leaving us in the dark. No point in pursuing Shakespeare's younger brother. Perhaps the cool night air would bring him to his senses.

'How are your teeth?' I said to Martin. 'Are you going to try horehound?'

'I would not take remedies from that charlatan, Nicholas. And another thing. He is not from Mantua.'

'How do you know?'

'My mother was from those parts, and his accent is quite different.'

# IV

As it happened, I did talk to William Shakespeare the next day on the subject of King Arthur and his bones. But it was WS who raised the subject while I tried my best to keep his brother Edmund out of the conversation. We were at the Globe playhouse and our morning rehearsal was done.

I passed WS in the passage outside the tiring room. He asked in his usual courteous style whether I had a minute to spare. That he wanted a private chat was indicated by the way in which he ushered me into a small office reserved for the shareholders.

'Nick, you remember when you called on me the other day in Silver Street and I showed you that, ah, relic of King Arthur?'

'The one Edmund gave you?'

'Yes. But it has disappeared from my room.'

'Stolen?'

'I would not think so were it not for another strange circumstance. As you know, I was working on a piece about the great king. I had not got very far for, in truth, the ink seemed to be flowing very reluctantly from my pen. But the manuscript sheets are missing also.'

I thought straight away of Edmund, wondered whether he had slipped into his brother's lodgings and for some perverse reason filched the bone and the sheets. But I said nothing. Perhaps the same idea was running through WS's head, for he seemed troubled.

'I hope you will not take offence if I ask you whether you told anyone of what I was writing.'

'Martin Barton may have got to hear of it,' I said, unwilling to say that it was Edmund who had mentioned the King Arthur play in the Mermaid tavern. 'But no one else as far as I know.'

'Barton can be a silly fellow,' said WS, 'but he would not stoop to thieving another man's ideas. He has too high a regard for his own.'

'No, he's honest,' I said, still grateful for Barton's action at Scoto's house the previous night.

'I might even believe my brother Edmund capable of it, but he would hardly steal back something that he'd given me in the first place. Or take a sheaf of my papers.'

I was glad that it was William who had raised the subject. I shook my head with almost as much conviction as I felt. Thieving on the quiet wasn't Edmund's style either. Besides, WS's brother was working as usual at the Globe this very morning, doing the bidding of the tire-man and the bookkeeper. We'd exchanged glances but no words. No longer cheerful, Edmund looked red-eyed and dishevelled as though he'd found somewhere to drink away his anger after quitting us last night.

'How does my brother do?' said WS.

'Well enough.'

'I can tell it from your tone that something has happened.'

'Nothing important.'

'No? Well, one day you might tell me. At least he is not in the Clink.'

He might have been, I thought.

'And I am grateful to you for keeping him company outside the playhouse.'

'I'm sorry for the loss of your royal bone and your royal play, William,' I said, wanting to change the subject since I didn't think I'd be keeping Edmund company much longer.

'A play can be written again and written better,' said WS. 'And if the bone really belongs to the great king, it cannot be lost. They say that Arthur is sleeping, ready to wake again in the hour of England's need, even if his bones have to be gathered from the four corners of the country.'

'Arthur may wake again on the stage,' I said.

'Yes, we can resurrect him,' said WS.

It was characteristic of the man that he should take such a relaxed view of his losses or thefts, although they troubled me slightly on account of the events of the previous day.

But that was as nothing to the trouble that came along the next day.

As I was coming out of my lodgings in Tooley Street in the morning, I was accosted by an individual with a narrow, pustular face who asked bluntly if I was Revill.

'Who wants to know?'

'That means you *are* Revill.'

He handed me a crumpled note. It was from Edmund Shakespeare. Scrawled as if written in haste or a poor light, it said: 'Ask no questions but come with the man who presents this, I beg you, Nicholas.'

It was signed 'Edmund'. I recognized the same hand I'd seen on the title page of *Venus and Adonis* where Edmund had inked his own name. But it wasn't the signature or the message which bothered me the most. It was the bloody fingermarks on the crumpled sheet. Edmund's blood? Or another's?

Despite Edmund's injunction, I did ask a couple of questions – basic ones like 'What's happened?' and 'Where are we going?' – but received no reply from this unhelpful individual. I rejected my first idea, which was that Edmund had indeed ended up in one of the several Southwark prisons. This spotty pinch-face was no gaoler. Gaolers are generally worse dressed than those they incarcerate and any approach to a friend of a prisoner always involves a demand for money, straight away. Nor did I fear some kind of trap for the fellow's garments had an official look to them. Indeed there was a badge on his jerkin which I hadn't had the chance to inspect.

I followed him down Mill Lane. There's no wharf here but a plain flight of steps and some mooring-posts. A boatman was waiting, and I realized that my guide had already been ferried across the river once this morning. I wondered where the trouble was. I had a nasty feeling that it might be found at Scoto's house on the corner of Tower Street.

In other circumstances I might have enjoyed being rowed across the Thames on a fine morning in May. The sun dazzled off the windows of the houses on the Bridge, the wind was invigorating and the boat rocked in a manner that wasn't too puke-making. But I was thinking about my best course: see what mischief Edmund Shakespeare had tumbled into, reassure him that we would do our best and then race back to the Globe to leave the matter in WS's hands. After all, he really was his brother's keeper.

I was sitting in the stern of the boat beside the individual who'd brought me Edmund's note. The boatman facing us was too breathless – it is a harder task rowing downriver below the Bridge – to make conversation or, more likely, to relieve himself with a stream of oaths. My companion still didn't say anything, and I was able to observe the little insignia on his jerkin. Then I looked up beyond the boatman's flexing shoulders and, squinting against the sun, saw that we were headed for a particular spot on the northern bank.

My heart and guts did a little dance. Or rather they both got up at once and ran into each other as if trying to flee from my mortal frame.

Even if I had never seen its precise equivalent before, the badge on my fellow passenger's jerkin was a royal one without a doubt. It showed a lion rampant, and everyone knows that the lion and the king are one. This and the direction of the boat confirmed our destination.

We were soon to put in at the wharf under the south-west corner of the Tower. There are plenty of stairs and berths along here, together with cranes and winches for unloading supplies. But nobody lands in this place for pleasure. Only for business. Or worse. Further along is that dreadful watergate through which traitors are conveyed into the bowels of the Tower. We were not headed there, thank God! – and a moment's sane reflection would have convinced me that there could be no reason why a humble player would have that honour – but it was bad enough to be conveyed to any point of the wharf fronting the Tower palace. Especially when summoned by a blood-marked note which was still screwed up in my gloved fist.

No longer much bothered about the fate of Edmund Shakespeare, I am hardly ashamed to say that I was more concerned with the immediate future of Nicholas Revill.

But even that was driven out of my head by the sight that now lay before me. The tide was out and a stretch of foreshore, muddy and pebbled, was exposed. Sitting in the sun by the water's edge was a bear. Almost every citizen of London from the age of six to sixty has seen captive bears dancing at fairs or fighting for their lives in the bear-pits by the Southwark theatres. But those bears are brown while the one sitting on the banks of the Thames was white. I had never seen this creature but had heard people talk of it. It was a gift from the King of Norway and its whiteness was a reflection of the desolate and ice-bound stretches of that distant land. In truth, the bear was more of a yellowy-white than snow-coloured.

I wondered why it did not swim away, then saw that it was tethered by a chain to a great stake sunk deep into the foreshore. Shackled like a prisoner, it was also muzzled.

Despite this, it looked contented enough, dashing a paw through the water in a playful way. Then it occurred to me that the white bear was being more than playful; it was trying to scoop up fish. There was no sign of any keeper.

Our boat squelched into the mud of the shore and the boatman hopped out with the skill of long practice to secure us to one of several posts driven into the mud. The bear paid us no attention but continued to strike its paws into the water. Nearby was a set of stairs. Pinch-face indicated that I should go first while he was settling with the boatman. I thought about taking to my heels. But I wasn't confident I could outrun him when all around was the territory of the Tower, unfamiliar to me. And given that he had found me once near my lodgings, he would find me again. And furthermore I had done nothing wrong. (Not that that's any defence.)

So, in a docile fashion, I slithered across the foreshore, giving the dirty white bear a very wide berth, and climbed the stairs and waited for my escort at the top. The air was not so fresh here on account of the tubs of rotting meat which, recently unloaded from the offal-boat, were sitting on the wharf. Lettering on the tubs indicated they were supplied by the Butchers' Company – no doubt for the other Tower animals which I could hear even now. A mixture of barks, brays, screeches and growls was coming out of the mouths of God-knows-what creatures over the wall on the other side of the moat. This south-west corner was dominated by the Lion Tower, which, to judge by the unfinished castellations and the scaffolding still clinging to the bright new stonework, was being enlarged.

It was widely known that King James had a special interest in the beasts of the Tower, not because he wished to study them but because he liked watching them kill each other. He enjoyed seeing his lions baited by dogs, bulls, boars and so on. Of course the lions tended to prevail, but I'd heard that any animal, such as a fighting mastiff, which acquitted itself honourably might be allowed to live out the rest of its days in peace. The grand animal contests were restricted to the king and his circle, but on other days any citizen might gaze at the Tower beasts either by paying three pennies or by bringing his own domestic animal – dogs, chickens, sheep – to be devoured by the larger ones. I had never seen the Tower beasts myself, though whether it was out of lack of curiosity or reluctance to open my purse I'm not sure.

By now the pustular pinch-face had joined me at the top of the stairs. He beckoned me to follow him, and we walked around the moat and the bulging western flank of the area that housed the animals. The moat had been almost drained, presumably for ease of work on the buildings in this quarter. Or perhaps it was that London no longer feared an attack on its greatest citadel. Beyond this was a drawbridge and a great gate. There were two soldiers sitting in a little sentry-house, but they were eating and drinking and hardly glanced up as we approached. We had come through more than half a circle so that ahead of us was the causeway leading back to the Lion Tower. My heart thudded louder in my ears than my feet sounded on the drawbridge. I felt as helpless as one of those domestic dogs being delivered over to the lions' pleasure.

We went through a second gate at the end of the causeway, where my guide nodded at a single soldier who didn't return the greeting, and into the cluster of buildings grouped under the Lion Tower. Still I saw no beasts, but I could smell their rank odours as well as hear them. Then it was up a flight of spiral stairs to an oak door on which pinch-face knocked, almost with delicacy. Receiving some reply, he unlatched the door and, putting a hand in the small of my back, as good as pushed me into the chamber.

'Here he is, sir,' he said, before shutting the door and leaving me alone with the room's occupant.

Like Scoto the Mantuan in Tower Street, this individual was sitting behind a desk, working on some papers. But there the resemblance ended. The room was neat and clean, with a view of the river through a glazed window. The desk-man was a kindly faced gent, with spectacles. I could have sworn he looked relieved to see me once he had taken off his spectacles. And for the first time in what was only a half-hour but seemed like half a lifetime, my terror started to subside. Perhaps I would escape incarceration in the Tower after all.

'You are Nicholas Revill of the King's Men?'

'I am – but I don't understand what I am doing here.'

'Be patient, Mr Revill, and I will explain our difficult position. I am Ralph Gill . . .'

There was a second's hesitation as if to give me the chance to recognize the name. I nodded but had no idea who he was. Luckily he supplied the answer.

'. . . Keeper of the King's Lions. Naturally there are other animals under my charge, but it is only the lions which matter. My father, Thomas Gill, also bore the same title, and I hope that my son will inherit it in due course. It is an honour, you know.'

I nodded again, although with no notion of where we were heading.

'This morning we made an unfortunate discovery. It involves a friend of yours.'

'Edmund Shakespeare?'

'Just so. Edmund Shakespeare. It was the name which gave me pause and made me agree to his sending you a note asking for your presence here. You are able to confirm, Mr Revill, that this individual is indeed the brother of William Shakespeare?'

'He is.'

'He was adamant that he did not want his brother to know of his . . . predicament.'

'Yes, that sounds like Edmund.'

'I must tread carefully where William Shakespeare and the King's Men are concerned. The king is patron to us all, you know. Plays are not so near the heart of James as are his lions, but I believe his queen is fond of the drama?'

'She is.'

'I thought so,' said Ralph Gill, almost mournfully.

'Sir,' I said, 'can you tell me what Edmund has done?'

'Oh, he has done murder,' said the spectacled gent. 'It may well be murder. Come with me.'

He came around from behind the desk and we left the room, going down the spiral stairs, across a lobby and down a further flight. Now that my personal fears were fading, anxiety over Edmund returned. Murder? Was it possible? Yes, I thought, remembering WS's brother threatening Davy Owen or brandishing a knife at Scoto's throat, it was possible.

As we descended through the building with its many twists and turns, I realized that this was not one edifice but several which had grown up and into each over the centuries. Meanwhile, the animal stench became stronger. Eventually we emerged from a tunnel-like passage into a yard via a barred gate that Mr Gill unlocked. The yard was in the shape of a great D, turned the wrong way about, and with the straight side formed by the buildings from which Ralph Gill and I had just come.

The surrounding walls were so high and the spring sky with its fast-moving clouds, seemed so distant that it was like being at the bottom of a well. A curved viewing platform with a canopy projected from the southern side, supported by scarred wooden struts. That would be where the king and his retinue surveyed the lions as they went about their work of dispatching the lesser beasts. And down here in the yard was where the killing took place, as evidenced by dark stains among the mixture of mud and shit and roughly levelled stone composing the floor. There was a large water trough and a platform-like area scattered with straw on the northern side for the animals to disport themselves.

Fortunately there were no beasts wandering free but in their place a couple of fellows garbed like the one who had collected me in Tooley Street. They nodded deferentially at Master Gill. I was glad of all the human company available because of the proximity of the beasts. They were at our backs in cages and behind doors set in the walls of the buildings nestling around the Lion Tower. I smelled and heard them. I felt their eyes on me and when I turned fearfully for a better look I caught glimpses of tawny fur, of yellow eyes, dark stripes, bedraggled tails. What I took for a wrinkled human hand thrusting out like a prisoner's from a panel in a low door belonged, said Ralph Gill, to an ape. There was a brown bear huddling miserably in the corner of its little chamber, and another creature which I mistook for a dog but which Gill informed me was a wolf, the very last in England. It was a lean, ugly thing, maybe on account of pondering its melancholy uniqueness.

In his pride at his collection, the lion keeper had for a moment forgotten why we had come to this level. But he soon led me off into yet another passage and past more cages and caverns set within the very foundations of the place. It was dark and noisome down here, with the only light provided by torches in iron wall-brackets. Feeble gusts of air indicated that there were hidden holes venting the place; otherwise every living thing would soon have been choked. The low noises, which might almost have been human, the bars and locks everywhere, could not but remind me of a gaol.

In this honeycomb or warren were little chambers set aside for provisions or the use of the keepers, but Ralph Gill led me to a pair of adjoining cells cut into the rock and meant for beasts. They were presently occupied by men. Candles had been brought in to help them see. In one cell a body lay face up, arms and legs splayed among the dirt. His fair beard and white ruff, his fine doublet and hose, all were dyed with blood. I feared very much that I knew his identity. It was the luxuriant beard that gave the clue.

In the other pen were three individuals, each of them alive. One was slumped, head in hands, in a corner, while on either side stood two of the fellows that I now recognized by their garb and royal insignia to be assistant keepers. They were holding cudgels, normally used, I supposed, to ward off the wild animals. We stood by the open gate since the interior was too small for five men.

Edmund Shakespeare looked up. His forehead was bloody and swollen.

'I did not do this thing, Nick. I am innocent, I swear.'

Not sure whether to believe his denial, I nodded at Shakespeare's brother and spoke instead to Ralph Gill. 'What happened here?'

'My men discovered early this morning that the lions were roaming in the yard, something never known before. They had a deal of trouble to drive them back to their cages with burning torches. It was only after they had done so that they heard human cries coming from this underground quarter. Here they discovered the sight before you, Mr Revill. A man dead by violence and another man cowering and shouting in this enclosure next door. I was summoned straight away and established this ... gentleman's name. I was for calling out the Justice but he begged instead to be allowed to scrawl a note to you. I was minded to refuse, but when I heard his name and that he was a member of the King's Men I decided to give him that, ah, benefit.'

I could see how Mr Gill had risen to his present eminence. He had quickly taken stock of what had occurred and, not knowing whether Edmund was really an important person or not, he responded with prudence. Clear-headed and diplomatic, Gill must have been a valuable servant of the Crown. I let it pass that Edmund was not a King's Man (or not properly so). It was more likely the Shakespeare name which had done the trick.

'Who is the dead man?' I said, though I was almost certain I already knew. Nevertheless Gill's answer gave me a jolt. 'He is called Leonard Leman. He and his wife are frequent visitors to the animals, not as ordinary Londoners but as members of the court parties who grace us with their presence.'

Leman was one of the group we'd seen arguing with the bookseller in St Paul's yard.

'How did he die?'

'He has many wounds on his body, Mr Revill, which could have been produced by a knife. And your fellow here was discovered clutching a knife this morning.'

'What happened, Edmund?' I said.

'I . . . I was tricked into entering this place,' said Edmund. 'I received a note telling me to come to the Lion Tower last evening.'

'A note? Who from? Where is it?'

'I don't know. It is gone. But once here, I was surprised by men I could not see and beaten about the head. My hat was lost. See . . .'

He leaned forward, the better to display the swelling on the front of his head. Hanks of hair which hung down were matted with dried blood. He touched the egg-shaped lump cautiously and then looked at his hands.

'I did not know where I was for a time, but when I came to myself it was here in this filthy sty surrounded by animal noises. I dimly saw the body of that man in the neighbouring cell. I made to leave but there were large beasts out in the yard, slinking through the dark. I was reluctant to move further, so I groped my way back to this place and did my best to secure the door with my belt. See . . . '

It was true. A girdle hung limp from the door. I did not think it would have kept a curious animal away for long.

'I must have slept, for the next I knew was shouting and growling from outside—'

'That was us returning the lions to their quarters,' said one of Edmund's guards, speaking for the first time. 'They didn't want to go in until we showed 'em fire.'

'—hearing the noise, I set up my own shouting from in here and was found. True, I was clutching a knife, but it was to defend myself against men, against wild animals, against God knows what. They'll tell you that I willingly surrendered the knife and that the blade was clean.'

The other guard nodded but said nothing.

'So, Nick, now you see me . . .'

'Now I see you, Edmund.'

I didn't know what else to say. Or, rather, I scarcely knew where to begin. The whole tale sounded like a pack of lies. Had WS's brother really been summoned by note to the Lion Tower, overcome by unknown assailants and dragged down to the animal level, there to wake with a dead man for company, and – too fearful to make his escape through an arena of lions – had he huddled for safety in a cage overnight? The only bit which was absolutely believable was the last.

I was reluctant to question Edmund in front of Ralph Gill in case I exposed too many holes in his story. In fact it was more holes than story. Yet whatever he was making up or leaving out of his account, it was hard to regard him as a murderer at the moment. Edmund looked hapless, not guilty. His face was smeared with dirt, but there was no blood detectable on him apart from the front of his head and his fingertips (I thought of the stained note, which I still carried).

Fortunately the Keeper of the King's Lions seemed to have come to the same conclusion and, having talked of murder, he was now anxious to discharge Edmund into my custody. I wondered whether he had played up the whole thing so as to get rid of Edmund. The dead man's body was an embarrassment to an official who had charge of the whole area. Strangers had penetrated what should be a secure place, wild beasts had not been shut away and had got loose. I had a sudden thought.

'Mr Gill, is it possible that the wounds on Mr Leman were caused by your animals? The lions? You say they were wandering free last night. It might be that the unfortunate gentleman was attacked in the yard and, mortally wounded, managed to crawl into the adjoining cell.'

'It might be, it might well be.'

'There is blood along the floor of the passage as if he might have dragged himself so far.'

Ralph Gill examined the floor and considered this idea. He said: 'But with such an important individual as Mr Leman, the Justice or the coroner will have to decide, and

Mr Shakespeare here will have to give evidence if it comes to it.'

I helped WS's brother to his feet and he reclaimed his girdle and even his knife, handed over by one of the guards. The blade and haft were, indeed, spotless (but they could have been cleaned after use). Then, accompanied by the head keeper, we passed the little chamber containing the unfortunate Leonard Leman before making our way into the yard, where the air, though heavy with animal odours, was a relief after the stenchy warren. Then up through the labyrinthine passages of the Lion Tower and along the causeway to the outer gate, the one with the sentry-house and the drawbridge. Here Ralph Gill put a hand on my arm to detain me. Edmund, meanwhile, was looking somewhat unsteady on his feet and taking down great draughts of air.

'Mr Revill, I will speak in confidence. You must see that I am in a delicate position. This is a royal palace and I would not like the king to learn of any, ah, irregularities concerning his lions. Nor would his majesty be happy to hear that the brother of his principal playwright has been caught up in any mischief. Or perhaps it is the queen who would not be happy. You would know better than I do. But a man is dead and must be accounted for, even if it was no more than a misfortune ... yes, a terrible misfortune.'

He paused, and I nodded. Taking his cue from me, Gill was evidently working himself into the belief that Leman's death was an accident.

'Your friend there has given a partial account of what happened. It would be to all our advantages if he gave to you a more precise account, perhaps leaving aside any talk of assailants and so on. No doubt he drank a little too deeply last night?'

'I will see what I can do, Mr Gill. But can you answer me one question? Whatever happened here last night, there seems to have been a great deal of coming and going. I thought this place was a castle, a guarded, secure castle.'

Ralph Gill looked uncomfortable. His hands flew to his head to keep his hat in place on his white head, even though there wasn't much of a breeze where we were standing.

'Sir William Ward is the aptly named Constable of the Tower and he has responsibility for our security. The inner wards where prisoners are held are truly fast, but an outer gate such as this is rarely closed. I cannot remember when the drawbridge was last raised. We have building work going on at the moment. There is always a deal of coming and going. Every day the public resort to this area to see the beasts.'

All of this seemed a roundabout way of saying that the south-west corner of the Tower was a common thoroughfare. The two soldiers in the sentry-house to our back had not noted our exit any more than they'd done with my earlier arrival under escort. Still, it was none of my business if the place was crawling with night-time assailants or if London was shaken by rebels who took it into their heads to storm the Tower. Instead I assured Ralph Gill once again that I'd do my best to get the full story out of Edmund Shakespeare.

'Good, good, Mr Revill. I can see you have a shrewd look to you.'

We shook hands. WS had recently called me shrewd before putting his brother in my charge. I would have preferred less of a reputation for shrewdness and less of my share of trouble.

Edmund and I quit the precincts of the Tower. We walked rapidly westwards as if to put as much distance as possible between ourselves and the animal den. Neither of us spoke a word until I suggested he clean himself up. By this time we were near a public trough at the Poultry end of Cheapside. Edmund dabbed cautiously at his face and washed his bloody hands in the running water which is supplied by the Great Conduit. The blow on his forehead was turning a shade of blue. It looked as though he had had an encounter with a doorpost.

Only when he looked halfway respectable did we enter a tavern. And only when we had finished a rabbit stew in near silence and started on our bread and cheese, washed down with second helpings of small beer, did I say to William Shakespeare's brother: 'Isn't it time for the truth, Edmund?'

# V

'First I must thank you, Nick. You have treated me better than I deserve, especially after the other night. I cannot tell you the roasting I would have got from William if he had come in your place. He might have let me rot in the animals' den.'

'Believe me, I was tempted. Enough, Edmund. The truth.'

But the story Edmund had to tell wasn't so different from the account I'd already heard. He had, he insisted, been attacked and overcome soon after entering the precincts of the Lion Tower. He had woken to find himself next to the cell containing the mortal remains of Leonard Leman. Too frightened to go through the yard with its wandering lions, he retreated for safety to the empty cell where he was found, knife in hand, by the morning keepers.

But there was one significant difference. Rather than

being summoned to the Tower by some mysterious note – that was a fiction to explain his presence to Ralph Gill, he openly admitted it – Edmund had been in pursuit of someone. Of three people in fact. The bookseller Davy Owen and the dead man, Leonard Leman, together with the dead man's wife, Alice.

'And this is no fiction, I suppose?'

'God's truth, Nick.'

WS's obstinate brother had been unwilling to give up his quest for those supposed Arthurian bones and was returning once more to Owen's shop. Again he arrived as the Welshman was about to close up and depart for the day. This time, though, instead of accosting him he had been more discreet. Had followed him at a distance to Bernardo Scoto's house in Tower Street and waited for him to emerge. Which he did after a time, accompanied by the large gentleman with the fine beard and the tall handsome woman. Edmund recognized them as Mr and Mrs Leman.

Detecting a plot and keeping in the shadows, for it was growing dark by now, he tailed these three up Tower Hill and so into the Tower itself. They passed unimpeded through the main gate, as did Edmund himself, and spoke briefly with the soldier on duty in the Lion Tower. Edmund wasn't certain but he thought money might have changed hands, and the soldier vanished. While he was engaged in watching, he was oblivious to his back for he was suddenly seized from behind and shoved violently against a stone pillar. He was sick and dizzy and the blood ran into his eyes. He heard voices but couldn't make out what they were saying. He was hit again and again, this time around the back of the head. Hands grabbed at him – three, four people, he couldn't be sure – and half-carried, half-dragged him down stairs and along passages. There was the stink and noise of animals. He was thrown into some cell and, for a time, lost all awareness of his surroundings. And after that he would have escaped but was driven back by fear of the loose lions, back into his own cage, where he did his best to secure himself until he was rescued.

'These attackers?' I said. 'Who were they? Davy Owen, the Lemans?'

'Possibly, but there was at least one other involved, the man who struck at me from behind.'

'Who was that? Scoto the Mantuan?'

'I have no idea. I was taken by surprise.'

'Ralph Gill would prefer it if you remembered no assailants.'

'Ralph who? Oh, the reverend-looking man who has charge of the animals. What story does he want me to tell?'

'That you were so flustered with drink you somehow wandered into the animal yard. Were you drunk?'

'No, Nick, I was not drunk,' said Edmund, taking a large swallow of his small beer.

'Did you kill Leonard Leman? Not deliberately kill him, but is it possible that while you were struggling you struck out at him with your little knife?'

'I was overcome, outnumbered. I did not even have time to find my little knife, let alone wield it. The little knife is clean. Truth to tell, although I may be too ready to wave it around, it has never been used in anger.'

'So you are one of those roaring boys.'

'Call me what names you please, Nick. I deserve it and you've earned the right. I confess I acquired a bit of a reputation in Stratford for bad behaviour, but I swear to you it was always more noise than substance. And I swear I had nothing to do with that man's death. Am I going to be called to give evidence?'

'I do not know. I think Gill wants to pass it off as some terrible misfortune, and that may cause him to avoid mentioning your name if possible. It depends how it is presented to the Justice or coroner. Then it depends how important Leonard Leman is – or was. How much trouble his family will raise over his death.'

'But they were there. At least his wife was.'

'Which suggests that she too might have an interest in covering things up,' I said. 'We need to discover more about them.'

'Martin Barton claims to know them,' said Edmund.

It turned out that Martin Barton was more than willing to tell us about the Lemans, and Leonard Leman in particular. Edmund and I called on Barton in his lodgings not far from the Blackfriars playhouse. He was scarcely out of bed, and his red hair was all awry, but he made us welcome enough. Barton was less regretful to hear the news of Leman's death than he was curious about the circumstances, which we presented as an 'accident in the house of lions'. Curious and a little suspicious.

'Would this accident have anything to do with that great egg on your forehead, Edmund Shakespeare?'

'Possibly,' said Edmund, automatically dabbing a finger to his wounded brow. 'But we will tell you more, Martin, if you provide us with a little information about the Lemans.'

'Where to begin? Leonard Leman used to be a fine figure of a man in his younger days. Nimble and lithe, although you wouldn't think it to see him now. Now he is a great bear of a man – or a great lion, given where he has apparently died. For certain, he is dead?'

'He is dead,' I said. 'How do you know what he was like in his young days, Martin? You'd have been at school.'

'I make it my business to find out about our patrons.

Do you want to hear what I've got to say or not, Nicholas? You as good as woke me up just now with your thundering at my door.'

'I apologize. Please proceed.'

'As I was saying, Leonard Leman once cut a fine figure. He even caught the eye of Queen Elizabeth with his dancing, and for a time he basked in the sun of her favour. Not in the hottest, brightest spot. He dwelled in the more temperate zones. Lucky for him, considering what happened to her closest favourites. Then young Leman grew older and larger and more bear-like, and long before the queen died he fell from whatever favour he enjoyed. But there's been talk recently that he is trying to worm his way into the favour of the present king.'

'Not much chance of that once he lost his looks,' said Edmund.

'Shush, we will have no talk of the king's tastes here,' said Martin Barton, waggling a finger. He looked almost offended, but it was probably on his own account rather than King James's.

'I apologize,' said Edmund.

'There is more than one way of acquiring favour with a monarch, you know,' continued Barton after a pause. 'It is said that Leman was devising some scheme for pleasing the king. And it was specially needful for him to gain favour.'

'Why?'

'Because, Nicholas, some unflattering remarks that he made about the Scots nation got back to the king's ears.'

Ever since James had come by the throne, two topics provided London's gossip: his preference for handsome courtiers (in this he was not so unlike the old queen) and his favouritism towards his fellow countrymen, or at least the nobility among them. They'd been flocking south to join him. So much so that it sometimes seemed as if half of Scotland had tumbled down the map into the bottom of England.

'So what is this scheme for regaining the king's favour?' I said. The idea flashed through my mind that it might be connected to the mysterious Scoto.

'I do not know everything, Nicholas.'

'You are much better informed than we are,' I said. This was flattery, but it was also the truth. 'What can you tell us about Alice Leman?'

'Not much more than you saw for yourself outside that bookseller's. She is younger than her husband by a good few years. She is large-boned and striking.'

'That she is,' said Edmund.

'The story goes that each married the other in the expectation of coming by a great fortune, and that both have been disappointed. Which I believe often occurs in a marriage.'

'And which made it even more necessary for Leonard Leman to regain the king's favour, if money was in question' I said. 'I wonder how his wife is taking the news of his death.'

'I could find out,' said Martin. 'I could call on her to present my condolences. I might even offer to compose a piece or two in memory of Mr Leman. She might welcome an elegy or a eulogy. She knows me, slightly.'

I refrained from saying that she hadn't even noticed him outside Owen's shop the other day and instead remarked: 'You don't write elegies but satires.'

'Like Edmund's brother, the great William, I can turn my hand to anything,' said Martin Barton. 'Besides, the widow's patronage would be useful.'

Martin grew more animated. I don't know whether he had suggested the visit out of simple curiosity or whether he was really on the watch for a patron. I was more

convinced than ever that all of Barton's satirical bile was
a cover for a fawning attitude towards those more powerful
and wealthy than he – which, in the case of a writer (or
a player), comprises nearly everybody. Nevertheless, and
almost against my will, I felt myself warming towards the
redhead. There was something artless about his guile.

'I will come with you,' I said. 'I too will condole with
the widow Leman.'

'What about me?' said Edmund.

'You? You will keep out of mischief,' I said. 'You'd be
recognized – particularly if Alice Leman was one of those
who attacked you.'

'What's all this?' said Martin. 'So you were attacked,
Edmund Shakespeare, and by a woman too. Now you
must keep your side of the bargain and tell all.'

It didn't take long for Edmund to recount his time in the
animal house in the Tower or for me to throw in my
ha'p'orth. Edmund was voluble enough now that his
immediate fear of being accused and incarcerated seemed
to be receding. In fact his chief anxiety was that his brother
might get to hear of his adventures. For myself, I thought
that he remained in great danger from the law and that
an interrogation by WS would be as nothing to what he'd
get from a Justice. He was still open to blame.

We left him nursing his wound in Martin Barton's lodgings
and likely to fall asleep after such a testing night. The
Lemans lived near the Strand and so the playwright and
I set off westwards. Despite everything that had happened,
it was not yet midday. The sun burned with holiday warmth,
and the air, softened by a pleasant breeze, was clearer than
usual. Naturally Martin had taken the trouble to find out
about the Lemans' dwelling, which was called Pride House.
'Not on account of the aspirations of the owner, Nicholas,'

he said, 'but because a religious foundation once stood on the site. The name is probably a corruption of "prayer" or "priory".' Martin was unusually cheerful and chattered away about widows and wealth and the corruption of all earthly things.

Leonard and Alice Leman did not have one of the great dwellings by the Strand, but Pride House was ample enough, with a main entrance in a high wall fronting a courtyard. There was a porter to whom Martin spoke in a lofty fashion, saying that we'd come to pay our respects to Mrs Leman. The porter said not a word but waved us through with a supercilious smile, as if he knew we were the mere sweepings of the public stage. Either that or he felt an obligation to live up to the name of the house. I might have thought it odd that the gatekeeper did not look particularly sad even though the master of the house was dead, but the idea never occurred to me.

What did occur was regret that I had offered to accompany Martin. I had no business being here, no part to play. Weren't we just prying? Prying in Pride House? But another, inner voice said that, if we could somehow discover the truth about what had happened in the animal arena the previous night, it would help to exonerate Edmund Shakespeare from blame. I had time to think these thoughts because the paved courtyard was empty and the house presented a blank face to us. There were no servants scurrying about, no open windows, no sounds. Perhaps this really was a place in mourning.

The silence was abruptly broken by a woman's cry. It sounded almost like grief and came not from within the house but from a wide walk that led down one flank of the building. Martin and I glanced at each other and together we moved towards the source. Flowering trees and shrubs clustered next to the pebbled path, and flakes of blossom floated through the air. The walk opened into a garden at the rear of the house, and at the point where it did there was an arbour so that the owner might sit in peace, shaded and secure, to survey his property. One side of the arbour was the outer wall of the garden, while along and over the wooden lattice which shielded it from our eyes there grew rosemary and roses which were not yet in full bloom.

But despite the foliage we were aware of figures, unidentified figures, on the other side of the lattice. There was the sound of rustling fabric, there were subdued sighs and groans. Grief? I did not think so.

We crept closer. Fortunately there was grass under our feet now. But I do not think we would have been heard anyway. The persons in the arbour were too occupied with their own concerns. Getting as close as we dared, Martin and I squinted between the interstices of the wooden frame, with the scent of rosemary tickling at our nostrils.

There was a long stone seat immediately below us. It must have been quite hard – the notion drifted across the back of my mind – quite hard to lie on, especially when you were bearing the weight of another individual. But Alice Leman did not seem to be aware of the stoniness of her couch. Rather, her eyes were tight shut and her arms firmly fastened around the back of the man who was lying on top of her, shoving away. I could have reached through and grasped one of the lady's shod feet since it and the corresponding leg were awkwardly propped on the back of the stone bench, while the other was out of sight, no doubt planted on the ground as a kind of buttress. The man's posture looked nearly as uncomfortable as hers, but he too was oblivious to his surroundings. I wasn't sure of the man's identity. It certainly wasn't Alice Leman's husband. Not only was he dead, but he had fair hair which was quite unlike the dark locks on the fellow assailing the widow.

We watched the scene for a while. Once we'd had enough, we crept backwards like villains in a play. When we were at a safe distance, we did an about-face and I said to Martin Barton: 'That puts paid to your idea of writing an elegy. Alice Leman has better things to do with her time than lament a dead husband.'

'Not at all, Nick,' said Martin. 'She'll feel guilty as sin after a while and welcome a lament.'

'Who was that man with her?'

'I believe it was the household steward, Jack Corner.'

I remembered the individual, thin as a rail, who'd been keeping company with Mr and Mrs Leman outside Davy Owen's bookshop. I remembered the way he'd been gazing at her. It is not unknown for stewards to enjoy a liaison with the lady of the house and, for every one who succeeds, there may be a dozen who aspire to it. The only surprising thing was the speed with which the affair was being consummated.

Then two or three things happened at once. We were about halfway down the path beside the house and, believing that the couple in the arbour were fully occupied, did not trouble to keep our voices down as much as we should. But the silence from that quarter might have told us that they were finished and more at leisure to pay attention to their surroundings. Then I was seized with a fit of sneezing. Something spring-like and itchy – the memory of the rosemary on the arbour lattice or a different plant beside the path – got up my nose, and I was convulsed with atishoos. At the same instant a person appeared at the point where the path met the courtyard at the front of the house. He halted when he saw us. There were shouts from our rear, a man and a woman. It was the steward and the widow.

Martin Barton and I took to our heels. As we neared the individual standing at the corner of the house, we swerved to avoid him, one on either side. But in all the confusion Martin and I managed to strike him a blow on each shoulder so that he tumbled backwards to the ground and almost took us with him. Though my eyes were still blurry from the sneezing fit, I recognized Davy Owen. He was carrying a rectangular box that flew out of his hands and up over his head, landing with a crack on the paving of the courtyard. Without thinking, I stooped to pick it up. I don't know why. Perhaps I was intending to return it to the St Paul's yard bookseller out of some sense of guilt. But there came more cries from behind us and Martin tugged at my sleeve to urge me on. We made for the entrance.

Alerted by the noise, the porter was too quick for us and, stepping out of his lodge, he slammed shut the door and stood there, arms folded and a grin on his face. Meantime, more figures had emerged from the house and were approaching Martin and me at a diagonal. We slowed, then halted, uncertain where to go next.

I glanced down at the box cradled in my arms. Made of wood but reinforced with metal at the corners, the box had been damaged by the force with which it had struck the ground. A panel on the top was cracked. The case was large enough to contain, say, a pair of pistols. But it was not pistols that I could glimpse through the splintered wood.

By now we were surrounded by the occupants of Pride House: Mistress Leman, her steward Jack Corner, the gatekeeper and several servants dressed in yellow livery. I noticed that Alice Leman and Corner looked flustered, with their clothes in slight disarray, but I suppose that could have been accounted for by their haste to raise the alarm. I also noticed Alice looking curiously at Martin Barton, as though she half-recognized him. Even so, it's possible we might have bluffed our way out of the place if it hadn't been for Davy Owen. He remembered us very well and, with the indignity of being tumbled on his back all too apparent on his face, he drew near.

'It is you,' he said. 'I thought it was you. A pair of rogues, you are. Give me back my property.'

He made to grab the case but I turned away and clutched it tighter. It was a pointless gesture. Martin and I could easily have been overpowered, and the box seized from my hands, but we had not yet reached the moment of physical force. We weren't exactly intruders – we'd been freely admitted by the gatekeeper – but neither were we welcome guests. Martin did a little bow and said: 'My condolences, madam, on the death of your husband.'

Alice Leman looked surprised as if she'd already forgotten about her husband. Then she recovered herself and said: 'Thank you, Mr . . . ?'

'Martin Barton. Of the Blackfriars Children.'

'That is where I have seen you.'

'And I you,' said Martin, all self-possession now. 'You and your husband.'

To give the widow credit, she did not indulge in any false tears or long faces. 'Well, my husband is gone. But I am here. Who are you?'

'Nicholas Revill, a player with the King's Men. I too am sorry to hear of your loss. In the Tower, wasn't it?'

I said this to prompt her to some expression of regret, although all she said was: 'A sad misfortune but an accident. Those animals!'

For an instant I thought she was referring to men behaving like beasts but, of course, she meant the lions that might have killed Leonard Leman. This was the story that would now be put about. She never asked how we had come by the news, and that in itself was odd. As was the arrival at Pride House of Davy Owen with his box. Or my box at the moment.

Jack Corner the steward coughed to draw attention to himself. He said: 'My Lady, we do not need to stand here listening to a couple of players.'

'I am no player but a playwright and poet,' said Martin, at which Corner wafted his hand as if the distinction was meaningless, while Davy Owen put in: 'Calls himself a playwright – oh, and a satirist too. He does not like the Welsh.'

'We know something of the death of your husband,' I said to Mrs Leman.

She glanced about at the servants standing at a respectful distance before saying: 'It is hot out here and tempers are getting frayed. We should all go indoors.'

So we did.

# VI

We assembled in a large chamber on the upper floor of Pride House. It was a tense, uneasy gathering even after the servants had been dismissed. I was still clutching the wooden box. Davy Owen kept his eyes on it rather than on anything or anyone else, but he did not attempt to wrest it from me. Jack Corner, whose height was made more apparent by a small head, regarded Martin and me with hostility. Alice Leman, meanwhile, seemed divided between curiosity and suspicion.

'What do you know of my husband's death, Mr Revill?'

'Nothing directly, madam. But an associate of ours was present when it happened, and he says that others were there too. He doubts that it was an accident.'

'Then let him come forward and speak out,' said the widow. 'We have nothing to fear.'

We? Presumably she was referring to herself and her steward. Was it known in the household that they were lying together? Certainly there'd been nothing very secret about the cut and thrust in the arbour despite the fact that it was taking place within hours of Leman's death.

'Nothing to fear? Not even a charge of murder?' I said.

Jack Corner took a step forward at that. An angry red spot burned high in each cheek. Mrs Leman put out a hand to restrain him and he halted. In that gesture and response were everything we needed to know: their closeness, her influence over him, his deference to her.

'Why do you say murder, Mr Revill?'

'Because I am holding here a box of bones and for some reason it makes me think of violence and sudden death. What are you doing bearing a box of bones, Davy Owen?'

I shook it, and inside the box the bones I'd glimpsed through the splintered panel rattled away. Having made this display, there seemed little point in holding on to the container any longer. It was heavy and, besides, an unpleasant odour was rising from it. I held it out to Owen.

'This is none of your business,' said the Welshman, snatching it from me.

'We came to you in quest of bones, I remember,' said Martin Barton.

'You got a dusty answer.'

'You sent us to Bernardo Scoto.'

I noticed the look that passed between Alice Leman and her steward at that. They obviously knew the man from Mantua. But then of course Edmund Shakespeare had seen Mr and Mrs Leman, together with Owen, going to Scoto's house before they went on to the Tower animals. What was going on here? I was baffled.

'To be round with you, Mrs Leman,' I said, 'it was you who were seen close to the scene of your husband's death in the Tower.'

'I was there, I admit it. My husband was drawn towards the Tower animals. They were a magnet to him. Like our king, he enjoyed watching the strange beasts. I sometimes accompanied him and our steward too. We were there yesterday evening. I grew tired, however, and found the air close and nauseous. So I left my husband to admire the animals by himself and returned home with Master Corner for company. I do not know exactly what happened after I left, but, with Leonard, valour or curiosity must have got the better part of discretion and he wandered too close to the beasts. He was savaged by the lions, was he not?'

This was remarkable. If she was telling the truth and had not been there at the moment of her husband's death, she could have heard the news only this morning. Yet she spoke in such even tones that she might have been talking about a stranger who had carelessly fallen victim to the lions. But then perhaps she was not very fond of her husband. Perhaps her attentions had long ago shifted in the direction of Jack Corner, who now so far forgot discretion as to put a soothing hand on her arm. Even if Martin and I hadn't witnessed them at it, we would have known them for lovers. Yet surely lovers, if they had carried out a murder, would put on a show of grief to allay suspicion? That they were not doing so could be construed as proof of innocence. Or indifference. Or brazenness.

'Is a little sorrow in order, madam?' I said. 'I ask only because, not being married myself, I am not sure how these things are carried on between husband and wife.'

'They are carried on as they are carried on, Mr Revill.

Be sure that you will be the first to know when I want to advertise my sorrow.'

Almost despite myself I was impressed by her cold dignity. There was nothing more we would be allowed to discover here. I said farewell to Mrs Leman, and Martin Barton made a more elaborate goodbye to her. We nodded to the steward called Corner and ignored Davy Owen, who was still keeping watch over his bone-box. No one tried to stop us leaving.

Martin and I said nothing until we'd made our exit from Pride House, crossed the courtyard and passed under the gaze of the supercilious gatekeeper.

'We shall get no further with them,' said Martin when we were back in the Strand. He was echoing my thoughts. 'Maybe it is as Mistress Leman says: her husband walked too close to the lions and paid for it with his life.'

'It's a story that would suit everyone. But there was mischief going on in the Tower. Edmund Shakespeare did not beat himself up.'

'And then there is that Welsh bookseller and his box of bones. You saw them, Nicholas?'

'Indistinctly – but they were bones, yes.'

'Human bones?'

'I suppose so. How could I tell?'

How could I tell? They might have been not human but animal. It was rumoured that what passed for the relics of saints in their crystal or metal settings were often no more than bones of sheep. I thought of the bone that Edmund Shakespeare had given to William and which had been supplied by Davy Owen, the large bone I'd assumed came from a human limb, even one of King Arthur's. I remembered the unicorn horn hanging from the ceiling in Scoto's den. That was nothing human. So where would one go for large, queerly shaped items of bone?

'What?' I said. Martin Barton had made some comment.

'I said, I would like to cause trouble for Mr Owen.'

'Because he is Welsh? Because he referred in a less-than-respectful way to your trade of writing?'

'I do not rise above malice,' said Barton as if claiming some special virtue.

There was certainly something unsettled, as well as unsettling, about the situation. We returned to Barton's lodgings and found Edmund recovered from his bad night and ready for action.

A notion was taking shape in my head, and I outlined to the others what we might do.

A few hours later we were sitting in the Black Swan, the tavern close to the narrow-windowed house at the corner of Tower Street. From our position in the front room of the Swan we could keep watch on Scoto's place. We were not rewarded until late in the afternoon, when we saw our old friend Davy Owen approaching the house. I half-expected him to be bearing books or bones, but he was carrying nothing.

Owen must have been a very welcome visitor for instead of knocking he was about to let himself in with a key which he retrieved from his jerkin. He would have done so had not I, closely followed by Martin and Edmund, raced out of the tavern to intercept the bookseller at the front door.

Davy Owen looked alarmed and, rather than fumble with the key, he banged on the door to be let in. That was a mistake, because it was opened almost straight away by Nano, the dwarfish attendant. Together with Owen, we jostled ourselves inside and stood in the hallway. There was an awkward silence. I had impressed on the others that we must not resort to force. Now I said, not to the little servant but to the bookseller: 'Forgive this intrusion, but we must speak to Scoto of Mantua. Tell him that we know the truth, about the bones and the king and the Lemans. Tell him that we have uncovered a plot and that we must see him now, even if he does claim to be a creature of the night.'

Owen nodded and scuttled off down the passage, disappearing into its far shadows. Meantime, Nano planted himself across our path and folded his arms. The three of us could have bowled him over, but it would have felt like attacking a child. Besides, he looked as though he might have put up a good fight.

After a time, and as if he were obeying some hidden signal, Nano stood to one side and with mock ceremony bowed us through. Once again, Edmund, Martin and I approached Scoto's den at the end of the passage. We knocked and were bidden to enter. Inside, there was no way of guessing the time of day from the smoky, ill-lit interior.

The Italian was sitting at his desk as before, his head covered with a cap and his shape largely concealed by the mantle with its cabbalistic symbols.

'You 'ave something to tell me,' he said. '*Il segreto.*'

'It is to do with King Arthur's bones,' I said, appointing myself as speaker. 'As you know, this gentleman here purchased one from a bookseller friend of yours – where is Davy Owen, by the way?'

'Signor Owen?' said Scoto, as if he'd never come across the name before. ''e is about the 'ouse.'

'No,' I said. 'I think he is sitting right in front of us.'

I took a couple of steps forward and, greatly daring, snatched the cap off Scoto's head. He clapped his hand over his scalp but not before the distinctive arrow-shaped pattern of hair was revealed.

It was Davy Owen. He stood up. His eyes flicked from one to another of us. Seeing that denial was useless, he said in an accent that substituted a Welsh lilt for the Italian cadence: 'My congratulations, Mr Revill. How did you guess?'

'The fact that the two of you were never seen together, the fact that Martin Barton here said that your voice was wrong for a citizen of Mantua, the fact that I'm a player and can usually tell when someone's acting a part. Your speech was seeded with Italian phrases, Mr Owen, like flowers in a garden, all carefully set out for the sake of ornament.'

'Well, well,' said Owen. 'I am uncovered in both senses. You may give me back my cap now.'

I did so. Martin and Edmund were looking at Owen (or Scoto) in surprise. Whatever turn of events they'd expected, it wasn't this. I was surprised too, for I had only been half-convinced by my own reasoning.

Owen resumed his cap and became Scoto once more. He went back to his place behind the desk while we three stood before him, half-suppliants, half-accusers.

'What is the point of this deception?' said Martin.

'Deception? Can a man not have two lives, can he not pursue two trades? *Due mestieri.* As a bookseller I have something of a line in herbals, while as a practitioner of the art I prepare and administer them. Under one name I stand with my own race and am proud to be Welsh. In the other part I assume the guise of an Italian. It's better for trade, you see.'

'Trade must be pretty good, judging by this house and your premises in St Paul's yard,' I said. 'But you don't just deal in herbs and remedies, Signor Davy; you also handle stolen goods.'

'Nothing stolen. Only what is rightfully acquired.'

'Then, if not stolen, you are attempting to pass off one thing as another. It's a type of forgery. You get bones from the dead animals in the Tower and you claim that they are the remnants of fabulous creatures – the unicorn up there, for example, or the mermaid's ribs.'

I gestured overhead, where the bones were suspended. The man in the cap and cloak raised his arms.

'Where is the harm in that? It is no great imposture. Have you never visited a fair where the monsters are exhibited, Mr Revill? Do you think that woman behind the curtain really has two heads or that the fish-man is covered with genuine scales?'

'The harm comes when you try to pass off some animal bones not as a unicorn's or a mermaid's but as a great king's. When you are selling them to Leonard Leman because he wishes to curry favour with King James and knows that one sure way of doing that would be to present the monarch with Arthur's remains.'

'I had those bones from a different source,' said Owen. 'I know that they are real. For I am Welsh, you know, and Arthur was of our tribe.'

'Perhaps some of the bones are real, but I think that you grew greedy and were prepared to use any old bones you came across. You sold one to my friend Edmund here and he in turn gave it to someone else. The Lemans found out you'd disposed of one and were angry with you. We saw you arguing the other day outside your shop. The argument continued last night at the Tower. Perhaps it turned violent. At any rate, Leonard Leman is dead.'

'Not by my hand.'

'Then whose?'

Davy Owen, who was also Bernardo Scoto of Mantua, hesitated for a moment. He looked wildly about the chamber. He was no longer the mysterious Italian mountebank or the canny Welsh bookseller. He was simply desperate to save his skin.

'It was the good lady, Alice Leman! She and that steward of hers. You must have seen the way they were acting towards each other this morning. They could not wait until the husband was cold in his grave. They had no interest in Arthur's bones or anyone else's bones. No one's bones except their own, which they want to grind against each other without let or hindrance.'

'You are lying!'

The tapestry, which stood against the left-hand wall, stirred and for a moment I thought one of the strange, demonic figures on it had spoken. My hair prickled. But there must have been another, secret entrance into the room that way. And a recess behind the tapestry to allow for eavesdroppers. From behind the arras there entered Alice Leman. She strode across to Owen.

'I have been listening to every lying word, Davy. Nano let me in, thinking I had come on business. I have always been a friend to Nano and so he is a friend to me. I heard voices coming from here and thought I would see who your visitors were. And hear what tales you were spinning. Just like the tales you spun to my husband. The king's bones, indeed! It is a fable.'

'No fable,' protested Owen. 'The bones – some of the bones – are real.'

'As real as your accusation of murder. Gentlemen—' she turned towards us '—what I told you this morning is the truth, if not quite all of it. We went to the Tower yesterday evening. I won't conceal from you that my late husband had business there, business that I did not approve of.'

'I was there too,' said Edmund Shakespeare. It was the first time he'd spoken. 'I was attacked. I bear the marks.'

Mrs Leman nodded. 'I regret that. My husband was fearful of some trap and my ... steward ... believed he had caught a spy, who was set on rather ferociously.'

'It was I,' said Edmund. 'I was dragged down to the animal yard.'

'That was none of my doing. I and Mr Corner left soon afterwards. As I said, I was nauseous. Not so much because of the air in that place as because I wanted nothing more to do with what was happening. It is not I or Mr Corner who should be accused of murder but this gentleman here, this bookseller, this mountebank. I want nothing more to do with him. We are returning the fresh bones that he brought to Pride House this morning.'

She raised her voice slightly and, on cue, a second figure stepped out from behind the arras. Really, this was as good as a play for its disguises, surprises and improbable entrances. This time it was Jack Corner. He was carrying the battered wooden box. He walked across to Owen and tipped the contents into his lap.

'I didn't do it! It was the lions!' said Davy. 'They savaged Leman to death. We quarrelled, true, but it was the lions did for your husband!'

'They may have done their own work,' said the widow, 'but be sure you led the way with your knife. I may not be in a great state of grief for my husband, but I would not stoop to murder.'

Davy Owen's nerve broke. The presence of five accusers was too much. He leaped up, scattering fragments of bone, and bolted past us to the door. It was some moments before we gathered our wits and set off in pursuit. There was no sign of Nano, but the open front door gave clear sign of where his master had gone.

The sun was beginning to go down, but we saw the still-cloaked-and-capped figure running up Tower Hill and then swerving to the left down Petty Wales. I wondered why he was doing this, then realized that it was probably the most direct route to the river. He would have to run down the flank of the Tower, the same path I'd taken that very morning.

We – Edmund, Jack Corner and I – were a couple of hundred yards behind Owen, with Martin Barton and Alice Leman bringing up the rear. He could not escape us, unless he managed to get a ferry across the river and lose himself in the meadows on the far side.

In blind panic Davy Owen ran alongside the Tower wall and across the quay where I had been standing earlier that day. He disappeared over the edge, down the steps. We reached the brink and halted. The tide was going out again.

We saw Davy Owen blundering and squelching across the mud and stone, head down, scarcely conscious of where he was going but doubtless hoping to reach the river and a ferryman.

There were no ferrymen in sight, but the bear was there, sitting by the water's edge, its yellowy-white coat distinct on the grey foreshore. For all I know it had been sitting there the whole day long, trying to catch fish. There was still no sign of any keeper.

We gazed, horrified, as Davy Owen blundered bearwards. When he was almost on top of the creature he realized where he was and slid to a stop. Too late! He toppled back in the mud and slime and the animal reared up. Perhaps it was aggrieved that it had spent a day in the sun without a catch. Perhaps it craved human company. Perhaps it wanted vengeance for years of captivity or had been maddened by them. Whatever the reason, it started towards Davy Owen as if to pursue the unfortunate Welshman. It swung one of its mighty paws against his head and I swear we heard the dull clout from where we stood on top of the quay.

Davy Owen swayed and then fell face down in the mud and lay still. If the blow had not killed him, then he would surely be stifled in the mud. The bear dropped back on all fours and, as far as the chain securing it to the stake would permit, snuffed around the body. I could imagine its breath, hot and stinky. Davy Owen did not move. After a time the bear resumed its sitting position by the water, although it no longer splashed its paws in the water. For some reason I felt sorry, not for the (surely) dead man but for the bear.

We stayed where we were, now joined by Martin and Mrs Leman, not certain what to do next.

# VII

But there was nothing for us to do and, when a few passers-by gathered to look at the dead man and the white bear, we walked away.

You may be interested to hear what happened to the few characters in this story. The death of Leonard Leman was accounted an accident. Maybe Davy Owen had killed him, maybe it was the lions. Rather like the famous Roman, Julius Caesar, the one-time favourite of Queen Elizabeth had been struck and gouged many times, and it was not possible to say who had done what, whether animal or human. All things considered, it was better to blame the lions. Nothing would happen to them; the king was too fond of his creatures. So the (more or less) blameless Alice Leman duly married her steward, Jack Corner, and they are established at Pride House. She took the dwarfish Nano into her employment.

Martin Barton continues to write his satires and grows more carping as he grows more successful. Edmund Shakespeare began to plough a kind of furrow as a player with his brother's company, with us, with the King's Men, and he was not doing too badly before things were brought to a premature close. Edmund had already been ploughing another kind of furrow. The woman I'd seen hanging about his ears at the Mermaid tavern bore him a child in the summer of the following year. You remember the one who was called Dolly or Polly, the one with dark curling hair and the big tits? Edmund was ready enough to acknowledge the child as his – which, in itself, marked him out as a decent enough fellow for a player – but the little thing lasted no longer than a few weeks. And the father followed a few months later, dying in the December of 1607. William Shakespeare paid to have the great bell at St Saviour's in Southwark rung in his memory. I am not sure how far WS lamented his brother's passing, and if Edmund hadn't been a Shakespeare I don't suppose anyone else apart from Dolly or Polly would have given him more than a passing thought or tear either.

Before any of this, we gave a selective account of what had happened to William Shakespeare, Edmund and I. We included the bear. We could hardly have left the bear out, for the fatal attack on an innocent bookseller was briefly the talk of London. We also mentioned some of the other mischief but not the whole story. WS probably guessed there was more to it, but he didn't press us. He did not even ask how Edmund had acquired the great bump on his forehead. We were sitting in his Silver Street lodgings, drinking, chatting. I was curious about WS's plan to write a play on the matter of Britain and King Arthur. I recalled that both the bone and some pages of his manuscript had gone missing. Stolen? It seemed not.

'My landlady took the bone. She thought it was an unhealthy thing to have in her house, and perhaps she was right. I am sorry, Edmund, since you presented it to me, but I fear it has ended up in some midden.'

WS did not seem unduly concerned by the fate of the relic, while Edmund too was unbothered. He seemed more pleased to be in WS's good books.

'And the sheets of manuscript?' I persisted.

'Nothing sinister, Nick. They must have blown out of the window. I found a few in the garden below. The ink had run and the snails had left silver tracks across them. I think I shall take it as a sign.'

'A sign?'

'That I should not pursue the subject of King Arthur. It is a doomed idea, or at least it is not one for me.'

'I have an idea for a play, William,' said Edmund. 'Or for an incident in a play. It would be exciting. A man chased by a bear.'

WS gazed at his brother in disbelief. 'Chased by a bear? And caught? And eaten? Like that unfortunate bookseller on the Thames.'

'He wasn't eaten,' I said.

'Good,' said WS. 'As I get older I find I am less inclined to put violence and horror on stage. Leave that to the rising generation.'

'You could have the bear chase the man offstage,' said Edmund. 'Then you wouldn't have to witness anything unpleasant. Sounds only. Cries. Crunching.'

'Exit pursued by a bear?'

'Why not?'

'I'll think on it,' said WS.

# ACT FIVE

'Yeeugh!'

The screech woke Joe Malinferno from his disturbed slumbers. He had been dreaming of a horde of Egyptian mummies rising from their stony sarcophagi and pursuing him down the dingy London streets near where he lodged. Just as the greyish bindings unravelled from the skull of the leading mummy, revealing its gaping, dusty jaw, the scream reverberated in his brain. He sat up abruptly, his tangled shirt sticking uncomfortably to his sweaty torso.

'Wh . . . aaat?'

His vocal cords were numbed, and he could hardly articulate his own cry of fear. He forced his eyes wide open, half-afraid that his nightmare might manifest itself in the grubby reality of his bedroom. Instead all he could discern in the darkness was a pair of pale, skinny buttocks poking towards him from across the room. He paused to admire them for a few minutes. The girl to whom the buttocks belonged then turned her pallid face towards him.

'Here. There's bones in this bag.'

'Come back to bed . . . Kitten.' He recalled her name just at the last minute, though its ridiculousness stuck on his tongue. Picking up a bawd in a gin-shop in Tooley Street was not his normal practice, and it wasn't conducive to remembering the girl's name later. Still, she had displayed a pleasing aspect last night, and he was drunk and in need of a romp. But by the cold light of day and in a more sober, if hung-over, mood Malinferno found her attractions less certain. However, the bed was still warm, and so were his passions. He beckoned her over to him, lifting the sheets enticingly.

'They are just some old bones that Augustus Bromhead left me for safekeeping. They are of no consequence.'

The girl pouted, her pinched face puckering ever narrower until she began to resemble a rat. Malinferno was familiar with the appearance of such rodents. Creechurch Lane was on a convenient axis between Billingsgate Fish Market and Spitalfields, and rats infested the neighbourhood around his lodgings. One morning he had awoken to come face to face with a bold example of *Rattus norvegicus* sitting on his chest. He had screamed, and the rat had scurried off back behind the wood panelling that clad the bottom half of Malinferno's bedroom. Kitten now looked less like the creature she was named after and more like a feline's best enemy. She was bereft only of a rat's whiskers. Though now that he looked closer, he could discern a fair sprinkling of hair on her upper lip too. He shuddered and let the sheets drop. Suddenly he was no longer in the mood to continue his amorous adventures. At least not with the pinch-faced Kit, who was now picking up one of the bones. A thigh-bone by its length and thickness, Malinferno reckoned. She waved it in the air.

'Ooooh! Is it from one of them E-gyptian mummies?'

Malinferno smiled condescendingly. The fashion for all things Egyptian had been occasioned by England's old enemy, Napoleon Bonaparte, and his invasion of that far-off land twenty years ago or more. Now, in 1818, it appeared that even a low bawd was influenced by the obsessions of the fashionable London set.

'No. These are a mere hundred and fifty years old. Augustus Bromhead is an antiquarian, not an Egyptologist.'

He could see by Kit's puzzled look that he had lost her already, and sighed. No use explaining to the girl the fine difference between his own interest in all things ancient and Egyptian, and Bromhead's immersion in the more mundane and recent history of England. Neither man had much time for the other's obsession, though both were eager to display their own knowledge to each other. It was only the previous day that Bromhead had thrust at Malinferno the bones that Kit was now playing with.

'Tell me how old you think these bones are, young Giuseppe.'

The elderly man always used the proper version of Malinferno's first name. Sometimes Joe thought it was done just to annoy him. Giuseppe was indeed the name with which he had been christened in his father's native town of Padua. But he had been brought to England as a baby by his mother after the unfortunate demise of his father in circumstances his mother never explained. And as he grew up he easily adopted the familiar name of Joe, though his surname remained exotically Italianate. But Bromhead was strictly observant of formalities, so Giuseppe he was to the rotund, little dwarf of a man. The antiquarian had been perched as always on a high stool in his study amid a perfect blizzard of old texts, ancient stones and maps. Without getting down from his seat, he pushed a large canvas sack across the table towards Malinferno. Joe wondered if this was some sort of test of his scientific abilities. He hesitated a moment.

'Go on. They won't bite.'

Bromhead waved his strangely delicate hands at the sack and winked grotesquely. As if by way of explanation of his excitement, he described their origins.

'I had them dug up myself. Witnessed the exhumation, indeed. At the Church of St Materiana in Trevenna in Cornwall.'

A wink once again contorted his wrinkled features, but it still left Malinferno in the dark concerning Bromhead's interest in the contents of the sack.

'How old are they, Augustus?'

Bromhead gave out a cackling laugh.

'That is what I want you to tell me. You are always dabbling in the unrolling fad. You must know truly ancient bones when you see them.'

The antiquarian was referring to a new trend among society figures for holding a soirée at which an Egyptian mummy was the central guest. But the embalmed body was not there to be treated with respect and honour. A grotesque delectation in unravelling the burial bindings and revealing the skeleton within had gripped the smart set. And it was not scientific curiosity but rather a morbid delight in causing feigned horror that was the purpose. Some ladies affected to swoon quite away when the skull was revealed. Much to Bromhead's annoyance, Malinferno had already taken part in two such unrollings. Joe, however, saw it as the only opportunity he would have to examine genuine mummies outside of the British Museum. So what if he had to play up to the upper-class set who frequented such events? He was already becoming known as 'Il Professore', and he quite liked the notoriety. Nor was he above purloining some of the jewels and other items that were sometimes bound within the funerary cerements. He waved aside Bromhead's scornful remark.

'So my perverting the true cause of science is acceptable now that it may be of some use to you, Augustus.'

'Yes, well . . . we will say no more about that. I suppose you can salvage some knowledge from the depredations of the smart set. Knowledge you can now put to good use by telling me how old these bones are.'

Once again he pushed the canvas sack towards Malinferno. Joe picked it up, and the contents rattled against each other as he hefted the sack over his shoulder.

'I will give you my considered opinion as to whether they are as old as an Egyptian pharaoh or as recent as something snatched from a grave by the Borough Gang.'

Malinferno's naming of the best-known gang of bodysnatchers caused Bromhead to glance around nervously. As a man of limited stature, and odd proportions, it was quite possible he was already on some surgeon's list. There was nothing that such eminent medical men as Astley Cooper liked more than giants and dwarfs to anatomize. And the Borough Gang served their voracious needs. Bromhead's room, with its dark corners and strange funereal collections of stones and bones, suddenly felt an unpleasant place in which to be. Malinferno laughed at his friend's frisson of fear, but in truth he too felt a cold finger of horror travel up his spine. The Borough Gang was not one to mess with, especially if you might be on their shopping list. For once, Malinferno gave private thanks for his nondescript appearance. He hurried from the antiquarian's lodgings and back across the Thames. He deposited the bones in his own rooms, giving them only a cursory glance before resorting once more to the south side of the river Thames. And the gin-shops of Tooley Street, where his meagre funds would stretch further. There he encountered the rat-featured Kitten, and in a rash moment smuggled her into his rooms.

Now he was faced with the task of retrieving the thighbone from her grasp and smuggling her back out of the house without Mrs Stanhope, his landlady, spotting her. He slid from under the bedclothes and, pulling his shirt down to cover his privates, he nervously approached the bawd, who was now giggling and poking at him with the large bone. Malinferno noted, not for the first time, that it was unusually long, and probably had belonged to a man who had stood more than six feet tall when he was alive. And it was all the more capable of braining him if Kitten swung it in the wrong direction.

'Now, come on, Kit. Don't be silly. You have to go now.'

'Not until you have paid me, James.'

'Joe, the name is Joe. And I have paid you. In advance in the gin-shop where I picked you up.'

The girl poked him even harder in the chest.

'Yes, but then I didn't know you was a resurrection man, with bones hidden in your place. You'll have to pay me to keep my mouth shut now, James.'

Malinferno cringed. Now he was being accused of being a sack-'em-up man himself. And the tart couldn't even get his name right. He would have to deal with this quickly, or Mrs Stanhope would be woken up by the sound of the altercation. And then he would be out on the street. His landlady did not like women in her gentlemen's rooms. He turned away from Kitten and began to pull on his long breeches, which had lain on the floor after being cast there the previous night in the heat of passion.

'Very well, Kit. Whatever you say. But I shall have to pass your name on to Ben Crouch. He doesn't like people poking their noses into his trade.'

On hearing the name of the legendary leader of the Borough Gang of bodysnatchers, Kitten went limp. She dropped the bone to the floor and scrabbled for her clothes.

'No, that's no trouble, sir. I was only joking. You can have this one on me. No need for Mr Crouch to know about it, is there?'

She didn't wait for Joe to answer but disappeared from

his room faster than the rat that had stood on his chest that other morning. The only difference was that Kitten used the door, rather than the hole in the wainscoting. Malinferno breathed a sigh of relief and picked up the long leg-bone.

Once again he wondered how Bromhead could be so uncertain of its origins. Though Joe couldn't tell a newly buried bone from a pharaoh's, he wasn't about to tell Bromhead that. Probably this skeleton was no more than a hundred or so years old. The location of its discovery should have told the antiquarian whose bones they were likely to be. If they had been dug up anywhere on the edge of the Cornish border, then they were probably the remains of some cavalier or roundhead who had met his end at one of the battles of Lostwithiel. By Joe's reckoning, that put the death in the year 1642 or 1644. There was no possibility that the bones had the age of the few mummified remains from Egypt that Malinferno had had the privilege to examine. But if Bromhead was so deceived as to wish the bones were as old as a mummy's, who on earth did he think they belonged to?

Malinferno had no more time, however, to ponder the eccentricities of Augustus Bromhead. He had an important meeting with a personage he had long wished to talk to. Someone who had actually been to Egypt and seen first hand treasures of which Malinferno had only heard tell. The problem was the man was French, and England's recent skirmish with that nation, and Napoleon Bonaparte in particular, had made it well-nigh impossible to speak to Monsieur Jean-Claude Casteix. But now Bonaparte was safely in exile on St Helena, the English mood had changed. Frenchmen were not viewed with such suspicion as before. In fact some members of the establishment had developed almost a fondness for their old enemy, Napoleon. Which suited Malinferno well, because Monsieur Casteix was not only French but a close associate of Bonaparte's from his Egyptian expedition of 1798. He had been one of the savants who accompanied Bonaparte on his campaign, and he had accumulated a large collection of artefacts. The problem was that, when the French forces had capitulated to the British in 1801, General Hutchinson had cast covetous eyes on the savants' collection of antiquities. Which had included the Rosetta Stone, reputedly the key to Egyptian hieroglyphics and most Egyptologists' Holy Grail.

Malinferno had ideas about deciphering the stone, and enhancing his own glory in the field. But first he had to speak to Jean-Claude Casteix, who twenty years ago had refused to be parted from the collection plundered by the British, and who had come to England with it. Today was the day he had finally got himself an interview with the great man, and he didn't propose to miss it. Despite a sick headache, resulting from his anxious imbibing of too much gin the previous night, he hastened to dress. Though his shirt was a little grubby from the night before, he thought it would suffice if he wore his best double-breasted waistcoat and a clean cravat over it. The problem was his fingers were too shaky to tie his linen in the latest fashion. And when he had managed it, it lay flat and irregular beneath his chin like a soiled napkin.

'Damn! It will have to do for now. Or I shall miss my chance with Casteix.'

He cast around for his Hessian boots, which had been discarded the previous evening at the height of his passion.

'Double damn. I shall have to go barefoot if I don't find them soon.'

He realized it was a clear indication of his anxiety that he was talking to himself in this way, and he resolved to stop up his mutterings. Finally, tight-lipped, he found his boots behind the aged chaise longue beneath the window. For a moment he had an image of Kitten drunkenly yanking his boots off and collapsing behind the chaise longue in a flurry of muslin and bare thighs. His sick headache gave a vigorous twinge, and he closed his eyes on the scene. Sitting down abruptly before his dizzy swoon tipped him over, he took a deep breath and yanked on his boots. At least his tall hat and Garrick overcoat did not require hunting for. They hung in their usual place on the back of the door. He pulled the coat on and slapped the hat rakishly on his head. It was only on an impulse that he then picked up the long bone Kitten had been waving at him and stuffed it in the capacious pocket of his Garrick. No harm in the great savant confirming it as being of no great age. He hurried down the creaky staircase and out into Creechurch Lane.

Young Malinferno's talk of bodysnatchers had upset Augustus Bromhead. It had taken the rest of the day, and several glasses of dry sack, before he had settled enough to go back to his studies. He had always done his best work at night, when the sounds of London had dimmed to a tolerable murmur outside his ramshackle house in Bermondsey. He was fond of the unfashionable area south of the river for its antiquarian associations. Somewhere beneath his feet stood the foundations of Bermondsey Abbey, and some said the very fabric of his house incorporated parts of the abbey. He fancied sometimes he could hear the shuffle of monks' sandals as they made their way to prayer. The sound had always been a comfort to him before. Tonight, however, the extraneous creaks and groans of the house and its environs were making him edgy.

'Damn you, Joe Malinferno, for your scaremongering. How can I concentrate on my task when all I can think about is sack-'em-up men.'

He leaned over his work table and tipped his eyeglasses at a more acute angle in an attempt to read the poorly printed book lying before him. He opened the cover and scanned the title page anew, his lips silently forming the words printed thereon.

*The British History*
Translated into the English from the Latin
of Jeffrey of Monmouth
Printed by J. Bowyer at the Rose in Ludgate Street
MDCCXVIII

Augustus licked his lips at the thought of this old book – an edition of a hundred years ago – telling the stories of the kings of Britain.

'Now, where was I?'

He skipped over the fanciful tale of the island of Albion, inhabited only by giants before Brutus of Troy came to found a nation on its shores. And ignoring the supposed origins of the name of the very city in which he dwelled as referring to a certain Lud who once ruled there, he again dipped into the prophecies of Merlin. He was particularly taken with certain references, which he could quote by heart that he thought referred to the demise of Napoleon.

'A bridle-bit shall be set in her jaws that shall be forged in the Bay of Armorica . . . Then shall there be slaughter of the foreigners; then shall the rivers run blood; then shall gush forth the fountains of Armorica.'

He stopped suddenly. His lilting voice had filled the dark chamber in which he sat, but he fancied there had been another sound. Like the creaking of the stairs leading to this room, which was set high in the eaves of the house. He sat in silence, the only sound being that of his own heart thudding in his chest. He essayed a laugh at his fears, but it came out as a nervous squeak. He spoke to himself again to bolster his courage.

'Hah! I'll be imagining its old Boney himself come to do for me. Despite his safe imprisonment on St Helena. Just because I can discern his downfall in Merlin's words, it does not mean he will come to haunt me.'

The ensuing silence convinced Augustus that he was truly imagining things. He turned the pages of Jeffrey's work and scrutinized the brief sentence that he came back to time and again. Once again it steadfastly refused to give up its secret meaning.

'The renowned King Arthur himself was wounded deadly, and was borne thence unto the Island of Avalon for the healing of his wounds.'

Behind Augustus' back the door swung silently open.

Malinferno felt he was in the presence of royalty. Monsieur Jean-Claude Casteix was attired in a sort of antiquated court dress that had gone out of fashion in England with the arrival of Beau Brummell twenty years ago. For a start he wore on his head a powdered wig, no less. His bulky form was clad in a heavily brocaded coat with a long waistcoat under it and satin knee-britches. Below the breeches, his white stockings were suspiciously well filled at the calf, as if faked with padding. His left leg was raised on a small footstool, and he held a silver-topped ebony cane in one hand. The chair he sat rigidly upright in was almost as heavily brocaded as his coat, and he was surrounded by small mementos of his time in Egypt. Malinferno's gaze was particularly taken by a group of four jars, made of limestone, that sat on the table at Casteix's elbow. The Frenchman saw Malinferno's interest.

'Ah. The canopic jars from the unnamed tomb in the Valley of the Kings.' Casteix's speech was still heavily accented, and he gazed fondly at the jars, recalling their discovery, which he had made along with two young engineers, Jollois and de Villiers. 'They represent the four sons of Horus. Each jar houses parts of the internal organs of a pharaoh.' He pointed first at the jackal-headed jar. 'Duamutef contains the stomach. Qebhsenuf, the falcon-headed one, the intestines. Hapi of the baboon head houses the lungs, and—'

Malinferno could no longer resist showing off his own knowledge. 'And the human-headed jar represents Imseti and contains the liver.'

Casteix tilted his own head, showing evident surprise that the ignorant young Englishman should know so much.

'I see I must revise my opinion of you, Mister—'

'Malinferno.'

'Ah.' Casteix now understood why he had made the wrong assumption about the youth's education. 'Not English, then, but from one of those myriad little states that makes up the Italian peninsula. There is a chance for you after all.'

Malinferno did not choose to correct the French savant. His father had been Italian, it is true, but his mother was English, and he had been educated in England. Still, let the old man think him a fellow foreigner, if it created a bond of sorts between them. Casteix eased the leg that was perched on the footstool and sighed. Malinferno assumed it must trouble him, but good manners prevented him from enquiring of the cause of his malaise. He manoeuvred the savant into reminiscing about his past.

'The Valley of the Kings, you say. And that was in 1799 . . . ?'

'Yes, two years before the British soldiers came and plundered our finds. The surrender list included several obelisks and statues, sarcophagi and . . . the Rosetta Stone, of course.' The old man's rheumy eyes glazed over once more at the thought of what the French had lost in 1801. 'If only Napoleon had been there at the time, things might have been different. But we were in the hands of the despicable General Menou. Do you know in what contempt he held us savants? Do you know what he said to the English general when we vowed we would not be separated from our collection?'

Malinferno shook his head.

'He called us *faiseurs de collections* – collection makers – as if we were nothing more than gatherers of random odds and ends. He said that, if we chose to travel to England with our collections of birds, butterflies and reptiles, he would not prevent us also being stuffed for the purpose.'

Malinferno suppressed a smile at the outraged general's comments. He could see that Casteix was scandalized still by Menou's words, even after almost twenty years. Years that Casteix had spent in exile in England along with the treasures that had found their way to the British Museum.

Casteix reflected on the misfortune that had resulted from him making the larger items in the collection his particular study, for they alone had come to England. The smaller items had in the end been left with the others savants, who to a man had carried them back to France in their personal baggage. Casteix alone had spent bitter years in the land of his enemy, becoming ever more and more irascible. Now, though the hostilities between England and France had ceased, he was still not able to return home. He had found himself something and nothing – a traitor of sorts, and now outside the charmed circle of French Egyptologists. His knowledge of value only to this ill-informed Englishman. Or was he Italian? Somehow it hardly seemed to matter.

Malinferno nervously produced the thigh-bone given to him by Augustus Bromhead, and he held it out for Casteix to examine.

'Monsieur, can you tell me if you think this bone has any age?'

The savant was at first inclined to dismiss the offered bone with a wave of his imperious hand. Did not this youth know it was impossible to age a bone with any accuracy? But then he decided to take the specimen and delay his observation. Truth to tell, he was an old man whom no one came to consult on scientific matters any more. At least he could coax another visit out of this Malinferno.

'Hmm. Leave it with me, and I will examine it properly. You can come back tomorrow or the next day, when I have had time to consider. Do you know . . . where it was exhumed?'

He knew that if the man said Egypt, then he could at least suggest it was old without seeming too ill-informed. But Malinferno was being cagey.

'I would rather not say just now. Suffice it to say that it has been nowhere near the British Museum. And talking of that institution, I wanted to ask you about the Rosetta Stone . . .'

His mention of the stone seemed to galvanize the old savant. Suddenly Casteix pushed himself up on his silver-topped cane and hobbled over to the heavy mahogany table in the centre of the room. He brought the ebony cane down with a thwack on the paper that lay on its surface.

'It was stolen from us, sir. Stolen. But now perhaps some restitution will have to be made.'

There was an edge of triumph in his quavering voice, which confused Malinferno.

'Why is that, *monsieur le professeur*?'

A self-satisfied leer distorted the old man's face.

'Do you not read your own newspapers, man?' It seemed for a moment that he had forgotten his assumptions about Malinferno's nationality, for he grabbed the newspaper from the table and waved it in his guest's face. Malinferno recognized it as that days' edition of *The Times*, which due to his dalliance with the rat-faced Kitten he had so far failed to peruse. He wondered what the Thunderer had reported within its pages that had so excited the old Frenchman. He was not in ignorance for long, as Casteix took delight in informing him. His face turned an unhealthy purple with the emotion of the moment.

'The Emperor Napoleon Bonaparte has escaped from his prison on St Helena and will soon be threatening these very isles with invasion.'

'Augustus! Gus . . . Gus. Are you there?'

Malinferno rushed up the winding staircase to Bromhead's study, which was sequestered in the loft of the dusty old house. He was winded by the time he got to the top and leaned on the banisters outside the door to regain his breath. The Frenchman's startling news had shocked him to the core. The last time Napoleon had escaped his island prison on Elba, he had raised an army of 350,000 and terrified Europe for a hundred days. Leaving Casteix's house and hurrying through the streets of London, Malinferno could see that the rumours of his second escape were causing equal panic. People were scurrying back and forth looking over their shoulders as if Bonaparte were already in pursuit. In one of the new town squares that he crossed, servants were even boarding up their masters' fashionable windows, as if invasion was imminent. He passed a butcher's shop inside which chaos reigned as a group of liveried servants, attempting to buy up all the meat on display for their masters, were carrying out a three-way tug of war on a haunch of pork. Fear of blockaded ports, it seemed, was concentrating the minds of the well-to-do.

Malinferno had intended to return to his lodgings, but he knew that Mrs Stanhope would be in a tizzy about Boney's escape. He did not have the time to waste reassuring her that all would be well. Especially as he was far from certain himself that disaster was not imminent. He wanted to talk to Bromhead, and tax the old man on what it was best to do. Crossing London Bridge, he had the uneasy feeling that someone was dogging his heels, a feeling he had had ever since leaving Casteix's residence. But every time he turned around to look, he could see no one following him. He put it down to his own mad fears. There were said to be so many sympathizers of Bonaparte's cause in the capital that Lord Liverpool's government had spies ferreting them out. Even the Princess of Wales was said to be an admirer. But then she was an exile from England in much the same way as Boney was.

Instead of going to Creechurch Lane, Malinferno had made his way over London Bridge, down Tooley Street and was now at the Court Yard in Bermondsey. The little antiquarian's house was in a row of tenements squeezed in between St Mary Magdalen Church and the noxious marshes south of the river. Bromhead would no doubt be oblivious to the news that was spreading like wildfire across London, immersed as he was in his studies. Malinferno not only wanted to gauge his reaction, but needed to talk to Augustus about the bag of old bones. He needed more information, if he was to see Casteix again and not appear an ignoramus. On the basis of the savant's reaction, he also felt less inclined to mock Bromhead's opinion that the bones were very old. In fact he was now very curious to discover whose bones Bromhead reckoned they were. Hence the headlong rush up the stairs.

His breath back, Malinferno burst into Bromhead's dark and gloomy study.

'Gus, have you heard the news . . . ?'

He paused, more than a little perplexed. The room was in utter darkness. There were no lamps burning, and the shutters on the windows must be closed for it to be so Stygian. Yet Bromhead should have been at home. The little dwarf of a man hardly left his house for fear of being mocked by the street urchins who frequented the run-down area. Malinferno often wondered why he continued to live in such a drab part of London, when he knew the antiquarian was of independent means. He could have afforded one of those new-style houses in Bloomsbury Square where the booksellers and cabinetmakers dwelled. But he seemed to prefer his creaky old residence in Grange Walk, and virtually lived on this upper floor surrounded by his collections of books and maps. So where was he?

As Malinferno's eyes adjusted to the unaccustomed darkness, he could see that the high stool that was Bromhead's throne was unoccupied. Nor was the man anywhere else in the room. And then he saw out of the corner of his eye that the heavy shadow below one of the high windows had shifted slightly. He gasped involuntarily and turned back towards the door. But before he could reach it, the shadow converged on the same spot and grabbed his outstretched arm. The hand was much more substantial than a shadow had the right to be. And the grip was vice-like. Malinferno felt as faint as one of his well-to-do female clients at the moment of an unrolling. His legs wobbled, and he tottered forward. Suddenly the hand was supporting his slumping body rather than restraining him. And the shadow spoke.

'Please. I did not mean to startle you. Only your arrival had me scared too, and for a moment I did not know what to do other than hide in the shadows.'

The stranger led Malinferno out on to the landing, where there was more light. Leaning once again on the handrail, Malinferno took a few deep breaths. He also took the time to take a look at the man who stood beside him. He didn't look much like a murderer. In fact his face was as pale and drawn as Malinferno assumed his was at that moment. He was a tall, thin man with a stoop that suggested he was rather reserved in company, and that he bent over to conceal his height. The top of his head was completely devoid of hair, though it grew long and dark about his ears. His clothes were not of the latest fashion, and when Malinferno gazed furtively at his hands, which twisted nervously around his sturdy cane, he saw they were stained. He guessed the man was a cabinetmaker, and thought it an odd coincidence that he had been thinking of those who lived in Bloomsbury Square only minutes before. The man suddenly thrust out one of the hands Malinferno had been examining.

'My name, sir, is Thomas Dale. I am a co-er-cabinetmaker.'

'And mine Joe Malinferno. Scientist.'

Malinferno's hand was taken in the firm and calloused grip of a man who used his hands for his trade, and then shaken vigorously.

'I am pleased to make your acquaintance Mr ... Malinferno. Once more I beg your forgiveness for my skulking ways.' Dale laughed nervously. 'I thought you were poor Bromhead's murderer come back to cover up the deed.'

'Bromhead's murderer? Is he dead, then? How do you know?'

Dale's face fell, and his hands twitched ever more vigorously.

'Oh, I don't know for sure. But the evidence is there to see. Come, I will show you.'

Malinferno followed Dale back into the room, still a little fearful that his companion might be the murderer, seeking to lay a false trail. Dale rushed over to the windows and flung the shutters back. As light poured back into the room, and Malinferno squinted around, uncertain of what he should be looking at, Dale strode over to Bromhead's work table.

'Look here. There are signs of a struggle – precious books scattered on the floor in a way Mr Bromhead would never have done himself.' He bent down to pick one up. 'This is a rare copy of Geoffrey of Monmouth's history of the kings of England. He would never have left it so.'

Dale folded back a creased page lovingly and, closing the book, laid it back on the table. Then he pointed at something far more alarming on the edge of the table.

'And look here. There are bloodstains.'

Malinferno's stomach lurched, and for once he was glad he had missed his breakfast. He gritted his teeth and looked more closely at where Dale was pointing. It was true. There was a large area of darkened wood, and evidence that something resembling blood had dripped off the edge of the table and on to the floor. He shrugged his shoulders.

'Perhaps Augustus cut himself and swept the books away from it before it stained them.'

Grimly Thomas Dale shook his head.

'No. I smell death here, and I know it well, believe me. I have some experience in these matters.'

Malinferno wondered why a cabinetmaker should know the scent of death. But before he could question the man, Dale was striding around the room clearly looking for something that he could not find.

'And where are the bones?'

Malinferno held his breath for a moment, wondering if Dale meant the same bones he now possessed. Did the man know Bromhead had passed the bones on to him, and were they valuable? He tried to inject his next question with an air of sincerity.

'Bones? What bones are these?'

Dale stopped his search, and a look of confusion came over his face. Malinferno could see that Dale had made an error in talking so openly, and was now deciding whether to confide in him. Finally he spoke in low tones that suggested he did not want anyone else to hear.

'Why, King Arthur's bones, of course.'

A dark figure passed under one of the newfangled street gaslamps outside Augustus Bromhead's residence and hovered for a moment. His coachman's overcoat had the collar pulled up so that, along with the wide-brimmed hat he wore, little could be seen of the man's face. To be certain of his anonymity, he moved a step or two away from the fizzing lamp and looked up to the windows at the top of the house.

It had been several hours since he had followed Malinferno from the Frenchman's residence to here, and he was unaware if anyone else was inside the house. He had seen some signs of movement at the upper window, but the angle was too steep from where he stood in the street to be sure. Darkness had fallen, and a lamp had been lit in the house, but no further activity had taken place. Nor had Malinferno exited the building. But the secretive stranger was addicted to his task and had a great deal of patience. Malinferno had greatly interested him now that he had revealed a connection with the Frenchman, Casteix. The lurker drew a notebook from the pocket of his voluminous overcoat and began to make notes.

Malinferno was seated on Bromhead's stool, pondering on the story he had just been told. The tale had been so long that darkness had fallen outside, and Dale had lit one of Bromhead's lamps. He had even revealed the ancient and battered wooden chest that sat almost hidden under Bromhead's large table. It was a squarish box, blackened with age and smooth to the touch as though it had been coated with some sort of resin. Crude metal hasps and hinges completed the sense of its being very old. Dale insisted that the bones had been found inside this very chest, though to Joe it looked so fragile that he couldn't imagine it holding anything at all. Having told his story, he now paced around the floor of the upstairs rooms, while Joe perched himself on the high stool by the table. He queried again the name of the group of men who met in the antiquarian's chambers.

'You call yourselves the Avalon Club?'

A deep flush came over Dale's face, and he looked down at his boots. It sounded foolish now, but the six who had met every month for the last two years had not thought so. They had been in deadly earnest.

'Yes. There are a number of us, all interested in the truth about King Arthur. About his life and death. If he truly did die, that is. There are some who say he never died but lies hidden near Snowdon. I am not of that school of thought, and neither is Mr Bromhead. We are both of a practical turn of mind, which is why he has been seeking the king's bones.'

Malinferno wriggled uncomfortably on Augustus's high seat. The thought of the bag of bones back in his rooms being those of the legendary Arthur made him uneasy. He had simply stuffed them under his bed to keep them from Mrs Stanhope's prying eyes as if they were no more than animal bones. Had Bromhead really discovered Arthur's bones? Is that why he had been so anxious for Joe to agree they were of ancient origin? He decided to return to his lodgings as soon as possible to retrieve them. He slid off the stool, carelessly placing his hand to steady himself on the edge of the table. It was only when he felt the slickness of the surface that he remembered Bromhead's supposed fate. He looked nervously down at his hand but could discern no stain on it. Was the mark on the table really the antiquarian's life's blood as Dale surmised?

The leading light of the Avalon Club suddenly grabbed his arm.

'If there is anything you know or can find out concerning Mr Bromhead's whereabouts, or of the bones, I and my colleagues will pay you well.'

Malinferno perked up at the mention of money.

'I may be able to help you, then. For a price. I should only expect my expenses to be covered, mind you. Though they may well be considerable . . .'

Dale dug in the pocket of his old jacket and came up with a handful of gold coins. He pressed them eagerly into Malinferno's palm.

'I am not without means, having established a steady line of business in these uncertain times. Here are a few sovereigns in advance of full payment. I hope you will help us. Never have Arthur's bones been as needed as they are now.'

Malinferno frowned.

'Why now?'

'Why, because of Bonaparte's invasion. The prophecy is that Arthur is not dead, but in hiding, only waiting to be called back to life when the nation is in dire need. What crisis can be more extreme than now, with our oldest enemy on the loose again?'

The stranger hiding in the dark watched Malinferno leave the house, carefully put his notebook inside the pocket of his big overcoat and followed him. He noticed that his quarry had a hand in the right pocket of his cutaway coat and appeared to be jingling coins. Malinferno looked extremely cheerful and was almost skipping as he hurried along Tooley Street towards London Bridge. For a moment Malinferno hesitated in front of one of the flash houses that his tail knew was a gin-shop and notorious rookery of thieves. The man surmised that if he went in there he would soon be parted from his money. And in not too pleasant a way either. But it seemed that Malinferno had second thoughts, because he shook his head and walked on. Having crossed the bridge over the Thames, Malinferno passed Billingsgate Market, and Custom House, then turned north. His follower assumed then that he was returning to his lodgings. But Malinferno did not turn west, instead carrying on up Aldgate until he came to Petticoat Lane. Though the street drew its name from the clothing trade that had located itself there a century or more ago, the garment referred to provided a connection with other more colourful establishments in the lane.

Malinferno cast a glance over his shoulder before approaching an anonymous black door set at the top of a small flight of steps between two sweatshops. The stranger hopped back into the shadows to make sure that his quarry did not see him. The door was opened immediately in response to Malinferno's rap on the knocker, and he disappeared inside. The stranger hurried up the lane and clambered on the railings that guarded one side of the door. From a precarious perch on top of the spikes, he could just see into the ground-floor window. The ladies who adorned the front drawing room were ill clad to be receiving gentlemen, but that did not seem to put Malinferno off. On the contrary, he was already pressing a coin into an older lady's hand. The madam of the bawdy house smiled greedily.

Madam De Trou bit down on to the gold coin. It had been a while since Joe Malinferno had visited her establishment, and last time he had left owing money. Still, the sovereign fully paid off his debt and left enough for some fresh credit.

'I have a new girl you might enjoy. As I seem to recall, you like the fuller figure.'

Malinferno, despite the pressing need to check on the bag of old bones under his bed, had not been able to resist the pull of Madam De Trou's bawdy house. The money from Dale was burning a hole in his pocket, and the skinny Kitten had been an altogether unsatisfactory encounter. He suddenly realized the madam had asked him a question.

'What? Oh, yes, I like them more voluptuous, certainly.'

The madam grinned, revealing a set of blackened teeth. Her latest recruit was a lass from Essex who went by the name of Dolly. She was a bit lippy, but keen enough for work to take on a poor payer like the Professor.

'Then I shall introduce you to Dolores from Spain. Come with me.'

Just as she led Malinferno from the room, there was a

clatter outside the front of the house, followed by a distinct groan. Madam waved her bony hands insouciantly.

'Pay that no mind. We are always getting peeping Toms trying to peer in the window. My doorman will call the charley, and get him seen off.'

The thought of a local watchman, popularly known as a charley, being called alarmed Malinferno. He did not want an encounter with the law until he had retrieved Bromhead's bag of bones. And discovered what had happened to the little man. He grinned nervously, wondering if anyone might have followed him to the bawdy house. Then he put it out of his mind. Who would be interested in the seedy goings-on of a mere meddler in all things ancient?

'Lead on, Madam De Trou.'

The scrawny madam led him upstairs to the bedchambers. So it was that Joe Malinferno came face to face with his fate – his nemesis you might say – in the form of a well-rounded and rudely confident Essex girl called Doll Pocket.

The encounter did not exactly start auspiciously. Having been ushered through a door, which had been abruptly closed behind him, Malinferno found himself in a gloomy room, lit only by a couple of candles. He hoped the dimness of the lights was not to conceal the imperfections in the bawd he had just paid handsomely for. Due to the dark, Malinferno was obliged to grope his way forward towards a big, high bed he had managed to discern across the room. He could just make out a pale figure sprawled on the bed. It was female, but it would be an exaggeration to say she was clothed, as she wore only tight short stays and a thin chemise. Thus, hardly anything of the delicious form was truly covered, and the stays held the figure's ample breasts high. Malinferno moved keenly towards the dark-haired beauty. And tripped over the rumpled rug, measuring his length on the floor.

'Ouch!'

The figure on the bed giggled and spoke in an accent that had never approached anywhere nearer the shores of Spain than Wapping Old Steps.

'Blimey! That must have hurt.'

Malinferno sat up, rubbing his nose that had cushioned his tumble on to the bare wooden floor. He examined his fingers and was glad to see they weren't covered in gore. He didn't have a nosebleed, at least, but then he realized his left knee hurt like hell.

'Hurt? I think my knee is broken.'

The giggle turned into a burst of out-and-out laughter. It was a gusty, uninhibited froth of good humour. A pale, languid hand reached out from the bed.

'Come here, you big baby. It's just a knock. It probably feels worse than it is.'

Malinferno staggered to his feet, his dignity now hurting more than his knee, though he did manage to feign a limp to gain some more sympathy. Sitting down on the edge of the bed, he stared at the round, plump breasts again. Until the bawd's hand firmly took hold of his chin and lifted his gaze to her face. In truth the woman was a pleasant sight, with long black tresses framing pale freckled skin. Malinferno put her age as no more than five-and-twenty. Her eyes were brown and oval, and her nose straight and shapely. He fancied he could see the Spaniard in her looks. Knowing how in awe the average bawd was of a man of letters, he opened with his usual gambit.

'I am a professor of Egyptology and of ancient bones. But I can see how young and fine your bones are, Dolores . . .'

His use of her name started another fit of giggles, and

she held her well-formed hand to her mouth in an attempt to stifle it.

'Dolores! Is that what the old madam says my name is now?'

'Yes, Dolores. It's a beautiful Spanish name.'

This revelation started another fit of laughter that Malinferno was not displeased to see caused her bare breasts to wobble in a most appealing way. The bawd snorted again.

'Dolores! Leave it out. Look, my name is Doll . . . Doll Pocket, and I'm from Essex. Pleased to make your acquaintance, Prof . . .'

She stuck her hand out as though they were meeting at a genteel soirée. Malinferno was quick to take it.

'Joe Malinferno. Just call me Joe for now, Doll.'

The girl leaned back on the bed at a rakish angle, her breasts oozing out over the tightness of her short stays.

'Good, I'm glad that's settled. And now you know who I really am, would you mind if I took this wig off. It's bleedin' 'ot.'

Malinferno was at least glad to see that Doll was not bald under the false black tresses. In fact her golden hair, free of the Spanish fakery, was luxuriant and glowing. She dragged her fingers through it, and shook out the curls.

'So, Prof, tell me about these old bones.'

Mrs Stanhope was worried. The girl had turned up in the early hours saying she was Mr Malinferno's sister just up from the country. That she had no accommodation yet, and had to see her brother so she could borrow some money from him. Mrs Stanhope had refrained from saying that if Mr Malinferno had any cash at all, then *she* wanted it in lieu of rent owing before this slip of a girl had any. The poorly dressed little girl looked as though she needed help, however, and sounded most anxious to see her brother. Malinferno's landlady doubted if she would get the assistance she needed from him, but in the end she had relented. She had let the little rat-faced girl into Mr M's drawing room with an injunction not to touch anything. The girl had nodded eagerly, and Mrs Stanhope had left her to it. It was only later that she sat down to thinking with a generous glass of Holland gin in her hand. She could not recall Mr M ever mentioning having a sister. Leaning back in her comfortable chair, she took a sip of her favourite tipple. And then another.

She did not know how long she had been dozing, but suddenly she was awoken by a loud thump from upstairs. It sounded like something or somebody landing heavily on the floor in Mr Malinferno's rooms. It had to be the girl, as no one else had gone upstairs, of that she was certain. Even though she could see the Holland gin glass was now empty, she was convinced its contents must have been tipped out by accident. She could have hardly closed her eyes for a second or two. No, it could only be the girl. She knew that child was trouble the first time she had set eyes on her. His sister, indeed. She was probably some bawd he owed money to, or even a Thames mudlark or scuffle-hunter on the scrounge. And she was up there right now, helping herself to his goods, which by rights were Mrs Stanhope's to seize if he failed to pay his rent. She had had her eyes for months on that little green stone shaped like an insect that he called a scare-bob, or something like. That rat-faced thief wasn't going to help herself to that, oh no. Mrs Stanhope heaved her not inconsiderable bulk out of her comfy chair and waddled over to the stairs.

Despite her weight, she was quickly up the fine curved staircase that spoke of more elegant days, when Mr Stanhope had still been alive and the house full of soirée

guests. She pushed open the left-hand door on the first
landing that opened on to Malinferno's living room.

'Now, look here, you little pilferer, I . . .'

Mrs Stanhope got no further than that initial imprecation.
For before her on the threadbare but once-pretty Persian
rug lay the battered remains of Kathleen Hoddy, otherwise
known as Kitten. Her life's blood was seeping darkly into
the rug, ruining it for ever. Mrs Stanhope screamed.
Whether from stark fear or horror at the ruined rug even
she did not herself fathom.

'So, this Rosie . . .'

'Rosetta.'

'This Rose Etta Stone has three different languages on
it.'

Malinferno nodded, already a little exhausted. Doll had
spent most of the night dragging out of him all he knew
about ancient Egypt and swallowing it whole. He had
never come across any man who could take so much in at
one sitting, let alone an uneducated female. And the way
her eyes had sparkled at his recital, he felt sure she was
completely absorbed by the subject.

'And you reckon we could use it to work out the ancient
language of the Egyptians and make a fortune?'

'Well, now . . .' He had to draw the line there. The girl
had said 'we' as though she was going to help him on the
gargantuan task that had already bamboozled several
polymaths in both France and England. She might be able
to swallow whole a mountain of facts, but as for cracking
the most complex problem of the age, well, there was a
limit. 'I don't think you could . . .'

Doll simply ignored his reservations. Sitting cross-legged
on the bed opposite him, he watched her breasts heaving
with the excitement of the moment. Malinferno regretted

it was not passion that was causing the flush on her cheeks. At least not the sort of passion he had at first imagined, when he had pressed the golden sovereign into the bawdy-house owner's hand. In fact he now saw that the light of dawn was filtering through the heavy drapes of the boudoir, and he had done no more than remove his jacket and boots. He leaned towards her buxom figure, his ardour returning.

'Doll, I wonder if . . .'

'And to imagine it was old Bonaparte who found it in the first place. Perhaps he's coming to nick it back. If he manages to reach dry land this time, that is.'

Malinferno sighed, knowing his chance had gone, and the day was calling him to more earnest tasks. The mention of Bonaparte had reminded him of the need to ensure the safety of the bones that lay under his bed. Not that he believed King Arthur would really come back to life. But perhaps they could form a rallying point, at whose centre would be Professor Joe Malinferno. He slid to the edge of the bed he had shared passionlessly with Doll and began to pull on his boots. Doll too made a move, bouncing eagerly off the feather mattress and grabbing her street clothes.

'Where we going first, then?'

'What?'

'You said you'd show me this Rosie Etta Stone. And I should like to go to Piccadilly to see the Egyptian Hall too. It costs a shilling, but you could pay for the both of us, couldn't you?'

Malinferno reached for his cutaway coat and began to pull it on, checking that the remaining sovereigns still nestled snugly in the pocket hidden in the coat-tail.

'Doll, I shall be delighted to escort you to the Egyptian Hall, and even the British Museum. But I have other pressing business to attend to right now.'

'Good. I'm ready.'

In the time it had taken him to pull his coat on and reach for his Garrick and hat, Doll had slipped into a filmy muslin dress, primped her hair and thrown a hooded black-gauze cloak over her shoulders. She was at his side, reticule and gloves in one hand and sliding her other inside his arm.

'Where are we going first, Prof?'

'We are not . . .'

Malinferno saw the determined look in the girl's eyes and bowed to the inevitability of this new force of nature. He crammed his hat on his head and led the bawd, now demurely attired as any lady, down the stairs and out into the street.

'Very well, come with me. There is something I have to collect at my lodgings. But you have to wait outside as Mrs Stanhope does not take kindly to young ladies in her gentlemen's rooms.'

'Orl right. What is it you have to pick up?'

'Well . . . Arthur's bones, actually.'

Doll squealed and pinched his arm in excitement.

'Bones? Which Arthur is that, then? Is he a relative of yours?'

Malinferno grimaced. 'More of an ancestor, shall we say. On my mother's side.'

Another of Mrs Stanhope's lodgers, who resided in the downstairs front, had called the Runners. One of the magistrates from the new office in Worship Street, Raleigh Pauncefoot by name, had turned up with one of his six constables in tow. And now the estimable lady was showing them the body. Pauncefoot, who was a starch-dealer by trade and who had got his position due to the patronage of a rich uncle, reeled back in horror. He held a lace-edged handkerchief to his nose and gagged. When he managed to control his stomach, he urged the constable into the room ahead of him.

'Mayes. Take a look, and tell me what you see.'

The lugubrious Archie Mayes, who had served under the Duke of Wellington and so was well used to messy bodies, slouched into the room and knelt beside the dead girl. He lifted her head, noting how loose it seemed from the rest of the body.

''er throat's been cut from ear to ear. Whoever did it nearly cut the head off completely. Savage, I say. Look 'ere, Mr P.'

He took great delight in showing the gaping wound to the magistrate, knowing the reaction he would get. Pauncefoot did not disappoint him, turning away and heaving into his lacy white linen. Mrs Stanhope took the pasty-faced magistrate by the shoulders.

'Come downstairs to my parlour, sir. I fancy I might have a bottle of spirits somewhere, left over after the death of my husband.'

She looked back at the constable and winked, divining he might prefer to be left alone to do his work. When his master had gone, Mayes paced the room silently, taking in anything that might prove of interest. The room was furnished sparsely, and the chairs and single table looked shabby. Clearly they were the property of a man who did not earn a regular wage but relied on his status as a gentleman to get by. Mayes had no time for such wastrels. Nevertheless, the man was tidy and, judging by the pile of books on the one table in the room, an educated man. He lifted the top book from the pile, and opened it to the title page. What he saw made him frown. For a start it was in French, that much he knew, though he could not read the language. But one word stood out among all the other jumble of foreign letters. The name – Bonaparte. Mayes had fought in the recent war against the little corporal and was not inclined even after his defeat to admire Boney as some now did. He had seen too many of his mates die around him. For the man in whose rooms the body had been found to also have a book all about Bonaparte was good cause to be very suspicious.

It was then he spotted through the bow window at the front of the house a man approaching with some half-dressed bawd on his arm. The man stopped and held his hand up to suggest the girl go no further. She for her part seemed not to mind, and stood next to one of those newfangled gaslamps on the street. The man, who was wearing a Garrick overcoat and a rakish hat, hurried up the steps of the very house the constable was in. To Mayes this looked ominously like the murderer bringing his next victim home. He pushed the door to the room closed, leaving a small gap he could peer through. He prayed that the magistrate was still preoccupied by the widow who owned the house. Much as he despised Pauncefoot, he didn't want the bad business of him having his throat cut while his constable skulked upstairs like a coward.

He need not have worried. The man – presumably this Malinferno character who rented the rooms – was making his way quietly up the stairs. Yet another reason for the constable to suspect him. Why creep up the stairs like a criminal in your own house? He tensed up, ready to leap at the presumed killer, watching as the man reached the head of the staircase. But instead of walking towards the door behind which the constable stood, the man turned the other way and opened the door to the room across the landing. Before Mayes could react, he disappeared inside the room, leaving the door open. Mayes crossed the landing quietly and pushed the door wide open. Malinferno, if it was he, was bending down under the bed that filled the small, dark room. A little embarrassed by what the man might be doing, Mayes coughed to announce his presence. Malinferno jumped up, knocking his hat against the side of the bed. It rolled across the floor and stopped at the feet of the constable.

'What the . . . Oh, constable. Is there a problem?'

Malinferno had been shocked by the sudden appearance of the Bow Street Runner. Did he know about Bromhead's death already? If so, how had he managed to track him down? And had he linked him to the murder? Malinferno thought back to that uneasy feeling he had had since leaving Bermondsey. A feeling that he was being followed. Put together with the incident of the peeping Tom at Madam De Trou's bawdy house, it added up to a worrying business. But a Runner in his uniform following him would have stuck out like a sore thumb, wouldn't he? And, furthermore, what did he know, if anything, about King Arthur's bones languishing under Malinferno's bed? He decided to brazen it out about Augustus, but keep quiet about the bones until he knew for sure what the Runner knew.

'The death is a very unfortunate matter, I am sure. Have you found the body yet?'

Mayes's eyes narrowed, assessing the brass neck of this man, who was practically admitting he did away with the girl.

'Oh, yes, we've found the body, sir. Did you think it was going to be difficult?'

'Well, where was it, then?'

Malinferno was deeply puzzled. The Runner seemed to think he knew where Bromhead's body was going to be. Did he suspect him of the murder? He hoped not. Mayes hooked a thumb over his shoulder.

'Where was it? Where you might have expected it to be, sir. In your drawing room.'

Malinferno gasped, the stuffing knocked out of him. 'In my . . . ? Show me.'

The constable stood aside and ushered Malinferno across the landing, a superior smirk on his face. He couldn't see how the gent was going to talk his way out of this one. He followed Malinferno through the door and into the room opposite. Malinferno stood as if transfixed, his mouth moving though no words came out.

'Bit of a mess, isn't it, sir?'

'But this isn't Augustus. It's . . . it's . . .'

He almost didn't recognize her at first because now her face was pale and slack. But in life she had not been all that animated, and despite the grisly wound and the splashes of blood, he could make out the pinched features of the rat-faced girl. But he couldn't for the life of him reason how she came to be a bloodied corpse in his own drawing room.

'Augustus, sir? Who's he?'

The constable's ominous tones woke Malinferno from his stupor. It seemed as though the man was mentally totting up the possible murders that Malinferno was guilty of perpetrating.

'Augustus? No, you misunderstand. He's a friend . . . who is sort of missing. When you mentioned a death, I thought . . .'

'I think it was you who brought up the matter of a death first, sir. You had better explain where you have been all night.'

'He was with me, constable. And a merry time he gave me too. Though I would prefer it if my husband didn't get to learn about it.'

The voice was that of a lady, and the tone peremptory.

Mayes turned to face the speaker, a blush already growing on his cheeks. It was the woman he had seen in the street returning with Malinferno. He had put her down as a common bawd, and close up her dress wasn't the most modest, with a hint of exposed bosoms beneath the muslin gown. But that was what he had come to expect of the upper classes now. When the Prince Regent himself chased mistresses all over the place, and the Princess, his wife, carried on with Italians abroad, you had to expect the rest of the nobs to be just as ill behaved. He turned his prudish gaze away from the lady's heaving bosom, and looked down at his own boots in embarrassment. Doll Pocket cast a glance at the astonished Malinferno and winked raffishly.

'Now, if you will allow this gentleman to accompany me home, we will be on our way. The streets of London are not a safe place for a lady, you know, even in daylight. Full of rogues, bawds, swindlers and grubbers, if you ask me.'

Mayes was thoroughly cowed, and for once wished Pauncefoot was in evidence. The constable felt awkward when having to deal with someone from a higher station in life than he was. And a female at that too.

'Yes, madam. I could not agree more. Rogues and itinerants. Though we Runners do our best, you know.'

Doll waved a ladylike hand, dismissing the constable from her consideration.

'I am sure you do. Now, Mr Malinferno has had a shock and will need to rest. Please arrange to remove the body and have his room cleaned up. Come, Joseph.'

Like a little poodle, Malinferno followed after Doll's imperious and very petite heels. When they had gone, Mayes hurried downstairs to find Pauncefoot and to arrange for the disposal of the gory mess in Malinferno's drawing room. Neither Malinferno or Doll Pocket, nor the constable and the magistrate noticed the shadowy figure lurking at the end of Creechurch Lane, waiting for matters to quieten down before he made his move.

'And where did that accent come from, Miss Pocket? I almost didn't recognize you.'

Doll giggled and hugged Malinferno's arm. On escaping the clutches of the Runners they had walked along the Embankment and into the heart of London. They had found themselves in Piccadilly, and Doll had dragged Malinferno to the Egyptian Hall at number 22. They were now standing outside, gazing at the ornate frontage, which was designed in the form of temple pylons with statues representing Isis and Osiris. Doll was not to be distracted by Malinferno's question though.

'Get yer 'and into yer pocket, Joe. It's only a shilling a head.'

Malinferno sighed and paid up. Soon they were lost in the obscurity of the crowds who thronged the aisles of William Bullock's exhibition. In the natural history section they marvelled at the central panorama of stuffed animals, including an elephant, a rhinoceros, a zebra and two ostriches. A realistic copy of a palm tree with a serpent climbing up it hung its fronds over the creatures. But Doll was interested in other curiosities.

'They say they have Napoleon's carriage taken at Waterloo on show, Joe. Can we see it?'

Malinferno allowed himself to be dragged to the room where the carriage stood. Doll was like a child absorbing all the wonderful sights and drinking them in. The Napoleonic relics only served to remind Malinferno of Bromhead's disappearance, and the bones he had promised to locate for Thomas Dale. If anyone was to call King Arthur to arms to save England from old Boney, then the bones under his bed were needed. He had come within an ace of collecting them before the Runner had interrupted.

'I learn accents quick. When I was young I wanted to be an actress.'

Malinferno realized Doll was answering his earlier question about her impersonation of a lady.

'You seem to learn lots of things quickly, Miss Pocket.'

Doll snorted. 'I don't know about that. But I was a lady's maid for six months and got to know how my lady spoke. Then I was sacked when she learned that her husband was paying me too much attention. A girl without work has to learn how to fend for herself quick enough, and that's the truth.'

It was the first time Malinferno had seen Doll looking anything less than ebullient. He suddenly saw in her hunted expression what a hard life she must have led. He took her arm gently as if she truly was a lady of quality.

'Come. I think we are both in need of some refreshment. We will find a coffee house.'

Doll grinned mischievously. 'I know one. It's called the Russian Coffee House.'

The man lurking in the shadows watched as a canvas sack was carried out of the lodging house in Creechurch Lane. At first he was confused as to what it might be, but then he saw the shape and obvious weight. It had to be a body. Especially as it made a soft thud as the two men carrying the sack tossed it casually into the back of the shabby black carriage that waited in the street. The horse in the shafts tossed its head but stood still, unperturbed by the load it was now going to pull. He eagerly opened his notebook and scribbled in it. One man went back inside and came back with a rolled-up rug that also went into the back of the conveyance. Then the two men mounted the driving seat, the horse was whipped up and the carriage slowly rumbled away with the mortal remains of Kitten in the back.

A large woman, with a mob cap on her head and dressed in an unfashionably heavy white gown, stood for a while at the door of the house. She watched the carriage with a sharp gaze until it had disappeared around the corner into Leadenhall Street. Satisfied that the messy problem had been cleared up, she turned and went back inside. A few minutes later a Bow Street Runner and a fancily dressed gentleman who had to be the magistrate also emerged. The magistrate, a little worse for drink apparently, almost fell down the steps. He was supported by the constable, and they both went off in the same direction as the hearse. The fat old woman closed the street door on the unedifying scene. The man decided he had done well to linger a while at Malinferno's residence. Besides, his fall off the railings outside the bawdy house had damaged his ankle and severely bruised his head. He had been in no mood to be dashing around London. He now had useful news to relate to his masters, and their goal may be in sight. But now the time had come to hunt Malinferno down. He decided to pick up his trail at the Frenchman's residence.

Having laid low for a few hours in the Brown Bear public house, Bow Street, better known to the low life of London as the Russian Coffee House, Joe Malinferno and Doll Pocket decided it was safe to return to his house. Joe was a little worse for wear, so Doll, who had imbibed as much but could hold her liquor better, insisted on going up to his bedroom on her own.

'You'll only wake the old harridan up, Joe. Whereas I can sneak up without disturbing a floorboard.'

Joe considered her voluptuousness, and would have

disagreed about who would make the stairs creak the more. In fact he considered her voluptuousness deeply for so long that by the time he came to object, Doll had left him in the street and had gone. He shrugged his shoulders and leaned against the gaslamp. It was indeed only minutes before he saw Doll scuttling down the front steps of Mrs Stanhope's house. As she hurried over to him, he was surprised to see that she didn't have the canvas bag with her.

'Where are the bones, Doll?'

'They wasn't there, was they?'

Doll Pocket's Essex accent was always more pronounced when she was excited or otherwise disturbed. And now she was very disturbed.

'Nonsense. Did you look under the bed where I told you to look?'

Doll hissed in annoyance. She was not used to being characterized as being deficient in common sense or guile.

'Of course I looked under the bed. And I looked inside and behind the chest of drawers, and under the only chair in the room. Gawd, your furnishings are so sparse, Joe, I was 'ardly likely to miss a big bag of bones, was I?'

Malinferno groaned and slid down the gaslamp post until he was sitting on the pavement.

'It's all up, then. Thomas Dale and the rest of the Avalon Club will want their money back. Which I have spent mostly on you, may I say. And what are we to do about Bonaparte and his invasion? There'll be no calling on King Arthur now.'

Doll gave a derisive snort. 'You don't believe all that rubbish, do you?'

'Well, you cannot be sure if he . . .'

Doll cut into Malinferno's admonishing with a peculiar, sing-song tone:

*'For when he fell, an elfin queen,*
*All in secret, and unseen,*
*O'er the fainting hero threw*
*Her mantle of ambrosial blue;*
*And bade her spirits bear him far,*
*In Merlin's agate-axled car,*
*To her green isle's enamel'd steep,*
*In the navel of the deep.'*

Malinferno was astonished. 'How do you know that? That's a poem by Warton, the old Poet Laureate.'

Doll sniffed. 'Don't you think a prostitute has any brains, then? I told you I wanted to be an actress. I learned the poem off by heart. Listen, the bit you would like is near the end.'

She began to rattle off the lines again as though they were some child's rhyme:

*'Thence to Britain shall return,*
*(If right prophetic rolls I learn)*
*Borne on Victory's spreading plume,*
*His ancient scepter to resume.'*

She snorted. 'What a load of old boll—'

'Yes, Doll. I think that's enough, don't you?'

He was glad she had not pursued her ambitions as an actress. Though she could con an accent and fool a simple policeman, her understanding of the beauty of Warton's lines was sadly lacking in Malinferno's opinion. And she somehow made the solemn and prophetic nature of Arthur's return sound quite foolish. So much so that suddenly he could not hold back, and a great gust of laughter rose up from his belly. This set Doll off, and soon they were both collapsed on the ground hooting at the madness of Thomas Dale's quest. But despite the hilarity, Malinferno knew he would have to have something to report to Dale. Then it occurred to him. Casteix, the French savant, still had the thigh-bone. He turned to Doll, who was still red-faced from all the hilarity. Solemnly he asked her the question uppermost in his mind.

'Do you think we can resurrect King Arthur from just his thigh-bone?'

Doll's face turned purple and crumpled as she tried to hold back another gust of laughter. She failed miserably. When she did manage to control herself, she tried to answer Joe's question as though it had been asked seriously. 'Maybe. I suppose he would at least be able to hop it when things get bad.'

It was Joe's turn to break into fits of laughter. Even so, he still reckoned it was worth retrieving the bone.

It was early evening but quite dark when they reached the home of Monsieur Casteix, and all the high, fashionable windows looking out on to the street showed no lights in them – save for one high on the second floor, where the bedrooms were likely to be located. Undeterred, Malinferno hastily mounted the steps leading to the front door, on which he hammered with his fist. Hearing the echo of his assault in the long hallway behind the door, he was not optimistic of gaining entry. But he felt tomorrow would be too late. A second attack with his fist brought a result. He heard the sound of bolts being drawn back, and eventually the door creaked open and a sour face peered out.

'The master is abed and may not be disturbed.'

As the door swung closed again, Malinferno inserted his sturdy Hessian boot in the gap.

'This is a matter of urgency. And a scientific one that Monsieur Casteix will want to know about.'

The sour face screwed up even further. 'Damn you scientists! And I would wager that it all has something to do with old Boney being on the loose again.' The servant stared at Malinferno suspiciously. 'You're not a Frenchy, are you?'

Malinferno wondered how a servant who despised both scientists and Frenchmen should have come to be working for the embodiment of both in one carcass. He reassured the man of his own antecedents, drawing on his maternal side and choosing not to mention his Paduan father.

'God bless you, my man. I am an Englishman through and through. But what we seek does have a bearing on the escape of Bonaparte from St Helena. The safety of the realm is in question.'

Malinferno felt a nudge from behind and heard the noise of a stifled giggle from Doll Pocket. He even heard her whispered comment on his stout rendering of a blue-blooded Englishman.

'Some ham of an actor, you are, Joe.'

The keeper of the door eyed Malinferno with concern. 'Who's that behind you?'

'That, sir, is my dear wife, whom I will not let out of my sight while Boney is on the loose.'

At this the servant finally relented and let Joe and Doll into the silent mausoleum of a house. Noticing a large spray of white arum lilies in a vase on the hall table, Malinferno hoped it was not a presage of the state of the master of the house. He needed Casteix alive. But it would seem he was, for the sourpuss of a servant led them upstairs past the large reception room on the first floor, where Malinferno had first been ushered into Casteix's presence, and on up to the level of the bedrooms. He stopped outside a grand set of double doors and asked them both to wait. First tapping on the doors gently, he opened the left-hand one and slithered in through the gap like a serpent. A muffled conversation followed, which must have had a positive outcome, because the servant returned the same way and said they could enter.

Once through the grand doors, they found themselves in an ornate bedroom at the centre of which stood an enormous bed with Egyptian motifs picked out in marquetry all over its scroll-shaped head and foot. Almost lost in a snowy expanse of white sheets and pillows lay Casteix, his wan face topped by a tasselled nightcap. He waved a hand at his visitors.

'Come forward. I cannot see you clearly without my eyeglasses.'

Malinferno and Doll Pocket complied. And Joe noticed the gleam in the Frenchman's otherwise strained face when he saw Doll's attributes.

'Ah, you have brought a companion, Signor Malinferno. And a very pretty one too.'

Doll simpered in a way Malinferno imagined she had perfected at Madam De Trou's. Old, leering men required an expression of admiration that had to be well simulated in order to feel they got their money's worth. Casteix was no exception. The Frenchman stirred in his bed, and Malinferno hoped he was not about to get frisky. Hurriedly he explained his mission.

'I wondered if you had yet come to any conclusions about the thigh-bone I left with you, monsieur. You see I need it returned, and am anxious to confirm its provenance.'

Casteix sighed. 'Ah, the thigh-bone. That item is the reason why you find me confined to my bed tonight. But let me answer your question first. There is no way of telling the age of the bone. It could be two years old or two thousand. My feeling on handling it was that it was very old, but that is not a very scientific assessment. Yes, very old.' He shifted under his covers again and slid a hand underneath the crisp sheets. Malinferno was getting alarmed at his behaviour. The Frenchman, however, continued to talk. 'As for returning it to you, I fear I am rendered unable to do so.'

'Why is that, sir?' It was Doll's turn to question his cryptic replies.

'Because it has been stolen.'

Malinferno groaned and was about to ask how, when Casteix provided the answer.

'After you left, another person came to the door. A man well muffled against the inclement English weather but with swarthy features. He reminded me of a short-arsed Breton peasant. My manservant let him into my presence, and this peasant practically demanded to know everything about you, sir. And what our conversation might have been about. I told him it was none of his business, but he overpowered me and . . . and sawed my leg off, sir.'

Malinferno heard Doll gasp, and he suddenly felt sick at the thought of the horrible attack on Casteix. Was this why the old man was now bedridden? Yet he should have bled to death, or expired with the shock. How had he survived such a gruesome attack? By way of explanation, the man brought his hand back out from under the bedclothes. In it he held two pieces of a well-turned mahogany table leg that had been sawed up. No, not actually a table leg, Malinferno realized, for it was not symmetrical all round. He saw suddenly why yesterday he thought Casteix had an unusually well-shaped calf. The leg was wooden, and his attacker had rendered Casteix incapable of pursuit by sawing it up.

'I lost my leg to a crocodile in Egypt, you see, many years ago. Mr Chippendale was kind enough to turn me a substitute. Now it is ruined.'

Malinferno, stifling a laugh at the absurdity of it all, managed to ask about Arthur's thigh-bone.

'And the bone?'

'Alas, stolen, Signor Malinferno. Though God knows why. Mummies are ten a penny these days.'

Malinferno and Doll did manage to get out on to the street before once again collapsing with laughter. Though they had no good reason to. The old man had lost his wooden leg, but they had lost the last part of Arthur's bones.

'Where to now, Joe?'

Malinferno, stymied, was ready to give up. But Doll was still eager to pursue matters and had a suggestion. 'We are forgetting one thing. Someone attacked the Frenchy for the bone, and killed Kitten for certain. If we figure out who it was, not only will we bring justice to Kitten, but we will probably find the bones. What other reason had he to kill Kitten other than to get his hands on the bones for himself?'

'You're right, Doll. But how are we going to find out who the murderer is? Augustus was no doubt murdered for Arthur's bones, before the man realized the box was empty and the bones were elsewhere. The man must then have waited to see who came to see Augustus, assuming any visitor might have possession of the bones. I was duly followed to Creechurch Lane, where Kitten was killed for the same reason. The man had traced the bones to my rooms, and Kitten was found to be in the way. But it still doesn't tell us who did in Augustus in the first place.'

Doll pulled a face. 'No, no, no. Don't you see the story as you tell it is full of holes. First, we don't even know if your friend Bromhead is dead. But leave that to one side. I am sure some bloke did keep tabs on the house, and saw you and Dale arriving and leaving. He had to choose one of you to follow, and perhaps it was you, as you said you were aware of someone. And we know he fell off the railing while trying to get an eyeful of me and my friends in our déshabillé. But does that make him the murderer?'

Malinferno made a mental note to verse Doll in the French language. Her accent was execrable.

'You mean, was he in any fit state after that to get to my rooms and murder Kitten? But who else knew of the existence of the bones?'

Doll stated the obvious. 'Only Augustus and the other members of the Avalon Club. But they already had the bones, so they wouldn't have murdered to get them. Once you had the bones, only Kitten knew about their location. With Augustus dead, the link must be Kitten, even though she didn't know they was King Arthur's. So why did she come back, when you had scared her off with talk of the bodysnatchers? She obviously came at a time when you were not going to be there, or her story of being your sister would not have stood up.'

A thought lit up Malinferno's brain like one of those gaslamps. 'Tell me, who would be interested in old bones, whosoever they were? And who would Kitten have blabbed to about a nice set of bones just ripe for the picking?'

'You don't mean . . . ?'

'Yes. The leader of the Borough Gang of bodysnatchers, Ben Crouch.'

Doll's face took on a fashionable pallor. 'Blimey!'

A trip into the Borough was not something an honest citizen would normally contemplate. A rookery of thieves operated out of the area, and the most feared were the resurrectionists – the men who dug up bodies and supplied them to the medical profession for gruesome anatomizing. Most feared of these bodysnatchers was Ben Crouch, who was the leader mainly due to the fact that he drank to excess less frequently than his comrades. But Malinferno knew that if he was to track down the killer of Kitten and Bromhead – who he was still convinced was dead – and perhaps find the lost bones, the Borough rookery would have to be invaded. However, it did not reduce his sense of terror when, a few hours later, he and Doll found themselves in a low dive somewhere off the Borough Road confronted by a pockmarked man with an evil grin.

'I'll have to hurry you, pal. It's a new moon tonight, and I am not in the mood to waste the hours of darkness when I have an order for five large.'

Crouch, for that's who the pockmarked man was, meant he had a request for five adult bodies to be supplied no doubt to Guy's Hospital down the road that very night. Flanked as he was by four lieutenants, resembling nothing less than Barbary apes from the hairy nature of their faces to their beady, animalistic eyes, Crouch was a fearful character at the best of times. Now he was in one of his bad moods, as today he had learned that Israel Chapman, a Jew to whom he owed money, had started up in the trade Crouch had thought to have monopolized. Israel had had the nerve to supply a corpse or two to St Bartholomew's. He had already had a drink or two while planning how to deal with the Jew, when these two innocents had had the nerve to fall into his rookery.

They had been observed asking about Kathleen Hoddy in a voice loud enough to irritate Crouch, who liked to keep his affairs dark. He had got his men to hustle them out of the gin-shop and into the back room Crouch used to plan his forays into the graveyards of London. So they had ended up in the very presence of the man they were asking awkward questions about. Now Crouch was wondering how to deal with them. He reckoned the man was easy meat, and maybe he could add him to the order for five large corpses by way of compensation for the nuisance he had caused. But the woman was another matter. A little on the plump side for Crouch's tastes, she would nevertheless be more useful alive than dead. He grinned, exposing his blackened teeth.

'Now, as for your request for information about the girl, I can't say I've ever heard the name. Nor do I know anything about this pile of old bones you are looking for. Though I might be able to help you for a consideration.'

Malinferno looked glum, knowing he had no money to offer the man as a bribe. Of course, if Crouch was the murderer they sought, no amount of coins would get to the truth. It was more likely that he and Doll would end up on some anatomist's slab themselves. He shivered, wishing they had never come to Borough to try to get some information from the locals. It was clear from the start that Crouch would learn of their prying. He watched in horror as Crouch stepped close up to Doll and leered at her, peering down her cleavage with clear intent in his mind.

'Of course, you could pay me in kind, if you know what I mean . . . arrgh.'

His lascivious tones were abruptly cut off, and Malinferno looked on in puzzlement as Crouch's face turned first bright red, then purple, his eyes bugging out of his head. Doll merely smiled sweetly, and told his nervous lieutenants to stand their ground.

'Or your boss's jewels will be crushed to powder.'

Malinferno looked down with curiosity at the front of Crouch's stained and crumpled pants. Doll had firm hold of a hefty portion of the cloth and, from the look of pain on Crouch's face, most of the contents too. Malinferno could not believe that such delicate hands, encased in virginal white gloves, could perform such a crushing task. He winced at the thought. Doll, however, was implacable.

'Mr Crouch, I don't believe that you never heard of Kitten. She spoke to you about the bones, and you sent her to get them, didn't you?'

At first Crouch's eyes shone with defiance, and he shook his head. Then he winced as Doll squeezed harder and lifted him a little by his crotch. His manner changed abruptly. He nodded vigorously. 'Yes, yes. I overheard the silly bitch talking about finding a bag of bones. I told her she should go back and fetch them for me, or she was in trouble. The next thing I knew she was dead.'

'Killed by you?'

'No. Why should I do that? She was on an errand for me.'

Malinferno leaned over Doll's shoulder and threw in his own question. 'And my friend, Augustus Bromhead? What of him?'

'Never heard of him.'

Doll gave a deft twist of her wrist, and Crouch squealed like a pig.

'Orl right, he was on our shopping list, the little dwarf was. But we heard someone else was after him. Someone you didn't argue with – a little Welshman from out of town. We left him to it.'

Crouch's eyes were by now screwed up in pain, and he could manage only a final croak. 'It's the truth. Honest.'

Doll relaxed her grip, and a great sigh came from Crouch. He sank to his knees, clutching his bruised tackle. Doll dusted off her pretty gloves and thought to retaliate in some way for Crouch's comment about Kitten being a silly bitch. It was not for the likes of Crouch to deride a girl who was now dead and due for a pauper's grave. Even if she was a silly bitch. Malinferno perceived Doll's intent from the look in her eyes and, grabbing her shoulders, steered her rapidly from the room. He wanted them both to escape before Crouch was sufficiently recovered to think of setting his faithful terriers on them. He didn't stop pushing her along ahead of him until they

were well down Tooley Street and halfway back to
Bromhead's house.

Sitting in the gloomy upstairs room that was Bromhead's
study, Malinferno tried to puzzle out the sequence of
events that had brought Bromhead's and Kitten's deaths
about.

'Well, it looks like Crouch didn't do it either.'

He rooted aimlessly through the impedimenta on
Augustus's desk, not sure what would be of relevance.
Sturdy modern leather-bound books lay side by side with
ancient curled-up scrolls, and various items served as
anchors for the latter, preventing the wind that whistled
through the ill-fitting windows from carrying such papers
away. One of the paperweights was a large skull, and
Malinferno quietly set it aside as a possible substitute for
Arthur's missing one. There would have to be some judicious
hammering of its surface, as he was sure Augustus had
once told him that Arthur's skull was damaged with a
sword blow. But it would be a start. After all, they had the
empty box already. He looked across at Doll, who was
occupying her time by scanning through a small and
battered tome that Malinferno remembered Thomas Dale
picking up off the floor at their first meeting. It was Geoffrey
of Monmouth's *History of the Kings of Britain*, and its position
on the floor had been the reason why Dale reckoned the
antiquarian had been killed. He said Augustus would not
have thrown down such a precious book. The recollection
gave him another idea – maybe the last chance of finding
the bones.

'Doll, put the book down. We have to go.'

Before she could ask where they were going, Malinferno
was down the stairs and out into the street. Only then, as
they hurried along, did Doll manage to get her question
out. 'Where are we going?'

'To talk to someone who might know who else is interested in Arthur's bones. Perhaps this Welshman of Crouch's knew about them from the start. Perhaps it's him who has been following me.'

Doll clutched Malinferno's arm and hung on tight. 'Well, I may be mistaken, but someone is following us right now. No, don't look around!' She pinched Malinferno's arm hard to stop him giving the game away. 'Ever since we left the Frenchy's place and in the Borough there's been a large cove with a big hat on right behind us.'

'Probably the same one as tried to peer in at the window of Madam De Trou's before he fell off the railings.'

'Well, that may explain why this one has a stick, and is walking with a limp.'

After a description like that, Malinferno could not resist it. He turned to look behind him. Suddenly Doll grabbed his face in both hands and planted a kiss full on his mouth. Her lips were wet, and she tasted of strawberries. Malinferno felt quite hot, and his hand sneaked up to Doll's bosom. She stopped his groping fist with one firm hand.

'Don't get the wrong idea, Joe Malinferno,' she hissed into his ear. 'That was just to stop you giving the game away. Though I must say it wasn't all that bad. Now, just look out the corner of your eye. It's the big man in the black coachman's coat and hat. You can't miss him.'

Indeed, Malinferno couldn't miss him. Not only was their pursuer supporting himself on a heavy wooden stick, but a bandage circumnavigated his skull underneath the hat. It seemed he had more than twisted his ankle when he fell from outside the window of Madam De Trou's house.

'Don't linger on him too long. And give me another of them kisses. I suppose I owe you from last night.' Malinferno needed no further invitation from Doll Pocket, and he tasted the sweet strawberry lips again. After a while they resumed their stroll, sure that the man was following again.

'Where *are* we going, Joe?'

'Why, to Thomas Dale, of course. We may not yet have the bones, but he may give us some idea of who might be interested in them besides us.'

Bloomsbury Square, once called Southampton Square because the fashionable area had been developed by the earl of that name, was lined with noble residences of the well-to-do. Malinferno guessed that Thomas Dale must have made a lot of money out of cabinetmaking. It boded well for his pockets if they could string him along until they found Arthur's bones. Or any bones, when it came down to it. The evil thought of substitution had more than once crossed Malinferno's mind, only for it to be put aside. If Arthur could be resurrected from his bones, then the bones of some utter nobody yanked summarily from his grave by the sack-'em-up men would give the game away. Of course, if Doll Pocket were to be believed, the whole idea was nonsense. But Malinferno, for all his love of science and engineering, could not discard the rags of a belief in the once and future king. After all, his English mother had told him all the tales. And like a foreigner who eagerly adopts the customs and ways of another country, Malinferno had become more English than a full-blooded Englishman. He realized Doll was saying something to him, and came out of his reverie.

'What did you say, Doll?'

'Here we are, Joe. Are you all right?'

Malinferno nodded and stared up at the fine brass plate on the grand house before which they stood. He mounted the steps, Doll on his arm. Pulling on the ivory handle of the bell-pull, he hissed in her ear. 'Put on that posh accent of yours. We don't want our employer thinking I consort with . . . with . . .'

Doll smiled sweetly. 'With bawds and grubbers?'

Malinferno blushed and was about to apologize when the door was opened and a liveried manservant stood before them.

'Yes, sir?'

'Is Mr Dale at home? He is not expecting us, but he will see us. My name is Malinferno.'

The servant sneered, though whether it was because of his name or Doll's presence on his master's pristine doorstep, Malinferno was not quite sure. But he did offer some information.

'Master is not at home.' He sniffed haughtily. 'He is still at his place of business.'

'And where might this place of . . . business . . . be?'

The servant named a street in a run-down area on the other side of the Euston Road and abruptly closed the door.

'Gawd, I didn't need my posh accent after all,' muttered Doll.

The place where Dale carried out his business was the very opposite of his residence. At first they couldn't find the address the snooty manservant had given them. But finally they located it down a narrow alley whence came a strange metallic stench. Three sets of sliding doors gave on to the alley, and one of them was open. Doll peered into the darkness, while Malinferno walked on to the last door behind which there was the sound of activity. She could only just make out the shape of strange cabinets piled high one on the other. Or that is what she thought they were at first, based on knowing Dale had introduced himself to Joe as a cabinetmaker. It was an easy mistake to make, until her eyes adjusted to the dark.

'Arrrgh, Joe!'

'What is it?'

Malinferno came scurrying back up the alley, worried by Doll's cry of alarm. She pointed into the warehouse.

'Look! It's coffins. Hundreds of them.'

Malinferno smiled knowingly.

'So it is. No wonder Dale stumbled on the word "cabinet" when he introduced himself. He was just about to say coffin-maker. A very lucrative business too, judging by the house in Bloomsbury Square.'

Just then, the end door in the alley slid open, revealing an unearthly red glow. A tall, lanky figure emerged from the smoke that billowed out of the open door. Doll clutched Joe's arm in fear. She hated anything to do with death, and this looked like the very devil himself come to fetch her to his lair. The voice of the apparition, however, was mild and well modulated.

'Who's that? Oh, Mr Malinferno, it's you. Have you any news for me?'

Thomas Dale came over to where Joe and Doll stood, and he took Malinferno by the hand. His face looked a little flushed, but that could be explained by the heat emanating from the end door of the narrow lane. He leaned across and slid the door closed next to where they stood, hiding the wooden coffins from view. He coughed nervously.

'I like to keep my business private, as it is not to everyone's taste in good society. However, that is all to change soon.' He rubbed his hands together with evident pleasure. 'I have just finished drafting an advertisement that will soon appear in all the best newspapers.'

He pulled a sheet of paper from his pocket with a flourish and gave it to Malinferno. 'Go on, read it.'

Malinferno did so. 'The violation of the grave is said to be needful for the instruction of medical pupils, but ask that of one who has interred a mother, husband, child or friend. Shall he devote this object of his affection to such a foul purpose? If not, **THE ONLY SAFE COFFIN IS A DALE'S PATENT WROUGHT-IRON ONE.** Thomas Dale performs funerals in any part of the kingdom, and those undertakers who have **IRON COFFINS** must divide the profits with **THOMAS DALE**.'

Dale positively beamed as Malinferno's inflection naturally highlighted those words written in bold upper-case letters by Dale's own hand. He indicated the red, glowing factory behind him.

'That is what we are embarked on now. And God help the bodysnatcher who encounters a Dale Patent Coffin.'

From behind Malinferno, Doll was heard to gasp. 'Gawd help us. What is the world come to, when we must lock our nearest and dearest away in a safe when they die?'

Dale nodded sagely. 'True, miss. But it is a business opportunity not to be passed up. Now, Malinferno, have you found the bones?'

Malinferno put on the most convincing tones he could muster, the sort of confident manner he used when unrolling a mummy for the edification and amusement of some duke or countess. 'We are getting very close, Mr Dale. What I wanted to ask you was if you knew of anyone beside yourself and Augustus who has shown interest in the bones?'

'What, recently? Or down through the ages?'

Silently Malinferno groaned, imagining from what Dale was saying that the coffin-maker proposed to expostulate on the whole history of Arthur and his errant bones. But in fact, what he did say proved very interesting.

'You see, there is a murky tale that very few know or have chosen to record of a family whose duty it has been to protect the legend and the bones of King Arthur.

Augustus had passed it off as another of the unsubstantiated myths surrounding the bones. But only a few days before he . . . disappeared, he asked me if I had heard tell of a family called Merrick in connection with the guardianship of the bones. When I laughed at the stories, he remained strangely quiet. In fact his face looked terribly pale, which I put down to the poor light of those candles he insisted on using. I have thought no more of it until recently. Do you think he was visited by someone from this family?'

Malinferno looked uneasily around him, aware more than ever of the hellish glow that shone through the factory doors and down the narrow alley. The walls seemed to be closing in on them as the sky above darkened. He was thinking of the Welshman mentioned by Crouch, and the man who had been following him for days. He noticed a shadow moving at the far end of the alley, and the click of a stick on the cobblestones. Could it be this Merrick fellow, hoping to hunt down Arthur's bones by following him? On an impulse he ran full pelt down the alley, bringing a cry of alarm from Thomas Dale. The shadowy figure made to skulk off into the growing gloom, but Malinferno was young and sound in heart and limb. The other man had taken a fall and could only limp away from his pursuer. Seeing that he was not going to escape, he turned to face Malinferno and waved his stick in the air. He swung it like a Turcopole's scimitar, slashing the air in front of his assailant's face, and for a few minutes there was stalemate. Then Malinferno stepped inside one particularly ferocious swing and took a blow on his shoulder. It almost numbed his left arm, but he was inside the man's defence.

'Got you, you devil.'

He swung a fist at the man's face and felt the satisfying crunch of a squashing nose. The man fell to ground, moaning and clutching a face that spurted red gore down the front of his capacious overcoat and down on to the cobbles. Malinferno might have thought he had captured a murderer at last, but he was to have his conviction shaken. The man who now lay at his feet was unrepentant and snarled his defiance.

'You are the devil, sir. And will find yourself in very great trouble soon enough.'

But Malinferno was in no mind to listen, and he grabbed the man's arm, dragging him along the cobbles towards the astonished Doll and Thomas Dale.

'Dale. Is your coffin store secure?'

'Why, yes it is.' He tapped the heavy, wooden sliding door, and slid it back a little. 'This is the only way in and out, save for a high window in the back that has bars over it.'

'Then it will serve as a prison cell for our captive until such time as we can call the Bow Street Runners.' He pushed the protesting man into the gloomy warehouse and slid the door closed. 'Besides, he will have plenty of choice for accommodation, provided he is not fearful of sleeping in a coffin.'

Dale produced a bunch of keys from his coat pocket and locked the bulky padlock that hung from the door hasp.

'There. It is done. Now let us have a little celebratory drink in my office, while I send one of my men for the magistrate. We may even discover where the bones are from this malefactor.'

Then all three left the 'malefactor' hammering in vain on the sturdy warehouse door. Unfortunately their celebrations were short-lived. Dale's workman had been sent to Worship Street to fetch the Runners who had attended at Kitten's death, and it was not long before Raleigh Pauncefoot and Constable Mayes were on the scene. Triumphantly Malinferno undid the padlock and let them into the coffin warehouse. The prisoner had given up his repeated hammering on the door, and for a long while after Pauncefoot and Mayes entered the store silence continued to reign. All three men eventually emerged, the prisoner leading the way. Malinferno was pleased to note that his nose had swollen to a size that meant it occupied most of the centre of his face, and that it was red and pulpy. Perhaps he would think twice about murdering innocent girls in future. Well, not so innocent in Kitten's case, but the principle was the same. However, Malinferno's smile was wiped from his face by the grim look on Pauncefoot's. Even Mayes looked shifty, as he scuffed his heavy boots on the cobbles.

'What's wrong? You have before you the man who so foully murdered Kit ... Kathleen Hoddy. And perhaps did for my friend Augustus Bromhead. Ask him if his name is not Merrick.'

The man's face had a look that resembled thunder. He turned to the magistrate. 'Tell him, Pauncefoot.'

The magistrate twirled his fashionable ebony cane with the Egyptian motif on the top, then cut Malinferno down with his words. 'I have seen this man's papers, and he is not called Merrick.'

'Then who is he? And why has he been dogging my footsteps for days?'

The man stepped forward and brandished his fist in Malinferno's face. 'Sir, I am a government official, charged with winkling out radicals and French sympathizers in this great state of ours. You have shown yourself through your choice of friends to be a most untrustworthy character.'

Though this outburst brought Doll closer to Malinferno's side, its effect on Thomas Dale was the very opposite. He gasped and took a step back.

'Is this true, Malinferno? And with Bonaparte at our doorstep too.'

The government spy laughed harshly. 'Napoleon is as safe as he ever was on St Helena. In fact the last I heard he has stated that he would rather be there than suffer the discomforts of flight. The rumour of his escape was planted in the newspapers by us to winkle out the likes of Monsieur Casteix, and his contacts such as Malinferno here. We wanted to see who would rush to his cause, so that we could deal with them in the future.'

Dale groaned. 'Then Arthur is not needed after all.'

'Arthur? Who is he?' The spy looked puzzled.

'Oh, it is nothing. It hardly matters any more.'

Raleigh Pauncefoot stepped forward and tapped Malinferno on the chest with the head of his cane. His question, however, was for the spy.

'What do you wish me to do with this chap, sir? He has after all assaulted you and accused you of the most heinous of crimes.'

'Though it displeases me greatly to say it, sir, I suggest we forget the matter of my assault. I do have to keep a low profile in my line of business, and a court case will not be conducive to the prosecution of my trade.'

Malinferno knew that the man, whatever his name was, would also be reluctant to reveal to his fellow spies and his employer that he had been bested by a mere dilettante in the field of investigation. He grinned insolently at the man, who added a chilling rider to his statement, however.

'I will, on the other hand, pass his name on to my superiors as a dangerous radical and Bonaparte sympathizer. Mayes, here, found a book in his rooms dedicated to Napoleon, so he cannot deny it.'

With his revenge on Malinferno complete, the spy turned to leave, his dramatic exit spoiled somewhat by the limp occasioned by his tumble from the railings at Madam De Trou's. Raleigh Pauncefoot and Constable Mayes followed on his heels, leaving Malinferno to deal with the now-wary Thomas Dale. He laughed unconvincingly.

'The book he referred to is probably my copy of the work by Baron Denon on the discoveries made in Egypt during Bonaparte's campaigns. I am an Egyptologist, you know.'

'Indeed, sir.' Dale's brow was clouded, and it looked like he now viewed his erstwhile employee as someone it was dangerous to be associated with. Especially if he was to be promoting his new wrought-iron coffin with the well-to-do. 'I am sure you are right. A book by a French nobleman, you say? In French? Hmm. Well, now, as the matter I had paid you for appears to be no longer of any urgency, I think we can terminate our relationship forthwith. Please do not bother to return any balance of accounts to me. Accept any money left as a just reward for your efforts.'

Malinferno breathed a sigh of relief. It was just as well Dale did not want any money back, as most of it had gone anyway in expenses incurred in the company of Doll Pocket. They took their leave of Dale, who disappeared back into his fiery furnace, and began retracing their steps to the beginning of this sorry saga – Malinferno's rooms, the place where the bones had been first lost. As they walked up Leadenhall Street, Malinferno was so deep in thought he began to drag Doll along at an ever-increasing pace. Outside the door to Mrs Stanhope's, she stopped him.

''ere! Pack it in . . . my slipper's coming off.'

Holding on to Joe, she bent down to pull on her leather slipper, the back of which had worked off her heel. It was late at night now, and she was glad of the yellowish light cast by the streetlamp to see by. Hopping on one foot, and clutching Joe's Garrick coat, she suddenly felt him pull away.

'Look out, or you'll have me over on my arse.'

'Doll, look at the upstairs window. What do you see?'

'What the 'ell you goin' on about?'

'Just look.'

She straightened up and looked at where he was pointing. A flickering light shone in one of the upper windows of the house. Malinferno looked scared, their previous encounter with Crouch having drained away all his courage. Doll snorted in disgust, though in truth she was not feeling all that brave herself.

'There's someone in your rooms. Well, come on, then. Let's take a look. It can't be a ghost – I don't believe in them.'

What they saw in Malinferno's rooms challenged her assertion for a while.

But first Malinferno had to sneak Doll past the beady eye and sharp ear of Mrs Stanhope. However, as soon as Malinferno opened the front door, he realized it was to be an easy task. He had not seen that recently his landlady's days had been full of horror and terrible encounters, what with dead bodies, blood ruining decent rugs, and Bow Street Runners everywhere. She had blanked out these irregular events with a strong dosage of Holland gin. She was deep in the arms of Lethe, and snoring like a pig. The reverberations carried from her quarters to Joe's and Doll's ears as they entered cautiously. Malinferno breathed a sigh of relief, and led Doll up the elegant but rather shabby curved staircase towards his rooms. He stopped her at the top of the stairs and peered across the landing. The door to his drawing room was slightly ajar, and a pale light shone through the crack. Someone had lighted one of his oil-lamps. It was a strange thing for a burglar to do. Or a murderer lying in wait.

Doll obviously thought the same. She edged past him and crossed the landing on her slippered feet before Malinferno could stop her. She pushed the door quietly open. Malinferno was at her back, both hands on her shoulders. What he saw made him gasp.

'It's Augustus!'

The body of the dwarfish little man lay sprawled in his comfortable armchair by the bow window, his large head lolling unnaturally over the side. Malinferno was wondering how he was going to explain a second body in his rooms when Augustus gave a great sigh and shifted in the chair.

'Augustus, damn you. You're alive.'

Malinferno's loud cry of relief woke the slumbering Bromhead, who started up and flung himself towards the window. Then he saw the person who had awakened him and stopped his headlong flight. He held his hand to his heart.

'Oh, it's only you, Giuseppe. Thank God for that.'

'Augustus, where have you been? We thought you were dead.'

'Dead? I would have been, if I had stayed in my house much longer. As to where I have been, I have been walking the streets of London and sleeping under archways with the beggars.'

For the first time Malinferno noticed how shabby Bromhead's clothes were. His cutaway coat was torn at the lapel, and mud stained its tails. His breeches were wrinkled and grubby, his stockings torn. Malinferno turned to Doll and slipped the remaining money from Dale's fee into her hand.

'Go down to Leadenhall Market. There are chophouses there open all night for the meat porters. Get poor Gus some food and a jug of ale if you can manage it. I don't think he has eaten for a while.'

Doll nodded and wound her cloak around her bosom. It was getting quite cold outside. When she had gone, Malinferno guided the antiquarian to the armchair again. Bromhead fell back into it with a sigh.

'Why did you think me dead?'

'Oh, it was Thomas Dale who thought that at first, because of the red stains on your table.'

'You have spoken to Dale, then. Red stains? Oh, I spilled some ink when I . . . Perhaps I should tell you why I have been in hiding since you last saw me.'

'Yes, perhaps you should. But let us wait until Doll returns, or I will not hear the end of it. Anyway, you should eat first, and tell us your tale afterwards.'

Bromhead's hunger was manifest in the way he demolished the potatoes, chop and gravy that Doll brought. Along with most of the jug of ale. Malinferno was itching to know what had happened to cause his friend to run and hide. But he held back his curiosity until the little man's belly was full. Then they all sat in the circle of light cast by the oil-lamp, and Bromhead told a story concerning strange noises in the night and dark men standing under flickering streetlamps.

'At first I thought it was the Borough Gang come to murder me and provide my body for some medical student's autopsy exercise. I am told they look out for men of – shall we say? – unusual stature.'

The antiquarian squared his shoulders in the chair where he sat, as if trying to stretch his body to a normal height. But there was nothing he could do about his large dome of a head which, set on his small frame, had earned him the nickname of Tadpole from the street urchins. Finally he shrugged the selfsame shoulders and continued his tale.

'Such a thought was bad enough. But when the lurker finally confronted me, it turned out I was as far away from the truth as I could be. It was in the evening after I entrusted Arthur's bones to you, Giuseppe. And lucky that I did so, because that is what the man wanted, and he was prepared to kill to get them. He slid into my chamber out of the darkness like some dark-skinned, slippery eel out of the Fleet. The first I knew was the vice-like grip I felt on my neck. I was terrified, I can tell you, and I waved my arms about trying to escape. That must have been when I knocked the inkwell over and sent my precious books flying. But I could not escape his grip, and he hissed a warning into my ear. "Keep still, you little worm, or I will snap your neck right now," he said. I stopped my struggle, and he released me. He demanded to know where the bones were, and I prevaricated – until he drew a sharp knife from under his coachman's coat. I'm afraid I told him you had them, Giuseppe. But even then I kept my presence of mind. I pointed at the old wooden box in the corner, which I had dug up at Trevenna. "The coffin is there," I cried. And when he bent over to lift the lid, I ran for my life. And have been running until this very night, when I could stand the cold and degradation no more. So I came in secret to my old friend's door.'

Malinferno leaned forward into the light and patted the old man's hand.

'I am glad you did, Augustus. But if only you had told me where you found the bones, I might have known earlier what this was all about. Trevenna meant nothing to me.'

Augustus gurgled with delight.

'I had to put you off the track. If I had told you straight away the church was half a mile from Tintagel Castle, you would have guessed the connection immediately.'

Malinferno smiled ruefully.

'And I might not have got into so much trouble. Never mind. We shall have a resolution to your dilemma very soon.'

Malinferno had a good reason to draw the evening out, as he was now expecting a visitor. That is, if his guesswork was correct. If it wasn't, the bones would be lost and Kitten's murderer would remain undiscovered. Though Bromhead was unaware of his friend's intense look, deep in his cups as he was, Malinferno noticed that Doll was eyeing him closely.

'Something on your mind, Miss Pocket?'

Doll narrowed her eyes and frowned. 'It's not me, Signor Malinferno, who looks like they got something to hide. Want to tell us what you're up to?'

Malinferno laughed. 'You are very perspicacious, Doll. I am hoping matters will resolve themselves pretty soon, actually. However, it will involve a little play-acting from you. But seeing as how you told me recently that such a profession was an aspiration of yours, you will not mind, I am sure.'

'I don't know who this Percy Caysius feller is, but tell me what you want, and I will oblige.'

'I am expecting a caller, but he will not come if you are still here. I suggest that, now Augustus has finished his meal and told us his story, you appear to take the remains of the repast back to the chophouse. Leaving me on my own.'

Bromhead belched gently and asked the obvious question. 'What of me, Giuseppe? Do I leave too?'

Malinferno put a restraining arm on Bromhead's. 'That will not be necessary, Gus. Our caller does not know you are here, I think. And I could do with your assistance when he arrives. All I suggest is that you place yourself behind the door here when I turn out this lamp, and retire to my bedroom.'

Bromhead shuddered at the possibility of a physical encounter, but he nodded his head in acquiescence.

'And what am I to do, Joe?' This retort was from Doll. 'Run away like some weak female?'

'You can run, Doll Pocket, but I suggest that when you have returned the dirty crockery, you run in the direction of the nearest magistrate, and bring him here forthwith.'

Doll gave him an angry look full of storm clouds and thunder. But she collected the empty plates and ale-jug and made her way down the stairs. When Malinferno heard the front door close, he took the oil-lamp and turned the wick low. Crossing the landing, he went into his bedroom, making sure that the lamp stood in the window there. Then he turned the lamp out. Anyone observing from the street would assume that Malinferno had retired for the night and that he was now alone.

Almost half an hour passed, and Malinferno began to doubt his own convictions. After the fiasco of incarcerating the government spy and then discovering he was not the man seeking the bones, he had been in a quandary. Then he remembered something Doll had said earlier on. When he tried to put the evidence together, she had said his story was full of holes. In fact it had been Doll who had said there was no proof Augustus was dead. She had been correct about that. It had set him to finding other holes, and he had seen it as they had been walking back to Creechurch Lane. Casteix had said it first. The man who sawed his leg in half had resembled a Breton peasant. Swarthy, he had said, and no doubt stocky. Dale had suggested the family interested in guarding Arthur's bones was Welsh, and Crouch had said the same. Bromhead had virtually confirmed that with his reference to a dark-skinned eel of a man. That he had not exactly said he was short was not surprising, taking into account Bromhead's own lack of stature. The only conclusion Malinferno could come to was that two men had been following him all this time. And the one who had killed Kitten was still on the streets of London searching for the bones.

Suddenly he heard a scuffling sound on the stairs, and the slightest of creaks. He knew exactly where the man now mounting the stairs had stepped. He had trodden there himself once when he had been sneaking a willing young girl to his room. It had alerted Mrs Stanhope, and he had never made the same mistake again. The intruder, unfamiliar with the stairs, had stepped on the middle step on the half-landing. Malinferno poked his nose out of his door, but could not see the pale face of Augustus staring back at him across the landing. He was afraid the old man had perhaps fallen asleep and that he was on his own. His heart raced, and he tucked himself in behind his bedroom door. After a few more seconds the door began to swing silently open.

How he then came to be disposing of a dead body was something of a mystery to Joe Malinferno. When he sat down with Augustus and Doll later, he reasoned that the man, who was clearly Merrick, had been a step ahead of him. He had felt the prick of a blade through the crack in the door on the side where the hinges were. Merrick had guessed he was hiding behind the door somehow, and attacked. He had stumbled forward, blood pulsing from the wound in his back. A wound that Doll had now expertly bound with a torn section of her muslin dress, so that she now revealed a satisfying expanse of white thigh to Malinferno's hungry gaze. Matters had from the point of being stabbed got quite confused for him. When Merrick fell on him, he had feared for his life. But a saviour had arrived in the form of Doll Pocket. It seemed she had spurned the idea of calling out the Runners on the grounds that they would not take too kindly to the requests of a common bawd. Besides, Malinferno hadn't expected them to come. He had only asked it of her to get her out of danger. But Doll had other ideas than being typecast as the weak and fainting female.

'I left the dirty dishes at the door of St Mary Axe church and sneaked back,' she explained. 'The man wasn't all that hard to spot, once you knew where he was hiding. I've hung around in plenty of doorways myself, making sure the charleys or the Runners don't notice me. When he entered the house, I followed him. And just as well for you it was, Joe Malinferno. For I pulled him off your back just in time.'

The man in question nodded sagely and glanced across at where Augustus Bromhead sat. The little antiquarian was ashen-faced and deep in thought, and Malinferno was unsure how to break into his reverie. It was Doll who spoke up boldly.

'And we must both thank Gus for his bravery. That sly little bastard Merrick was as slippery as Gus said, and he would have done for us both if he hadn't come in when he did.'

Bromhead gave a despairing cry. 'But I killed him.'

Doll walked swiftly over to him and buried his head in her ample bosom. Malinferno looked on with envy. 'No. It was an accident. You tried to wrest the knife off him, and his arm got twisted around. He fell on his own blade, if you ask me.'

Bromhead's sobs subsided, but he kept his head between Doll's breasts longer than Joe thought necessary.

The disposal of the body had been relatively easy. It had merely required calling on the services of Ben Crouch, who with a free 'large one' on offer ended up bearing them no more ill will. He even made light of Doll's assault on his jewels.

'I do like a good tussle before the main event. It perks up the spirit, don't it?'

But he was quick to exit with his body, when Doll offered to reacquaint him with the force of her grip. Merrick, the killer of Kitten, was soon fated to decorate the autopsy slab at St Bartholomew's, where he would be drawn and quartered in the most modern of ways. Justice of a sharp and rough kind, but justice all the same.

'But we still don't know what happened to Arthur's bones apart from this one,' moaned Bromhead, swinging the thigh-bone they had retrieved from Merrick's coat pocket. 'If Merrick didn't have them, then where have they gone?'

It was Mrs Stanhope who solved the mystery, by entering the room at that very moment with a familiar canvas sack over her shoulder.

'Mr M, if you don't want these old bones I hid away for you before the Runners came round, I will throw them on the local tip.'

Malinferno strode across the room and gave his startled landlady a long and lingering kiss.

The final act of the three conspirators was to agree to hide King Arthur's bones away securely so that a future generation may call on them in a time of real need. It was Bromhead who had voiced all their fears about the bones.

'They have been nothing but a curse since I uncovered them. We should put them somewhere secure where they will not be found for a very long time.'

They had called on the services of Thomas Dale, who provided them with a newfangled wrought-iron coffin, inside of which was placed the bones, along with the battered and scarred remains of the ancient wooden chest that had once housed them. From Bromhead's house at dead of night, they had solemnly processed to the run-down building across the yard that was ironically called Pope's Mansion. The cellars beneath it were the original undercroft area of medieval Bermondsey Abbey, and it seemed a fitting place for Arthur to rest a while longer. With the aid of four of Dale's men, sworn to secrecy with a plentiful supply of ale, they secreted the heavy coffin behind an old, crumbling wall, which they patched up after them. Malinferno silently prayed it would be a considerable time before the bones saw the light of day again.

# epilogue

## *London, August 2004*

The rescue dig at Bermondsey Abbey was coming to an end, as the contractors for the huge development project, which would bury the ancient foundations for ever, were itching to send in their piledrivers. Only two archaeologists remained, sitting in their Portacabin over mugs of instant coffee, while their solitary student volunteer was somewhere outside, grubbing through the basements with his metal detector.

'Never gives up, does he!' muttered Edward Asprey. 'The last day and he still hopes to find a pot of gold with that thing.'

Gwen Arnold jumped to the defence of Philip Grainger, as she knew that Asprey, the rather depressive team leader, disliked the student, probably because he was unfailingly cheerful. 'Come on, he's harmless enough. And he has found a few coins and bits and pieces with that gadget of his.'

Gwen was a physical anthropologist on secondment from Cardiff University, an earnest woman of thirty drafted in to advise on the human remains found when they excavated the abbey cemetery, though some unexpected finds had been unearthed elsewhere in the dig.

Edward Asprey grunted and looked despondently around the cabin at the piles of papers, books and assorted debris that would have to be packed up and removed this weekend. He was a small man, with a wispy beard and a mop of black hair. 'It'll seem odd to be back in my office after months in this place,' he observed. 'Are you going straight back to Wales?'

'No, I need to write up this project first. Then I must get back before term starts, as I've got to get my lectures sorted.'

She had plain but pleasant features, with rather lank brown hair pulled straight back and secured with an elastic band.

Abruptly the door was thrown open and Philip's amiable face appeared around it. He had a pair of headphones pushed down around his neck and seemed excited, but he was always one to be enthusiastic about everything.

'You'd best come and have a look at this, folks!' he chanted, waving a gadget that looked like a walking stick with a black dinner plate stuck on the end.

'Oh, God, not that bloody thing again?' whined Asprey, but Gwen was more sympathetic. 'What have you found this time, Phil?' she asked.

'Not actually found anything yet,' he answered, rather crestfallen. 'But I've had the strongest signal I've ever had with this.' He waved the detector again. 'Almost burst my eardrums. There must be a huge piece of ferrous metal there.'

'And where's that?' asked Asprey wearily.

'In the cellarer's undercroft, against the north wall.'

The senior scientist groaned. 'Not that bloody place again. It's cursed!'

They had had several misfortunes there during the dig. It was the site of the storage vaults beneath the cellarer's building of the original eleventh-century priory. First, a volunteer had fallen into the excavation and broken a leg, then a new JCB had crashed over the edge – and finally lightning had struck a bizarre discovery behind a false wall.*

The more sympathetic Gwen went out with Philip and followed him as he almost danced across to the ladder that went down into the long excavation. It was criss-crossed with the remains of walls from haphazard building over almost a millennium.

At the bottom he led her over to a ruinous patch of masonry about six feet high, which showed stones, bricks and crumbling mortar from many different periods. Philip brandished his detector again and fiddled with some of the control knobs.

'I'll put it on the speaker, rather than the headphones, so you can hear,' he offered excitedly. Raising the dinner-plate end towards the wall, he moved it slowly along, just above ground level. The steady whine suddenly erupted into a rising shriek, which persisted for about six feet as he closely traversed the stonework. 'Something big in there, Gwen!' he said gleefully.

Next afternoon the three of them stood in a cluttered preparation room next to a laboratory in the Archaeology Department, just off Gower Street. A badly rusted metal coffin sat on the floor, its lid propped against a nearby wall, the corroded holding bolts cut off with an angle-grinder.

A spreading pool of rusty fluid seeped across the floor, even though a large volume of water had been drained out at the excavation site.

'No doubt about it being early nineteenth century,' said Edward Asprey. 'It was from the time when there was this

* See *House of Shadows*.

real fear of grave robbers – the "resurrection men" and all that.'

'Stealing bodies to sell to anatomists, you mean?' asked Philip. He was still on a high from being the finder of this strange contraption. When a section of the decayed wall had been pulled down, the iron coffin had been found under pile of waterlogged rubble and had to be hauled back to the laboratory before it could be opened by their technicians.

'But what was left of that box inside certainly wasn't nineteenth century,' objected Gwen. 'Nor are those bones, though God knows how old they are.'

They moved to a metal table against the wall, where at one end a pile of mouldering wood had been separated from a collection of fragmented bones at the other.

'So what are you saying about these?' asked Edward, pointing at the remains of a fragile, brownish skeleton. Gwen carefully picked up a length of thigh-bone, with the round knob of the hip joint at the top. 'It's a partial skeleton, very badly decayed – the bone is sodden and porous. Probably the last two centuries in that leaking metal box did it more damage that it suffered in all its previous history.'

'Which is how long?' demanded Edward Asprey.

The anthropologist shrugged. 'Impossible to tell! Environment affects the appearance of bone far more than time itself. Without carbon dating, it would be sheer guesswork.'

'What about the remains of the box?' asked Philip. 'Those bits of wood lying all around the heap of bones must be what's left of some sort of container.'

Asprey claimed this as his expertise. 'Again, impossible to date it, given the rotten state of the timber. It looks like oak and there seem to be some bits of rusty iron left, which were probably bands or hinges.'

'What can you tell from the bones themselves?' persisted the student. 'Even I can tell that the remains of that skull are male.'

Gwen Arnold hefted the partial thigh-bone in her hand. 'It's a man, all right – and a big fellow too, judging by the diameter of this femoral head. But I'll need some time to look at all this stuff properly.'

'What about carbon dating?' asked Asprey. 'Can we afford it from what's left of our budget?'

'Probably, but if there's a shortfall I'll wangle it from the Cardiff grant. As soon as these have dried a bit, I'll drill some samples and send them off to Oxford, together with some from the wood.'

'When you write this up for publication, can you mention my name?' asked Philip wistfully.

Three weeks later they met again in Asprey's office, which was even smaller than the Portakabin he had had at Bermondsey.

Gwen Arnold held a few sheets of paper in her hands, the results of the tests carried out by the Oxford Radiocarbon Accelerator Unit.

'I can't tell you much more about the skeleton, which is very incomplete and in a bad state of fragmentation and decay. He was a man probably between forty and fifty years of age. As I said before, he was a big chap, at least six feet tall, with no evidence of bone disease, but, although his skull is badly crumbled, it looks as if he had a severe head injury which didn't have time to heal before he died.'

'All that could apply to a million people over the last few hundred years,' observed Edward cynically.

'Make that fifteen hundred years,' said Gwen, waving her papers at him. 'The carbon dating on four bone samples all agree on a date of AD 530 plus or minus forty years!'

Philip whistled in surprise. 'Dark Ages, be damned! We didn't expect him to be that old.'

'What the devil's he doing in a nineteenth-century iron box in South London?' exclaimed Asprey, for once too astonished to be cynical. 'But what about that wooden case that he was in?'

Gwen again cast her eye at her papers. 'That's even more curious! Two samples both showed it was late twelfth century. So nothing ties up – a sixth-century skeleton in a twelfth-century box inside a metal coffin possibly contemporary with the Napoleonic Wars!'

They discussed the conundrum for a while, but concluded that there was no way in which the matter could be resolved more definitely.

'So what are we going to do with them?' asked Asprey finally, gesturing towards a brand-new plastic storage box that sat on a bench. 'They obviously have no bearing at all on our medieval abbey. They must have been dumped there by some bloody antiquarian two hundred years ago.'

'I'd like to do some more work on them back at our department,' offered Gwen. 'There are new techniques we're developing about discovering what food people ate in ancient times. We might get some clue as to where they originated.'

'Take them, then,' said Asprey. 'One less box of junk for us to store here.'

The little Ford crested the hill on the M4 motorway west of the Almondsbury interchange and began rolling down the incline towards the Severn Bridge. In the distance shone the river, and beyond it the hills of Wales came into sight. The back seat was piled high with her belongings, the boot being almost filled by the plastic box.

Happy to be going home after three months in London,

Gwen began to sing softly, crooning an old folk melody in Welsh, as she was born and brought up in Carmarthen. Some of her contentment was also because, during her stay in Bermondsey, her divorce had finally come through and she intended reverting to her maiden name of Merrick.

As the car reached the approach to the huge bridge, a feeling of well-being crept over her and she was somehow suddenly aware of the anonymous bones sharing in her happiness, an extraordinary feeling that intensified as she neared the two huge towers at the centre of the bridge.

Sixty miles further west, at the top of the Vale of Neath, the remote rock of Craig y Ddinas reared above the little village of Pont Nedd Fechan. In a huge cave, deep within the crag, sixty armed warriors slept in a circle around another sleeping figure, a taller man dressed in finer clothes and armour reminiscent of the Roman legions.

As the Ford crossed the centre line of the bridge, he briefly opened his eyes and a beatific smile creased his strong face, before he turned over and contentedly went back to sleep.

POCKET
BOOKS

# The Medieval Murderers

# House of Shadows

**Five enthralling interlinked mysteries from Michael Jecks, Susanna Gregory, Bernard Knight, Ian Morson and Philip Gooden.**

Bermondsey Priory, 1114. A young chaplain succumbs to the temptations of the flesh – and suffers a gruesome fate.

From that moment, the monastery is cursed and over the next five hundred years murder and treachery abound within its hallowed walls.

A beautiful young bride found dead two days before her wedding. A ghostly figure that warns of impending doom. A daring plot to depose King Edward II. Mad monks and errant priests . . . even the poet Chaucer finds himself drawn into the dark deeds and violent death which pervade this unhappy place.

**ISBN 978-1-41652-680-3**
**PRICE £6.99**

POCKET
BOOKS

## The Medieval Murderers

# The Lost Prophecies

A mysterious book of prophecies written by a sixth century Irish monk has puzzled scholars through the ages. Foretelling wars, plagues and rebellions, the Black Book of Bran is said to have predicted the Black Death and the Gunpowder Plot. It is even said to foresee the Day of Judgement. But is it the result of divine inspiration or the ravings of a madman?

A hidden hoard of Saxon gold. A poisoned priest. A monk skinned alive in Westminster Abbey. Only one thing is certain: whoever comes into possession of the cursed book meets a gruesome and untimely end.

'The various excellent crime writers each weave a clever and inventive tale around a central theme' *Good Book Guide*

**ISBN 978-1-84739-121-6**
**PRICE £6.99**

**POCKET
BOOKS**

This book and other **Pocket Books** titles are available from
your local bookshop or can be ordered direct
from the publisher.

| | | |
|---|---|---|
| 978-1-41650-213-5 | **The Tainted Relic** | £6.99 |
| 978-1-41652-190-7 | **Sword of Shame** | £6.99 |
| 978-1-41652-680-3 | **House of Shadows** | £6.99 |
| 978-1-84739-121-6 | **The Lost Prophecies** | £6.99 |

**Free post and packing within the UK**
Overseas customers please add £2 per paperback.
Telephone Simon & Schuster Cash Sales at Bookpost
on 01624 677237 with your credit or debit card number,
or send a cheque payable to Simon & Schuster Cash Sales to:
PO Box 29, Douglas, Isle of Man, IM99 1BQ
Fax: 01624 670923
Email: bookshop@enterprise.net
www.bookpost.co.uk

Please allow 14 days for delivery. Prices and availability
are subject to change without notice.